THE
MOTHER

BY

SHOLOM ASCH

·········

Translated
by
NATHAN AUSÜBEL

Preface by Ludwig Lewisohn

AMS PRESS
NEW YORK

Reprinted from the edition of 1930, New York
First AMS EDITION published 1970
Manufactured in the United States of America

Library of Congress Catalog Card Number: 73-114047
SBN: 404-00408-3

AMS PRESS, INC.
NEW YORK, N.Y. 10003

The Mother

Preface

▪▪▪▪▪▪▪

ALL that the average cultivated American knows of Sholom Asch is that some years ago his play *The God of Vengeance,* excellently interpreted in a New York playhouse, was made the object of one of those amusing attacks by policemen and other guardians of our public morals that occasionally add their comic touch to American life. The play itself is a serious, sagacious and most moving work. But it is high time for American lovers of letters to become acquainted with the fact, fully known, for instance, in Germany, that Sholom Asch is primarily a novelist and, as such, one of the most original and eminent now writing in any language.

Asch, long famous in his own world and speech, arose as their interpreter and "maker" from the Jewish masses of Poland. He had the felicity, granted to few Jewish writers of modern times, of being rooted in a spiritual soil, unreflectively integrated with his people and therefore able to function as an artist as spontaneously, as naturally, as—let us say—the Fleming Timmermans or the Norseman, Knut Hamsun. I compare him not at all idly to these two: he has a comparable simplicity of narrative rhythm, a similar devotion to the humble, significant, eternal things that go to make up the life of man, the same absorption in the concrete from which the uni-

v

Preface

versal and permanent has the best chance of issuing
at last.

He began with delineations of the Jewish proletariat in
the cities and small towns of Poland. And to this subject,
which is closest to his heart, he has always returned. But
his long residence in America gave him the additional
theme, epic in quality and subtle in psychological pat-
tern, of the transfer of great masses of this proletariat to
America. It is about this theme that he has built his
novels: *Uncle Moses, The Electric Chair* and, more recently, *The Mother*. It is the latter strong and tender
work—strong without effort, tender without sentimen-
tality—that is herewih presented to the American reader.
But I am less eager to commend this now accessible book,
than to dwell for another moment on Sholom Asch's
quality and stature among the writers of our age. And
hence it should be added that a third theme, the history
of his people, has engaged his creative attention and has
been the subject of those two noble tales: *The Sorceress
of Castile* and *The Sanctification of the Name*. Nor will
I deny myself the pleasure of saying that of a great
trilogy of novels, *Before the Flood*, two volumes, *Peters-
burg* and *Warsaw* have already appeared in Yiddish and
in German and show Asch at the height of his development so far, as an artist of such creative sweep, power
and grasp as to link his name unquestionably with the
most eminent names of our period.

LUDWIG LEWISOHN

Paris, March 7, 1930.

Contents

•••••••

PART ONE

PART ONE

Chapter 1

FATHER, MOTHER AND THE
WHOLE FAMILY

■■■■■■

FATHER was practicing the cantillation of the Book of Esther.

It was before Purim, after a long and severe winter. Outside the thaw was already in progress. The ice-encrusted earth began to shed its garments of winter gloom and revealed all that lay hidden underneath them throughout the long, silent months. The unpaved street became so muddy that it was impossible to cross from one side to the other. Great puddles, like miniature lakes and oceans, emerged from under the thin layers of melting ice and flooded the thoroughfares so that all ways of communication were cut off. It was only possible for people to shout across to one another.

A gentle warmth and an indefinable gayety penetrated into the house from the outside. The frosted little windows at last were liberated from their traceries of ice-flowers which blossomed on the panes throughout the long, bleak winter. The windows became smudged with wetness. It was impossible to look through them. The house was steaming and filled with smoke. It poured from the small kitchen because it could not pass through the sooty chimney. The winter-clothes, which throughout the cold weather had felt as if they had grown to the body and become a second skin,

9

The Mother

now proved annoying and heavy as lead. One felt the irresistible impulse to throw them off. It was at this time that father commenced to practice the cantillation of the Book of Esther. And when father sang the earth seemed to grow lighter and airier and a new hope arose like the first greetings of spring.

Whenever father cantillated the Book of Esther a dead silence had to reign in the house. In fact, whenever father was at home all disturbing and unseemly sounds became properly subdued and hushed. It was obligatory upon all to tread on tiptoe and to hold their breath. Since father did one of two things: either he lay down on the sofa for a nap or he practiced intoning sacred Scripture, proper decorum had to be observed by all. To keep all animate existence sufficiently muted for him was no easy task for mother. Her brood was large (may no Evil Eye fall on any of them!). Her oldest was Shloimè, the "young man," who sewed uppers for the custom shoemakers in the town. Her youngest was a mere infant who bore his grandfather's name and who propelled himself across the floor with the aid of his tiny hands.

All the children had their own individual ways of letting themselves be heard from. The trouble began with little Moishelè, nicknamed "The Ox," who had been barred from Hebrew school because his mother had not paid his tuition for three months. Just now, while father was chanting the Book of Esther, he found the most fitting time to teach his little brother Yoinè (he also bore another name but because of our natural refinement we cannot mention it) how to whistle through his nose while his mouth was closed. Mother, who stood guard over the soup that was cooking on the stove, made an ineffectual effort to silence them. She slapped the one and pummeled the other of the mischief makers. But the little fellow named Yoinè burst out laughing and whistled through his nose.

Father, Mother and the Whole Family

This was just one bit too much for father to bear. He raised his eyes sternly from the Bible, lifted his spectacles to his forehead and steadily regarded first his wife and then the little fellow with the ingratiating nickname. While doing this he modulated his cantillation to a shrill pitch:

"In those days when the King Ahasueros sat on his throne."

Hearing the implied reproach in the changed key of his chanting, mother turned significantly to Moishelè, "The Ox," and said:

"Well! See what you have done now?"

The boys suddenly became grave and subsided. Then they ran out into the street. Although shod in badly patched and dilapidated shoes they began to navigate the "oceans" and the "lakes" with great ardor.

Silence reigned once more in the room. The only sound that could be heard now was the monotonous beat of the foot-pedal of the sewing machine at which Shloimè, the "young man," the sole provider of the household, sat sewing uppers. Father's singing grew constantly louder, livelier and more ecstatic. He now competed with the steady rumble of the sewing machine to drown out its hoarse squeak, to outdistance it in rhythm and tempo.

There was no happier man than father when he practiced the reading of Scripture with the traditional melody. Then the whole world of dross, poverty and struggle disappeared. What he saw only in his imagination then became real. Best of all father loved the Book of Esther. While reading it he felt himself carried bodily away into King Ahasueros' palace to be present at the great feast where wine was served in golden vessels, where one was not forced to drink, but only according to one's inclination.

When father reached that passage which narrates how King Ahasueros waxed expansive: "When the heart of the king was merry with wine," and how he commanded his

The Mother

seven royal chamberlains "to bring Vashti the Queen before the King with the royal crown, to show the people and the princes her beauty, for she was fair to look upon," he fondled the notes in his throat in such a, long cadenza as if he grieved ever to let the phrase pass out of his mouth, as if it were an indescribably delicious morsel that a gourmet regretted to swallow.

His excitement visibly increased when he sang of "Mordecai the Jew." Here he felt perfectly at home. He had the indubitable conviction that he himself was the great Mordecai. As if by enchantment he conjured up out of his imagination the radiant figure of Queen Esther. He preached at her sternly, reproaching her for not making intercession for her people before the King:

"For if thou altogether holdest thy peace at this time, then will relief and deliverance arise to the Jews from another place."

A moment later and father has completely identified himself with King Ahasueros. He now sees himself sitting on his throne with golden scepter in his hand. Before him kneels the beautiful Queen Esther, magnificent in her regal crown. And she finds favor in the eyes of the King and he extends to her the golden scepter and says, gurgling the sounds with a caressing tenderness:

"What wilt thou, Queen Esther? For whatever thy request, even half of my kingdom shall I give unto thee."

And when mother stands over her pots in the kitchen and listens to father's cantillation, how he trills and turns every word as if it were a priceless pearl, then her heart overflows with happiness. How proud she is that he is such a fine scholar! In her silent thoughts she glories over her great fortune. Why had she been blessed so by Providence, she asks herself? Perhaps it came only as the reward and payment for all the pain and anguish that life had piled upon her?

Father, Mother and the Whole Family

When father's chanting went well so that he himself felt pleased, there was no happier man on earth than he. For father was blessed with a rich imagination and at no other time did it soar as high as when he was cantillating the Book of Esther. Then all that appeared impossible became real. Permeated with the haunting magic which hung over King Ahasueros and his court, he completely took on the personality of "Mordecai the Jew."

Mother always sensed when father was in a light-hearted mood. At such times she enjoyed being peevish. She then became expansive in her complaints. At no other time did she indulge in such a luxury. Surè never uttered a single complaint. She was never peevish. But when she knew that Anshel was in a good mood she took pleasure in grumbling before him. Had she any cause to grumble? On the contrary! It was just a pleasurable self-indulgement. . . .

Father now closed the Bible with great ceremony — and groaned while doing so. No doubt also out of pleasure. He walked good-humoredly up to Surè who stood at the oven with her infant in her arms — slapped the little one playfully on his buttocks and with affected ill humor grunted:

"What are you cooking for dinner to-night, Surè?"

"Cooking? Heavens! What is there to cook?"

"Oh! Let me see!" laughed Anshel with good-natured irony. "Certainly not the kind of dinner that was prepared for King Ahasueros in his capital at Shushan."

And Surè, knowing that Anshel was in a jolly mood, retorted gayly:

"Well, who can equal the wonders that Holy Scripture tells us about?"

With the corner of her apron she now wiped the perspiring forehead of the infant who nestled snugly in the curve of her arm.

"Anshel," said she poutingly, "I have already nursed many children, but none like this one. What a perfect can-

13

nibal! He sucks the very life out of me! God bless his little
soul! May he be protected from the Evil Eye!"

The "cannibal," overcome by his heroic exertions, still
oozed streams of hot perspiration. Once more Surè mopped
his little forehead with the corner of her apron.

"Do you know what, Surè?" remarked Anshel suddenly.
"I have a mind to buy you a goat. You will always have
fresh milk then. So many people in town have goats. It is
so easy to keep one. You just feed it with the kitchen
left-overs."

Anshel delivered himself of these words with such casual-
ness, verve and conviction, as if the animal were already
standing outside tethered to his doorpost.

Surè stared at him with astonishment. His matter-of-
factness disconcerted her:

"Tell me—husband dear, where will you get money for a
goat?"

"Let it not be your concern. If I tell you I will buy a
goat, rest assured you will have a goat. Don't you know
Anshel?" And he drew himself up proudly to his full height.
"Don't you know that whatever Anshel says he means? If
Anshel promises you something you need question no
further."

Mother didn't answer. To all this she kept silent. She
only sighed deeply — one of her well-known disturbing sighs.

The skepticism of her sigh made Anshel's pride suffer. He
fairly exploded:

"Here I come and promise you a goat and all you do
is sigh. Evidently you don't believe me. I see that my
promises haven't the least value for you."

Mother feared she had gone too far! As approachable as
father was when in his good humor, she well knew the
extent of his temper. How she trembled for fear of over-
stepping the boundary! She now tried to pacify him — to
soothe his ruffled pride:

Father, Mother and the Whole Family

"What is the use of my quarreling with you? Just bring home the goat. Then we will see."

This was just one bit too much for Anshel.

"In other words Anshel's words have no significance for you. What? eh!" he asked angrily.

"Who ever said so? You speak just as if I didn't want a goat. Just bring one home. I will look forward to that happy day."

"I thought — I thought" — stammered Anshel, already mollified. Then he drew on his cotton-padded winter coat. Mother helped him to rub the dried mud from its hem. She brushed his hat for him. Anshel smoothed the fringes of his beard with his fingers and picking up his walking stick, left the house to say the twilight prayers at the synagogue.

Mother well knew that it was out of the question for her to expect from father money with which to purchase food for dinner. For, when father returns empty-handed from the market place he — but no! that is not so! Anshel never returns home empty-handed. If it is not money that he brings, it is most certainly a fabulous "goat," a "business" or even "a steamship ticket to America." . . .

So was it this time also. No sooner did Anshel begin to speak about the "goat" than mother understood well enough that he was without a red copper. For whenever father earns a gulden or two as his commission in some commercial transaction, he does not speak about a "goat" but he hums to himself with unspeakable delight a snatch of some melancholy synagogue hymn. And when he enters the house he exclaims with great solemnity:

"Well, wife! You probably want money for dinner. What — no?"

Then with a magnificent sweep of the arm he draws the two glittering gulden from his pocket and lays them on the table. No knight of old ever did deliver his captive enemies to his liege lord, as Anshel delivers his two gulden to Surè.

The Mother

While doing so he elegantly twirls his mustache with two fingers, then playing with his beard, he says:

"There, wife, are Behemoth and Leviathan! Slaughter them — cook or broil them and serve them for dinner."

But after his oration on the "goat" mother knew that that night she could not expect anything from father for dinner, nor from the "young man" — who sewed uppers. The latter was putting by his money for a steamship ticket to America. Only after much quarreling and abuse did she ever succeed in obtaining a blessed groschen from him. She felt now disinclined to exchange bitter words with him. She wanted to preserve as long as possible the tender mood which Anshel's cantillation of the Book of Esther had woven round her like a spell. So she turned for aid to her well-tried friends of last resort: her pots.

What wonderful pots mother had! They seemed but ordinary clay pots — no different from other pots of their kind: earthy, black with soot and flame-baked. Yet they were different from all other pots. Even when it appeared that they contained nothing in them, still mother succeeded in exorcizing, as if by witchcraft, a dinner from their fabulous insides. Mother's pots were milch-cows. She drew nourishment from them like milk from an udder. They always remained true to her. She poured water into them, and they returned her a highly seasoned soup or a delicious borscht. She poured into them hot water and lo and behold! there issued forth dishes fit for a king. Mother exorcized her pots with one magic charm: a sigh. No sooner did the pots hear mother's sigh than they gave forth their pitifully meager nourishment with which to feed her many hungry mouths.

That was hardly to be wondered at. For mother's pots were not just mere pots. She had formed a close alliance with them many, many years before. Some she knew when she was still a little girl, when her mother, by that self-same secret power, forced them to surrender their begrudging bounty. From her mother too she inherited her pots.

There stands the earthen pot with the black band painted on it. Always has it served as the savior of the family. Mother regards it as her best friend. Never has it failed to fulfill her wishes. Wonderful to relate — it has acquired the power of preserving in its innermost recesses the essences of cooked carrots and of pickled meats. On its bottom always rests a thick layer of fat, as if it cannily understands — Oh, that clever pot! — that poor folk may not recklessly indulge themselves in eating up all of their food at one time, but must prudently leave some of it for an evil hour. Always in time of dire need mother turned to it for help. Also now when Anshel left her alone and bewildered with her mirage of a "goat" she turned imploringly to it once more.

She uttered over it her most potent charm: a sigh — poured into it water and the left-overs of yesterday's dinner and seasoned it with a few curses which she leveled at the youngsters who now burst into the house with muddy feet after having navigated all the "oceans" and "lakes" on the street. As if by magic the pot soon released from its secret parts all the fat which had accumulated on its inner surface throughout the years of its service. It gave forth the different aromas of all the foods ever fried and cooked in it. These appetizing, pungent flavors rising up with the steam from its depths, filled the entire room with such tantalizing effect that soon all the children stopped in the midst of their play and ran in to inquire of mother what it was that she was cooking. When Anshel returned from the synagogue he was greeted at the entrance of the house by a titillating aroma so that his mouth began to water. A passage from the Book of Esther, under whose spell he still labored, then recurred to him with a curious persistence:

"Now when the turn of Esther the daughter of Abihail the

17

uncle of Mordecai, who had taken her for his daughter, was
come to go in unto the king —"

He too felt like a royal personage now.

"Wife dear," he exclaimed impulsively as he entered, "do
you know what? I will buy for you a permanent seat in the
synagogue so that you may be the equal of all other decent
folk and not be forced to sit with the riff-raff and the
beggars."

Surè was overcome with astonishment.

"What? You will buy me a seat in the synagogue!" she
gasped.

"Most certainly I will," proudly declaimed Anshel. "A
seat has been left vacant by the wife of Reb Leibish who has
just died. Don't you stand in need of a permanent seat in
the synagogue?"

"Stop your joking!" laughed mother good-naturedly.

Inhaling the delicious aroma which the good pot gave
forth, Anshel's fantasy burst into full bloom. He dwelled
fondly in his imagination on foods salted and foods pep-
pered, to whet his already quite stimulated appetite.

He pulled from his pocket some cigarette paper and rolled
for himself a cigarette to be smoked luxuriously after dinner.
After which he began to think out loud, speaking as if to
himself alone, enumerating all the varieties of pickled and
canned herrings:

A herring — mused Anshel — smothered in onions —
drenched in vinegar. Ah! If only it were served to him he
would surely not refuse it! Or for that matter — even a
white, fleshy herring, dripping in fat, spiced with red pep-
per and served with slices of sour pickle would also prove
a tempting morsel. For a last resort it might also be a
smoked herring — preferably one not too much smoked —
not too dry — from which there still dripped fat. That too
wouldn't be bad. Oh no!

When Surè sees how sorely tempted Anshel is for a bit of

Father, Mother and the Whole Family

herring, she becomes unhappy. The thought gives her no peace. Whenever one of the children clamors for bread and she has none to give it, she does not take it to heart as much as when Anshel mortifies himself for a bit of herring. At such times she turns imploringly to the only savior of the family. She opens the door and calls:

"Dvoyrelè! Dvoyrelè!"

At this outcry, Anshel suddenly reminds himself of his parental duties. He begins to fume and rage:

"Where is that wench? Among decent folk the likes of her already contribute to the income of the household. Only she runs about idling her days away."

After much calling Dvoyrelè enters the house from the street.

From the hullabaloo raised by both father and mother one would be led to imagine, the Lord only knows, what kind of personage this Dvoyrelè was. In reality there entered a little girl of ten or eleven who looked more like eight or nine. Her thin long neck made her head appear like a strange flower stuck on a narrow little pipe. Her meager body was supported by thin little legs which gave the illusion of tiny twigs, such that the slightest gust of wind would surely break. Like a little flower peeping out through the grass, her little face looked naïve in its frame of black hair which poured down like a waterfall to her shoulders, concealing parts of her face, eyes, cheeks, neck and back. She carried in her hand a small unfinished jacket on which she was obviously teaching herself how to sew. But at the same time she carried as if he were glued to her arm, her little brother Meyer, the "big boy." Before the infant whom mother now nurses came, Meyer was known as the "suckling child." After that he became the "big boy." And little Dvoyrelè was henceforth saddled with him. So there he sits — the "big boy" on sister's aching hands like a coiling vine round a tree. From early morning until late in the night, loaded like a

The Mother

beast of burden with him, she plays in her leisure moments a game with pebbles. And with the "big boy" glued to her arm she also teaches herself how to sew.

"Where were you all day long? How is it one never sees you?" began father angrily.

"What do you want of the child?" Mother tried to appease his wrath. "She is quite a young lady, as you see, and must be thinking already of how to earn a livelihood. So she spends most of her time with Feigelè the seamstress and learns how to sew."

Then turning to Dvoyrelè, mother said:

"Run, Dvoyrelè, to the grocer's and see if you can get a herring on credit. Your father would like to have something salty to eat."

Chapter 2

AMERICA

:■■■■■■

AFTER Dvoyrelè had served Feigelè the seamstress for one year she began to bring home her earnings, two gulden a week. Mother sought out a certain pot, one of her "best friends" on which she could always rely, and deposited in it the money Dvoyrelè brought home every week. She swore with a thousand binding oaths that even were she to know, God forbid! that the whole household were to go to the dogs, she would never touch her child's hard-earned money. No! Never! She would put it by until Passover — to buy Dvoyrelè a new pair of shoes and a holiday frock. "The poor child has never worn a decent rag on her back," mother had always reproached herself as long as she could remember. In fact, the child had never worn anything new. All her clothes were either remodeled or patched up beyond recognition.

And truly — it was as if the curse of excommunication hung over the pot. Mother battled like a lioness over her child's small hoard earned by her "blood and sweat." Neither hunger nor cold could move her to weaken in her decision not to touch a groschen of it. Even Anshel's devouring passion for a bit of herring, which ordinarily moved her mother's heart to pity, left her unshaken. She did not make the slightest movement to get near the pot. It was sacrosanct — a forbidden temple.

How difficult it is for the poor to keep their vows! Mother

The Mother

was strong in her determination. But her need was still stronger. And during one critical hour she stealthily approached the pot and "robbed the child." This happened when the Hebrew teacher sent Yoinè home from Hebrew school because he had not been paid tuition for three months. The boy went about aimlessly — doing nothing — and mother's heart ached when she saw that he did not study. Yes! Everything was justified for the sake of learning — even stealing, thought mother determinedly! . . .

When Passover time approached mother removed the pot from its hiding place in a dark corner and took from it the hoarded silver guldens. At first she resolved to ignore all the other pressing household necessities and to spend the money on Dvoyrelè. "After all — it is the child's hard earnings!" But a mother's heart knows strange inner promptings. She thought of the other children and she faltered. Yoinè's breeches were so badly patched that they already had lost their original color, and shamelessly flaunted through their open lattice-work — parts of his underwear. Yet terrible to think — in such tatters was he to accompany his father to the synagogue. Furthermore, how disgraced and humiliated Anshel would feel when standing on the rostrum at the synagogue and cantillating Holy Scripture, and beside him would stand Moishelè dressed in a cap from which the brim was torn.

So night after night mother turned everything over in her mind, made all sorts of calculations. But they all were to no purpose. She at last came to a decision. Whether he wanted to or not the "young man" had to supply the household with shoes. He made an outcry — charged that he was being held up and because of them would never be able to emigrate to America. Despite his protests he nevertheless cut and sewed four pairs of uppers. For Yoinè and Dvoyrelè he made them out of the very best leather; for Yoinè because he was his father's favorite son and a good scholar to boot, and for Dvoyrelè because he loved her.

Therefore, for the money that Dvoyrelè earned mother bought calico for a dress for her, cloth for two pairs of breeches for the boys, and an extra remnant for patches on the "men's" coats.

When the boys put on their new breeches and patched coats during the Passover holidays, mother first noticed that their tattered shirts were not in perfect harmony with their new clothes. Also she suddenly realized the need for giving the boys new caps. So mother sat through half of the night and by the light of a small kerosene lamp, mended the shirts.

Now when Dvoyrelè saw this she could not fall asleep. So she got out of bed in her shift and said:

"Mother, I will help you."

"Get back to bed, Dvoyrelè — it is already late. I can manage all by myself — never fear."

"I am not at all sleepy," remonstrated Dvoyrelè, and quickly threading her needle she tore the shirt from mother's hand.

"Here, you have Yoinè's shirt," said mother. "I will do father's myself."

It is late in the night. All are asleep in the home of Anshel the Synagogue Reader of Scripture. Outside, the voices of the night are heard in muted, sad cadences. A cricket chirps in a monotone up in the chimney and the clock with its heavy, swinging pendulum rumbles out the time. The hour is late. The darkness of the night peers through the slits in the shutters. On the white shirts which lie on the little table falls the ghastly light of the kerosene lamp. And on the half-darkened walls become silhouetted in strong relief two huge shadows, petrified and immobile. One of the shadows is large. The other is small. Both go through the pantomime of sewing. . . .

But when the Passover Feast of Liberation arrived and

The Mother

Surè beheld all her children in their dazzling finery, her eyes lit up with pleasure. She watched them seated about the table one beside the other. Their white collars were stiffly starched and pressed. Moishelè wore a new cap and Yoinè purposely had drawn up his coat in order to display his new breeches. The new boots of all the children creaked alarmingly. The youngsters did nothing but walk about in order to hear their boots creak. The sound was diverting and made them feel important. Dvoyrelè, washed and combed — her hair hanging down in two black braids — looked adorable in her new calico frock, trimmed with a red sash that had somehow survived the years since mother was a girl.

Mother's joy in regarding her children was but short-lived. She had been so fatigued with her preparation for the holiday, that she fell asleep at the table. But next morning when she looked down from the women's balcony in the synagogue and saw Anshel in the pulpit, reading from the Holy Scrolls, flanked on either side by Moishelè and Yoinè, resplendent in their new caps, boots and breeches, her heart swelled with pride. Who could compare with her in joy? It was for the first time in her life that she had seen her children rigged out in such holiday magnificence.

But alas! The holiday which began in such festive mood ended very sadly. On the third day of Passover week, Shloimè, the "young man," began making ready for his journey across the seas.

"Father — mother," said he. "I am sailing to America."

Although everybody well knew that Shloimè was putting money by for a steamship ticket, and all, including father and mother, looked forward to his ultimate departure, his announcement came with the impact of a thunderbolt. More than once, when the family was seated at table, Anshel would turn to his eldest son and in Biblical metaphor would ask him:

"When, O my son, will you redeem us from our everlasting exile? When will you leave for America and lead us all out of bondage to the Promised Land?"

Anshel even put this question in a briefer form. He would say:

"Tell me, my son — when will the Messiah come?"

Yet, when the much expected, much talked-about event arrived, and the "young man" was already thinking of getting ready for the journey, father looked dazedly at mother and mother looked mutely back at him, as if some great calamity were about to take place. Father regarded it all as preposterous and incredible.

"Ah! You are just talking nonsense."

"But, father, I am in earnest! Immediately after the holidays, I will travel with the emigrant wagons to Kohl and then steal across the border," insisted Shloimè with resolution.

"Just think of it! He wants to journey to America," chaffed father, much amused. "Do you think going to America is child's play? I want you to know that America is not Tischnowitz! Just look who wants to go to America!"

When, however, it began to dawn upon them that their son was in earnest, for he had now called in Shmuel the Singer-machine agent to sell him his machine, then mother's heart grew sad and father became thoughtful.

"Tell me, my son, what will you do in America?" asked father disconsolately.

"Work."

"Do you think that America stands in terrible need of workers such as you?" continued father derisively.

"A worker in America is highly esteemed. He is 'all right' there!" confidently answered the "young man," using the only English words he knew, the words that every emigrant to America learns even before he sets out on his journey.

"But not such workers as you," persisted father in his disparagement.

The Mother

Mother would not permit that the machine be sold. It had been their only source of livelihood — she argued. No matter how stingy her son was, no matter how much she had to scold before he gave her a single groschen, he nevertheless was their only support. Whenever bread proved scarce in the house and all that father brought home was a "goat" or a "seat in the synagogue," then the "young man," whether he wanted to or not, was forced to loosen his purse-strings. And mother was convinced that it all came from the machine.

"Don't sell the machine!" pleaded mother and her voice trembled. "You will take the bread from our mouths."

"What will you do with the machine, mother? Of what earthly use is it to you?"

"It is my breadwinner!" she doggedly insisted.

And mother embraced the machine in a manner as if she would defend it against some aggressor.

"When there is a machine in the house there is some possibility of earning a groschen," she debated.

"But who will sew on it?" wonderingly asked Shloimè.

"Who? Who?" asked mother, herself looking perplexed. "Don't worry! Some one will be found to sew on it," she confidently added.

Despite her assurance, mother became frightened when she thought about the matter. She, as well as every one else, knew who it was that would sew on it....

When father saw that the "young man" was in earnest about going to America he changed his tone. Instead of ridiculing him, he suddenly became very thoughtful. He now gave him solemn advice as to how to deport himself out in the great world:

"Don't for one moment think that to travel to America is a very easy matter. Remember — you first have to cross a great ocean. To travel to Germany is also no trifle — understand me well! You have to travel, my son, through many countries and after you pass over the great ocean and reach America and finally find yourself in Castle Garden, then ..."

Anshel regarded himself as a man of the world. In his youth he had come in slight contact with the Enlightenment movement among the Jews, and read little Hebrew books on secular subjects. Even now, after so many years, he still found pleasure in occasionally reading a Hebrew journal which he borrowed from the local Hebrew teacher. Yes, Anshel was convinced that he was a thoroughly worldly man. He described to his son, most graphically, what he was to encounter along the journey — the numerous boundaries he would have to cross, all the great cities he would visit in transit, about the ships that sail on the ocean, about America, and finally about Castle Garden. He spoke of them as if he had seen them with his own eyes.

"Most important of all," Anshel cautioned his son, "don't speak to a soul on the way. The world is full of charlatans and you might find yourself in deep waters as a result of having had anything to do with them. Also, when you will have crossed to the other side of the border, see that you do not run. Walk slowly and casual-like — so that people may not recognize that you are a stranger. And when you will meet a German, say to him: 'Gut Morgen, mein Herr.' The Germans are a fine people and if you will say to them: 'Gut Morgen,' they will not ask you for your passport or anything else. A day before you embark you must eat absolutely nothing except a lemon.

"And when with God's help you will reach America — But wait! Should a storm — God forbid! — break out while you are on the sea, you mustn't look down into the sea but lie down flat on your belly, bury your face in the pillow and recite a psalm. Throughout the voyage read about Jonah and the whale and when God in His mercy will help you to survive your ocean ordeal and you will be admitted into Castle Garden and should the Americans ask you: 'For

The Mother

what have you come here?' Then you must answer in your most polite manner: 'I have come to earn my bread by the sweat of my brow.' You must also tell them: 'I have an address to an uncle.' Then they will do you no harm. The Americans, I would like you to know, are a very fine people and very rich. When you come to them, especially if you happen to be a Jew, they receive you with open arms. . . ."

When father lectured Shloimè on how he should behave out in the wide world, all the children stood about listening with mouths agape at the strange things he told him. They now stood in awe of their eldest brother. To them it appeared as if in the folds of his coat there were already concealed the biting winds and the shrieking gales of the terrifying ocean.

Father now sent for a sheet of paper and a new pen-point, which he moistened with his lips and dipping it in the inkwell, wrote in a highly embellished hand, a letter to Uncle Pinchas in America. His exertions over the letter made father perspire very profusely. The writing took a few hours and all this while every one was forced to keep quiet and walk on tiptoe. . . .

The letter was duly signed and sealed, but when it came to writing the address on the envelope, father was stumped. He had completely forgotten the address of Uncle Pinchas in America.

Father ransacked all the drawers in the house — looked feverishly among old letters and papers but of the address there was no sign. In as much as the letter was already written and Anshel felt that it would be a great pity to let such eloquence and beautiful calligraphy go to waste, he without further ado wrote on the envelope and in Yiddish: "To Uncle Pinchas in America." Then he handed it to his son with the following words:

"When you will get to New York you will inquire of some one where Uncle Pinchas lives. It won't be very difficult to find him. What is the difference between New York and America? Same thing."

None of the children, not even the eldest, Shloimè, knew exactly who this Uncle Pinchas was, whether he branched from mother's family or from father's.

Surè offered no advice to her son. Neither did she give him a letter to his uncle. Of such matters she knew but little. Only, together with Dvoyrelè, she sat up night after night until the wee hours of the morning, mending his shirts and socks. Every shirt she packed into his box was accompanied with her blessings and moistened with her tears. . . .

The day after Passover, father folded the letter written to Uncle Pinchas and his son's money into the little bag that Dvoyrelè had sewn for her brother. He then hung it about his neck for safety. He also gave him a pair of phylacteries and a prayer-book, and made him swear a solemn oath that never would he forswear his Judaism. For the last time mother laundered for him his fringed prayer under-shawl and made him faithfully promise that he would wear it throughout the journey. It would thus shield him against all harm. She also put a slice of bread and some salt in his sling-bag and wrapped it in a piece of paper to ward off the Evil Eye.

Then Shloimè, the "young man," took up his box. Father and mother accompanied him to the place where the carts stood. When the wagon which carried emigrants to the border town, Kohl, arrived, they took farewell of him.

All this while mother had not betrayed a single sign of grief. She had succeeded in stifling her feelings. But when her son took her in his arms and kissing her, said, "Farewell, mother!" she burst into bitter weeping.

"Do not forget me, my child!"

"Never fear that, mother!"

The wagon bore her son away into the dark night. . . .

Chapter 3

A NEW BREADWINNER

■■■■■■■

WHEN the eldest of her brood had left for America, mother felt as if her right arm had been cut off. Now for the first time it became clear to her how correct she was in her valuation of the sewing machine. Despite his stinginess her son had nevertheless helped her occasionally with a gulden or two. Now she did not know what to do. She found herself in a state of utter helplessness. Where was money for bread to come from? Who would help her now? To whom could she turn?

The sewing machine, however, still stood in the room. Mother forbade any one to touch it. There was no one to operate it. But one evening when father and mother sat quietly talking together after dinner the subject of a means of livelihood turned up. Mother lamented:

"When Shloimè was still here, no matter how bad times were, I nevertheless saw a blessed groschen before my eyes from time to time. And now, we might as well die of starvation."

Said father: "What about the machine?"

"Can I eat it?" answered mother exasperatedly.

"What about Dvoyrelè? She's a big girl already. Why should she continue to slave for complete strangers and receive nothing but a gulden or two a week, when—"

"Why must you always begin about Dvoyrelè over and over again as if there were nobody else but she on earth?"

"Why should Dvoyrelè toil to enrich others when she might open for herself a little dressmaking establishment?" heatedly persisted father.

"I will not permit you to enslave Dvoyrelè — to put her under the yoke! She is so young! I know only too well that once we harness her to the machine, she will always remain strapped to it."

"What do you think she is doing now? Dancing?" growled father irately.

"But she is only a little child!" remonstrated mother.

Mother's protests were of no avail. It was she herself who summoned Shmuel the agent and had him exchange the machine so that Dvoyrelè might sew dresses on it instead of uppers. She was to pay for it in weekly installments of half a ruble. The contract with Feigelè the seamstress was also broken.

When Dvoyrelè sat down to sew at the machine, mother said to her tremblingly:

"I know very well, child, that I am yoking you like an ox to a plow. How else can I help myself? There seems to be no other way out. Perhaps it is the bitter fate of both of us that it be as it is."

Dvoyrelè could not understand why her mother lamented over her so. On the contrary, she regarded herself as fully grown up. Was she not working for herself now? This thought filled her with pride.

"Mother," she said gayly, "it is better so. I will be my own mistress now and not a slave to others."

Dvoyrelè was fifteen years old. She was proud of the fact that she was already grown up and was of help to her mother. But mother continued to lament over her:

"My daughter, it is as if I have placed a leaden yoke on your young shoulders."

The relationship between mother and daughter was a

curious one. It seemed as if they had been fused into one being.

No one understood mother's pain as much as Dvoyrelè. She had become aware of it from the very first day that she began to think for herself. And if she worked for her it was not because she wanted to, for Dvoyrelè did not regard herself as an exemplary or virtuous daughter, but because she felt that her mother's duty was hers too. The burden of that duty she had cheerfully accepted when she was still a little girl. For this very reason she was filled with wonder at her mother because of her incessant lamentations over her.

"How can you help yourself otherwise, mother? What can you do?" she asked, folding her little hands over her little breasts just like mother was wont to do.

"After all you are but a girl! It is quite time enough for you to be concerned over your own affairs," answered mother.

Dvoyrelè became lost in thought. At first she did not grasp the sense of mother's last words. Afterwards, when their meaning first dawned upon her a hot flush suffused her pale cheeks.

"I will have time to worry about marriage later, mother," she stammered.

Always, since Dvoyrelè was a child, mother imparted her troubles to her. She had no one else to whom she might pour out her overburdened heart, discuss her problems with, or from whom she could seek advice — only Dvoyrelè. She found it impossible to discuss these matters with father. He was always absorbed in innumerable and wonderful plans for getting rich. Each day, when he returned home from the market place, it was invariably with a brand-new plan. When the drinking of soda water came into fashion he decided to go in for its manufacture. At one time he had even secured a partner for leasing a windmill. On another occasion he was on the point of buying a lottery business. The carrying out of each successive plan hung on a hair. But as always, it all came to nothing.

Then again, Anshel was always up to the hilt in communal politics and public scandals. In this he was without a peer in town. For every one of his failures father found a fitting excuse. And in case mother cornered him in argument, and that happened very seldom, father with skillful evasion and with much enthusiasm commenced to dilate upon a dazzling new plan:

"Have patience, wife! Just give me sufficient time to carry out my plan — then you will have all that your heart can crave for the Sabbath — as well as wood for the winter. You will be short of nothing. Wait and see!"

Since mother stood in such great need of counsel, she drew Dvoyrelè into the net of her troubles. She fully realized that she was doing her an injury. And often she lay in bed awake, brooding on the wrong she was doing her:

"What do I want of the child?" she would ask herself. "Why do I enmesh her in my misfortunes?"

Despite it all, Dvoyrelè was the only one to whom mother could bare her heart.

Now that Dvoyrelè became her sole breadwinner, it was quite natural that mother should come to consult with her about all the household affairs:

"What shall I do, child, about Gedaliah? The teacher has sent him home again from Hebrew school."

Hearing this, Dvoyrelè put aside her work and folded her hands over her little breasts just like mother was wont to do. Her childish brow became furrowed with thought.

"Perhaps you ought to take the two gulden out of the pot and send it to the teacher on account?" she faltered.

"If I do that father will have no holiday clothes. I have been stinting and scraping together these few miserable groschen to buy him at least a ready-to-wear suit of clothes.

The Mother

How I blush with shame on the Sabbath and on holidays
when I see him mount the rostrum in the synagogue, dressed
in his week-day tattered coat!"

"I will soon have ready the shirts I am sewing for
Leyelè," cheerfully consoled Dvoyrelè. "Then you will be
able to return the two gulden to the pot."

Then something unexpected happened. Mother found a
new source of income. Moishelè "The Ox," who only a short
while before was but a schoolboy, began to earn money
which he conscientiously brought home. It came so unexpectedly that mother found it hard to believe.

Moishelè was two years younger than Dvoyrelè. His pet
name, "The Ox," father gave him because there was no
power on earth or in heaven that could persuade, cajole,
bribe or threaten him into studying. Nothing availed, neither
blows nor abuse. He stubbornly refused to be educated.
And all the wisdom and knowledge that his teacher tried
to cram into his young head was wasted on him. On the
basis of this mental obtuseness father logically and somewhat maliciously deducted that he had inherited it from
his maternal ancestry....

Moishelè "The Ox" was cut out to be a business man
instead. He first began to barter and trade when he attended school. He was always buying and selling things
to his schoolmates. His business genius was innate. He
would, for instance, purchase a pocketknife for twenty
groschen, and then raffle it at a groschen a number. There
being one hundred of such numbers he would net a clear
profit of eighty groschen. Once he had disposed of the
knife he would raffle a pocketbook or a pair of gloves. When
he grew older he bought tobacco and paper and manufactured cigarettes by hand which he afterwards sold in
the town. His ingenuity and resourcefulness knew no bounds.
Every Purim he organized his own troupe of players and
made the rounds of all the Jewish homes — giving per‹

formances from which he collected a tidy sum. On the eve
of the Passover holidays he would remove for burning all
the crumbs of unleavened bread from Jewish homes for
two groschen a home. When Shevuoth arrived he would
engage a few wagons, have them driven for him to the
river's end and then load them with water reeds. These
he would cart away to town and have them sold at a considerable profit. Similarly, during the Feast of Tabernacles,
he would sell to the pious fragrant pine branches with
which to cover their improvised pastoral booths. Every
season and every occasion brought its own variety of business. During the summer he stood guard over the clothes
which the bathers left on the banks of the river. In winter
time he sold paper lanterns of his own manufacture.

Until he was thirteen years old he stood in mortal fear
of father. He dutifully attended Hebrew school and went
to services at synagogue. But no sooner had he been con-
firmed than he decided to declare his independence from
his father. After the "great revolution" he refused to attend synagogue and Hebrew school any more. And so
Moishelè hung aimlessly about the market place, and following the example of the other Jewish merchants, he
lounged outside the candy shop where the Polish gentry
and landowners would come to buy confections. If a peasant
came to town, Moishelè was the first to climb onto his cart
and hastily pushing his hand into the straw, discover for
himself what the peasant had brought to sell. Was it perhaps eggs that he was carrying — then Moishelè would
run helter-skelter to the egg dealer with the good news.
Or if it was wheat — the wheat dealer would be quickly
apprised. For which service Moishelè would receive his
reward.

When he had saved a few gulden, Moishelè became a
trader on his own account. On occasion he dealt in eggs or
in butter and even in live poultry.

The Mother

On one beautiful summer's day "The Ox" brought home from the fair a dozen eggs.

"Mother," said he, "here are a dozen eggs."

Surè regarded him with amazement. She could not believe her own eyes. At first she turned deathly pale. She was afraid she was going to faint. Surely, the boy must have gone and stolen the eggs from a peasant's cart.

"Moishelè! In Heaven's name — what have you done? Get out of my house! Do you want to bring misfortune on us?"

"Why do you excite yourself so, mother? The story is very simple. I bought from a peasant for Lézèr, the egg dealer, a gross of eggs. He gave me a dozen of them as my commission on the purchase. If you don't want to take my word for it — you may go and ask him."

Surè wrapped her shawl about herself and went out to the market place to look for Lézèr the egg dealer. When she discovered that her son had not deceived her, she became radiant and accepted the eggs.

Henceforth Moishelè brought home from every fair either a dozen eggs or some butter. On a Friday he would even bring home a live chicken. He thus became a great help to mother.

But Moishelè was not satisfied with his petty triumphs. He aimed at bigger deals. He wanted to engage in "big business" — like an honest-to-goodness merchant. With the aid of some boards he hammered together a booth and on every fair day he made a brave display of his merchandise. Sometimes he sold remnants of ribbon, or damaged goods. He was not any too fastidious as to what he sold; one day a dry-goods merchant — the next day a dealer in wheat. It wasn't long before Moishelè contributed half of the household income. In town he had already attained to the distinction of a merchant.

When Anshel, who thought highly of his own abilities as

a business man (only, the Devil take it — he had no luck),
saw how his son succeeded in his affairs and in fact had
already outstripped him, he could not fully understand the
miracle.

"Just look at your merchants! Look who becomes a business man to-day!" said father disdainfully one day as the
family sat at table. "There is the new world for you!" And
he pointed mockingly at his red-headed, freckled boy seated
next to mother who figuratively, like a colony hen, pro-
tectively spread her wing over her chick.

"What is the difference? Well — have it your own way:
so he is not a business man!" answered mother with some
irritation. "Isn't it better to be a business man and to earn
money than to be a business man and not to earn any?"

Hearing these words, father took the spoon from his
mouth and angrily pushed his soup bowl from him.

"What did you say?" he stammered.

Mother now regretted having put Anshel to shame. His
discomfiture cut her to the heart. How she would have liked
to recall her words! But she did not know how. She kept
silent.

Then father began to wallow in his self-torment and
bruised vanity. He commenced to interpret mother's words.

"In other words," said he, "you think Moishelè is a better
business man than I because he earns money and I don't.
Isn't that what you have been trying to prove to me?"

"Woe is me, Anshel! Who, God forbid, is trying to draw
a comparison between you and him?" exclaimed mother, all
aghast at the mere thought of it. "You are a scholar and
what is he? Only an ignorant loafer!"

And not succeeding in stifling a groan, mother ladled some
more soup into Moishelè's bowl and said to him:

"Naturally I would prefer that you go to the synagogue
than that you bring me a fortune."

The Mother

Hearing which, father became reconciled to his dinner. He drew his soup bowl to him.

"But you, my child," said mother to Gedaliah, who liked to study and was an apt pupil, "you must follow in your father's footsteps rather than in your brother's."

And she put into his plate an extra lump of meat.

Chapter 4

A LETTER FROM AMERICA

■■■■■■■

THEN came the great fortune.

A letter arrived from America and some money with it, too. Another letter had already preceded it. As soon as he had landed in America the "young man" had written:

"Dear Father and Mother:

"I have survived the journey across the terrible sea and have safely reached America. Everything that you, dear father, told me about the ocean was nothing compared with what it actually was. For fourteen days I lived in a smelly cellar together with the other passengers. I buried my face in a blanket throughout the journey and I did not know for certain whether I was dead or alive. And regarding your advice that should I meet a German on the other side of the frontier I must say to him: 'Guten Morgen' I wish to inform you that I did not see a single blessed German all the time. No sooner had I, together with the rest of our party of emigrants, stolen across the border after dark, than they took me and all the others and locked us in a railroad car just as if we had been convicts. Then they transported us direct to the ship. For this very reason it was impossible for me to alight at any of the railway stations we passed and have the fortune of at least having one good peep at a German."

Father was amazed that the Germans should do such a

thing! The Germans were, after all, such fine people.... He blamed it all on his son.

"Very likely," said he, "if the Germans once cast their eyes on such a Schlemihl...I would like to see if they would dare lock me up in a railroad car were I to travel to America!"

After this letter, none further came for many, many months. Surè believed that her son, God forbid! had met with a sudden death. This fear tormented her so that she could not fall asleep. A new source of anxiety was added to her already unbearable burden of woe.

"Anshel!" she would call across to father's bed at night, when she found sleep impossible. "What do you think has happened to our son? I have the most terrible forebodings. We should not have sent him away — to face unknown dangers alone — to cross the dreadful seas and to die in a foreign land!"

"Most likely the scamp wasted all the money that he earned and then went to the dogs. Once a profligate always a profligate," declared Anshel prophetically.

Month after month passed by. The Passover again arrived. It always was the best beloved and the happiest of all the holidays for Anshel and his family. If a miracle was to happen to any one of them it was sure to be then. And this time the miracle did happen. A letter arrived from the "young man." In it was also enclosed his photograph and a money draft for twenty-five gulden. Surè looked dazedly at the photograph. She could hardly believe her own eyes.

"Is this my son?" she gasped.

Her son looked out at her from the photograph as if he were alive. He wore a short, elegant coat. A gold chain dangled on his vest. This induced Anshel to deliver himself magnificently of an ingenious deduction:

A Letter from America

"If he wears a gold chain most likely he also owns a gold watch, too."

For who ever heard of a man wearing a gold chain without having a watch on its end?

Father was now thoroughly convinced that his son had prospered in America. Wasn't the "young man" photographed standing near a tea-table that was loaded with many dainties and good things to eat? And was there not placed close by an immense basket of artificial roses? And did he not stand hatless as no good orthodox Jew should? And had he not written:

"Dear Mother—do not think I have forgotten you. Just as a mother cannot forget her son, so is it impossible for a son to forget his mother who has given him birth."

At this passage in the letter Surè burst into tears. Had she been reading the Book of Lamentations during the Memorial Fast of the Destruction of the Holy Temple, her tears would not have flowed faster and hotter. Anshel found it difficult to quiet her. He shouted at her:

"For God's sake let me go on reading! You can cry afterwards!"

Father resumed reading:

"I have not written to you all this while because I really had nothing to write. I have experienced much—suffered much in America. If the water in the sea were turned into ink, the trees in the forest into pens, and the dome of the sky into paper, yet they would not suffice to record the bitter struggles I have endured during the past year in America. . . ."

"What else would you have? We have taken our son and cast him away to the other end of the earth!" moaned Surè, and she burst out anew into weeping.

"In Heaven's name calm yourself! Let me read!" shouted Anshel, and he turned once more to his letter:

"Yet, praise God, all that is already behind me and I

can happily write you of it. I did not write to you all along because I wanted to send you more than mere empty words."

"Do you understand his meaning?" asked father, much pleased. "He did not want to dispose of matters with mere empty words! Surè — I would like you to know that America is making a man out of our boy!"

"And now, dear father," the letter went on to say, "I will write you of everything that I have gone through. When I landed in America I immediately inquired after Uncle Pinchas for whom you gave me a letter. But no one seemed to know him. I asked our fellow countrymen about him. They did not know either. In this manner I succeeded in wasting many weeks of my time looking for an Uncle Pinchas that no one had ever even heard of. Had you not given me that letter to Uncle Pinchas it would have been much better for me. You would then have spared me much trouble, time and energy which I should have given to earning a livelihood."

"And all that results when you send a fool to the fair," interjected father sagely, repeating an old saw.

"If the water in the sea were turned into ink — the trees in the forest into pens"— father and mother became much alarmed. May God have mercy upon us! What really could have happened to Shloimè? Their alarm, however, was utterly unjustified, as the remainder of the letter soon convinced them. It appeared that during the first week he spent the nights in the home of one countryman — the second week in the home of another. Another countryman introduced him into the shoe factory where he worked and it resulted in his employment there. And now, at the time of the writing of the letter, he was sleeping at the home of a fourth countryman whom he paid one dollar a week for the privilege.

"Do you understand, wife?" exclaimed Anshel with incredulity. "He pays the equivalent of two guldens a week for lodgings — and that for sleeping privileges only! In America one gulden has as much value as two gulden for us here."

"Most likely he cannot help himself!" commented mother, attempting to explain away the unheard-of extravagance of her son.

... Shloimè wished to console his parents, however, with the fact that he was doing well, God be praised! Only how much he was earning he did not mention. Nevertheless he promised:

"Have no fear, mother! I will never forget you. I think of you both night and day."

"May God grant him health and happiness for that!" murmured mother, and she stealthily wiped the tears from her eyes with the corner of her apron.

"Of course, I am concerned about my future"— wrote the "young man." "But most of all I am concerned for Dvoyrelè. What will become of her if she continues to stay at home? In America young girls earn well. Very often they meet with good fortune and they get married. A girl like Dvoyrelè could become happy here. In America girls don't need dowries in order to get married. Here it is a topsy-turvy world. The man has to supply the dowry — not the woman. Dvoyrelè could get happily married here. Girls from the old country are in great demand because the American girls are very brazen and spoiled."

Anshel ceased reading and caught his breath.

"Haven't I always told you that it was senseless for us to remain here? Isn't there a land called America on God's earth? Why do we stay here?" heatedly asked father.

"But read further," begged mother impatiently. So father continued:

"And the boys too can become something worth while here. American children work and they bring home their earnings. Father also will do well here. Readers of Scripture are very scarce in America. No one here can read properly. Father could easily procure a position in a synagogue as Reader. Therefore, mother dear, cease your worrying. Surely God will help us and we will yet be reunited in great happiness. Then you won't need to work so hard and to worry yourself sick over us. Things are different in America. Children work for their parents and not the parents for their children. Here you will sit in the 'poller' on a 'rockin chair' and the children will work for you, and not you for the children."

Even though mother did not know what "poller" and "rockin chair" actually meant she imagined that they stood for something good. This generosity of her son once again released in her a flood of tears. Only this time they were tears of joy.

For the first time in her life that was without hope and without joy — some one out of his own free will had offered her consolation — had breathed into her soul the hope for a better and a happier existence. Her son from America consoling her! Was it not in reparation for all the years of torment and poverty that a kindly Providence was bringing to her now, she asked herself tearfully? ...

It never occurred to Surè that she was working herself to death or that she was eating her heart away because of the many cares that rested on her. Was it not for her children that she was doing it all? Then what did it matter? And now her own son came and consoled her!

"My dear son, may God console you as you have consoled me with your kind words."

She made Anshel include these words as her personal message to Shloimè in the letter he wrote to his son in reply. At first he put up a struggle against its inclusion. Wouldn't people laugh at her in America for writing such things? They would say: "These are but the foolish words

A Letter from America

of a woman." Only Surè remained obstinate. She gave him
no rest until he had written what she had asked him to.

"How then must I write — not like a woman?" she protested. "Am I not a woman?"

It is hard to imagine fully the sensation that the letter
from America created in Anshel's home. The fact of the
money alone that the "young man" had sent, had set the
town agog. Everybody spoke with bated breath of the great
fortune that had befallen Anshel. And Anshel too regarded
himself as the most fortunate man on earth. He could
henceforth speak of nothing but of "his America." And as
he sat among his cronies in the synagogue he would describe to them in the greatest detail the wonders of America, as if he had already beheld them with his own eyes.

"In our America things are done different," he would
say with great disdain. The impression he tried to give
was that he was only a guest staying for a little while
in his home town and that in reality he was a man of tremendous importance — an American, if you please. It even
came to pass that when some local gossip of communal affairs, which he previously had so relished, was imparted
to him, he would shrug his shoulders and say:

"What does all that concern me? I don't belong here
any more. I am already on my way to America...."

That Passover mother not only clothed all the children
from head to foot and ordered new garments for Anshel
but she also indulged herself the luxury for the first time
since she was married, of a new dress and a pair of shoes.
And before her neighbors on the women's balcony in the
synagogue, she would boast:

"Because my dear husband cannot buy me shoes, what
does the dear Lord do? He has my son send me money
from America for a pair."

And all the women envied her. And Surè's heart rejoiced.
During this Passover, the congregation at the little syna-

gogue listened to a new and marvelous kind of reading of Scripture. Never had Anshel's voice sounded so clear and vibrant. He trilled like a bird, prolonged his *fioritura* deliciously and crooned every sacred word until the color of ripe apples came to mother's cheeks. For the first time in many years her eyes glowed with pride and happiness. All the shadows of an unhappy life disappeared from her forehead as if by magic, and her youth blossomed forth again. Tears welled up in her eyes and blinded her.

"God!" she exulted in her heart. "Why is all this coming to me?"

And she believed that she was the happiest woman on earth. And all the other women envied her too.

Chapter 5

HENECH

•••••••

W HEN Dvoyrelè became an independent seamstress and opened her own establishment, she began to meet young men — workers. One of these pleased her more than all the others. His name was Henech. Because Dvoyrelè bccame much attached to him and because he exercised a great molding influence on her character — we shall now concern ourselves exclusively with him even though he plays no part in the development of our story.

All the time that Henech was a child he slept with his mother. His two little brothers also slept in the same bed. On cold winter nights when there were not enough coverlets in the house to keep everybody warm, the children, as if by mutual agreement, snuggled into mother's bed. Then all the old discarded coats and tattered quilts were unearthed and piled in a small mountain on the bed. But none of these could give as much warmth as did father's fur coat, which he had received as a wedding gift from mother.

Father was a Talmudic scholar and even in his youth had been famed for his great learning. The fur coat was already frayed and threadbare and its collar, which in better days had given its wearer such an air of distinction and prosperity, now presented a woebegone and bedraggled appearance. Just the same, when the coat was spread over the bed, it wrapped about the entire family with its warmth. No sooner was it removed, than it was as if the sole pro-

tector of the home had been snatched away and mother
and the children had the curious sensation that they were
lying stark naked out in the bitter cold.

In truth, the fur coat represented in itself the person
of father — the protector. Every day before dawn, in the
coldest weather, father sat down to study the Talmud
aloud by the light of a kerosene lamp. The great shadow
that his body cast sprawled over the wall and filled half
of the room. He intoned the ancient words in a sad and
depressed monotone. They sounded as if they were coming
from afar — so far, that they must have come from within.
Most of the nights it was bitterly cold in the room. The
night struggled to creep into the house through the little
window, but it could not. For the panes were filigreed
with frosted flowers. And father, dressed in his thin and
tattered summer coat, sat huddled over his Talmud and
swayed to and fro like the pendulum of a clock. And as
he swayed forward and backward, the shadow he cast on
the wall also swayed with him. Mother knew but too well
the reason why he sat studying in the cold room instead
of in the well-heated synagogue. It was because he would
not remove his fur coat from mother's bed. It happened
more than once that mother threw his coat from the bed
and angrily bade him put it on:

"Why do you sit here in the cold room? Is it not warmer
in the synagogue?" she would reproach him.

Father did not answer. He was a silent man by nature.
He never uttered an unnecessary word. And so he continued
sitting over his Talmud and intoning the sacred words to
himself. Gradually the cold room and all the hard times
that it stood for vanished from father's consciousness. It
was as if he were already basking in the warm sun that
shines in those warm countries in which he found himself
in his imagination. . . .

Little Henech snuggled close to mother in bed, under the

Henech

warm fur coat, and regarded father with his black sparkling eyes. He was much more absorbed in the shadow on the wall than in father. Looking at father's shadow so intently he became grave and thoughtful. The little room then became full of that sanctity that father's studying conjured. The cold and the poverty that hung over the bed and the children disappeared. In the half-darkness, under the light of the shadow-spinning lamp, the bed and all that was piled on it became transformed into an awesome mountain — a mountain of human heads. . . . Every broken chair or bench appeared as if it were about to spring into life. Every pair of breeches that hung on a chair — every little frock, every pair of shoes, every pot on the stove — seemed as if they were become metamorphosed into living creatures — into wild horses, cows, animals and chickens. Everything lived — breathed — had a soul. All these inanimate objects were but souls in straying transmigration that had gathered to listen to father studying aloud the Talmud and by that means to find salvation and be elevated to a higher sphere. . . .

And Henech lay with mother . . . he, a young man of ten years, who already studied the Talmud, whom every one praised because he was such a bright boy. He it was who lay with mother in the same bed — just as if he were a girl! Overcome with shame Henech hastily tumbled out of mother's bed. And so that he might torment himself the more and in order to overcome the Evil Spirit that tempted him to remain in bed, he first of all exposed his little bare feet to the cold. Then he sprang out of bed and pulled on his tattered breeches, shirt, and his little fringed prayer shawl that was worn underneath his shirt. In vain mother cried:

"Are you mad, Henech? You will catch cold!"

Henech, just like his father, answered nothing. He only muttered something under his breath. So that even father

49

interrupted his study for a minute, and half as if to himself he muttered:

"It is early yet. Go back to bed. The water is still frozen."

Henech answered father — also indirectly:

"I don't want to sleep any more."

Henech hurriedly made ready to say his prayers but before doing so he had to make his ablutions. He put his hand into the water pail. The water was frozen. Recollecting what father did, he took a meat chopper and broke off a piece of ice. This he held in the palm of his hand. It burned into his flesh like a hot coal. So he juggled it gingerly from one hand to another — rubbing it for an instant between his palms.

"Just see, Gedaliah, what the boy is doing," called his mother from the bed in alarm.

Gedaliah knew what the boy was about. He did not answer.

A few minutes later — two shadows move to and fro across the wall. One is huge, bearded with thick, accentuated eyebrows. It sways slowly and rhythmically, like the pendulum of a clock. The other is small and restive, and moves impetuously, like a brooklet leaping among the rocks. Two voices are heard. One sounds earnest and sad and distant, like the overtones of an echo. The other sounds nervous, tense and impatient. It is that of a child.

. . . .

Henech remained deeply religious until he was about thirteen or fourteen. He had inherited from his father that unostentatious piety that wrapped his spirit about like a prayer shawl. A silent prayer, like unstruck music, always sounded within him. Since childhood he had that happy faculty of seeing before his mind's eye all the happenings of the Bible in the most graphic and colorful manner. These mental pictures formed of Holy Scripture inflamed his imag-

ination. He vicariously lived through them. The patri-
archs, Abraham, Isaac, Jacob, Joseph and his brethren,
Moses, and all the other heroes of the Bible were for him
living, contemporary creatures. He was more absorbed in
their lives than in the prosaic, poverty-stricken existence
at home. His childish heart was full of longing for all the
holy places in the Land of Israel and for the religious life
so rich in spiritual experience.

With that passionate hunger for ideal truth that only
the young are capable of, he wholeheartedly believed that
the Messiah would come and that he would bring salvation
to all suffering humanity. So he waited daily his coming
and the advent of the eternal life. To Henech the Mes-
sianic redemption was inevitable. He waited for it with a
simple, indestructible faith and crystal-clear vision — as if
he were only waiting for an everyday reality to take place.
Oh! that the happy and far-off Passover from the life of
pain and travail to the glorious existence of perpetual beati-
tude might soon arrive — prayed Henech in his childish
heart that was consecrated to God! ...

Henech's piety was always unobtrusive. In the synagogue
he would hide in a corner and pray unnoticed. Often when
he came to those prayers that dealt with Jerusalem, the
Temple and the Messiah, he wept and prayed to God with
all the naïveté of his childish soul, that He should be moved
to pity for the suffering of mankind and send the Messiah
without delay. Those passages in the prayers that spoke of
the Messiah he regarded as the holiest, the most intimate
and the most important of all. He lingered over them the
longest and most fondly.

This deep religiosity Henech inherited from his father.
It left an indelible impression on his outlook, life and character. His father was a silent man. He eked out a livelihood
initiating rich men's sons into the wisdom of the Talmud.
However, the principal breadwinner of the family was

mother. She was the proprietress of a dry-goods stand in the market place. She also peddled with linens, cottons and woolens. And often she was to be seen, loaded down with her pack, and trudging from house to house to earn an extra groschen. On fair days she had her booth in the square and carried on a lively trade with the peasants. Father helped her in his unobtrusive, silent way. He put her booth in place and laid out the goods on the shelves and counters. He would have helped her sell too but he was not cut out for a business man.

Father's soul was like a walled-in garden. He never uttered a superfluous word. He never betrayed any sign of emotion. Were he to hear some unpleasant news or even of a great misfortune he would display no agitation. He was wrapped in a fatalistic calm. Despite his aloofness and seeming indifference he was a deeply devoted father. If an accident happened to a child of his, he refused to go to bed, but sat up all night keeping vigil. He helped pass the interminably long hours then by browsing in some ancient Hebrew tome. Silently, without a superfluous word or gesture, he attended the sick child. At all times he did not go to sleep until he had tucked all the children comfortably in their beds and had covered them with his tattered old coats and those in mother's bed with his frayed fur coat.

He would rise early, before dawn, and study the Talmud in an undertone so that he might not disturb any of the children in their sleep. And he never left the house for the synagogue without first making a fire in the little stove so that when mother and the children awoke they would not find it too cold to dress.

The most astonishing thing about the man was his tender and unostentatious devotion to his wife. Even though she was the breadwinner of the house and his activities were entirely limited to supermundane matters, he never allowed her to carry her packs of merchandise nor the boards of her stand to the market place. He put up her booth and laid out her wares. It made her feel very unhappy to see her husband do such manual labor for her. But what was she to do? It just could not be helped. He continued carrying her packs for her like a common porter. He even was obliged to come late to the twilight services at the synagogue because he insisted on carrying home her packs of merchandise.

Whenever his wife returned home, tired and worn, from the market place, she already found the table set for dinner. A brisk fire was blazing in the stove and a pot of water was sizzling merrily. This she came to regard as a great tragedy. She felt guilty for what she believed was degrading him, an unworldly scholar, a superior and sensitive creature, a pious man of God. With simulated reproach and a loving tender look she would say to him:

"Have you ever heard of a man of your kind occupying himself with such things?"

When the children were yet small, he would often sit late into the night rocking the cradle to still the weeping infant so that Feigè might snatch some sleep for herself. Even now, whenever he hears her complain with a groan of some internal pain or sunburn which she suffers as a result of her exposure to the broiling sun in the market place, Gedaliah finds it difficult to fall asleep.

He softly slips out of bed, and taking infinite pains not to make too much noise, he chops some wood. Then he builds a fire in the stove and makes tea for his wife. He places it beside her bed without a word. When Feigè finds the tea near her bed she becomes conscience-stricken for depriving Gedaliah of his sleep. So she grits her teeth and suppresses her groaning.

A loud or angry word was never heard in the house. Husband and wife were united by a chaste and shy love which sounded in the drabness of their life of poverty and struggle like a song without words. They never spoke to one another of their love. They felt it too keenly to have the need of giving utterance to it. They were fused into one another as if they were but one body and one soul. At the very best Feigè, the more demonstrative of the two, would express her affection for her husband with mock anger and a tender look. If she ever found him engaged with household matters which in her opinion were not befitting a man of his sensibilities, she took it greatly to heart. She even found a secret pleasure in the thought that Gedaliah loved her, so that there was nothing he would not do to please her. And her appreciation of his love was expressed in pretended irritation:

"Just look what a man occupies himself with!" she would grumblingly exclaim. "Such work is proper only for a woman!"

He answered nothing, and instead cast a stealthy, shy look at her. . . .

Their reserved and chaste love not only was mirrored in their daily life but also permeated the entire household with its spirit. The children were devoted to their parents as well as to one another with a deep-welling, overflowing tenderness.

The relations between his father and mother made an indelible impression upon Henech's young soul. It molded his character and indicated the destiny he was to follow during the course of his life.

.   .   .   .

Gedaliah was an ardent disciple of the Rabbi of Ger — the mystic saint whose feet trod the earth but whose soul soared always in celestial regions. Once every springtime, during the holiday of Shevuoth, he would piously set out on a pilgrimage to the holy seer. And when Henech was twelve years old he accompanied him on this annual visit, so that he might receive the blessings of the man of God before he reached his confirmation. The Rabbi, his little court, the festive spirit, and the religious ecstasy of the multitude of disciples, became deeply engraved on his impressionable mind. What moved him most deeply, however, was the comradely spirit — the unifying bond of brotherhood and the common religious ideal which dominated them all. Henech and his father lodged in the same inn with hundreds of other pilgrims. There was a complete absence of "mine" and "thine" among them. They ate together — slept together like one big family. Men who were complete strangers to one another readily slept in the same bed, alongside each other, on the same tables, benches and any other convenient perch. The dividing distinctions between rich and poor were completely forgotten. Whether in the courtyard of the Rabbi's house, at his great table or in the synagogue, they acted all like one man. They sang the sonorous songs of praise to God in mighty unison — entwined an arm about each other's shoulders, or clasping hands for the dance, they formed the mystic circle. Closer and closer, without deliberation, as if by magnetic attraction, the whirling dancers drew near to the Rabbi who sat in the center of the room with face hidden in his hands and moaning without end.

And when the holy man began to expound Scripture before the multitude all felt as if they were being fused into one body — into one soul — and eagerly leaned forward the better to catch his words of illumination. If a disciple broke into song then all joined with ardor until the rafters in the room shook with their exultation. In the dance, affectionately intertwined, the rich embraced the poor and the learned the ignorant and in a concentric circle they stamped to the rhythm of their stirring hymns of praise to the Almighty.

In this unforgettable manner five days passed.

The Mother

To Henech it appeared as if the stern, eternally harried and despondent gray-beards had once more become children. Like a flock of boys let loose from school they made the air resound with their laughter and their sheer joy of living. The whole world seemed liberated from its everlasting burden of gloom, poverty and suffering.

That is how it will be when the Messiah will come, thought Henech joyfully. Only then all the Jews of the world, and not only the disciples of the Rabbi of Ger, will be united in such brotherly love. They will live amicably together, dance together, sing together and serve the dear God together. The Messiah will then be like the Rabbi of Ger and all the people of the world his disciples. Yes — all the people of the world will be his disciples, except, of course, the Gentiles! They will all be annihilated on the Day of Judgment, then there will remain on earth only Jews! . . .

With all the inner ecstasy and mystic religiosity that only a child of his age and naïveté could feel — Henech was filled with a devouring passion to hasten the coming of the Messiah. He began to practice austerities — fasted, prayed long and devoutly and was convinced that the Day of Judgment was not far off. He is coming — he is coming — the Messiah of the Lord — galloping on a fiery white charger — bringing eternal peace and happiness for all men! . . .

A day arrived when Henech's dreams, alas! went up in wraiths of smoke. Shattered was his faith in God. Pale was his hope in ultimate redemption.

This is how it happened. Since the days of his childhood he had been beset by many disturbing doubts of which he ineffectually tried to rid himself by pushing them back into the dim recesses of his mind. At first he was frightened even to think about them and tried hard to explain them away with the usual time-honored theological sophistries.

Henech

To the first doubt, which at one time or another besets every believing child's mind: "What is good and what is evil?" he was glibly answered with the stock-in-trade explanation given by all the wandering preachers when they visited the town and which are contained in the little Hebrew books on faith and morality, viz: that the final choice rests with man. Such is the will of God!

One question logically leads only to another. The first doubt soon became overshadowed by another— a far more formidable and perplexing one. The very thought of it filled Henech with terror. But ultimately he had to face it with fortitude. It was this:

"Why did God create Gentiles and Jews as well? And why so many different faiths? Why did He not in His surpassing wisdom arrange it so that *all* should believe in Him? If He has bungled His work then why are the poor Gentiles to blame because they were not born Jews? Is it then just that on the Day of Judgment they be annihilated?"

These disturbing questions led Henech with irresistible logic to the fundamental doubt which, try as hard as he would, he could not shut out from his feverishly probing mind:

"How can I be convinced that the Jews are the Chosen People and that their God is the true and only God? Aren't there more Gentiles than Jews? The whole world is full of them and are not the Jews but few in number? Then how can I accept in good faith the belief that the Jews are the only people on earth that worship the true God?"

And if matters were really as he feared they were, then why pray to Him?

"Why does God stand in need of my prayers and my songs of praise? For what purpose does He desire my good deeds?"

Henech's first heresy and test of God's powers was to reduce the number of his prayers. Remarkably enough —

nothing happened! He did not die. And the selfsame world continued on its selfsame course undisturbed. God seemed to have no intention of destroying it as a result of his blasphemy. . . .

How Henech stood in need of confiding his doubts to another human being! There was no one, he felt, who would understand and sympathize with him. He did not dare discuss the subject with his father, the ever-silent, self-contained man. When at last driven by desperation he did attempt to speak to him, he met with the brief reply:

"You must have faith!"

"But what am I to do if I have no faith?"

Father kept silent.

When with great trembling Henech picked up sufficient courage to broach the subject to his teacher of Scripture, the latter became purple with rage and sending a resounding box on Henech's ear he roared:

"It is quite clear that nothing good will ever come of you."

A young man who tutored him in the Talmud at the synagogue listened to his confession much aghast.

"You must read sermons on faith and morality," he advised him.

So Henech penitently devoured pietistic books. They did attempt with a great display of learning and logic to answer all the disturbing questions that a heretical-minded young skeptic might ask. But to no avail. The explanations given even strengthened his doubts. . . .

For a long time Henech walked about in a daze — immersed in chaos. They were years of anguish and self-torment. The world that he had so laboriously built up as a child was now rapidly crumbling. Where was there another world to take its place? He now turned to much praying — so that he might drown out his doubts and his despair by frantic exhortations to God. His prayers were lifeless — without spirit. Then he flung himself angrily into his Talmudic studies. But his heart lay elsewhere. They had no longer any meaning for him. He might have saved himself from the sea of doubt in which he was drowning by his own efforts but fate willed it otherwise. A young friend of his gave him heretical Hebrew books to read. These not only made clear to him the nature of his doubts but they also robbed him of the last vestige of faith that he still clung to frantically.

So Henech went about like one who was both lost and damned. There was no one to extend to him a helping hand and to guide him out of the wilderness of his spirit. Occasionally there did fall into his hands by sheer accident some secular Hebrew book which threw some light on his inner problems and pointed rather vaguely towards some solution that lay along a still untrodden path. But this light did not endure long. It soon vanished and Henech's path became as dark as it was before.

He still went to the synagogue but that was merely out of habit. Yes — he continued to pray and to study the Talmud. That was because there was nothing else to do. But his heart was desolate and there was nothing he could live for.

How can one live without an ideal—a Messiah?

Gedaliah did notice that something was wrong with the boy, but as was his habit, he said nothing. One evening, though, he suddenly broke his taciturn silence and speaking as if addressing no one in particular he remarked quietly:

"How can one live without an aim?"

But where was one to find an aim? brooded Henech. Had he not been seeking one ever since he lost his belief in God and in the justice of His Will?

He now spent all the long summer days roaming through the woods and lingering over the quiet graves in the ceme-

The Mother

tery. In these retreats, far from the disturbing life of the world, he feverishly devoured one secular book after another. When the cold weather arrived he sought seclusion in the deserted women's balcony in the synagogue or in the home of the Hebrew teacher of the town, and there, all by himself, he painfully groped his way through the intricate mazes of Russian grammar. He also found a sympathetic ally in a Jewish student from Lithuania who was also a secular teacher. Him he visited secretly. This student opened a new world of thought to him. He gave Henech books by the enlightened Hebrew writers Smolenskin and Mapu and even by Russian authors. And if he had not yet found his aim, thought Henech, so what? Wherein then lay his guilt? Life must be lived whether with or without an aim.

One fine day an unknown young man from Zochlyn descended upon the town. Altogether he remained but a few days. He came to the synagogue and drew the young men into conversation. He also asked Henech to accompany him on a stroll into the woods. He then told him of many things that Henech did not know before — about life in the great cities. He made clear to him the meaning of true justice and brotherly love and vehemently adjured him to work for their realization with his whole heart and soul. Everything can be accomplished, he urged. One must only will it — only will it.

And better yet, the young stranger from Zochlyn left him some books that were written in Yiddish. These books created a revolution in Henech's thinking. What he read in them he had long known about and yet but half understood. Now the storm subsided and the great calm set in. Out of the whirling chaos order was being born in his mind. Everything that was formerly confused seemed so clear to him now! ...

Two of these books were by Peretz — the mystic revolutionary in Yiddish literature. In them he called upon the Jews to renounce their Christlike meekness and slavish Ghetto spirit and proudly to take their place in the sun with the rest of an enlightened humanity. Reading Peretz, Henech felt as if red-hot coals were being placed over his heart. They seemed to sear into his soul and left a gaping, bleeding wound there.... But in the end they brought him healing. They destroyed his old faith. In its stead a new faith was born. Henech's wound closed.

The selfsame ecstasy and piety that had moved him in his belief in the Messiah he now transferred to his new faith. He believed in a new Messiah — the Messiah of a liberated humanity.

Henech was only fifteen now. But he had already succeeded in destroying one inner world and in creating another.

As a direct result of his reading he now decided to become a working man. He apprenticed himself to Getzl the printer. For his services he received twenty-five gulden a season. At home this was regarded as a great calamity. He had abandoned his sacred studies only to become a common day laborer!

Gedaliah, as was his wont, said nothing. Worst of all, he appeared to become completely oblivious of his son's existence. They lived together in the same house, ate at the same table, slept in the same room, yet it was as if Henech had ceased to exist for him. Gedaliah pretended to notice nothing. He refrained from questioning his son. He avoided the necessity of addressing him. The boy was as if dead for him.

For his mother, Henech's becoming a workman added a new anxiety to her already too numerous anxieties. Her suppressed groaning at night became more audible and more frequent....

It was at this time that Henech came to know Dvoyrelè.

Chapter 6

THE FIRST RENDEZVOUS

••••••••

ONE bright afternoon on a summer Sabbath day, Henech first met Dvoyrelè in Itte's orchard which served as the promenade for all the young people of the town.

The sun stood high in the sky and the apples and pears on the trees were ripening under its benevolent light. The plums looked still green but the berries were ready for picking. Of cherries there was no longer a trace. It was at this time that the older boys and girls of the town sauntered forth among the trees — the former with books under their arms — the latter resplendent in their stiff taffeta frocks. The "young men" strolled arm in arm along one footpath; the "young women" with arms about each other's waists along another. At the leafy arbor near the great pear tree, marking the convergence of the two paths, both groups would meet! The first meeting was usually marked by mutual embarrassment and well-bred constraint. Not a word was exchanged. The second time they met — one of the boys would burst into provocative laughter. This proved too infectious for the fun-loving girls. They giggled hilariously and like frightened hares ran past the boys. When they met for the third time one of the more courageous among the boys would pass a sly witticism about the girls.

"Red cherries fall from the trees," he would say rather pointlessly.

The First Rendezvous

"Green apples are sour," retorted one of the least shy of the girls witheringly.

At the fourth meeting, Leibish, the sewer of uppers, who had lived for six months in Lodz and had learned there how to behave properly with girls, stepped forward gallantly and with great ceremony introduced those who had not been previously acquainted. Henech Lipski presented Leibish the sewer of uppers to the company. Then Dvoyrelè Zlotnik, nothing daunted, introduced Hanelè, a spinner in a stocking factory, despite the fact that she was already well acquainted with all the boys.

Dvoyrelè was sixteen years old then. Because she had set up her own little dressmaking establishment, she earned for herself an enviable social distinction among the other girls of the town. The older girls were therefore anxious to be her friends. Because of the heavy burden which rested on her frail young shoulders since childhood, Dvoyrelè, despite her sixteen years, did not appear much older than when we first introduced her into our story. It is true she had grown slightly taller but nevertheless still gave the impression of only a precocious child. In vain mother labored to confine her torrent of curly hair into two braids. She failed in her attempts even after she had tightly bound them with two red, silken ribbons. Her hair rebelliously overflowed the confines of her braids and fell like a shower of silken down over her delicate face and concealed her forehead and eyes.

With a toss of her head Dvoyrelè would brush the hair from her eyes. She was small for her age and looked like a mere child that in play had disguised herself in mother's clothes and pretended she was grown up. . . .

When the "young man" began to send home money from America and Moishelè "The Ox" began earning money in the market place, mother became concerned over Dvoyrelè's attire. She was, after all, a "young lady," she would apologetically explain to Anshel. So she bought her a pair of dainty slippers for the Sabbath and, wonder of wonders! a new Sabbath frock, cut in the latest fashion with a tight little bodice and a cushioned elevation behind.

This was the first time in her life that Dvoyrelè had become "acquainted" with a young man. Not that she did not know all the young men in the town but she had never before been formally "introduced" to any of them. And when she was "introduced" to Henech—she lost her composure completely. She did not know what to do with herself or what to say to him. She turned pale and her eyelids began to quiver from fright. The blue veins in her throat stood out swollen and taut. Her heart beat wildly so that she could hear its agitation. Her pallor now gave way to a crimson flush. She wanted to run. Her feet would not carry her. Then she recollected she was dressed in her Sabbath frock which was, after all, cut in the latest fashion. The thought of the cushioned elevation behind gave her a sense of security. She felt more at ease now. . . .

Henech felt even more embarrassed than Dvoyrelè. He, Henech Lipski, foremost among the young men of the town, in whose presence they became restrained in their remarks because of his superior learning, he it was who completely lost his head in the presence of girls. He dared not look into their eyes and spoke with averted glance in an incomprehensible mumble. Henech stood before Dvoyrelè deathly pale, uneasily playing with his fingers and smiling foolishly.

When the boys and girls had joined company in Itte's orchard that Sabbath afternoon they continued walking in a group. Leibish the sewer of uppers and Hanelè the hosiery spinner carried on the conversation for the whole company. Little by little they broke up in pairs and meandered away among the leafy aisles. The only two who remained standing as if rooted to the spot were Henech and Dvoyrelè. It

The First Rendezvous

was their first entry into "society" and they did not know how to behave.

For a long time they strolled along the pathway without uttering a single word. Their hearts beat alarmingly fast. They avoided each other's glances and did not know how to begin their conversation. Dvoyrelè sought support in the self-consciousness of her new frock and new shoes, and Henech in the celluloid collar he was now wearing for the first time in honor of his stepping out into "society." ...

While passing by an apple tree that was heavily laden with fruit they half mechanically, without thinking — shook it slightly. A ripe, red apple fell from the tree before their feet. Henech stooped and picked it up. For a long while he held it in his hand. He had not the slightest notion of what he was to do with it. Suddenly, on an impulse, he extended it to Dvoyrelè without a word.

The suddenness of his gift frightened Dvoyrelè. She was ashamed to accept it and yet was afraid to refuse it. Henech might perhaps think her too countrified and ill-mannered. No! she did not want him to think that of her. So she took the apple, also silently, and in her embarrassment did not know what to do with it.

"Dvoyrelè," said he with shyly averted gaze, "I would very much like to meet you sometimes when you are alone."

"Alone! Why alone?" wonderingly asked Dvoyrelè, not understanding his intention.

"I would like to meet you when no one else will be present," reiterated Henech with rising courage.

Dvoyrelè did not answer.

After a long pause he began again:

"I have to tell you something very important."

"Why not? Of course we can meet alone," answered Dvoyrelè. Her little heart leaped up in her breast.

A sense of guilt suddenly overcame them — as if they

had committed some wrong. They lapsed into silence. It was Dvoyrelè who now recalled Henech to the necessity of being practical about their newly formed relationship.

"And where shall we meet?" she asked, quite reckless of the consequences.

"If you will come to the old water mill, I shall be waiting for you there," timidly ventured Henech.

Before Dvoyrelè had time to answer one of her girl friends approached them and slyly asked:

"Is it a secret that you two are having between yourselves? In that case I beg of you a thousand pardons."

"Not at all!" hastily interjected Dvoyrelè. "There is no secret between us. We were not talking about anything in particular."

They then rejoined the rest of the company. The hosiery worker sang a song and Henech and Dvoyrelè found no opportunity to talk to one another again. But when they came to the great pear tree at the junction of the two footpaths they shook hands all around in parting. And when Henech extended his hand to Dvoyrelè it was she who reminded him of their rendezvous. Would she really meet him? he asked, getting red as a beet in the face.

"Yes," answered Dvoyrelè softly.

This word she uttered so suddenly and in such a far-off voice that for a long, long time after that Henech marveled much over it. In her "yes" he thought there sounded so much hidden beauty — such ineffable charm. He was overwhelmed by the mere recollection of it.

"Yes," she had said to him. He repeated the word a thousand times to himself as if it were some haunting melody.

"Yes," she had said to him. And he dashed through the streets like a wild goat. In his joy he could have embraced the entire world. Ah! If only he could find some one to confide in. . . .

Neither Henech nor Dvoyrelè had a wink of sleep that

night. Dvoyrelè produced a tiny mirror from some hiding place, and rubbing on its surface very hard, she at last succeeded in seeing herself in it. When no one saw she stealthily regarded her reflection. Before going to bed she braided her rebellious shock of hair more carefully than ever and tightened it with her scarlet Sabbath ribbon.

Before Henech went to bed he carefully washed his celluloid collar. . . .

The next morning, as Dvoyrelè sat sewing at her machine, she was so absent-minded that it was necessary for her to rip several times what she had sewn on Reisel's trousseau shift. Mother even insisted most vigorously throughout the day that some malicious person must have cast the Evil Eye upon her for she looked as if she had high fever. There was a hectic flush on her cheeks. And father, noticing this, sagely corroborated mother's fears. Yes, he had for a long time already noticed that all was not well with Dvoyrelè.

"I have suspected all along," said he, "that something was ailing her. Only I have prudently held my tongue."

"You frighten me, Anshel, with your words," apprehensively exclaimed Surè. "What is it that you have noticed?" she pleaded.

"Well!" explained Anshel with a shrewd wink, "she has been walking about these past days like one possessed by evil spirits."

"Be quiet! In Heaven's name, don't say any more!" begged Surè, much alarmed.

When night began to fall, Dvoyrelè placed herself before the house "mirror." It really wasn't a mirror, but an improvised affair invented by the ingenious Moishelè "The Ox" and was effected by placing mother's black dress in the clothing closet. Dvoyrelè did not tire of looking at herself in this "mirror." She braided her hair and intertwined her scarlet ribbon in its plaits. Mother persisted in questioning her about her unusually elaborate toilette. It aroused her suspicions.

"What are you doing, Dvoyrelè?" she asked wonderingly. "Why do you take greater pains with your appearance to-day than on other days?"

Happily for Dvoyrelè, father was just then at the synagogue saying the twilight prayers. So she carefully dressed herself in her new Sabbath frock and explained with embarrassment to her mother that she was just going out for a stroll.

At the signpost on the road to the water mill Henech waited for her. He again wore his freshly washed celluloid collar. He had drawn a curious strip of ribbon through it into a fantastic bow tie. He had secured from God-knows-where a walking stick that was not much for elegance — only an umbrella handle — but he twirled it with ésprit and elegance as if it were quite the real thing.

When he saw Dvoyrelè he hastily buttoned his coat — manipulated his cane like an honest-to-goodness dandy and eagerly ran forward to meet her. When he came close to her he suddenly remained standing in embarrassment.

"Dvoyrelè," he began eagerly but cut himself short.

She did not reply.

They walked side by side until they reached the woods. They exchanged not a word. When they came to the water mill they seated themselves on an old log. It was she who broke the constrained silence:

"Why have you asked me to come down to meet you here?" she pouted girlishly.

"Nothing!" he answered smilingly.

"Why then did you ask me? Just so?"

"Just so," replied Henech.

"Does one ask to see another because of 'just so'?"

"I wanted to read you something," explained Henech evasively.

The First Rendezvous

"What did you want to read to me?"

"A poem."

"A poem!" echoed Dvoyrelè with astonishment.

"Yes, a fine poem by a new writer."

"Good! Read it to me then!"

Henech opened a new Hebrew anthology of poetry which he had brought with him and began to read. The poem contained references to Spring, Maytime and Freedom. When he read the verses on Freedom, Henech waxed quite ecstatic and felt more at ease.

"Do you understand what the poet means by 'Spring'?" he asked solemnly.

"No! I am afraid I don't at all," guiltily confessed Dvoyrelè.

"He doesn't actually mean the season called by that name. What he really refers to is Freedom — the time of liberation — when mankind will cast off its chains of slavery. Then the 'winter' of sorrow will be past, and the 'springtime' of joy will have arrived. The waters will break through the 'ice' and — now do you understand what the poet meant?"

"No!" said Dvoyrelè still more guiltily, and she hung her head.

Nothing daunted, and superhumanly patient with such mental obtuseness, Henech once more attempted to explain:

"The poet meant that mankind should cast off its chains that tyrants have loaded it with. When it will free itself from its yoke of slavery then will come the happy 'springtime' and everlasting freedom will rule over the earth. Do you understand now?"

"Yes," said Dvoyrelè, vigorously nodding her head.

At this Henech ceased reading and became lost in thought.

"What are you thinking about?" asked Dvoyrelè.

"Nothing," answered Henech.

The Mother

"Do you want to know why I have called you here?" he burst out suddenly.

"No," said Dvoyrelè and she began to tremble for fear at what he was about to tell her.

But Henech was stricken dumb. He could not utter a sound.

"Why don't you speak?" asked Dvoyrelè.

"Not just now — I cannot tell you now," mused Henech. "It is a very serious matter that I want to talk to you about — a matter of life and death."

Hearing these ominous words Dvoyrelè became frightened. Yet she was overjoyed because Henech would condescend to confide to her, a mere girl, a matter of life and death. She did not dare, though, to ask him what it was that he wanted to speak to her about —"the matter of life and death."

Both remained silent for a long while. Night fell slowly and silently. Shadowy veils began to steal from the woods across the fields and enveloped the clouds. The sun had set and its last ruddy glow was drowned in a sea of nocturnal blue. On the earth descended an awesome religiosity and melancholy.

Henech and Dvoyrelè sat watching the dark sea of blue devouring every sun-flecked cloudlet. It grew ever darker and darker.

They did not utter a single word and averted their eyes from each other. When they arose to return to the town they both discovered that they were holding each other's hands in a tight clasp. . . .

Chapter 7

FOR THE HOLY CAUSE

·······

A NEW life began for Dvoyrelè — a life replete with hope and expectation. It was as if her blood had begun to blossom. Dreams, mysterious and haunting, like blue veils, wrapped about her soul. As she sat at the sewing machine, making dainty shifts for brides and expectant mothers, she sewed into every stitch a dream, a blessing or a desire. . . .

Towards nightfall, after she had dressed to go for a stroll in the orchard outside the town as she dissemblingly had explained to her mother, she hastened to the signpost on the road to the water mill. Henech already stood waiting for her, swinging his umbrella handle with great elegance. A new book was tucked under his arm. With a bashful little smile he sprang forward to meet her. Without a word they sat down on the old log near the water mill which stood half concealed by a copse of tall poplars.

Each time she came to meet him it was as if he were listening to a new song. Each time, when silently they walked to the water mill with loudly beating hearts, it was a new love-play, a new "bride and bridegroom" sensation. . . .

They exchanged no words. But when they sat down on the old log Henech bashfully opened his book and asked:

"Shall I read you something, Dvoyrelè?"

"Yes," she answered.

The Mother

So Henech read from his book. He explained and inter-preted everything to her. Reading books was his great pas-sion. And whenever he found the opportunity to read aloud he grew quite breathless with excitement. He lost all his shyness then. He was not reading just mere words to her. Through them he attempted to communicate to her all his feelings for her. . . .

It is true that she but half understood him. But was it really necessary for her to understand? Henech's books were to her as sacred Scripture was to her mother. She looked up to him with pride and reverence. She was grateful to him for every word he uttered — grateful that he asso-ciated with her — that he read aloud to her. She could not understand why he should take the trouble to do all that for her — just a slip of a foolish girl!

Dvoyrelè felt the same joy when Henech read aloud to her from his books as when mother listened to father's cantillation of Scripture. . . .

Once at dusk, after he had read to her at their trysting place, Henech fell into a strange musing. He said to Dvoyrelè:

"Dvoyrelè, I would like to talk to you about something — something very important and serious. For a long time I have been thinking of talking to you about it but I did not know whether —" Henech began to stammer. "I did not know whether you would like me to. Do you, Dvoyrelè?"

"Please do tell me about it," said Dvoyrelè. Her heart leaped with excitement.

Very gravely Henech began:

"Do not for one moment think that life is such a simple matter. It is a difficult and often a tragic burden. Every one must have his duty to perform and must fulfill his obligations. Do you understand me, Dvoyrelè?"

"Yes," stammered Dvoyrelè, and vigorously nodded her head even though she did not quite understand.

72

For the Holy Cause

"Would you too like to take upon yourself the burden of this duty, Dvoyrelè? You must accept it out of your own free will and without coercion."

"What duty is it?" asked Dvoyrelè uneasily.

"Your duty to 'The Holy Cause.'"

"What is that?" asked Dvoyrelè, perplexed.

"The Holy Cause? Why, that is the Revolution," Henech enlightened her.

"The Revolution!" exclaimed Dvoyrelè. And she shook with fear.

"Yes!" emphatically answered Henech. His shyness was now completely gone. "The Revolution aims to make all men free and equal. That is what is meant by the Holy Cause."

These solemn words struck Dvoyrelè dumb with amazement. She looked at Henech with her large velvety eyes and all the sincerity and earnestness of her childish soul became fixed in her look. Terror paralyzed her tongue. She looked mutely at him.

Once more Henech spoke in a solemn voice:

"Do you, Dvoyrelè, agree to take upon yourself, as we all do, the burden of the duty for the Holy Cause — to seek freedom for all mankind?"

"And what must I do if I accept this obligation for the Holy Cause?" stammered Dvoyrelè. She reverently mentioned the Holy Cause as if she were afraid to pollute the sanctity of these words with her earthly lips. With a mute look of devotion she turned to Henech that he teach her the nature of her obligation.

"You must be ready, Dvoyrelè," began Henech earnestly, "to bring sacrifices for the Holy Cause at all times."

"At all times!" Dvoyrelè furtively echoed his words.

"Even with your very life," adjured Henech.

"Even with my life," mechanically repeated Dvoyrelè, already distracted with fright.

"Do you understand what I mean?" asked Henech.

"I do," answered Dvoyrelè.

"Are you ready to pay with your life for the Holy Cause?" persisted Henech mercilessly.

Dvoyrelè did not answer. She was too terrified to speak. She only nodded her head dazedly.

"And if it will be found necessary that you pay with your life for this duty — will you give it?" asked Henech point-blank.

Dvoyrelè was under the impression that her life was needed immediately as a sacrifice for the Holy Cause. And with all the ardor of her young soul she was ready to lay it down that very instant.

"Yes," said she, "I will lay down my life for the Holy Cause.

Dvoyrelè uttered these words with a trembling and pious voice as if she were standing before the Holy Ark of God.

"In that case," said Henech joyfully, "we are brother and sister." And he clasped her hand in his.

This pact they closed with all the earnestness, piety and deep-welling faith of their young souls.

"I will introduce you to our comrades next Saturday afternoon in the woods," said Henech.

"Splendid!" answered Dvoyrelè with gratitude.

"One thing though you must remember," cautioned Henech. "When you enter 'The Party' you are sworn to absolute secrecy. You must not divulge any of our secrets even were it to mean your death."

"My death!" gasped Dvoyrelè.

They both kept silence now.

A great, indefinable joy descended upon them. For joy they did not speak. They had nothing more to say to one another. Only Henech swung his "cane" with great gusto.

"Good! good!" Henech repeated to himself.

"What is good?" asked Dvoyrelè.

For the Holy Cause

"Life — the world. It is good to live. It is even good to die. Don't you think so, Dvoyrelè?"

"Yes," agreed Dvoyrelè.

And suddenly, without warning, she impulsively blurted out:

"Henech! I am so happy that I have met you! Are you, too, happy?"

For a while Henech kept silent. He averted his glance. Then he burst out:

"Why, of course, I am happy! . . ."

Then both flushed and paled in turn. And their hearts beat so loudly that they could almost hear them.

For a long while they sat in silence, wrapped in tender musing. Then suddenly *it* happened. Dvoyrelè impulsively threw her arms about Henech and kissed him on the lips. Great tears gushed from her eyes in an outburst of joy. At first she attempted to hide them with her hands, with her handkerchief. Seeing that it was of no avail, with quiet resignation her head drooped against Henech's shoulder and she wept unrestrainedly.

Henech rudely stroked her hair without daring to look at her.

"Why do you cry, Dvoyrelè? Why do you cry?" he asked her.

"I don't know," Dvoyrelè gasped between sobs.

Henech did not question her any more.

By the time Dvoyrelè had calmed herself it was already dark. They retraced their steps to the town in silence. But before parting Henech said to her:

"For the Holy Cause you must be ready to sacrifice everything — even love. Do you understand, Dvoyrelè?"

"Yes," answered Dvoyrelè guiltily. "I understand."

All that night she lay in bed awake. She brooded upon her own unworthiness. She had not controlled her "carnal"

75

passions but had blasphemed against the Holy Cause with her "sinful" love.

.   .   .   .

Repentance flayed her like a scourge. She had blasphemed against the Holy Cause with her love. Henech had initiated her into a holy secret. Henech had lifted her spirit up and carried it away with his into another, a higher and a more beautiful world. Now she had desecrated it with her foolish earthly love.

Even though she was certain that what had transpired between her and Henech was the true, the "holy" love about which she had read in the story-books, that the kiss they had exchanged had irrevocably united them for all time, she also well knew that her "sinful love" was of little significance in comparison with the Holy Cause.

The following days she avoided meeting Henech at the signpost. She was ashamed to come face to face with him again. Also she was certain that he was not waiting for her there any more and that everything between them was at an end.

When she saw him again the following Sabbath on the promenade in the orchard with the other young men of the town, her heart leaped to her mouth. She felt both abashed and afraid to look in his direction.

How astonished she was when Henech, approaching near, whispered to her in an undertone:

"Dvoyrelè, I would like to speak to you."

She flushed to the roots of her hair and pretended that she had not heard him, for the other boys and girls were standing about them.

Despite her caution and reticence, the entire company knew that Henech and Dvoyrelè had "an affair" between themselves. So they considerately pretended they noticed nothing — arranged it so that the young pair walked side by side and in an opportune moment wandered off and left them to their own devices.

"Why didn't you come to the water mill?" asked Henech reproachfully. "I waited for you every evening."

"I crave your pardon ten thousand times," said Dvoyrelè, employing an elegant expression out of the romantic novels that she had read. And she unnecessarily studied the tips of her little slippers.

"Why?" insisted Henech.

"You know why."

"I also crave your pardon ten thousand times," said Henech, formally repeating her elegant expression. "There will take place a secret gathering of our comrades to-day in the woods. Would you like to come with me? I will introduce you to the comrades. 'Important News' will be announced."

Dvoyrelè raised her eyes to his. There was a look of gratitude in them.

"I do not know if I will come," said Dvoyrelè stammeringly.

"Why? Have you changed your mind?" asked Henech ruefully.

"No, Henech! Only I — I have desecrated the Holy Cause."

"No, Dvoyrelè! It is I who have done the desecrating," murmured Henech in a low voice.

They did not speak for a long while.

"Will you come with me?" ventured Henech timidly once more.

"Shall I come?" asked Dvoyrelè with indecision.

"Yes, Dvoyrelè! Come with me. I will await you near the highway."

The boys and girls now sauntered up. It was impossible to talk any more.

Chapter 8

THE LAST MEETING

....

MANY times Henech had walked up and down past Anshel's dilapidated little hut and had cast stealthy glances through the opening between the white curtains in the front window. He was sure he recognized Dvoyrelè's silhouette against the white curtains. She was sitting near the window reading.

In her silhouetted form cast against the curtains he could discern her round little head that was bent over her book, framed in its avalanche of hair. The few wisps of hair that had strayed rebelliously from her braids concealed part of her face. The second time he passed the window he caught a glimpse of her bent neck on which lay coiled the two heavy braids. Later on he even saw parts of her face and her delicate little chin that rested on her arm. He regarded her silhouette fixedly. Against the curtain it appeared like a reflection seen on the surface of a clear pool. It gave him greater pleasure to regard her shadow than the actual form which cast it. To him the shadow appeared to emerge more from her inner being and character than from her body.

Each time that Henech peered into the curtained window his heart overflowed with happiness. He felt as if he were being enriched by some priceless treasure. Each time he caught a glimpse of her head, face or hand, or even her silhouetted form, he discovered in her a new source of joy and a new charm. This filled him with great elation.

The Last Meeting

Dvoyrelè was utterly unaware that Henech was haunting her door. And as if she had deliberately designed to tease him she sat near the window. The light of a kerosene lamp fell upon her face and brought into clear silhouetted relief all the charm and sweetness that she possessed ... the refinement that lay impressed upon her long, delicately chiseled face, the pensiveness of her drooping eyelids and all the pity that her tender, young throat awakened in the onlooker....

All this Henech saw etched in shadow against the little white curtains. Her charm flowed like unending music into his veins and appeased with joy the thirst of his longing heart.

It happened on an evening in early fall, when the sad weeping days had already set in. The days were getting shorter and the evenings brought with them a longing and a disturbing melancholy. All the earnestness of the gloomy days hung like a depressing thought in the air and weighed one's spirits down. Each heart became consumed with longing and restive with desire for an aim in life. The dread specter of repentance for the years that are gone, and fear for the years that are yet to come, stalked across the earth. And when these nights arrived, when their melancholy descended upon men's spirits, Henech turned into the synagogue street and loitered about Anshel's house, if only to capture one single glimpse of the beloved face or the shadow of her form silhouetted against the little white curtains.

It was already more than an hour that Henech had loitered about Anshel's house. The day had retreated slowly and night had set in imperceptibly. Dark shadows stole one by one across the heavens, and as they advanced, flushed out the light-rimmed clouds lit by the setting sun. Like live goldfish in a pool, these clouds still quivered in the light of the dying sunbeams. They cast their wan, shimmering light through their dark, diaphanous veils. But the curtain

The Mother

of night swiftly swept over them, flushed out their flickering light, and with its folds wrapped them about one by one in a revery of sleep. Every dark veil that flittered across the ravening sky cast a sable shadow on the earth below. Thin, transparent shadows fell from the sky and with their dark flimsy draperies wound themselves about the houses, the trees, the fields and the meadows. The green grass turned dark, the trees loomed up grotesquely as if they had suddenly sprung up from the earth. Spirals of smoke curled from the chimneys of the houses. Lights began to flicker in many windows. The street became deserted. The children's merry laughter ceased. Their mothers had anxiously called them indoors. Through the street ran a belated worshiper to the evening services in the synagogue. The cowherd drove his flock hurriedly home. A peasant girl led a stubborn goat by a rope. The goat demurred. It had a will of its own. The girl tugged frantically at the rope and wept bitterly. A form emerged from Anshel's house and drew the shutters down in preparation of the long night.

And Henech still loitered about the house....

How overjoyed he would have been if only Dvoyrelè would have noticed him and come out to greet him! Yet he dared do nothing to attract her attention. And if she would come to him what would he tell her? What reason could he offer for calling her? If only it were possible to go with her now to the tall poplars near the little water mill and there, sitting by her side on the old log, look deep into the dark pool whose transparent bottom was green with moss. Side by side they would sit and utter not a word. And the night would descend upon them gently as it had so often done on summer days....

Henech well knew that it might be the last time that they would meet. Yet he felt that he had to speak to her before parting. He felt the irresistible impulsion of ap-

80

proaching the window and by a slight tapping attempt to draw Dvoyrelè's attention, yet he did not dare to do so. It was not fear that held him back. An inner voice, unbeknown to him, prompted him not to — restrained his will and chained it with bands of steel.

And as he stood yearning for her, an indistinguishable form appeared in the doorway. Could it be she? Perhaps it was only her mother or a brother, thought Henech despondently. He worked up enough courage to approach warily. As he came nearer he became conscious of the presence of something very familiar. It was the rare joy that hovered over her little childish figure like a nimbus. He was aware, even though he could not clearly discern her in the dark, of the curling wisps of hair that straggled over her face.

Should he or should he not approach her? he debated within himself. He regarded her from a safe distance. She returned his steady look. And before even he had time to collect his thoughts she was already standing by his side and smiling into his eyes.

"Henech!" she exclaimed and hastily looked about her to see if she was being observed.

"Yes, Dvoyrelè," stammered Henech.

"I did not recognize you at first," she continued and fearfully looked once more about her.

Henech stood as if tongue-tied. He did not know what to answer.

Dvoyrelè still looked uneasily about her.

"I am afraid some one may come out and see us together," she said.

"Then I must go away," answered Henech and immediately turned to go.

"Meet me at the old log near the water mill," said Dvoyrelè. "I will come soon." These words she uttered in such low tones as if it were a secret she was confiding to him. Then she ran into the house.

Henech stood as if dazed with "the secret" she had confided to him. He was overwhelmed with regret, grew angry at himself. Why, he did not know....

He walked slowly the entire way to the mill, as if in a trance. At the old log he stopped to wait for her. Her familiar form soon appeared in the distance. In the dark it seemed as if she were swimming toward him through a sea of mist. For the first time since they came to know each other he did not advance to meet her. Instead he waited for her to approach. She wore a kerchief on her head. It made her look so different, thought Henech. It was for the first time he had seen her in this kind of headdress.

"Henech," she commenced when she stood near him. "Did you really want to see me?"

"Yes," answered Henech, "both yes and no...I wanted and at the same time I didn't want to see you."

"What do you mean by that?" asked Dvoyrelè, much puzzled.

"Just that," gravely replied Henech.

And without at all being aware of it he began to play with the fringe of her kerchief.

"So you wear a kerchief! I have never before seen you wear a kerchief."

"It is mother's. I was in a hurry."

They both fell silent.

"What did you read? I saw you read — through your window," resumed Henech once more.

"I was reading the book that you gave me."

"Which one?"

"Don't you know?" asked Dvoyrelè, blushing furiously. "The Russian book."

"How do you like it?"

"I am afraid I don't understand it very well."

The Last Meeting

Once more they fell silent.

"Do you know, Dvoyrelè, that I am going away?" said Henech very suddenly.

"Where to?"

"To Warsaw. There is nothing for me to do here."

"What about the Holy Cause?" she asked in a low voice.

"In Warsaw it will be possible for me to serve it better."

"Yes," said Dvoyrelè simply and nodded her head.

"I can learn nothing here," bitterly complained Henech. "I am completely cut off from the rest of the world. No books — no teachers! In Warsaw I will be able to study, to obtain teachers, and meet many people who know a thing or two."

"Yes," said Dvoyrelè and thoughtfully nodded her head.

"I would like to learn something," explained Henech anxiously. "An ignorant person can hope to do but little in this life. I want to study languages and sciences. Not just to be able to pass examinations, but to become a wiser man. I want to know, to understand everything."

"But you know so much already!" said Dvoyrelè with undisguised admiration. "Why must you learn more?"

"What do I know?" savagely burst out Henech. "For the ignoramuses in this town I know a great deal. I have read a few books that I only half understood. I am only an ignoramus myself. I know nothing. I never studied. Life is so empty! What can one make out of one's emptiness? I have no faith in myself and in nothing and in nobody else. And that is because I have nothing to live for."

"If only I but knew half of what you know!" Dvoyrelè consoled him blushingly.

"Believe me, Dvoyrelè, I know nothing, understand nothing. I deceive everybody. To the ignorant fools in this town I appear as wise and learned. But what do I really know? Where have I studied? Who were my teachers? Sometimes I have a guilty feeling that I am but an empty

83

braggart, that I am moving in a circle of ignoramuses and am myself only a dreadful ignoramus and a poseur. I pretend superior learning for all I am worth! What really can I do for the Holy Cause when I am only an ignorant person?"

"So, what do you intend doing?" asked Dvoyrelè.

"I will go to Warsaw. I will set out immediately after the holidays. I am already packed for the journey. A few gulden have been promised me. They will be of great use to me at first. I will look for work. If I don't succeed in finding any, I am quite prepared to starve. It really doesn't matter one way or another. I know for certain that I will meet with many interesting people. I will join some intelligent workers' circle. I may even join a workers' co-operative society that holds courses of lectures. I will also borrow books from a public library. This way I will learn much. If I learn something, then I will be able to decide what to do with my life. Perhaps I will be able to become of some use then. But now! — what am I?"

"You are right!" Dvoyrelè shook her dark little head vigorously. "You are right! I know that you will reach any goal that you may set yourself."

And she looked into Henech's eyes with open admiration and faith. Her eyes glowed with an inner light.

"I do not know," faltered Henech, "if I will ever be of much account."

And sadly, as if to himself alone, he murmured:

"I do not know if I will ever be of much account."

"You will accomplish a great deal, Henech!" Dvoyrelè said staunchly.

"What makes you be so sure?" asked Henech and he smiled indulgently.

"I am certain of that! Please don't laugh at me, Henech! I know that you will be a great man some day. You will, you must reach your goal."

"How do you know all that?" asked Henech, secretly flattered.

"Because I know. I believe everything you say. When you speak one cannot help but listen to you and be convinced. Whenever I heard you speak in the woods, I thought that you were like a great Rabbi. How can one help but do what you ask? Can one disobey a great Rabbi?"

Henech felt abashed at hearing these words of praise. Little by little he grew drunk with her encouraging words. A new stream of energy and faith in himself and in his powers filled his spirit. He refused to share her sentiments about himself. The very thought of them filled him with a sense of shame. Why that was so, he did not know. He said:

"I would like to be of some use to myself and to others. If not, what is the use of living at all?"

"You are right," assented Dvoyrelè.

"Are you leaving too, Dvoyrelè? I have heard that you and your folks will soon emigrate to America."

"Yes. My brother who is in America has sent us steamship tickets. We do not know yet when we will set out on the journey. But what difference does it make where I go?" asked Dvoyrelè gloomily.

"Don't speak that way, Dvoyrelè!" mildly rebuked Henech.

"Is there anything I can do with my life?"

"Every one can achieve something. When you live in America you will be able to work for the Holy Cause and I will do my share here. Our common work will unite us —" and in a low tense voice he added — "for the great ideal."

Dvoyrelè looked at him mutely. Her large eyes became still larger.

"A common ideal," Henech assured her, "unites people wherever they may be."

"So we will be united!" murmured Dvoyrelè happily and raised her dark grave eyes to his.

The Mother

"Yes! The Holy Cause will unite us no matter where we may be."

"It is good so," whispered Dvoyrelè softly.

And two great tears rolled down her cheeks. She looked at him through her tear-blinded eyes, and he read boundless gratitude in them.

Now the Holy Cause arose in her imagination as something holy and godly and miraculous, which one must serve with boundless devotion and with joyful sacrifices.

Her tender girlish heart broke under the ordeal. She felt the sudden impulse of wanting to kiss Henech's hands. This filled her with shame and she was seized with a fear that she might bungle matters by doing so. But Dvoyrelè could not restrain her tears. They flowed thick and fast.

For a long time Henech stood silent. Suddenly he raised his hand and gently stroked her shoulder.

"Why do you weep, Dvoyrelè?" he asked.

"I don't know," said Dvoyrelè, wiping her eyes with the edge of her kerchief.

"You musn't cry!" rebuked Henech. "True revolutionists must advance to battle with brave hearts."

"There! I'll stop crying soon!" promised Dvoyrelè, much mortified at the feminine weakness which she, a devoted revolutionist, was now displaying. She smiled wanly up to him through her tears.

"Revolutionists must never weaken!" Henech admonished gently.

"Yes!" Dvoyrelè nodded her head.

Then they both seated themselves on the old log. It had already grown completely dark. They could hardly discern each other. But each sensed the other's presence. Both sat in utter silence, hand clasped in hand. It was Dvoyrelè who first spoke.

"I too would like to make some use of my life," she said when she felt her hand in Henech's.

The Last Meeting

Henech did not answer. He felt as if his spirit had grown wings. An indescribable joy filled his heart. All doubts and fears vanished. He saw his path lying clear ahead before him — dazzlingly illuminated — to the very goal....

.   .   .   .

Before parting, Henech, with a simple gesture, placed into Dvoyrelè's hands a little, paper-bound book. Without a word he left her.

When Dvoyrelè reached home she looked at the book. It was by Peretz. And on the title-page in Henech's own handwriting she read the following words:

"The Holy Cause will forevermore unite us."

Dvoyrelè never saw Henech again.

Chapter 9

NEWS FROM AMERICA

∙∙∙∙∙∙∙∙

A T last a letter arrived from Shloimè "the young man."
Previous to that he had written that he would send
steamship tickets for only Dvoyrelè and Moishelè "The
Ox." After this cheerful communication nothing further
was heard from him for fully nine months. And after the
family had already completely abandoned hope of ever
emigrating to America, there arrived unexpectedly a large
envelope containing steamship tickets not only for Dvoyrelè
and Moishelè but for the rest of the family as well. And
to top the climax he also sent one hundred gulden with
which to defray the family's railway expenses to the port
of embarkation. The tickets, wrote Shloimè, he had purchased on an installment plan. And furthermore, he added,
on their arrival in America they would find prepared for
them a completely furnished home. He advised mother to
leave her old pots behind her, for, he wrote rather uppishly,
pots were also obtainable in America. . . . Also they must
not waste too much precious time in preparing for the
journey. They must make no bones about it but do it in
the American style: *"hurry up."*

"After all, you won't have so much to bring along. So
pack up your few rags and come over as fast as you can
in order that you may be in time for the new season. See
to it that you arrive during the 'busy season' and not during the 'slack season.' Otherwise there will be trouble."

88

News from America

Although Anshel did not at all understand what "busy" or "slack" season meant, nevertheless, as was his wont, he painstakingly commenced to explain it all to his wife.

"Shloimè means that we must arrive for the new season when the children first begin to attend Hebrew school. In other words, Surè, our son has gone stark mad!"

"Mad! What are you talking about, Anshel?"

"The boy must be mad to ask us to pack up our belongings helter-skelter, as if the Devil were behind us, and bundle ourselves over to America! Does he think that to go to America is like jumping over a garden fence? Does he think emigrating to America is a trifling matter?"

Father grew as red as a beet with anger.

"But haven't you always been most impatient to leave for America, Anshel?" asked mother. "How often have you written to Shloimè, as if the Day of Judgment had already arrived, begging him to tell you: When will the Messiah come at last?"

"Must one always do what one says?" asked Anshel irately. "What is the great hurry ... I would like to know? There will be plenty of time to go to America later, should we decide to do so. Don't you think it were wiser to wait and see what great fortune befalls Shloimè before we venture such an important step?"

"How can you talk this way, Anshel? Shloimè has slaved away so hard — sacrificed so much for us, sold all his belongings — literally pawned himself in order that he might bring us over to America! And here you come and want to spoil all his plans!"

"Can you think of nothing else but of America?" bellowed Anshel. "Is there anything wrong with this town? Are you certain that things will be better for us in New York? Why rush? What is the great hurry?"

"Hurry?" asked mother indignantly. "The hurry is certainly not on me! It is you who have always dinned into my ears about wanting to go to America. You have kept writing one letter after another to Shloimè, begging him to hasten our departure. And now when the possibility to do so has arrived you turn on me abusively. Did I want to go to America? Did I think up the idea?"

"Who then did — I?" roared father.

And Anshel and Surè began their interminable squabbling. To both it appeared as if some terrible misfortune had befallen them. As usual, Surè capitulated and tried to pour oil on the stormy, conjugal sea.

"After all, no one is forcing us to go! If you think it best so, send the steamship tickets back."

"What! Send the tickets back! Do you call that talking sense? If instead of these useless tickets he would have sent us the money that they cost we would have had America right here in this Polish town and not have to drag ourselves over terrible seas and face so many untold dangers!"

"Well, there is still time to do something about it," soothed mother.

"Of course, we still have time to do something about it," agreed Anshel, his anger subsiding. "We will first see what we can accomplish with the hundred gulden that he has sent us. Quite likely it won't at all be necessary for us to go to America!"

And Anshel began to drum merrily with his fingers on the table.

His head overflowed with all sorts of fantastic plans on which he might employ his hundred gulden. He oscillated in his decision between a windmill, a small general merchandise shop and going into partnership with the soda-water manufacturer of the town. Was there anything that might not be accomplished with a hundred gulden?

In the synagogue he chatted vaingloriously with men

of affairs who came forward to congratulate him upon his great fortune.

"I thought," said Anshel, "that my son was only joking when he proposed sending a steamship ticket for his sister and possibly for his younger brother too. But can I describe to you my astonishment when I received a whole packet of tickets for the entire family? It must have cost him a tidy fortune!"

"And what do you intend to do?" they asked him.

"What do you mean by what I intend to do? I am already an American! I am no longer one of you. I will perhaps wait a week or two longer, and perhaps not even that long. My son writes me that he has everything prepared for my coming, furniture, and all the furnishings; in other words, a real palace. So why should I remain here — what?"

"And who will take your place as Reader of Scripture?" they asked.

"Is there any good reason why I should be concerned about everybody and everything? Why don't you let the sexton read? He just frets himself ill with the desire to take my post. At any rate the town is so full of asses that they won't notice the difference between his and my reading. And besides," hastily added Anshel, "my son informs me that in America Readers of Scripture are being paid fully twenty-five dollars for just reading the weekly portion. And despite this they cannot find any competent readers! It is only by a miracle that a good Reader of the Book of Esther is found. My son writes me:

" 'You will earn enough on Purim, reading the Book of Esther, to live on for the rest of the year.'

"How stupid it would be of me to remain here any longer! What do you say? Am I wrong?"

However, when Anshel sat rolling a cigarette after dinner at home, he said to his wife:

"Do you know, Surè, what I have decided? We will

91

put away the steamship tickets for the present. With the hundred gulden I will enter business. If Moishelè and I will engage in business with one hundred gulden we'll become millionaires in no time, I'll guarantee you that."

Mother rejoiced on hearing that father had intentions of drawing Moishelè into his business.

"And if, God forbid, our business does not prosper," gushed Anshel in a Talmudic singsong, "we still have the steamship tickets to fall back upon. We will then go to America? Don't you think I am right?"

"Who knows?" answered mother noncommittally. "And what about Shloimè? What will he think?"

"Don't talk foolishly," said Anshel impatiently. "It will be the same thing to him whether we are happy here or in America."

"Then do whatever you think best, Anshel. You know better what to do than I."

And Anshel puffed leisurely at his cigarette and, looking very mysterious, said:

"I have a certain plan which, if it proves successful, will bring America to us right here." And he pointed to the floor. "Then it won't at all be necessary for us to emigrate. Be assured that in that case our son the cobbler and all of his damned America will come to us and not we to them."

"May God heed your words!" sighed mother piously, with one of her familiar, disturbing sighs.

. . . .

Life flowed on in the selfsame undisturbed manner. Signs of increasing comfort began to be evident in Anshel's home. Dvoyrelè's dressmaking establishment grew and prospered. She already employed three assistants and was recognized as the town's official dressmaker. The trousseaus of all the brides in the town were prepared by her. Mother continued to make solemn vows not to touch her daughter's hard earnings. With one hand, as it were, she put Dvoyrelè's earnings into the favorite pot. With the other she withdrew them.... What she had succeeded in doing, however, was to put enough money by to prepare Dvoyrelè's trousseau for a possible marriage. She acquired a sackful of plucked feathers sufficient for three large pillows — also a roll of fine linen which she bought from Hanelè, the dry-goods merchant, on installment.

"If I cannot save for a dowry — let me at least prepare a trousseau for her," thought mother silently in her heart.

By this time Moishelè "The Ox" had already grown into a young man. There wasn't one kind of merchandise that he had not at one time or another traded with. He had sold grain, had bought eggs from the peasants and sold them in the large towns at a tidy profit. He already seemed in a fair way to establishing himself. But an adverse fate willed it otherwise. One day a wheel came off a wagon carrying a load of eggs for him. All the eggs were smashed, and he was irretrievably ruined. The little money he had saved was wiped out. But Moishelè, an indomitable optimist, did not despair. He now began to trade in calf's leather. Not finding it very profitable he lost neither time nor heart and instead became an agent of gramophones.

As soon as the talking machine came into vogue, Moishelè, with the foresightedness of a true man of business, saw its commercial possibilities. The first thing he did was to bring down from the city a gramophone with pipes attached. For the price of two groschen, with a pipe placed into the ear, one could listen to a snatch of synagogue music, or a very moving tune from *The Ruined Bride*. Every evening there foregathered in Anshel's house all of the curious and most of the young men and women of the town to listen to the gramophone. Mother was nearly deafened by the noise made by the gramophone and the enthusiastic shouts of the audience. It gave her a fearful headache. So she walked

The Mother

about with a wet towel tied around her head and stuffed her aching ears with cotton. And she uttered a terrible curse against Moishelè and the gramophone as well — that both he as well as his "hurdy-gurdy" should be damned for all eternity.

For father, on the other hand, the gramophone exercised a great fascination. He marveled over an instrument that could play by itself and he was extremely anxious to penetrate the mystery to its bottom. He pottered about the machine until he succeeded in breaking it. Moishelè then sent it to Warsaw for repairs. There is a strong suspicion that the hundred dollars which his cobbler-son had sent his father for traveling incidentals to America, had some relation with the gramophone venture.

The only happiness mother found, the only compensation she received for her life of torment was Gedaliah, her third son. Mother's fondest wish was that one of her sons might become a scholar. She left nothing undone in order that she might give her children an education. She stinted herself, deprived herself of even the barest necessities that she might be able to pay school tuition for her boys. Above all household obligations stood school tuition. Even food was subordinated to it. . . . If payment had to be made and money was lacking, mother would carry a pillow or a pair of brass candlesticks to the pawnbroker. And on Friday night she ushered in the Sabbath Bride with a prayer over lighted candles that were stuck crazily into raw potatoes. . . . Perhaps this explains the numerous depredations mother had to carry on against Dvoyrelè's little hoard earned by her "sweat and blood" so that she might keep her three boys in the path of God.

Her pride and boast was Gedaliah, who was already involved, together with all the grown-up scholars in the synagogue, in the intricate mazes of the Talmud. Then came Meyer "the big boy" and Nutè "the suckling child"

News from America

— both of whom Dvoyrelè had nursed until the time came
that they could propel themselves across the floor by their
own exertions. The two boys were still too tender in age
to study with the grown-ups in the synagogue. So they
continued to attend Hebrew School. Thus it was that most
of the money Dvoyrelè earned at her sewing was spent on
them. The two eldest sons were not over-anxious to study.
Since childhood they had resisted every effort to educate
them. It was only by sheer force that mother succeeded
in keeping them at school. Every morning she drove them
to their sacred studies with the aid of a stout cudgel. How
mother grieved at the thought that her first-born had become a workman and the second, her breadwinner, only a
petty merchant!

But Gedaliah was different. At thirteen he was counted
a prodigy and at fourteen he was already unraveling the
knottiest of Talmudic dialectics with all the grown-ups.
Father himself maintains:

"Gedaliah is the only child who has inherited my brains.
All the others have yours, Surè."

Nevertheless, Anshel generously conceded that Surè was
after all Gedaliah's mother. She had given birth to him
and had brought him up. Yes, there might be something
in that!

Gedaliah was a rigorous pietist. He would rise at dawn
during the severest winter weather and, defying the frost
and the cold blasts, he would hasten to the synagogue,
there to pore over a folio of the Talmud until noon. He
was never idle — always studying. And when he wasn't
studying, he read. Gedaliah's fame spread far and wide in
the neighborhood. Mothers sermonized at their small sons
and referred to Gedaliah as their model of virtue and piety.
Numerous blessings were showered upon his head by the
righteous, and the universal wonder was how it ever came

95

The Mother

to pass that such a phœnix should have been born to a man like Anshel the Reader of Scripture!

From sitting overlong at his Talmud in the stuffy synagogue, the boy grew thin and pale. Mother moved heaven and earth to make him eat a lot. Even when there happened to be but little food for the rest of the family, Gedaliah was always served the costliest and most appetizing dishes. Mother's principal concern in cooking was for Gedaliah.

"The child sits all day in the synagogue. He must get sufficient nourishment to continue," said Surè pityingly. She left no stone unturned in order that he might have a piece of tender meat for dinner. Two or three times a week she would make him a fine chicken broth. And whenever she passed the fruitseller's, for her last groschen she would buy her darling a ripe, luscious apple. And she baked it to a nice brown so that when he returned from the synagogue he would find something delicious to eat. At the time when the other children were forced to wear their old threadbare clothes during holidays, Gedaliah had always something new to wear — whether it was a coat, a pair of shiny boots or a shirt.

And none of the children would question Gedaliah's privileged position. They had no envious feeling for him. They thought it was all coming to him. Was he not a prodigy and a scholar?

Now, whenever mother walked through the street on which the synagogue stood there came to her the palpitating sound of young voices chanting the sacred Talmud in rapture. And above them all she heard the clear, flute-like voice of Gedaliah. Surè's heart was ready to burst with pride and happiness.

Chapter 10

GETTING READY FOR THE JOURNEY

■■■■■■

ANSHEL, the Reader of Scripture, wrote a letter in which he availed himself of all the rhetorical flourishes that he still remembered from his younger days when he had written extravagant "bridegroom" letters to Surè, his betrothed. He wrote the salutation thusly:

"To my son, the excellent youth, the fruit of my loins, the yearning of my soul."

Who, not knowing Anshel, would have imagined that these encomiums referred to none other than his son Shloimè, the lowly sewer of uppers?

After this high-sounding and reverential introduction, Anshel tried to explain to him what had happened to the one hundred dollars which he had sent him for railway and other incidental expenses to America.

"I want you to know, my son, that I missed becoming a wealthy man by a mere hair. And what wealth! Had my plan succeeded it wouldn't be Anshel that would be going to America but you, and your America to boot, would spryly come to me, yes, indeed!"

Then followed a wearisome account of the possible glories and good fortune that might have ensued had only his soda-water venture succeeded. As always, this plan failed because of an insignificant trifle —"a mere hair." The machines that he had bought for the purpose of manufacturing soda water proved to be no machines at all, but just rusty

97

old irons. And to overhaul them, to make them function properly, would require a fortune. The upshot of it all was that he had at last firmly made up his mind to leave "the old home" and to seek his fortune in "the new world." The tickets, he added, he had kept:

"They are still in the same condition as when I received them. Even the envelopes are the same. The only thing that is missing are the hundred gulden for expenses."

Of course, wrote Anshel, he believed he could, by his own exertion, raise sufficient funds to enable him to reach even to the very gates of America. But was it not perhaps taking too great a hazard to start out on a journey, on which all money calculations usually go awry, with what might prove to be insufficient funds? Therefore he asked his son to send him another hundred gulden without delay so that they might set out on their journey immediately after the holidays.

"I am already sick of 'the old home,'" complained Anshel. "I don't want to remain here any longer — even were I asked to become the governor of the province. And please don't think that your money, God forbid, is thrown away on us. I want you to know, my son, that I have scrupulously written down every groschen and every gulden that you have advanced me. And when with the help of God I come to America, I will return it to you a thousandfold, the principal with all the interest and the interest on the interest. So help me God!"

Some weeks after Anshel had dispatched this letter to his son he received an answer with the requested money for traveling expenses included. Then also came this curt warning:

"If for the third time you will ask me for expenses I won't give it to you. I simply haven't got any more money!"

Feverish preparations now began for the journey.

Until departure became imminent, neither Anshel nor

any one else in his family really knew what emigrating to America would be like. They had spoken so long about it that it was finally accepted as a matter of course. They developed the naïve conviction that to cross over to America was like moving from one house to another. It was quite difficult for them to face the reality.

The most vexing problem for mother was how to dispose of her beloved pots. Were they not her most devoted friends from whom came sustenance for all her fledglings? They knew her sorrows and her privations and they had never, never failed her; they had surrendered to her their fatty treasures from their innermost recesses even at a time when there was nothing to cook in them. Mother was certain that never would she find other pots like them. They would not know her culinary secrets and as a result they would be quite useless to her.

Weeks before their departure Anshel's family already waged fierce battles over the question of the pots. Mother issued an ultimatum that she would take them all with her. This made father wax derisive. He said:

"Why, all America will laugh at you! Do you think there are no pots to be gotten in America?"

"What do I care if all America will laugh at me?" answered mother stubbornly. "At least I will be certain that I will have decent pots to cook in."

"Foolish woman! Hasn't your son prepared for you in America a magnificent palace, with furniture and pots and everything? Why must you bring along this junk?"

But mother remained obdurate.

"When I will have new pots then there will be time enough for me to throw away the old ones."

When the packing of the household goods began Surè had her way. She carefully wrapped up all her pots, dishes and the old spoons. Even the lids of the pots she safely put away in the bedding. Then she tied it all up in a white sheet, as if America were only the house next door to which she was moving.

"How will we carry all that?" asked Anshel in dismay.

"Don't worry! The ship is roomy enough," answered Surè curtly.

Anshel felt certain that even though the residence his son had prepared for him might not be a palace, it surely was an elegant roomy house, with new furniture which also included a comfortable sofa on which he could stretch himself luxuriously after meals for a nap. Otherwise, of what earthly use would America be to him?

Mother not only insisted on taking all her pots with her but everything else as well, including her decrepit-looking furniture. She felt a deep affection for every object in her home — distinctly remembered their histories, the hardships entailed in acquiring them and the length of their loyal service. They had become a part of her being and when the time came to part with them she felt heartbroken. It was like bidding farewell to dear and well-tried friends. At first she did not permit any of them to be sold to the junkman. She wanted to take them all along with her — the tables, the benches, the day-bed and other cumbrous and bulky household articles. But when she realized how hopeless it all was she reluctantly sold them to Hayyim the junkman. She wept over each article separately before she parted with it — as if in mourning over the dead. . . . And when the day-bed was carried out it was as if a beloved corpse were being taken away.

Anshel uttered no word of protest when Surè packed away the brass candlesticks and the chandelier together with the pots, but when she insisted on including the sewing machine, he balked.

Mother simply would not go to America without her sewing machine! She was so deeply attached to the dumb thing.

Getting Ready for the Journey

"If the sewing machine will remain with us we will never be in need of bread," she asserted.

Of this she was certain. It had been her lifelong experience. But how was she to transport the machine? It threw her into a fever.

But Anshel showed battle. He argued: "Is it really necessary that you bring the sewing machine to America? If all sewing machines come from America, does America stand in great need of your old barrel-organ? . . ."

"But isn't the machine our sole breadwinner?" pleaded mother.

When, however, Shmuel the sewing machine agent later came to take it away, mother instinctively threw her arms about it as if she were saying farewell to a dear friend for the last time.

"She fed me like a —" sobbed Surè. But she could not finish her sentence. The tears choked her voice.

Two weeks after the holidays Anshel and his household were ready to leave their old home, where he and his ancestors had lived for untold generations, to wander forth to a distant and foreign land that lay beyond strange lands and a vast ocean. His eldest son, like Joshua of old, had preceded him to spy out that land — to see if there was enough bread to eat there because in his own land there raged the great famine! . . .

Prior to their departure, an understanding had to be reached with Nutè, the emigrants' agent, to smuggle them across the border and to lead them safely to the port of embarkation. Also mother went to the cemetery and bade a solemn farewell to her children who lay buried there under the cold sod.

She did not visit the graves of her parents. They lay buried in a distant town and she could not afford the cost of the journey. . . .

The last Sabbath preceding his departure, Anshel outdid himself in cantillating Scripture in the synagogue. It was more than cantillation. It was an unforgettable song recital. He fondled every tone and dwelled long and mellifluously on every word in the text. His reading created a furore in the town. It was universally agreed that never had such reading been heard in the memory of the oldest gray-beard.

"Now they will have something to remember me for," rippled Anshel boastfully a little later.

That very night Anshel departed from his birthplace. Together with other emigrants, Nutè's cart carried him away far from the house where he, with his wife and his children, had lived.

Half of the town's population came out to bid them Godspeed and a happy journey. And the sound of weeping and lamentation that took place at parting rose like a forlorn wail to the impassive heavens.

PART TWO

Chapter 1

CROSSING THE RED SEA

· · · · · · ·

THE departure of Anshel the Scripture Reader's family from the old to the new world passed by uneventfully. Otherwise thought Anshel, his wife and their children. To Surè it often seemed as if the end of all things had come. And Anshel, as was his wont, generously blamed his son in America for whatever trouble and discomfort they met with on their way to the ship.

They had but barely succeeded in reaching the border town when Anshel, to his great chagrin, discovered that his true worth and distinction passed by unnoticed among the strangers with whom he lodged in the inn. No one made a fuss over him nor seemed to care very much that he was Anshel the Reader of Scripture and that together with his family he was traveling to such a legendary country as America. Numberless were the Jews like Anshel who stopped at the inn in transit to America — Jews from every part of Europe — Lithuanians, Russians, Ukrainians, Poles and Galicians. And there were other Jewish mothers like Surè, weighed down with the responsibility of providing for a large and hungry brood. They too were carrying along with them to America their well-tried, precious pots.

At first Anshel held himself aloof from all the other emigrants. He stood on his dignity. Was he not Anshel the Reader of Scripture, the best in the whole country? Then again, was he not journeying to his own son in America who probably by this time had become a real American himself? Yes, he would like every one to know that in America there had been prepared for him a house with furniture, bedding and every conceivable luxury. Who could compare with him? But Anshel soon discovered that there were many such worthies as he in his company of fellow emigrants. If one was not a Reader of Scripture he very likely had some other distinction equally as great or even greater. And every one as well was journeying to America to join some relation — a father, a brother, an uncle or a cousin. And each one spoke of America as "my America." Only one among the emigrants, a curious little man, a simple cobbler, was traveling alone. His wife and children he had left behind him at home. He had no one waiting for his coming in America and no house with new furniture was prepared to receive him. Marvelous to relate he did not even know where America was nor could he explain why he was going there.

"Isn't everybody going to America?" he remarked naïvely. "So why shouldn't I go too? Surely, the whole world hasn't gone crazy over America for nothing."

Was any one expecting his coming to America? Most certainly! It was a very dear relation of his, the nearest of all, who was richer and more powerful than all the sons, uncles, brothers and cousins rolled in one: God the Father was waiting for him there. . . . Was He not to be found in every land to protect the weak, the fallen and the righteous?

Anshel finally condescended to companionship with a certain personage who passed under the name of "The Palestine Jew." No one knew exactly who had fixed this name to him. He was called so because he said he was a Zionist and because he maintained that Jews must not emigrate to America but instead should settle in the Holy Land, and there become farmers.

"We Jews must prove to the entire world that we can earn our living from the soil by the sweat of our brow and

the toil of our hands," he argued heatedly. "We must cease
to be petty storekeepers and peddlers!"

No sooner would he reach the shores of America, he
boasted, than he would turn farmer and convince the Americans that besides being merchants Jews can also be good
farmers. As a matter of fact, even better than the Gentiles
at that — if only they wanted!

No one really understood how the Palestine Jew could
possibly make good his boast. Every one knew that he suffered from heart disease. Every evening at table he fell sick.
Seeing which the women screamed — that the Palestine Jew
was giving up the ghost. As many bottles of smelling salts
as were to be found among the emigrants, which they had
taken along with them as a safeguard against seasickness,
were pushed under his nose. He refused to open his eyes if
the women had not first lamented piteously over him. He
enjoyed having them make a fuss over him. He persisted,
however, in his claim that his ailment had nothing to do
with his heart. That, no doubt, came from his kidneys, said
he. Of course he had some trouble with his lungs, too, as a
result of a bad cold. And an enlarged liver even came to
him by inheritance. His father and his grandfather, as long
as he could remember, always suffered from an enlarged
liver. Oh, no! He had no trouble with his heart!

"But all that is just nonsense!" he deprecatingly dismissed the subject. "No sooner will I begin to till the soil
than all my ailments will vanish of themselves."

Anshel and the Palestine Jew together formed the aris-
tocracy of the emigrant company. They held aloof from the
others and looked with disdain at them. What were they
after all? Just workers, ignoramuses! It was Anshel and his
new friend who were the spokesmen for the group before
the steamship agent. They sternly threatened to complain
of him to the emigrant aid committee and to write a "correspondence" to the newspapers exposing all skinflint agents

and their nefarious doings in robbing and maltreating poor, defenseless emigrants.

Anshel compared their journey to America with the Exodus from Egypt and applied to it the Biblical language of the latter to describe its various stages. Thus, when they spoke of their "flight from Egypt" they meant only their crossing of the border: "Crossing the Red Sea" was their passage over the Atlantic and to safely pass through the portals of Castle Garden, the old United States immigrant station in New York, was to "conquer the land of Canaan."

Their "flight from Egypt," which took place on a dark night, left an indelible impression upon them all. Huddled close together, holding each other's hands in terror, with the children clinging wildly to them, they advanced in the dark. Passing through a forest they were forced to wade knee-deep through a muddy stream. And from time to time, the agent and his two Christian assistants who preceded the group bade them to fling themselves upon the ground and to hold their breath. More than once Surè resigned herself and her children to God's mercy for she thought that it was all over with them.

But "crossing the Red Sea" was a comparatively easy matter. It proved thoroughly uneventful. The women, who throughout the journey had quarreled incessantly, became the fastest of friends the moment they boarded the ship. They piled their bundles in one heap and shared with one another all the edible tidbits they had brought with them. As for the men, they prayed together, discussed politics and dwelt long and fondly on the new world they were about to enter. They also spoke with great extravagance and boastfulness of the wealth of their relations already in America. And the women prepared their food together and shared the little they possessed. If one dished up a herring, or opened a jar of preserves, every one else had to taste of them. They lived in communal amity and bliss.

Crossing the Red Sea

And Anshel and the Palestine Jew strutted about as if they were the actual owners of the ship. Their curiosity was insatiable. They explored all the boilers and the engine room and were determined to seek out the captain himself and have him show them the great compass. But the "anti-Semite" who guarded the door leading from the steerage to the rest of the ship sternly barred their way. No matter how much they threatened to expose him in the newspapers and to ruin his virtuous reputation as a gentleman and a sailor, so that no Jew would ever want to travel with his ship again, the "anti-Semite" remained obdurate and would not let them see the captain.

Even though they were not fortunate enough to see with their own eyes the great compass, they saw it nevertheless very vividly in their imagination. And when Anshel stood talking to the other Jewish emigrants between the boilers in the long galleyway, he described to them the wonders of the great compass in such detail that they opened their eyes wide with wonderment. It was as if Columbus himself were describing to them his first voyage to America. The Palestine Jew did not altogether agree with all the fine points of Anshel's description of the compass, but he had to admit that in knowledge of the sea and navigation he was his peer. Needless to say, Surè received much honor from the other women because of Anshel's great maritime knowledge. And she would then say regretfully with one of her famous sighs:

"Ah, if only God willed that he earned as easily as he acquires knowledge!"

Shloimè awaited them at Castle Garden. And when Surè saw him through the iron grating which separated them, she lifted her eyes in thanksgiving to heaven. The world about her grew light and joyous. She no longer had any fear of America....

Chapter 2

REST FOR THE WANDERER

■■■■■■■

THE reception that Anshel received entering America was not the one he had prepared himself for in his fond imagination. He was astounded, even deeply outraged. The rude questions he was asked in Castle Garden by the immigration officials, and his being placed in a penlike enclosure behind an iron grating, filled him with dismay.

"Was it for this I have come to America?" he asked. "I could have had the same thing in Russia!"

But his dismay and amazement grew still greater when Shloimè led him from the pier to their own residence which he had prepared for their coming. If not a palace, Anshel had expected to find at least a comfortable, snug little home, with beds and bedding, a clothes closet, sideboard and other respectable household necessities. Was it not to improve his condition that he had left his old home and came over land and sea — liquidated his own home — sold to the junkman for a song all his household effects, including machines and a factory? (Dvoyrelè's single, rheumatic sewing machine now loomed large in Anshel's excited state as a whole squadron of machines and her little dressmaking establishment blossomed into a factory.) Instead, "the young man" led Anshel the famous Reader of Scripture, his wife and their six children, together with all their belongings, down steep stairs into a dark cellar under an elevated iron structure across which incessantly rumbled and shrieked innumerable speeding trains. True enough, the cellar also contained a little alcove which possessed a tiny little window opening against a gray wall, but as it was covered thickly with dirt it was impossible to look through it. Above it, on the ground floor, a Rumanian restaurant had established itself. As the cellar was in close proximity with the kitchen of the restaurant, it was constantly filled with smoke and a symphony of pungent odors. These aromatic fragrances irritated the throat and nose and made one cough and sneeze. Since onions were being ground and peeled all day long, the eyes were forced to tears incessantly. Anshel's amazement was so great that he could not utter a word.

The myriad noises and shrieks of the street poured down in waves into the cellar through the two little windows and the open door. Only the shuffling feet of the passers-by could be seen. All day long they came and went, disturbing, unnerving feet of human beings. Every minute there galloped by overhead on the elevated structure a roaring train until the senses reeled and one felt the train thundering through one's exhausted brain.

Surè remained standing in the middle of the cellar with folded arms. She was dazed and did not understand what was taking place about her. Later on when she began to collect her painful thoughts she had the sensation as if she, her children and their belongings had been put out upon the street and that she had been told:

"You will make your home here."

Nevertheless she made no comment. It was quite enough for her that she had at last safely found a resting place for herself and her children.

In the meantime Anshel, with hands folded behind him, roamed about the cellar in methodical exploration and silent scrutiny of his "palace." Half of the cellar was occupied by large iron beds on which lay long and heavy mattresses. In the center stood a round table crazily supporting itself on only three iron legs. In place of the missing leg a wooden crate stood guard. There were also two chairs but for the rest wooden boxes had to serve the purpose. In compensation for all these shortcomings a rocking-chair stood invitingly in a corner. Before mother had even time enough to note its presence, Meyer, the "big boy," and Nutè, the "suckling child," were already engaged in a fight to the death for its occupation. The furniture for the alcove which was to serve as a parlor was still missing. It waited for better days that were to come — in America....

To distract them from the depressing first impression of their new home, Shloimè had prepared a magnificent breakfast. Anshel drank a little brandy. The children tasted for the first time crisp American rolls. Then came Itzikel, their countryman, to bid them welcome to the new world. In the old country he had taught girls how to read and write. But in New York he had become sexton of a little synagogue formed by his fellow countrymen. No sooner did Itzikel smell the possibility of a good bracing drink, than he lost no time in realizing it. It was for this very reason that he now appeared in Anshel's new home — to drink his health — also to invite him in the name of the president of the synagogue to read Scripture on the following Sabbath.

After her initial amazement had somewhat worn off, mother unpacked her beloved pots and began to look about her. She could not grow accustomed to the noises of the street and the roar of the elevated trains. Each time they thundered by she had the curious sensation that invisible spirits were cavorting like furies through the cellar. Even that could be endured, thought mother. But the thick odors of Rumanian cooking that penetrated into the cellar through the walls gave her a tormenting headache. Nevertheless, she kept her peace. She did not want to mar her son's joy in their reunion, nor to increase Anshel's depression. So

she tied a wet towel about her head and continued unpacking.

Shloimè went out for a while on the street and soon
returned with a basket of fruit which he placed near the
little gas stove. One by one Surè unpacked her old friends,
the pots, and regarded each one of them separately with a
little groan. It was as if she were confiding to them her
new crop of troubles, and reminding them of their ancient
alliance, beseeching them to remain true to her in her hour
of need even as they had in olden days.

What completely reconciled not only mother but also
father to the cellar was the faucet of running water. When
the "suckling child," quite by accident, discovered the
nature of the faucet, mother at first became frightened. She
was under the impression that some terrible accident was
about to happen. But Shloimè quieted her and with great
pride spoke about the virtues of modern plumbing just as
if he were its inventor. He said:

"There will be no more need for you, mother, to fetch
water from the town pump. Here in America you can draw
water from the wall."

"Just as easily as the water that Moses drew from the
rock by striking it!" added father with undisguised admiration, his good humor quickly returning. He approached the
wondrous faucet and contemplated it earnestly. "I can well
see that you will not find it necessary to lead your flock
to the well for water," remarked he to mother, employing
a Biblical figure. "For that purpose this contrivance has
been made." And he pointed with an air of superior understanding to the sink. Its workings fairly intrigued him.

"How cleverly it is done!" he exclaimed. "It pours from
the wall and then it disappears into the wall."

These physical conveniences made living in the cellar
more tolerable to the immigrants. Little by little father became reconciled to his humble abode, to the noises of the

street and to the shuffling feet of innumerable passers-by. Anshel rediscovered his old enthusiasm for America and went about chanting its praises. One by one the smaller children ventured into the street for exploration purposes. And mother, concerned with putting each one up for the night, went about the cellar making her calculations in beds and bedding.

Mother was not permitted to cook dinner that day. Shloimè went shopping and returned laden with wurst, rolls and brandy. When night began to fall, father commenced to say the prayers of the twilight service. And Shloimè taught mother how to light an American gas stove.

That very evening there came many of their townspeople from the old country to bid them welcome and to inquire after the folks at home. There came Henech, the pastry cook, who in America had prospered and had been elevated to the position of president of his synagogue, Baruch the shoemaker, Itzikel the sexton, and Taubè, an old friend of Surè's. Each visitor brought cheering words and a handsome gift. Shloimè lit a gas jet, and the immigrants regarded it with great wonderment. A few tins of beer were placed before the guests and the conversation turned on the little town of their birth. Anshel listened avidly to the heartening words of his fellow townsmen. They painted in glowing colors the great fortune that was awaiting him in the new land of his adoption. In a burst of parental pride he paraded before them his children. They underwent a close scrutiny from the guests.

"What can she do?" demanded the synagogue president, pointing to Dvoyrelè.

"She was my breadwinner at home," said mother with a light in her eyes. "She is a seamstress and wonderfully handy with the needle."

"It will be an easy matter to procure work for her," said the synagogue president. "If you like, I will recommend her to a relation of mine, a dress manufacturer. He will surely find work for her."

"And what can this young man do?" he asked, referring to Moishelè.

"Oh, he is a merchant!" said mother boastfully. "There isn't another like him in the world."

"Well, my boy, have you brought along with you some dollars?" asked the former pastry cook of Moishelè, with an attempt at humor.

For an instant Moishelè felt flustered. He flushed furiously and lost his speech. Then rapidly collecting himself he rejoined tartly:

"It is easy to be a merchant with money. Show me how I can become a merchant without money."

This remark evoked a hearty laugh.

Then mother introduced Gedaliah to the company.

"He knows enough already to put all your American Rabbis to shame," she boasted.

"American Rabbis aren't much for learning," commented Itzikel the sexton with an air of contempt.

Mother suddenly realized that her "scholar" was wearing a tattered cap. So she tried to conceal it with her hand.

The visitors regarded with great curiosity the prodigy that Anshel had brought with him to America. One of them even waxed prophetic.

"One never can tell! You and your children may bring yet great honor on us, Anshel," said he.

The pastry cook now arose and drawing Shloimè into a corner whispered secretively into his ear:

"Have your folks enough money to get along on for the next few days?"

He pressed a few dollars into his hand and raised his voice so that mother might overhear:

"Tell your mother that I want her positively to come to my bakery for bread and rolls. She can have everything she needs on credit and when the boys will begin to earn money she will repay me."

"And you can always get your meat on credit in my shop, too," added Avrum the butcher.

"Just as in the old country!" exclaimed mother joyfully, and tears of gratitude welled up in her eyes.

After the guests had departed mother finished unpacking her belongings and made the beds for her little flock. She grew more cheerful now. Everything appeared more home-like and the cellar took on the aspect of familiarity.

"Do you know what I think, Anshel?" mused she. "The whole world is one. People are the same everywhere."

Anshel said nothing.

"Father in heaven!" mother winged her impassioned prayer, "grant us that we, our children, and our children's children may find here a resting place from our wanderings!"

Anshel said nothing.

When the Sabbath arrived Anshel made his appearance in the synagogue to give a trial reading of Scripture before the townsfolk of the old country. He had prepared himself for the occasion during the preceding week as he had done at home with the Book of Esther for Purim. The Biblical portion of the week dealt with the Lord's command to Abraham:

"And leave the land of thy forefathers!'

This admonition Anshel had in his thoughts identified with his own migration to America.

He was warmly received in the synagogue. Every one wished him welcome and rejoiced aloud over the fortune that brought to them the Reader of Scripture from their home town.

"To-day," said every man to his neighbor, "we will hear a Scripture reading, not in the silly American style, but as we used to hear it in the good old days at home."

Rest for the Wanderer

Before Anshel began his reading he cleared his throat elaborately. Then he commenced:

" 'Leave the land of thy forefathers!' said God to Abraham."

And Anshel absorbed himself with the story that he was cantillating. He trilled every syllable and coquetted with each phrase, adorning it with all the pretty musical conceits he was capable of. At first the townsfolk listened with the greatest rapture. One winked to the other meaningfully and called out in a stage whisper:

"This is what I call reading!"

But when the reading became protracted and seemed never to draw to an end, the congregation became restive. Hunger was undermining its pleasure in Anshel's virtuosity. The young folk with characteristic American irreverence threw off their prayer shawls and deserted the synagogue for the street. The older members in the congregation still remained attentive in a sort of strained piety. But when Anshel continued to decorate a musical façade over each separate word and the hour was getting to be late, impatient mutterings were heard.

"Who is that greenhorn?" called maliciously one across to another so that Anshel could hear.

"Does he think to-day is the Day of Atonement?" asked a gourmand, regretfully thinking of his dinner waiting at home.

In vain Anshel's friend, the former pastry cook who was president of the synagogue, tried to call the congregation to order, to quell the mutiny. He pounded on the pulpit table for silence. What followed was complete pandemonium. So that poor, distracted Anshel was forced to abandon all his artistry and finished the reading in the American style, "hurry-up." He left the synagogue alone and humiliated. . . .

Chapter 3

ANSHEL CHANGES HIS CALLING

■■■■■■

ANSHEL had descended upon America with eight souls —
but souls that stood in need of very earthly nourishment.

The first few days of their sojourn in the new world was marked by a festive and carefree spirit. Their countrymen came to bid them welcome. They rejoiced over their arrival. Some brought gifts. Others foretold to Anshel happy and prosperous days. Nothing, however, was mentioned about earning a livelihood. Shloimè supplied all the needs of the household. And Anshel felt exceedingly pleased with America.

But life is not a perpetual holiday. The prosaic, drab reality began to obtrude itself. The problem of earning a livelihood had to be faced. Mother still obtained food on credit, but both the baker and the butcher, their countrymen, who had so heartily and voluntarily offered to help them tide over the dog-days, now asked insinuatingly whether the boys had not already obtained work.

One evening, Shloimè said to his father unexpectedly:

"Father, I want you to know that things are not done here as in the old country. America is quite another world."

"In reference to what do you say this?" asked Anshel eagerly unsuspecting.

"I mean in reference to earning a livelihood. Work is not

regarded as disgraceful in America. Here every man works to provide for his wife and children."

"Truly — what an excellent custom! Only provide me with some work that will enable me to earn a livelihood for my wife and children! Wasn't it for this you brought me here?"

"Do you remember Duvid Goldschmidt? I met him on the street to-day. He told me that he works in a shirt factory in Brooklyn. Many elderly, pious Jews are also employed there. The boss is very orthodox and shuts down his plant on the Sabbath. Duvid would like to take you along with him. Perhaps you might find something to do there!"

"Shirts! Did you say shirts?" gasped mother, utterly taken aback. "Do you think father is suited for that kind of work? It may be all right for Dvoyrelè, but for father!"

"Dvoyrelè is quite another matter," said Shloimè determinedly. "She will find a job at women's waists. The season hasn't begun yet. I have been promised work for her in a week or two."

Father's head drooped.

"I thought," he faltered, "I thought you had found for me some honorable post as Reader of Scripture in a large synagogue."

"Reading Scripture is no business in America," unfeelingly rejoined Shloimè.

"What then?" asked mother with a lump in her throat. "Do you want him to turn tailor in his old age?"

"There lies no disgrace in being a tailor," heatedly answered Shloimè. "Many respectable Jews have become tailors in America — even former Rabbis. America is a free country. Here no one is ashamed of working with his hands."

"In other words you would like me to take up tailoring," said father aghast. "Could you think of nothing better for me to do than tailoring?"

The Mother

"For my part," retorted Shloimè, taking offense, "you can become a Rabbi! I must say though, that in this country every one must swim for himself. These are your wife and children — not mine. I have provided for you long enough. As yet I have not managed to pay off the debt on your steamship tickets. The next payment soon falls due on them as well as on the furniture. The little ones will soon have to be put to school — else the Truant Officer of the Board of Education will come down and will want to know the reason why. An American public school is not a Hebrew school. The children must be sent there clean and neatly dressed. If they are not, you can be certain that their teacher will send them home. You mustn't forget for a minute that this is America. I do believe though that the wisest thing for me to do would be to move out of the house. Then you would be forced to shift for yourself."

The implied threat that lurked in Shloimè's last words proved more effective than anything else he might have said. Mother looked frightenedly at father and father, suddenly lapsing into a piteous whine which was entirely foreign to his nature and which now sounded terrifying even to his own ears, murmured:

"What! You want to move! What will become of us then? We will all die of starvation."

"What else is there for me to do?" cried Shloimè with a despairing ring in his voice. "I have gone and cut my own throat because of you. Other young men in my circumstances have already tidy sums salted away in savings banks. But I — I have sacrificed my whole life for you."

Shloimè was submerged by a wave of self-pity. The tears sprang to his eyes.

Father and mother sat in stony silence. Dvoyrelè who had listened mutely to the entire conversation bit nervously at her fingernails. She flushed hot because of her parents'

120

humiliation and the crushing weight of their poverty.
"Perhaps I can take father's job in the shirt factory for
the present," she ventured with a forlorn little voice.

"No! You will have your own work to do — Moishelè
too. Even your scholar Gedaliah will have to find himself
a job in some shop," snapped Shloimè, steeling himself by
a painful effort. "Things are different in America than in
the old country. Every one must work. He who doesn't
work doesn't eat. I suppose it's easy for you to forget that
we still owe three hundred dollars on your steamship tickets.
As for the little ones — they will have to be supported until
they graduate from public school. America doesn't tolerate
idlers. Every one, without exception, must work."

Moishelè, without being noticed, tiptoed out of the cellar.
And father, mother and the other children sat frozen and
wretched in a leaden silence.

Then Anshel began to boil within. He arose suddenly —
his old self-possession and pride rekindled, and striking the
same heroic attitude as when he stood on the synagogue
rostrum reading the Law, he declaimed:

"Right you are, Shloimè! Every one must work in
America. What says Holy Writ! 'By the sweat of thy brow
shalt thou earn thy bread.' " These last words he cantillated
with his well-known trills, turns and quavers. "Lead me
then to that shop of yours, my son!" he commanded sternly.
"I will become a sewer of shirts, by the Will of God!"

Hot, scalding tears rolled from Surè's eyes. She wiped
them away with a corner of her apron and amidst her sobs
cried:

"Alas! That I have lived to see this day when Anshel,
the celebrated Reader of Scripture, must become a sewer
of shirts like a common woman!"

"Idiot! What are you crying about?" shouted Anshel
angrily. "Of what earthly use are Scripture Readers in

America? What America needs most — are garment workers. Now give me my coat and walking stick."

With the tears coursing down her cheeks, Surè handed her husband his coat and his walking stick. And Anshel accompanied his son to the factory in Brooklyn — there to hire himself out as a sewer of shirts, which he was to remain for the rest of his life.

What was Anshel's great amazement when he found among the patriarchal Jews and Italian women workers in the shirt factory — none other than his shipmate the Palestine Jew, who had boasted that he was coming down to America only to show the haughty Gentiles that Jews could be good farmers. When Anshel first saw him sitting bowed over a work-table with a shirt in his hands, and beside him an Italian girl teaching him to sew buttons, he fairly gaped. With a cry of joy they embraced one another like old and tried friends.

"Is that how you fulfill your holy mission as a farmer?" asked Anshel teasingly.

"Not here but in the land of our forefathers, in Palestine, will you find me with a spade in my hands," replied the Palestine Jew.

"And when will that be?" asked Anshel mournfully.

The Palestine Jew did not answer. He was racked by a suspicious cough which made it impossible for him to utter a word.

"When the Messiah will come," Anshel answered his own question with the deepest emotion. He left the shop with a lightened heart. He had found a friend.

That same evening Moishelè returned home late, after they had all dined. All day long mother had gone about distracted with anxiety. She had feared that he had somehow lost his way in the Ghetto labyrinth. So Shloimè went out to look for him. He found him washing dishes in the Rumanian restaurant on the floor above. When Moishelè was brought home he shamefacedly slipped a silver half dollar into mother's hand. . . .

.　　.　　.　　.　　.　　.　　.

It happened on a summer morning several weeks after. Without, the light was still gray and dim. Dawn was just breaking. In the cellar the ghastly flare of a gas jet wrestled with the murky shadows. It lit up the adjacent objects. All the others were swallowed up in indistinctness and mist. Surè, with a cold compress about her forehead, stood at the little gas stove making coffee. The knotted edges of her towel cast huge shadows on the walls. They looked like the ears of some fantastic monster. She prepared the lunches of her menfolk in neat little packages. From time to time she called:

"Anshel! Anshel! It's getting late."

"Eh! What!" groaned Anshel in his sleep, uncomprehending, and he soon dozed off again.

It grieved mother to wake him. So for a little while she let him be. The previous night he had fallen asleep over his dinner — so dead tired had he been. He was not at all used to physical labor, mother pondered pityingly, and heaved a deep sigh.

Anshel lay in a stupor. He dreamed that he was standing in a synagogue that was full of sewing machines. Tailors, innumerable ones, sat before each of them, furiously working their iron foot-pedals. The machines whirred and rumbled and he saw himself standing on the rostrum cantillating Scripture.

When Surè realized that if Anshel slept much longer he would not be able to say his morning prayers before leaving for the factory, she steeled herself and called out sharply:

"If you don't get up right away, Anshel, you will have no time to say your prayers."

When Anshel heard the word "prayers" he awoke with a

start. It took him some time to recollect who and where he was. He staggered dazedly out of bed, dressed hurriedly and washed himself at the sink.

Suddenly Dvoyrelè appeared at her mother's side near the gas stove. Her disheveled hair fell over her bare arms and neck. She wanted to help with the breakfast. But mother brushed her gently aside:

"Better dress quickly before the boys get up," she urged.

Anshel's resonant voice rose in prayer. Even his toil and poverty could not restrain its vibrancy and overflowing ardor. He sang out full-throated and joyous with the ecstasy that was of ancient days. Surè even reminded him that those days were past.

"What are you doing, Anshel?" she exclaimed in amazement. "You have no time for this. You'll be late on your job!"

Before father had ended his prayers and put away his prayer shawl and phylacteries, a steaming breakfast had been prepared as well as lunch bags and coffee tins for all the menfolk. Without a word, like hundreds of thousands of their kind, the men went to their work — father to his shirt factory, Moishelè to help a customer-peddler carry his packs of merchandise from door to door and Dvoyrelè to her dingy waist shop.

After the grown-ups had left, mother got the children — Meyer "the big boy" and Nutè "the suckling child"— ready for school. Both were unrecognizable now, for they had undergone a complete transformation during the few weeks since their arrival in America. Their side-curls had been clipped and they looked resplendent in dazzling-white shirts which mother washed for them every night after they had gone to bed. Every morning now a pitched battle took place between them and her over the prescribed number of prayers that they were obliged to say. She would not give them their buttered rolls before they had covered at least half of the prayer-book. But the cunning little rascals, by shrewd bargaining, kept on reducing their songs of praise to the Jewish God. They needed more time to devote to their school lessons which they had neglected to do the night before. For mother this was a sign that in the ungodly new world they were becoming heretics and unbelievers and that they ultimately would renounce their Judaism.

Only one of their brood father and mother succeeded in saving from the hungry jaws of American sweatshops and the godless public schools. That was Gedaliah, their Talmudic scholar. Mother battled with might and main to protect him against the virus of American assimilation which was rapidly transforming her other children into creatures foreign and alarming to her. What a pity to waste such a brilliant intellect on an American school, lamented mother! And Anshel, as was his wont, kept postponing from one Sabbath to another, to inquire after a good Rabbinic College for his son.

Chapter 4

LONGING

■■■■■■■

THE frantic noises of the street continued to flow through the walls, windows and doors of the cellar like a roaring torrent. It was evening when the workers returned home from their factories and the street peddlers displayed their merchandise on the stands and testified, with ear-splitting eloquence so that all the world might hear, to the cheapness and excellence of their wares. An old Jew had stationed himself directly opposite Anshel's windows and boomed out in a bass, hoarse voice the virtues of his bananas. One's senses reeled with the tumult. The walls trembled with the fury of the elevated train as it roared by, its steel wheels shrilling unnervingly on the steel tracks. It almost appeared as if the ceiling were bending like an elastic and the panes in the little windows rattled like breaking glass. Most of all, the uproar was heard within one's self. Each time the shrieking of steel crushing against steel was heard overhead, one felt as if the speeding train went roaring through one's brain. . . . Opposite the windows opening on the street little urchins were tirelessly building bonfires at night. From time to time there flared up tongues of flame which illuminated the cellary gloom of Anshel's humble dwelling. This was accompanied by childish shrieks of delight and wonder.

A procession of feet marched endlessly by on the street past the cellar. The panes did not cease rattling and all

126

the noises, shrieks and insufferable clatter became petrified into a continuous hum which throbbed through the walls from the Rumanian restaurant. It was as if hundreds upon hundreds of crickets were incessantly chirping in a fearful monotone which they never, never would cease.

The Sabbath peace throbbed silently in the cellar.

Four lit candles flickered piously on the table at the head of which sat Anshel. With half-closed, sleepy eyes he droned his songs of praise to the Almighty. With stern glances he would from time to time intimidate the bored youngsters about him to join in the sacred singing. They were already calloused to his rebukes and showed but little inclination to comply with his irksome requests. With their hearts and minds they were with the other boys building a bonfire on the street as they did every other night. They displayed unuttered resentment towards their father for forcing upon them his old-world customs. None of the other boys was obliged to sit at home on Friday nights and sing interminable hymns of praise — only they, ruminated Anshel's children bitterly! So they squirmed restively in their chairs and with infinite longing looked out upon the street through the little windows. They waited impatiently for that happy moment when father would doze off. They would then steal quickly out upon the street before the bonfire had died out.

Shloimè was conspicuous by his absence. He was busy courting a young lady and rarely was at home of an evening. He had even served timely notice on his mother that she should look about for a boarder in his place. He was planning to get married. Moishelè "The Ox" was also away from home. During the brief period since his arrival in America he had already, with breath-taking speed, changed his name to Moses. No one knew exactly why he had taken on a new name. He had displayed a remarkable attitude of independence from the first moment after he had touched American soil. He was the first of the newly arrived immigrants to earn money. Every day he engaged in some new employment. Now he was a clerk in a grocery store. He thus managed to supply mother with all the household necessities. Because of this he drew up a solemn treaty of peace with Anshel whereby his father would not "bother" him and demand that he remain at home on Friday nights and Saturdays. Friday night, pleaded Moishelè piteously, was the busiest night during the week in his store. He had to fill orders for Sunday.

Only Gedaliah stayed at home and helped father usher in the mystic Sabbath Bride. He had no employment — neither did he study. Father still promised to make inquiries about a good Rabbinic College where tuition was free. He wanted his son to be "an American Rabbi," learned in the Talmud, yet capable of delivering a sermon in English. But as he always pleaded preoccupation with more mundane matters, he never came to the point of inquiring. Gedaliah, however, grew restive; his active mind needed some outlet. He somehow obtained books and began to study English by himself. He mysteriously spent his days away from home and invariably returned with a pile of English books. He seemed to have little use now for the sacred Hebrew books, although he continued to say his prayers aloud every day and faithfully observed all the ritual laws and religious practices. He was the only one of the children who still helped father exalt the Sabbath of the old world in the strange, noise-ridden cellar in the New York Ghetto.

Dvoyrelè too remained at home on Friday nights and helped welcome the Sabbath into the damp cellar. Since of old she had been in the habit of washing and carefully combing her hair before sundown brought the Sabbath peace over the earth, now, too, in far-off America, she observed this ancient custom religiously. But in as much as she returned from work at a late hour she was forced to sit near the stove and dry her moist hair over it.

Longing

The candles sputtered chastely and in a festive spirit in their brass candlesticks which mother had brought with her from the old country. True, the candlesticks no more wore their high polish as of old. Mother merely contented herself now with wiping the dust off them with a wet cloth. Yet the mystery of the Sabbath glowed in them as of old. The red gleaming brandy flagon too, that mother had brought to America, helped give the illusion of bygone and long-cherished days in the little Polish town across the seas.

All week long, as Anshel sat over his work, deafened by the ceaseless whir of innumerable machines about him, he felt as if all of his past life had been amputated from him. But each time he saw the Sabbath candles on the table, flickering bravely in their ancient candlesticks, saw the old, familiar red, glass flagon in which the brandy glowed like a priceless elixir, the cellar became transfigured for him. The spirit of the old days had stolen silently into their humble new-world abode. Everything else was blotted out. . . .

No matter how tired and sleepy Anshel felt, after sitting humped up over his work all day long, when he returned home on Friday nights, the Sabbath advanced joyously to greet him. The tumultuous street vanished from his consciousness. He no longer heard the roar of the elevated trains overhead, or the clatter of dishes in the Rumanian restaurant. Silence and peace reigned in the cellar as if turned abrooding into itself. Anshel struggled to keep awake, sang his hymns of praise with greater ecstasy, and spurred on his bored children to greater vocal efforts, with imperious glances from his half-closed eyes.

When Surè placed a steaming dish of noodle soup before him he wearily placed his head in his hands and became lost in thought.

"What are you thinking of, Anshel?" asked mother, pushing his plate of soup nearer to him.

"To-morrow there will be read in the synagogue the

weekly portion of Scripture beginning with: 'Give ear, ye heavens,' " murmured Anshel regretfully, as if to himself.

At this Surè too became melancholy and thoughtful. She felt a lump rise in her throat. Her old, sad eyes grew moist.

"And if the Scriptural portion is: 'Give ear, ye heavens,' do you regard that as enough cause for you to go back to the old country?" she bitterly asked as if she were angry with herself. "Better drink your soup. It's getting cold."

Anshel drew his soup plate towards him with a groan.

And as if in explanation Surè asked mollifyingly:

"And if this is a topsy-turvy world, must you feel guilty? This is a country only for the ignoramus."

Anshel kept his peace but before saying the final benediction he quite casually opened his Bible. At first he hummed to himself in an undertone, then his voice grew ever louder and louder until in a flood of melody he burst out:

" 'Give ear, ye heavens, and I will speak;
And let the earth hear the words of My mouth.' "

Surè sat at the table. Her head rested heavily on her hands. As she listened to Anshel's cantillation tears rolled down her face.

There was still another soul that was consumed with longing. . . .

Four months had elapsed since Dvoyrelè came to the great city and was swallowed up among the millions of other people. She was like a plant that is torn up by the roots and then transplanted into a wilderness. She knew no one and no one knew her. She felt herself completely alone among the many. She arose at dawn and went to her work. All day long she sat among strangers. And at night she returned home, one among many hurrying millions. At first she found this experience of solitude among many very interesting.

Longing

The novelty of it fascinated her. She was eager for new sensations. Afterwards it began to bore her. She felt its hollowness, its futility, its purposelessness. It was all so strange to her!

How she longed now for the little town in Poland! For those unforgettable twilights near the water mill, and for Henech! For Henech himself she felt no longer any longing — only for that which the recollection of him made her think about: the twilight hours near the water mill, the woods, the Saturday afternoon promenade in the orchard. Then, life had some meaning — a purpose. How she longed for that *purpose!* She called it by the hallowed name that Henech had given it: *The Holy Cause.* Because of it life then had a fascination and a justification. Now her world had changed. Then she felt herself identified with something. She belonged to some one. But in the new world she was alone — all alone — among so many. Was it possible then that the Holy Cause could be found in the large forbidding brick houses with their many gloomy windows — a Holy Cause which made life worth while and meaningful? No! She could not believe that.

Had not Henech told her that the Holy Cause would unite them even though they would be far apart from one another? Where then was the Holy Cause? In which of the immense tenement houses in the city did it dwell?

In her little chest that she had brought to America, Dvoyrelè had placed a few books. One of them had been given her by Henech before parting. Many a time in her hours of sorrow and longing had she turned to it for consolation. She had already read and reread this book a hundred times. She knew it almost by heart. Yet it tempted her to reread it again and again. And on Friday night, when longing filled her soul, Dvoyrelè sat down to read her precious book before the sputtering Sabbath candles. She became absorbed in it, as if it were the first time she was reading it, as if in its well-thumbed pages she could once more find the Holy Cause that she had lost, lost, apparently forever, in the great alien, cruel New York Ghetto.

Chapter 5

THE FIRST DISILLUSIONMENT

▪▪▪▪▪▪▪

THE shop in which Dvoyrelè worked was a non-union one. In those years the workers in the needle trades were but poorly organized. Accordingly Shloimè found employment for her where it was easiest to be gotten, without asking too many questions. The shop was small. With her worked a few other girls. They were older than she and looked haggard and overworked and gave Dvoyrelè the impression that they were thoroughly submerged in a sea of trouble and responsibilities and had no time to give her any thought. They were hardly acquainted with one another. They were of various nationalities, and included both Jews and Gentiles. There were even some orthodox Jews of past middle age among them. The boss himself was a young man wearing a little goatee. He was newly-wed and was anxious to get rich quick. He was boss, foreman, cutter, finisher and operator all in one. His wife would often come in during the course of the day and assist him at the sewing machine.

So the boss speeded up his workers, not with words, but with work. He and his wife worked at lightning speed — preparing the garments for his "hands." He often remained in the shop until after midnight for this purpose, so that when the workers came in the following morning they found everything in readiness for them. They worked silently, swiftly, absorbed in their work, wrapped up in their thoughts. Dvoyrelè never learned to know any of them.

133

The Mother

No one ever addressed her. Neither did she speak to any of them. Alone she went to her work, alone she returned home.

She found it difficult to imagine that this steady, endless grind was all the life the great city could offer. Perhaps this was, she thought, because she did not know a soul yet, had no opportunity to come in contact with the finer aspects of the workers' lives. More than once she felt tempted to ask one of the women workers what sort of social life she and her friends were leading, but being too bashful and constrained she never did anything about it.

A time came when she could endure her loneliness no longer. Her existence in the shop became obnoxious to her. Life at home was a complete void. She began to seek for that mysterious essence that would give some meaning to her life. So Dvoyrelè found herself a friend among the workers in the shop. She pleased her more than the other girls. She was older than Dvoyrelè, yet not so old that she need stand in awe of her. For three months they had sat working together with hardly a word exchanged between them except in reference to their work. Dvoyrelè laid the blame of their distant relationship on her own reticence.

One day, when closing time came, she purposely delayed her departure, so that she might leave the shop at the same time with the girl. They descended the stairs together. Although the girl seemed in a great hurry, Dvoyrelè caught up with her.

"I beg your pardon! I am only a *greenhorn!*" she blurted out with a guilty little laugh. "I would like to ask you something."

"Please ask!" said the girl looking with some surprise at Dvoyrelè.

"In the old country," began Dvoyrelè, "I belonged to the Holy Cause. I would like to do the same here. Isn't there some group among the workers that concerns itself with the Holy Cause?"

"What is that?" asked the girl amazed.

"Don't you know what I mean?" Dvoyrelè became flustered.

"I don't!" curtly answered the girl.

"Well — I mean a place where men and women workers get together. Don't workers meet here as in the old country?"

"Ah! I see what you mean — meetings in public halls in time of a strike. Of course workers hold meetings here! Why shouldn't they?"

"In what halls?" asked Dvoyrelè.

"If you want to take my advice — you'd better not speak about it. Our boss would be very angry. You might lose your job."

Dvoyrelè flushed with fear and embarrassment.

"Oh, it's quite all right to talk to me about it," the girl hastily reassured her. "Never fear — I will not betray you. You must guard yourself though with others. Should the boss ever find out what you are inquiring about he will send you packing instantly."

Dvoyrelè became confused.

"I beg your pardon," she mumbled.

The girl then parted from her. But after walking a few steps she turned back.

"Have no fear that I will betray you! But don't forget to guard yourself while talking to others, if your job means anything to you at all."

Dvoyrelè did not answer.

"Do you also take the elevated train?" asked the girl.

"Yes — my folks live downtown."

"Are you long in America?"

"No, only a few months."

"That's quite clear," said the girl smilingly. "Most likely you belonged to the Socialist Party in the old country."

"Yes," said Dvoyrelè, nodding her head.

The Mother

"I too was in the movement once. Now I have no time for it. It's too bothersome to think about it in America. You must pardon me for having answered your question the way I did before. I had a good reason for it. You see, it was so difficult for me to get my present job. I was without work more than six months, and I have a sick mother at home. I am simply frightened to think of the possibility of losing my job. Once I have managed to land one I am determined to hang on to it with all my might. Our boss is a hard man. He asked me an awful lot of questions before he gave me the job. He only engages recent immigrants. A union worker stands no chance of getting a job from him. He is afraid of a strike. One must always guard one's tongue. One can never tell to whom one speaks. Do you understand what I mean ... ?"

Dvoyrelè did not understand what the girl meant, but in order not to give her the impression that she was too "green" and partly because she wanted to remain alone, she nodded her head and hastily parted from her. Before doing so the girl had said to her:

"Please don't think that I would not prefer working in a union shop. But what can I do? Work is very scarce these days. Surely you know that yourself. Haven't you the same trouble?"

After this conversation Dvoyrelè had no desire to return home immediately. Instead of taking the train she walked home, as she had so often done before. She was not thinking of anything in particular, only a great yearning gnawed away at her heart. For the first time she felt a deep feeling of self-pity. Was she not alone — alone in the great city? Had she not lost her way in a barren wilderness?

A light snow was falling. It barely covered the pavements. And through its transparent curtain gleamed the yellowish-gray refulgence of the gas jets in the shop windows. The streets were teeming with a seemingly endless stream of workers returning home. After working all day long in stuffy factories, they greeted with delight the transparent, childishly playful snowfall. In the furniture shop windows were displayed entire bedroom and dining-room suites. They beckoned invitingly to the passers-by. Before the shop windows stood young couples inspecting the furniture and making plans for their future homes. Others stood before the dress shops and regarded the waxen manikins that stood clothed like human beings in elegantly appointed display windows. How happy they looked! Dvoyrelè too stopped to gaze with envy at the happily-smiling wax manikins that looked so at peace with themselves and with the world. They did not have to look for jobs — only sit in pleasant company and drink tea. They were either dressed for a ball or for an afternoon walk, adorned in expensive gowns, furs and jewels.

Of a sudden the thought of her work in the factory, with all its deadening monotony and endless grind, became obnoxious to her. But what was the use of rebelling against it? It was at this moment, as she stood before the illuminated shop windows in the falling, merry snow, feeling about her the movement of gay throngs, that it became clear to her that it was impossible for her to rebel against selling her young life to traitorous work. When she recollected that she was employed by an enemy of the workers she became frightened at herself. How could she ever have forgotten the oath she had taken to remain true to the Holy Cause? She saw before her the woods in the little town where she was born. Then Henech and his comrades arose; they were singing. The oath of allegiance to the working-class. . . . Suddenly she felt as if she were being pushed off the edge of a precipice. Frantically she clutched at bushes and rocks and with difficulty clambered back to the top.

An indefinable resentment arose in her breast towards her mother and her brothers. How she would have liked to free herself from them! Ah! if only once to be alone, to live with one's self and for one's self! This feeling was soon displaced by pity for her mother. Then she became angry with herself for weakening — for feeling pity....

Dvoyrelè found every one at home. Father, who was still sitting at the table, had already dined. Shloimè was washing his hands and face at the sink in preparation to going out. He was "taking out" his girl that night. Mother was anxiously awaiting her arrival, but instead of expressing relief when she saw her enter, began to rebuke her:

"Where have you been? I was afraid you had met with some accident."

"Why do you tremble over me so?" remarked Dvoyrelè with nervous irritation. "Why must you guard me so closely? Why must I remain chained to you always?"

Dvoyrelè repeated the word "chained" a few times. She felt that it most perfectly expressed what she was feeling at the moment.

Surè became frightened. She did not understand what Dvoyrelè meant.

"Chained! Who has chained you? What are you talking about?" she stammered.

Dvoyrelè did not answer this. Instead she walked over to her bed in the corner of the cellar, her only sanctuary, and sat down upon it without taking off her hat and coat which were wet with the snow.

"What is wrong with you?" murmured mother, frightened. "Why don't you take off your things? Have your dinner — it's getting cold."

"I am not hungry," pouted Dvoyrelè complainingly like a little girl.

"What ails you? Are you ill? Did anything disagreeable happen to you?" asked mother uneasily.

"I am not sick and nothing has happened to me either."

"Then why do you sit so glum? Take off your things.

The First Disillusionment

They are wet. In Heaven's name, what is ailing the girl?"

Anshel, who had recently begun to cultivate the habit of reading a Yiddish newspaper every evening after he returned from work, sat now at the head of the table, his spectacles perched comically on the tip of his nose, and deeply absorbed in the news of the day. The large newspaper concealed his face and all that could be seen of him was the spiral wreath of smoke curling from his cigarette which his eldest son had supplied him rather ungraciously after dinner.

Hearing mother's exclamations of alarm, he put down his paper and peered intently through his glasses into the corner where Dvoyrelè sat on her bed.

"I don't know what has happened to the girl!" said Surè, turning to him.

"What's the matter?" called out Shloimè, now already known as Solomon, as he stood shaving in front of the little mirror that hung over the sink. He uttered these words indifferently, without even turning his face away from the mirror.

"What kind of shop have you sent me to work in anyways?" suddenly burst out Dvoyrelè angrily, not being able to contain herself any longer.

Solomon began to find this interesting. He turned his face from the mirror and for a moment looked speechless at his sister.

"What's wrong with the shop?" he snapped.

"I don't want to work there any more."

"Why not?"

"It's not a union shop."

At this all looked astonished. Anshel put his newspaper aside. Mother, who did not understand what it was all about, stood helpless and confused and looked pleadingly at Anshel to come to her assistance. But Anshel was himself completely at sea.

"What did you say: 'a union shop'?" asked Solomon surprised. "How on earth have you found out the meaning of a union?"

"I know," answered Dvoyrelè briefly.

"How do you know? Who told you about it?"

"I have known it all along even before I came to America."

"Really!" began Solomon sarcastically. "It would have been better had you remained in the old country. In this country, sister, you won't get very far with such ideas."

"I wish I had never come here," murmured Dvoyrelè sadly to herself.

"What's all this rumpus about?" eagerly asked Anshel of his son.

"Your daughter is a socialist. She is displeased with the shop that I have found for her to work in because there are no other socialists working there. So let her look for the kind of shop that will suit her."

"Oh!" drawled Anshel in his astonishment. "So that's what it is! She is one of those who would like to throw the kings off their thrones. Who would have suspected that I had a socialist for a daughter? This is a free country, after all," said Anshel, pointing proudly to his newspaper for authority, "and you can be a socialist if you like."

"You are mistaken, father, she was a socialist even before she came to this country," said Solomon.

"Ei! Ei! Ei!" exclaimed Anshel with rapture. "Then she belongs to the truly great! Well — if so, Dvoyrelè, tell me what you know about socialism."

The subject began to interest Anshel.

But mother could not well see them poking fun at her daughter. She was sorry for her. So she turned furiously on the menfolk in rebuke:

"What are you teasing the child for? Is it because she

wants to dethrone the kings of the world? Dear, dear —
how serious!"

And mother turned soothingly to Dvoyrelè and said:

"If the shop in which you work doesn't please you —
you don't have to go back there. You'll find another job.
Now be a dear and sit down to your dinner. It's getting
cold."

"She won't find a job so easily nowadays!" bitterly remarked Solomon.

"Under no circumstances will I ever return to my present
job!" said Dvoyrelè with a determination that she had
never shown before.

Solomon ceased shaving out of astonishment and gazed
mutely at her.

"Surely you don't intend to sit idly at home like that one
over there!" asked Solomon, pointing witheringly at Gedaliah who, whenever any reference was made to his not working, became filled with a sense of guilt and hid himself in a
corner to sulk in his humiliation. "Father wants to make of
him a Rabbi! Swell chance! His is one more useless mouth
to feed. Do you want to do as he does? If so, who will pay
the rent, gas and grocery bills? And what about the payments on your steamship tickets — who will pay that? Of
course, it will be I — I — always I!"

Since he had begun to work in the shirt factory, Anshel
felt all his old pride returning to him. So now, when he
heard his first-born abusing Dvoyrelè, he called out
sharply:

"Things are not so bad, my son, that you will have to
pay for all that. God be praised that there is still some one
else who can do the paying besides you!"

This slight to his pride was more than Solomon could
endure. With only one side of his face shaved and the other
still creamy with lather he placed himself in the center of
the room and wallowed in his self-pity.

The Mother

"Who was it that sent you money — more than three hundred dollars? And steamship tickets and an extra hundred dollars? Who engaged an apartment for you and bought furniture and everything? Because of you I have not married and am wasting my life. And no sooner have I decided to become concerned about my own interests than you burden me with that idler over there whom I have to support because you are determined to make a scholar out of him. And Dvoyrelè chooses to work only in a socialist shop. Since such jobs are not to be gotten I will be forced to support her too. You are all greenhorns no longer. So shift for yourselves. What do I care what you are going to do? In this country every one must worry for himself."

"His girl must have prompted him to say that," said Anshel grimly.

"All right!" said Solomon exasperatedly, wiping the lather from his face, forgetting that one side of it was still unshaved. "In that case I will move out of here to-morrow. Then you will see how easy it will be for you to get along without me."

As always, Solomon's threat to move frightened Surè. Swiftly there shot through her mind the thought of the bills that would soon have to be paid: The rent, the grocer, butcher and other indispensable household nightmares. Terror seized her. Anshel, as well, was a little shaken by his son's declaration of secession, but his pride made him mask his inner turmoil. The Anshel of the old country was still alive within him. Striking a contemptuous attitude, he said:

"So move! Who is keeping you? God did not abandon us in the old country. He will keep us in His mercy here too."

Surè's heart kindled with pride at Anshel's resolute stand. She made a final desperate attempt to appease Solomon's anger. With a gentle, conciliating smile she said to him:

The First Disillusionment

"Don't be offended, my son! Father's words were not so terrible that you should take offense."

"So long as I will continue living with you in the same house you will all never amount to anything and will always remain greenhorns."

Saying this Solomon hastily drew on his coat and rushed out of the cellar.

Chapter 6

HARD TIMES

▪▪▪▪▪▪▪

THAT night Solomon did not return home to sleep. But next morning when all were away at work and mother was standing bowed over the tub doing her washing, Solomon entered the cellar and without uttering a single word began packing up his personal belongings. Mother tremblingly wiped the suds from her hands, and approaching him with a pleading gesture, asked:

"Dear son, what are you planning to do?"

"I must get out of here."

"Then what do you think will happen to me and the children?"

"I will let your husband worry about that."

"Good God! Why must you take offense at father's rebukes? That's his privilege as a father."

Mother made an impulsive movement to embrace her son, but Solomon turned coldly away.

"It's not that at all!" said he. "I am not moving because of father's insults. For a long time already I have been planning to move from here. It will be better for you and for me as well."

"And who will pay for the upkeep of the home?" asked mother tearfully. "Father only earns seven dollars a week. And Dvoyrelè makes but little slaving away in her sweatshop. My heart just breaks looking at her. Since her arrival to this country she has become the mere shadow of herself.

Now how can I possibly manage without you? I am worrying myself to death already about the rent!"

"And because of that must I remain an old bachelor?" shrieked Solomon with anguish. "Because of you I have gone to the dogs!"

Mother did not answer. She leaned her shrunken, haggard face on her hand and for a while remained standing in the center of the room, ruminating on her son's despairing outcry. Then she said as though to herself:

"You are right, my son. It is about time that you began to do something for yourself."

"Haven't I worked for you all my life, first in the old country, and afterwards over here? Will it never end? Sooner or later I will have to shift for myself. Now I have met a fine girl. Her father owns a shoe store. Perhaps he will consent to take me into partnership with him. If not now, when will the time come for me to plan for a future?"

"You are right, my son, you are right!" muttered Surè, nodding her head vigorously.

"Believe me, it will be better for you if I will move out," earnestly reiterated Solomon. "You have become accustomed to my taking care of you and I too have fallen into the swing of it. It is bad for both of us that things remain as they are."

"May God help you, my child!" burst out mother fervently, and she embraced him with warmth and pressed her shrunken face to his. "What can I do when misfortune constantly dogs our steps and never chooses to leave us?"

Solomon gently slid out of her arms and silently resumed his packing. When he wanted to take away his soiled shirts, socks and underwear, mother snatched them from his hands and said to him:

"Let me at least wash your things for the last time."

.   .   .   .

The Mother

Hard times arrived for Surè. "The young man's" departure made a deep dent in the family's income. To crown all her misfortunes, Dvoyrelè did not return to her job. She now stayed at home. The first few days the effect of these financial defections was not in evidence. The first of the month was still distant and both the butcher and the grocer continued to extend credit. Finally, when the first of the month arrived and the landlord appeared with his but too-well-known salutation:

"Have you got the rent ready for me, Mrs. . . . ?" and the boys, whenever they were sent to make purchases at the grocer's, returned home with the latter's insistent invitation that mother come to see him . . . Surè grew sad at heart. She lay awake night after night, vainly plotting how to meet her most urgent obligations, until her head grew heavy and tired and her senses whirled round and round.

Mother's one pillar of strength during these trials proved to be Moishelè "The Ox" who now called himself Moses — the Anglo-Saxon equivalent of his Hebrew name. Since he had hired himself out as delivery boy to a grocer he invariably brought home a little package of groceries and delicatessen: tea, sugar, coffee, wurst, cheese, butter, eggs, cake or even a bottle of sweetened brandy. And he adjured Surè not to let any one else taste of them but herself. She was not in the best of health and stood in need of these delicacies, he had told her.

"I know, mother, that when a woman reaches your age she stands well in need of a bracing drink. I assure you the brandy will not do you any harm."

Moses did not stay much at home. Neither did he come for his meals. He would drop in unexpectedly every few days and he never came with empty hands. When he heard how affairs stood at home his parcels of foodstuffs grew more frequent, bulkier. . . . Mother would say in the silence of her heart that first came God and then Moses in preserving them from need and misfortune. She did not say this aloud, in order to spare Anshel any humiliation.

Accordingly, mother experienced little difficulty in the way of food. But the most troubling problem was the rent. In the old country there was no disturbing question of rent or the possibility of eviction should one not be in a position to pay. If one occupied a home one continued living in it no matter what happened. Superfluous questions such as the ownership of the house were never asked. Who had ever heard there of trouble over the payment of rent between landlord and tenant? If it chanced that a hard-hearted landlord insisted on the rent due him from an impoverished tenant, the whole community would rise as one man and damn him publicly. And if he dared threaten his tenant with the law he would be branded as an informer. If he still persisted and evicted his tenant he and his seed would be piously anathematized for ages upon ages. And when he died the Congregation of the Pious would refuse to bury him. Instead, hired pallbearers would carry him to the cemetery and his grave would be dug near the fence where all apostates from the Faith lay buried. . . .

In America things were different. The nights preceding rent day were passed without a wink of sleep by Surè. She worried herself ill with the problem. Where was she to get the money for the rent? And no sooner did the first of the month arrive, than there appeared the "rent collector," bright and early, with his impudent, clean-shaven jowls, and a fat cigar stuck provokingly in the corner of his mouth. Chewing hard on the tip of his cigar he would tap significantly on his collection book and growl the one eloquent word:

"Missus!"

And if the rent of fifteen dollars was but one quarter of a dollar short, he would reject it angrily, and pulling his heavy gold watch from his vest pocket, and chewing excitedly at the tip of his cigar, he would shout:

"Missus! The court closes at three o'clock. I give you time until then to pay the full amount of your rent."

The first of every month was like the Day of Atonement in Anshel's home. Despite Surè's careful calculations, despite her scrimping and saving throughout the month, when the first of the new month arrived she was always short of the required amount. Other bills also had to be paid. The gas bill had to be met, a child's shoes had to be soled, and often sickness would unexpectedly make a dent in their finances. At such times a full family council would be held and after much abuse and acrimony, Solomon would reluctantly make up the difference in the rent.

The thought of the approaching first of the month frightened mother to death. At night she lay in bed staring helplessly before her in the dark. How was she to manage with the rent? Solomon, who occasionally dropped in to see the folks, solemnly advised mother that the only way out of her difficulties would be to take in a boarder in his place. As a matter of fact, he had found a highly desirable boarder for her.

To this proposal Moses offered violent opposition.

"I will never allow mother to be a servant to a stranger!" he said.

Solomon countered that this was the custom in America and that every household kept at least one boarder.

"That may very well be," retorted Moses. "It may be quite the thing to keep boarders in America — but I will never permit my mother to wash a stranger's underwear. That — never!"

Said Solomon with cutting sarcasm:

"In that case, if you really are such a good son, why not pay the rent for mother?"

"Very well," said Moses, "I will pay out of my own

pocket for mother's rent, but never will I permit her to work for a stranger. It is bad enough that she is forced to do so for her own children, but for strangers — never!"

But mother would have none of it. As it is, she said, Moses was doing more than his share. Thereupon she embraced him most tenderly. And Moses shamefacedly dug into his pockets and produced fifteen dollars which was the full amount of his weekly wages and gave it to his mother to pay the rent with. When Solomon saw this he grew confused with embarrassment and remarked that as it is he had already sufficiently fulfilled his obligations to the family. Henceforth he would let some one else concern himself about them. To which mother made answer that he was not at all obligated to help her — that she had never asked him to do so. She realized fully that it was now time for him to worry for his own future. After all, was he not getting on in years? And it was high time that he married.

The others held their peace.

Having successfully surmounted the difficulty of the rent, a new misfortune loomed up suddenly. The Passover was rapidly approaching.

The advent of this holiday had always been a source of great anxiety for Surè. It was still possible for her to cope somehow with the exigencies of everyday life. But those festive days of obligatory rejoicing brought her only terror and worry. She abstained from sharing her troubles with Anshel. Poor man! He worked so hard! Let him sleep peacefully at night! So she stifled her sighs that she might not disturb his sleep. Despite her precautions he heard her one night and awoke. Much alarmed he asked:

"Why do you sigh, Surè? I thought the rent was paid already."

"The holidays are fast approaching and I don't know how we will ever receive them."

"You have always had something to sigh about — some-

thing to worry about. If it isn't the rent it is the needs of
an approaching holiday."

"You are right, Anshel," said Surè guiltily as if she were
all to blame.

Anshel was quite right. There was no need for her to
worry. Moses supplied them plentifully with "Matzos" with
which his employer dealt. When the time for the holidays
came nearer even Solomon's heart began to soften.

"Mother," said he, "the holidays will soon be here. I will
not be with you then but I would like to give you some
money anyway."

He handed mother a ten-dollar bill.

"If you won't be home for the holidays," said Surè,
offended, "I don't want your money either. It is our first
Passover holiday in the new world and I would like that
all of us be together then."

"Right you are, mother!" answered Solomon, "but I have
already promised my girl to spend the holidays at her parents' home."

"Do I mean less to you than your girl?" asked mother a
trifle hurt. "Have I not given birth to you and brought you
up? Therefore I must be your first choice in this matter.
Why not bring your girl to us for the first feast night? You
can spend the second night with her people. Perhaps it is
because we are green that you are ashamed to bring her
here?"

Surè did not know the exact meaning of the word "green"
and was under the impression that it meant "poor."

Solomon blushed with shame. He knew mother was right
in her reproach, so he did not answer.

Mother wiped away the tears from her eyes with a corner
of her apron.

"I don't even know," she said bitterly, "what your girl
looks like. It is clear that you are ashamed of us, my child."

Solomon fell into deep thought. Perhaps mother was

right. It might not at all be out of place for him to invite his girl to his parents' home. But when he looked about him and saw the dismal poverty, the gloomy cellar, the broken chairs and the unstylish beds he hardened his heart. He now added another five dollars to the proffered ten and in a conciliatory voice said:

"Buy the children some clothes with this. During the holidays I will take you and father on a visit to my girl's parents."

Then he quickly left the cellar.

When Anshel came home from work and Surè told him that his first-born had been to see them and had given her fifteen dollars for holiday purchases and also added that he had proposed to take them on a visit to his girl's parents, Anshel grew purple with rage. In his resentment he compared her in a very uncomplimentary way with all manner of beasts and fowl.

"Cow! Calf! Donkey! Sheep and foolish hen! Why did you accept that cobbler's fifteen dollars? And for that he wants us to accompany him to meet his future wife's father — that cobbler and son of a cobbler! He wants to drag me — Anshel, Reader of Scripture — like a common beggar, to do a cobbler honor! And you, foolish old hen, agreed to that and accepted his fifteen dollars! He can go to hell first! If Solomon wants me to become acquainted with those cobblers, his future parents-in-law, let him do himself and them the honor and bring them down to me, in *my cellar!*"

Surè realized that Anshel was justified in his resentment. So she kept silent and only nodded her assent.

"Right you are, Anshel! Right you are!"

"So swear to me by all the holy laws of Moses that you will not touch any of his fifteen dollars! Let them be as unclean and forbidden to you as pork! Do you hear what I am telling you?" shouted Anshel, beside himself with fury.

"I hear! I hear!" gasped Surè with fright.

The Mother

"Better hand me the money!" ordered Anshel peremptorily. "I am afraid you might be tempted to use it."

"I promise you, Anshel, I will not touch it! I would sooner eat pork. Don't you believe me?" pleaded Surè plaintively.

"I would like you to fling it back into his dirty face!" roared Anshel, pounding with his fist on the table and lashing himself into a frenzy.

Surè stood intimidated and subservient before Anshel. Her heart swelled with pride and admiration for his noble character.

"I am afraid I didn't know what I was doing when I accepted the money," she confessed guiltily. "My troubles have confused my reason."

Chapter 7

THE FIRST PASSOVER IN THE LAND OF THE FREE

■■■■■■

WHEN Solomon once more came to see his mother, tempted, no doubt, by her excellent cooking to which he was accustomed, he found his father deep in his newspaper. Solomon had about him an air of condescension, sweep and benignancy. His gift of fifteen dollars to his mother must have had something to do with it. Surè placed before him a plate of steaming soup. He drank it with great relish.

"Well, mother," asked he vaingloriously, thinking, no doubt, of his contribution of fifteen dollars. "Are you all set for the holidays?"

Surè did not answer. Only Anshel began to show audible signs of excitement behind his newspaper. He turned the pages feverishly.

"I have already informed my girl's father that I will bring both of you to see him on the holidays," said Solomon as he gulped down his soup.

Again mother made no reply. And Anshel once more turned the pages of his newspaper furiously.

"And you, Dvoyrelè, still have no job!" sarcastically mused Solomon as he regarded his sister sitting huddled over her sewing near a gas jet. "You want a union shop — don't you? Why doesn't the union give you a job?"

At this point, without a warning signal, Anshel unexpectedly put down his newspaper, smoothed his beard and his mustache with great self-pride, and with an ironic note in his voice, said:

"In my opinion, Dvoyrelè is doing well by refusing to work in any but a union shop."

Solomon was just raising a spoonful of soup to his mouth; on hearing his father's words he held it suspended in mid-air.

"Yes!" added Anshel solemnly. "That is the way *we workers* feel about it."

Solomon's eyes grew big with amazement.

"You don't mean to tell me, father, that you too are planning to become a member of a labor union?"

"What then do you suppose? Do you want me to rely only on your kindness of heart? You have gone and sold me like a Canaanite bondsman to a skinflinting boss!"

Solomon was visibly stricken dumb. He just stared at his father in a dazed manner.

"Why don't you say what you are supposed to say, Surè?" called Anshel rebukingly to his wife.

So Surè took the fifteen dollars from the bottom of the pot and laid them near Solomon's plate, without uttering a word.

"What's that?" gasped Solomon, not understanding.

"We don't want any money from you exploiting bosses! We don't need it," proudly declaimed Anshel and buried his face again in his newspaper.

Solomon looked in a bewildered manner from father to mother.

"My dear child, I will tell you the whole truth," called out Surè. "It is true that we are very poor folk but we have nothing to be ashamed of. Because you feel ashamed of us it is impossible for us to accept your money. God will help us without your aid!"

And Surè folded her hands piously.

"Do you understand now?" asked Anshel with a sneer as

he lifted his eyes for a moment from his reading. "I very well know who I am exactly. I am but a worker, a poor man, a greenhorn. But whether those low-born cobblers, your girl's parents, are my superiors, I still have to discover."

And Anshel once more became oblivious of his son and composed himself to read his newspaper.

"The young man" stopped eating, pushed his plate away from him and in a despairing voice said:

"What shall I do now? I have informed my girl and her parents that I will bring you to see them during the holidays. They are expecting you. What will they think of me if you won't come? How will I ever be able to face them again?"

Anshel now laid down his newspaper.

"Do you want to bring us to them, those low-born cobblers, ha? Do you think it is easy to make fools of us because we are fallen from our high estate, because we are poor and greenhorns? I would like you to know that I am an honest worker!" roared Anshel suddenly with a pride and boastfulness that not only shocked Solomon but also startled Surè to speechless wonder. "I earn my bread honestly, even as it is prescribed in Holy Scripture. And who are your cobblers anyway? Can they read at least? Do they know their prayers? Perhaps they can even cantillate the Scripture portion of the week? Who can tell? Your America is just full of miracles. And to such people you want to bring your own father and mother! If your cobblers are so anxious to meet us let them come down to me, Anshel, Reader of Scripture, even if I live in a cellar. They are no cripples!"

And Anshel flung out his chest, like a general displaying his medals.

Solomon became frightened at father's words. For the first time since he had come to America, Anshel grew back to his old stature. Solomon wisely held his tongue. He looked about him and once more noticed the dire poverty. With all the good will in the world, how could he possibly bring his girl and her parents down to such a hole? This impasse made him turn with self-pity on himself. He lamented:

"By my blood and sweat I had put by a few hundred dollars in order that I might get married. Can you expect me then to furnish this miserable cellar with that money? And if I do so, where will I again get the money to get married with?"

"Who ever asked you to do so?" growled Anshel, somewhat milder.

Mother stepped forward now as the conciliator. Her heart reached out to her first-born.

"We don't stand in such great need of new furniture," she told him. "You can tell your girl's parents that we are but new arrivals to this country, greenhorns, and so we have not yet had time to furnish our home properly."

"Surely it's not a question of furniture," interjected father in quite a friendly voice. "It's the kind of people that we are and not the kind of furniture we possess that should really matter with them."

Solomon sat in despair, racking his brain for some satisfactory way out of the dilemma. Then Moses came in. As usual he brought with him a package of groceries. He called mother into a corner and gave her a pound of macaroni which he had abstracted from his employer's grocery store.

"Cook this macaroni for yourself, mother. It will be quite a treat for you," he urged her.

"Foolish child!" called out mother. "What for do I need this? I will keep it instead to treat the bride with when she will come to visit us."

"Bride!" exclaimed Moses. "What bride are you talking about?"

"Solomon is bringing his girl to be with us during the first Feast of the Passover," said mother in a loud voice so that Solomon might hear her. She badly wanted to soothe his ruffled pride.

"How can I possibly bring her into this cellar?" asked Solomon. "Just see how it looks!"

"Now don't worry," coaxed mother. "I will sweep the cellar clean, sprinkle fresh sand on the floor, spread a nice cloth on the table on which I will place our pretty brass candlesticks. Dvoyrelè stays at home now and she will help me. Believe me, your girl will have no cause to be ashamed of us, Solomon."

"So let her be ashamed! The cellar is our home. This is the way your parents live, Solomon. She must come into our home if she wants to be my daughter-in-law," growled Anshel with irritation.

As always, Moses proved to be the only practical-minded person in the house. Looking about him he remarked in his rather cold-blooded way:

"It's out of the question. You can't bring a bride into this cellar."

"What then can we do?" asked mother in a hopeless sort of way, while father stuck his head curiously out of his wilderness of newspaper.

"We've got to furnish this cellar first," said Moses decisively. "We need a new table, chairs, dishes, knives and forks. In what will you serve food to the bride? You have only a few broken dishes!"

Surè was filled with housewifely shame.

"He's right," said she to Anshel.

"Just listen to my second jewel of a son!" snapped Anshel annoyed.

"But he's right!" loyally persisted Surè.

By this time Solomon's sinking courage had revived. He turned on his father wrathfully:

"Why do you heap so much abuse on my girl's parents?

The Mother

What if her father is a cobbler? Aren't you a worker too? Why this uppishness on your part?"

"A worker, yes! But I am no rotten boss."

"Calm yourself! By abusing one another we will never come to a decision," said mother, stepping forward as the peacemaker. She now turned to Moses as if from him alone could come a solution to the knotty problem confronting them. "Tell us, Moses dear, what you think we ought to do."

Moses knitted his brows and, scratching his red head, thoughtfully answered:

"If you, Solomon, want your girl to be present at the first Passover Feast you must give mother one extra dollar each week. I will do likewise. For two dollars a week we can furnish this cellar so that it shall look like a king's palace." (This elegant metaphor he had learned from the street peddlers he had been associating with.) "We will buy furniture and other furnishings on the installment plan. I know just the store where we can buy it that way."

Tears sprang up in mother's eyes.

Solomon groaned and replied: "If you will be able to buy furniture that way, I am ready to pay my share. But how long will I have to do so?"

"Don't worry! In six months' time we will have it all paid for. Then mother will have a decent home to live in."

Solomon heaved a deep sigh and consented to the plan.

After solving the problem of furnishing the cellar to make it appear more presentable, a new trouble appeared on the horizon. The entire family was disreputably clad and shod and stood badly in need of new clothes. Father's suit was threadbare and shiny with wear. Mother stood greatly in need of a new dress and the boys of shirts, trousers and new caps. Could they sit down to the Feast of Passover in their tatters? Hardly. Then again, money was lacking for the holiday preparations, for meat, fish and other necessities.

The First Passover in the Land of the Free

The thought of these things made Surè's heart grow heavy within her. So she said to Moses, her one rock of salvation:

"Better let things be as they are, my child! Our poverty is so great that there can be no remedy for it."

Only Moses, formerly Moishelè "The Ox," saw a way out of every difficulty. So he said to his brother:

"After all, you are anxious to bring your girl down to see us. I too look forward to it. If you will give mother money to buy shirts and pants for the boys I will supply her with both meat and fish for the holidays. Besides, if you will buy father a high silk hat I will furnish mother with goods for a holiday frock. Dvoyrelè will sew it for her."

And mother, seeing how downhearted all this made Solomon feel, gushed consolingly:

"Don't you worry, my son! God is good. You will have for everything. Only clothe us decently for your wedding so that we may not be put to shame before others. After that, God willing, there may be no necessity for you to spend so much money on us."

Hearing the cheering word "wedding" Solomon brightened up. It sounded like sweet music in his ears. With a good-natured sigh he assented to everything.

.   .   .   .

Since olden days the Passover proved always a joyous holiday for Anshel's household. In the new world too it brought nothing but promise of happier days. Not only was Surè fated to celebrate the Passover in a manner not to make her feel ashamed before God and man as she had so often feared while she lay awake in bed, but she did so amidst the magnificent setting of new furniture, clothes, a future daughter-in-law, and a piece of sparkling "cut glass" which the ingenious Moses had unexpectedly brought home on Passover eve to make a grand impression on the

159

bride. . . . The cellar was completely transformed. It radiated well-being and peace. At the head of the table, awe-inspiring in his immense second-hand silk hat, sat Anshel. Solomon had bought it for him. After Anshel had cantillated the Haggadah, that ancient commemorating narrative of the Jewish liberation from Egyptian bondage, and Surè, resplendent in her new frock, began serving the meal, Anshel, expansive and radiant, addressed himself to his household:

"Very often, as I sit sewing in the shop, certain strange thoughts pass through my mind and I begin to wonder about many things. When one sews one cannot help but think. What else is there to do? The fingers become accustomed to the monotony of needle plying. So they sew. But the head continues its own labors. Try and stop it! At such times many and curious thoughts flit through my brain — the years that are no more, the little town where we all were born and raised. But most of all I am filled with wonderment over the thought that I, a former synagogue Scripture Reader, who am somewhat of a Talmudic scholar, should, by a trick of destiny, be forced to work with common Gentile wenches and do such manly work as sewing buttons on shirts! But when I think further about the matter I suddenly begin to realize that the old Anshel is no more. In his stead a new Anshel has arisen. He is finer, better, more honest, more proud, more erect. He serves God with greater devotion than ever before. What was I in the old country? Just a ne'er-do-well and an idler. How different in this country! When I hold a shirt in my hands and sew buttons on it, I well know that it will be a human being who will wear it. In other words, my labor is of some use to somebody. I serve others with my labor. I no longer eat bread that I have not earned, and therefore I thank and praise the Almighty, who in His goodness and mercy has seen fit to make of me a worker. Thus I fulfill the sacred injunction:

'By the sweat of thy brow shalt thou earn thy bread.' Yes, children, to sew shirts is not such a commonplace thing after all. It is a very grave matter. It offers much food for thought."

Every one kept silent. Only Solomon, who was sitting near his girl and who in a moment of embarrassment and fleshly weakness during the beginning of his courtship had boasted vaingloriously before her that his father was a Rabbi, hearing the latter disgracing him so thoroughly, turned his eyes away and flushed red as a beet. He couldn't look his girl straight in the eyes. . . .

Chapter 8

A NEW CIRCLE

■■■■■■■

DVOYRELÈ still had not found employment in a union
shop. Also Gedaliah had not yet entered a Rabbinic
College where he was to prepare himself to become a Rabbi
in the "American style." Both he and his sister remained
idling at home, although in a way they contributed to their
support. Gedaliah distributed the morning newspapers among
the tenement dwellers for which he received a few dollars
weekly. This money he did not keep for himself but gave
to mother. As for Dvoyrelè, her talents were diverse. Each
day she brought home something to work upon in order
to earn a dollar or two. Sometimes it was hair for wig-
making. At another time an old dress of a neighbor's which
she remodeled. She also mended all the old garments at
home that stood in need of it. She sewed shirts and pants
for the boys as well as an occasional dress for mother. But
of regular employment she had none.

Because of their plight, Gedaliah and Dvoyrelè found
sufficient time to perfect themselves in their English. Gedaliah had discovered an evening public school where
English was taught to adult foreigners. He and Dvoyrelè
attended it every evening.

Their fellow students were of a varied assortment. There
were Jews, Italians and Poles among them. The prepon-
derant number, however, were Jewish young men and
women. The atmosphere in the classroom was intimate and

A New Circle

Dvoyrelè felt thoroughly at home. Miss Furster, their teacher, by her tact and sympathy created this intimacy among them so that they all felt as if they belonged to but one family.

Miss Furster was descended from immigrant parents. Although she had spent most of her life in America, her upbringing was replete with memories and customs of the old world. As in a dream she recollected the broad, green steppes of Russia with their sparse, erect birch trees that somehow had blundered into the fields of her childhood home. As in a dream she remembered the journey to America — the crossing of the border, the fatiguing railway ride, the harbor and the ship which carried them across the ocean. Her parents, although they had belonged to the "intelligentzia" in Russia, experienced the same poverty, privations and problems of maladjustment to the new American environment as all other immigrants. They too sewed pants in sweatshops, took work home from the factory, and together with their children, by the ghastly flare of gaslight, sat up far into the night working. They too kept boarders in order to give their children a decent upbringing and a good education. It was by such sacrifices that they enabled their daughter Isabel, one of a substantial number of daughters, to finish the Teachers' Training School. The nature of her early surroundings influenced her entire life. It inbred in her a light-heartedness and a gayety typically American and gave her an air of self-assurance and determination.

Because of her early home environment Miss Furster felt deeply drawn to the immigrants. She was happy to instruct her class of foreigners. A radical by inclination, she felt much more at ease among her immigrant students who came from revolutionary Russia than among her outwardly formal, vacuous, Americanized Jewish acquaintances. She had many friends among the intelligent immigrants and she

163

readily came socially in contact with her pupils in the evening school.

She became interested in Dvoyrelè through Gedaliah, to whom she gave special attention because of his unusual brightness. Dvoyrelè's appearance, her small, helpless and yet arresting personality, her dark curly head and large questioning eyes which looked at her in such a sorrowful way, struck a responsive chord in her own restive and groping spirit. After they had met a few times they became fast friends. Acquainting herself with Dvoyrelè's economic situation, Isabel's interest in her redoubled. So one day she introduced her in the classroom to two sisters whose name was Salkind.

The sisters Salkind were also greenhorns. They studied English in the same class with Dvoyrelè. The latter had already noticed them for a long time because they were dressed in an extraordinary manner. One could not help noticing the blazing colors of their attire. They wore multi-colored Russian peasant kerchiefs and Turkish shawls and this lent to them an exotic attractiveness.

The elder of the sisters, Rose, was a spinster and already well advanced in years. She had large brown eyes and a great shock of black hair that lay coiled about her head in two heavy plaits. Although her face was no longer fresh and young it appeared sweet and sympathetic to Dvoyrelè. She was certain that they had met before. The very first time they met, Rose succeeded in drawing her out.

"Where do you come from?" she asked immediately after they had been introduced.

"From Poland."

"Great! We are countrywomen. So you also insist on attending kindergarten in your old age!" she said with a laugh.

"I have no job and more time on my hands than is good

for me. Why shouldn't I turn it to profit and learn something useful?"

"What is your trade?"

"A dressmaker."

"Really! In that case we belong to the same branch of the clothing industry."

A certain confidence-inspiring quality in the girl's face caused the usually laconic Dvoyrelè to become talkative.

"Do you think you could find work for her?" asked Miss Furster coaxingly. "I know you could if only you would want to."

"That's quite possible," said Rose hopefully. "I will talk to mother about it."

"Do so, I beg of you!" said Miss Furster with a melting look. Then she left Dvoyrelè and the girls alone in order that they might become better acquainted.

The three girls left the school building together. Rose introduced Dvoyrelè to her younger sister.

"This is my sister Bronia," she said.

The girl she introduced was short, with black curly hair and small white teeth.

Bronia beamed a sweet, half-shy smile at Dvoyrelè and said nothing.

"I am called Dvoyrelè," said the latter.

She did not attempt to hide the fact that both of the sisters pleased her.

"Excellent!" said Rose.

"Why excellent?" asked Dvoyrelè with surprise.

"Because Dvoyrelè is a very lovely name. We had a dear friend in the old country. Her name too was Dvoyrelè."

They continued walking through the streets.

"Are you attending school for a long time already?" asked Rose. "No doubt you know a great deal of English already."

"Not at all! I have just begun. Only my brother Gedaliah" — and she pointed with pride to him — "is attending school for more than three months. He already knows English well."

Gedaliah, not accustomed to female society, had walked along with them and remained tongue-tied all the while. He trailed along behind in a helpless sort of way. But when his sister presented him to the two girls he became so frightened that he almost stumbled off the pavement into the gutter.

"In the old country," said Rose, "we read only Polish books. But without a proper knowledge of English one gets lost here somehow. My sister and I would very much like to be able to read an English book well."

They parted and agreed to meet the following night after school.

When they met again the next day Dvoyrelè greeted Rose as if she were an old friend.

"Have you a job already?" was the first question Rose fired at her new friend.

"No!" answered Dvoyrelè. "It's very hard to get a job."

"Would you perhaps like to come and work with us?" hazarded Rose. "I discussed the matter with mother. We have our own little workshop at home where we sew dresses for private customers. If you like you may work for us."

Dvoyrelè looked at her with gratitude. She did not consent to her proposal immediately, only transfixed her with her large, luminous eyes:

"Do you really mean it?" she finally asked with incredulity.

"What then? Do you think I am joking? We are in need of another 'hand,' so come over and see if you will like to work with us."

"What a question! Of course, I will like to work with you! Thank you so much!"

"We don't live far from here, near Avenue A. Won't you take my address?"

A New Circle

Dvoyrelè returned home hot with excitement. Her disheveled hair fell riotously over her face. Her cheeks were flushed and her eyes sparkled for sheer joy.

"Mother!" she cried, "I have a job! I begin work tomorrow."

And mother, who stood at the sink washing dishes, murmured piously:

"God is good. May you keep the job for years! ..."

Next morning betimes Dvoyrelè went to her new task. She found everything just as the girls had described. Together with their mother they occupied a tiny apartment on the third floor of a dingy tenement house. In the "parlor" stood a few sewing machines at which the girls were working. Rose introduced Dvoyrelè to her mother, a good-natured fat woman.

"This, mother, is our new hand," said she. "Her name is Dvoyrelè, and she comes from Poland."

"How nice!" said her mother, scrutinizing Dvoyrelè with kindly eyes. "From what town do you come?"

"From Gostynin."

"Really! I had an aunt who lived there once. She was a saint. She is probably dead by now. If so, may she dwell with the angels in Paradise!"

The character of the new "shop" was entirely in contrast to the old one in which Dvoyrelè had worked. The sisters sewed dresses for their friends, acquaintances and country-women, most of whom hailed from Warsaw. They worked industriously but without rushing, according to their pleasure. Occasionally they paused in their work and burst into song or good-humored play. Their mother would serve them refreshments — tea, cakes and fruit — several times during the day, to lighten the tedium of their work. She would say:

"Children! I have brought you some beautiful apples. It

is a pleasure to look at them. Just taste them and see how good they are."

Occasionally she prepared for them a delicious hot soup which she would coax them to drink:

"Just see the wonderful soup I have cooked for you to-day! If you will drink it you will get new strength to work."

During the afternoon of the first day there came to visit them a short-legged, thickset young man. He wore a tight-fitting suit of clothes that was several sizes too small for him. He gave the impression that at any moment and without warning he might burst through. The girls introduced him to Dvoyrelè as their countryman. The young man seated himself near the girls. He took from his pocket a bar of chocolate and after he had divided it into three equal parts insisted that he himself deposit them into their mouths. After he had solemnly gone through this ritual he pulled from Bronia's lap the unfinished silk dress she was working on and began to play with her soft white fingers. Apparently she found this attention quite diverting for she roguishly complained of a headache. She said that she did not feel like working any more that day. Then she put her work aside.

"Mother, mother!" called her older sister in boisterous jest. "That terrible Bonchik is keeping us again from working!"

"Bonchik darling, let them work!" pleaded mother, stroking his little fat jowls. "The customer who is having this dress made will soon be here for a fitting and there will be hell to pay if the dress won't be ready in time."

"Dear Granny," he jested lightly, "I have bought you some whisky at the Rumanian restaurant, and you won't find its like in all Poland."

And Bonchik pulled a whisky bottle from his pocket.

A New Circle

"Now, now, Bonchik! How can I possibly drink it? No sooner do I taste a drop than it affects my heart."

She accepted the bottle after all and returning to the kitchen left Bonchik to tease the girls with his good-humored chaffing.

After a little while another young man turned up. He had long wiry hair and because it was moist it stood up like bristles on his head. Affecting the artistic, he wore a Windsor tie and carried a book under his arm.

"Hello, Berl!" Rose greeted him as he entered, and pointing to Dvoyrelè quickly added: "This is the young lady I spoke to you about. She too reads only Yiddish books."

"My name is Berl Glassman," mumbled the young man with an awkward bow.

Dvoyrelè flushed deeply and also told him her name.

"Berl, do be a good fellow and recite for us your poem: 'Mid-Ocean,' " wheedled Bonchik.

"What for?" demurred Berl, smoothing the moist stubble on his head with his fingers.

"Do so in honor of our new friend — I beg pardon, Miss, but what is your name?" asked Bonchik of Dvoyrelè.

"Dvoyrelè Zlotnik," answered Rose for her.

"Recite for Miss Zlotnik then!" pleaded Bonchik very gallantly. "Now be a good fellow and out with your poem!"

"What for?" persisted Berl like a prima donna who enjoys being coaxed.

"Mr. Glassman is an actor," explained Rose to Dvoyrelè. "He plays all the romantic leads in the Jewish Literary and Dramatic Club. Now, Berl, be good and begin."

"But what for?" repeated Berl with artistic coquetry.

"Berl!" burst out Bonchik under a tidal wave of generosity. "I promise you that next Friday night we will all come to see you play at the Club Theater, provided you recite for us now. On my word, I will buy tickets for all of us here!"

The Mother

"Is it a promise?" eagerly asked Berl.

"Sure enough!" said Bonchik.

"Fine!"

Berl now cleared his throat and had just opened his mouth to recite when Mrs. Salkind appeared in the kitchen door, bearing a plate of hot, steaming soup.

"Bonchik sweetheart," said she, bubbling over with good spirits, "here is a plate of soup — the most delicious you have ever tasted in your life!"

"Oh, for God's sake!" cried Berl in exasperation, feeling that his artistic honor had been slighted by this rude interruption. And Mrs. Salkind stood in the doorway, still holding the plate of hot soup, and with mouth agape looked bewildered at Berl.

Chapter 9

A JOLLY COMPANY

■■■■■■■

A NEW life began for Dvoyrelè. Unconsciously she had been desiring it all her life. The need for it had lain dormant in her for years. The sisters Salkind dressed tastefully in quite an original manner. It was sufficient for the younger sister Bronia to drape her slender little body in a strip of flowered material to create a new style. She and her sisters frequently went bargain hunting among the Italian pushcart peddlers. They bought colorful Italian stuffs and large Turkish shawls from which they made exotic looking dresses, jackets, and cloaks. They wore multicolored strings of beads which made them look like gypsies. Dvoyrelè lost no time in copying their mode of attire. She did it most naturally as if she had been accustomed to it all her life. The colorful stuffs she wore were well adapted to her sinuous, graceful form. They enhanced her charms a hundredfold. She spent more time now than ever before the mirror, and, wonder of wonders! seeing how the Salkinds took such meticulous care of their nails, she too manicured her own at every opportunity although at first she felt shy about it and did it by stealth.

In this new environment she soon learned to forget the old country, the summer twilights and the Holy Cause. They receded from her consciousness into the misty past. A great burden was lifted from her fragile young shoulders.

The Mother

Her spirit grew lighter and more cheerful as if it had undergone a great liberation.

As time went on Dvoyrelè became more intimate with the Salkinds. She felt happier there than at home.

What pleased her most was the carefree spirit that pervaded their home, their singing and joking while at work, their mother's light-hearted way of joining them in their fun like an overgrown child, and most of all the young men who frequented their house.

Besides Bonchik, who, thought Dvoyrelè, must surely be a wealthy man, because whenever they went out for a good time he always paid for everybody, and Berl the actor, who recently began to pay her marked attention, there were other callers at the Salkinds'. They had many friends. It was hard to tell whether that was because of the girls or because of their mother's excellent cooking. Mrs. Salkind had a passion for cooking and baking as long as there was somebody ready to appreciate her culinary talents. The young men, whenever they called, brought with them all kinds of delicacies. That was in polite payment for the *gefülte* fish and other old-world Sabbath dishes which the old woman served them. When the holidays arrived the young men gave her money to cook for them those festival dishes in which she excelled. This delighted her immensely and she stayed up nights making dough, baking all sorts of delicious cakes and stuffing chicken necks and the intestines of tender young calves.

One of Mrs. Salkind's favorites was a certain Mr. Silverman, a labor union official. He was fat and jovial and loved to sing for the girls operatic arias, and the latest hits from the Yiddish theaters. He possessed a strong manly voice. That served him in good stead as a labor leader. At meetings he outshouted all the rest. Yet stronger than his voice were his hands. Whenever his powerful voice failed to convince an opponent his hands were of great use to him.

A Jolly Company

Another of Mrs. Salkind's favorites was a young man whom everybody called "Mischa Elman." His real name was Sascha Cohen. He played first violin in an obscure orchestra and often took part in East Side concerts devoted to charitable purposes. His ardent dream was some day to enter some well-known music conservatory. He so wanted to be an artist, a real Mischa Elman! But he never scraped together sufficient money for it. So he continued dreaming and played often at the Salkinds'. Music and declamation were the cultural fare at their home. But most of all their company loved to discuss to tatters all the arts and artists and the common gossip emanating from them. There wasn't a Jewish editor that did not get his share of abusive criticism. They were all painted black enough to suit the Devil.

One evening, in the midst of a vitriolic discussion, there entered an extraordinary-looking individual. He was tall and gaunt as a birch-rod, and had a long, lean neck. Without as much as a "good evening" he entered the room and quietly seated himself next to Bronia. He took her hand and completely ignoring every one else in the room he said:

"What! Cold hands again, Bronia?"

"I feel so cold!" murmured Bronia, ostentatiously wrapping her red gypsy shawl closer about herself.

"A new gypsy shawl!" exclaimed he with admiration.

At this moment he saw two large, naïve and almost frightened eyes turned on him. He looked questioningly at Bronia.

"Haven't you been introduced to one another yet?" quickly interposed Rose, banteringly, as usual noticing everything. "Freier, meet the beautiful *Litvak* (Lithuanian) Dvoyrelè Zlotnik. Dvoyrelè meet Freier, the great Yiddish poet of the future. He is a countryman of ours. We know him since the old days."

Dvoyrelè, who had heard much about Freier and already knew that he was an author and wrote verses, reddened and

173

became frightened. She had never met an author in the flesh. The very idea of meeting one struck her as bizarre. She had never imagined that a poet could look so commonplace. So she opened her eyes wide and regarded him closely.

"Are you really a Litvak?" asked Freier in mock astonishment of Dvoyrelè. "That can't be!"

Without himself being aware of it he rose from his seat near Bronia and came over to Dvoyrelè's side.

"Why can't that be?" asked Dvoyrelè, flushing.

"Litvaks don't look like you," said Freier with conviction.

"How then do I look?" she insisted.

"Like a calf," answered Freier without twitching an eyelash.

The girls burst out laughing and Dvoyrelè, to hide her discomfiture, laughed with them.

"You feel by no means offended, do you?" asked Freier innocently.

"What kind of a compliment is that anyway?" asked Rose.

"One of the greatest. Very few people are worthy of such a compliment."

"Better don't make such compliments in the future," Rose advised him with a wry expression.

"Are you really a Litvak?" asked Freier again, seriously this time.

"No, I come from a small Polish town."

"Then why don't you say so? I suspected it all along. Why did you make a Litvak of her?" asked Freier of Rose.

"Because she carries on like a Litvak," answered Rose. "She is always brooding, always worrying. The Lord only knows why!"

"Now that's an entirely different matter," agreed Freier.

"Leave the girls alone, Freier!" demanded Silverman, the union official.

"Just one minute, one minute!" pleaded Freier.

A Jolly Company

"Now, Freier, be a good fellow and recite for us your 'Eyes'!" wheedled Berl the actor, himself anxious to display his declamatory talents before the company. By calling on Freier first he thought that everybody's attention would next be focused on him.

Instead of offering excuses, as all had expected, Freier was eager to comply with Berl's request.

"Of course I will!" said he. "It will be in honor of my new acquaintance, the young lady here. But instead of 'The Eyes,' which I think is quite terrible, I will recite for you a new poem. I am not sure that you will understand much of it. It really makes no difference. I will read it to you anyway."

Freier began to recite his poem. At first it sounded incoherent. One phrase had not the slightest connection with the next one. The poet spoke of joys that go fluttering over the earth like transparent white veils, of hidden springs that gush forth in forest seclusion, of clouds that float in invisible skies, of women who dance on street pavements, of yellow lights that appear and disappear. No one knew what it was all about. Every one kept silent for fear of betraying that dread secret, and sat lost in thought. Only the labor union official, who was braver than the others, burst out:

"Kill me if you like, I don't understand a blessed word of what you have been reading, Freier!"

Instead of registering wounded vanity as he invariably did whenever any one dared criticize his verses, Freier laughed good-naturedly.

"Of course you haven't understood!" he chided. "What conceivable relation can there be between trade unionism and poetry? They are as harmonious as fire and water."

"Then why do I understand your 'Eyes' so well?" challenged Silverman in a withering tone.

"The very fact that you understand it so well is the best

proof that it must be quite rotten. I can promise you that it won't be included in my forthcoming volume," snorted Freier with contempt.

"What's the use of all this talk, Freier? I once recited your 'Clouds' on a literary-dramatic evening before our club members and it created a furore," broke in Berl, anxious to conciliate him after the union official's bitter words. He succeeded in bringing the poet into a better mood.

"It's not a bad poem at all," modestly agreed Freier.

"Would you like to hear it? Good! I will recite it for you," cried Berl eagerly. For a long time he had been chafing to recite something for the company. Now the happy opportunity appeared.

After Berl's declamation, the union official issued a vigorous protest:

"Do you intend to feed us to-night only on poetry? It may be good enough nourishment for poets. As for us — do send some one down, Bonchik, for some more brandy."

"He's right," said mother. Throughout the recitation she had stood listening with a bored air in the kitchen doorway. She had wanted to make the same suggestion to Bonchik all along only she was afraid to appear impolite. Even Freier had no serious objection to a good drink.

"The Devil take it!" he cried. "Let's have a good bracer! Will you drink too, Miss Zlotnik?"

"Will you run down, Berl, and get the brandy?" asked Bonchik.

Berl needed no coaxing.

"I'll go along with you, Berl. I'll run over to my house and fetch my fiddle," said Sascha infected by the general excitement.

"Good boy, Sascha!" everybody assented.

To give the proper tone to the festivities, Mrs. Salkind now appeared in the doorway bearing a great bowl of cooked carrot-dessert.

A Jolly Company

"Children!" she cried. "You must taste my carrot-dessert!"

"Carrot-dessert!" exclaimed Rose in astonishment. "What holiday is to-day?"

"I have nothing else with which to serve our guests," apologized Mrs. Salkind profusely.

"What about potato pancakes?" asked the union official, his mouth watering.

"I have no oil to fry them with," murmured Mrs. Salkind, much embarrassed.

"Bonchik will get the oil," suggested some one.

"Go along with Berl, Bonchik!" they all cried. They pushed him through the door with their coaxing eyes. They knew that if he went along all the necessary articles would be purchased. One good fellow, that Bonchik!

With a good-natured smile, Bonchik prepared to go, unwillingly though.

"Bring me, my child," asked Mrs. Salkind, "a quarter pound of raisins, a half pound of almonds, a pound of potato flour and a bottle of oil, as well as a dozen eggs, but all of the very best. Now what else?" she pondered.

"Oh, yes! How stupid of me to forget — also buy a few tins of sardines, a fresh pumpernickel and a *schmalz* herring."

"And see that you don't come back without a herring!" admonished the union official.

"I'll just go crazy trying to remember so many things!" lamented Bonchik.

He finally returned laden with all the good things. Soon Mrs. Salkind stood in the kitchen frying the potato pancakes. The delicious aroma floated into the living room and titillated all the appetites. Then Sascha brought his fiddle and played both Jewish and classical airs. Freier read his own verses that no one understood. Berl and the union official sang Yiddish and Russian folk songs. Everybody joined in the singing. After that Berl and the union official sang

177

couplets from Yiddish musical comedies; Berl sang the romantic lover part and the union official the prima donna rôle. And to crown it all Mrs. Salkind, with a flushed, happy face, placed on the table a great platter of fat, steaming potato pancakes. Everybody grew expansive....

Chapter 10

A MEETING

■■■■■■

EARLY one morning, when Dvoyrelè emerged from her home on her way to work, she had a strange meeting. She saw Freier walking up and down the street past her house. His coat collar was turned up although it was a clammy, warm day. A cigarette stuck rakishly from a corner of his mouth.

"What are you doing here, Freier?"

"I have been waiting for you."

"For me!"

"Yes! I would like to take you from your work to-day. Come with me! Let us go walking outside the city."

"To walk now! So early in the morning!"

"Do you know a better time for walking? Midnight perhaps? It's getting cloudy. Let's go. Come! We'll have a swell time."

Dvoyrelè remained standing in stupefaction. Such a proposal as Freier had suggested would never have occurred to her. How absurd! To walk in the country when all workers were busy at their tasks!

"Are you afraid?" asked Freier. "If so, of whom?"

"I am not afraid," explained Dvoyrelè apologetically. "Only I am not accustomed to such luxuries."

"Then get accustomed to them," advised Freier.

"Honestly, I don't know what to answer you."

The Mother

"Do indulge yourself this pleasure. What are you afraid of?"

"I am not afraid."

"All are afraid of starvation in America!" began Freier bitterly. "In the old country it was no disgrace to go hungry. To starve was entirely a personal matter, and every one had an indisputable right to it. But here, in America, it is strictly prohibited to go hungry. The very thought of it is enough to terrify one, be he rich or poor. Bosses and workers, socialists and bankers, editors and poets — all stand in mortal fear of it. Take me for example: Heavens! What have I got to lose? By all tokens, who has a better right to starve than I, a poet? But in America not even poets have the right to starve. As hard as I try to starve a bit, I fail in the attempt. I must continue working and make enough for food."

"Do you work?" asked Dvoyrelè much surprised

"Because I do not wish to work with my pen, therefore I must work with my hands."

"At what do you work?"

"What's the difference? I work at anything that turns up. Only sometimes I feel like mutinying. His majesty, the poet, awakens in me and insists on his divine and inalienable right to starve. And as I sit in my shop over my work, I, the well-fed one, hunger — for starvation. As I lie in bed at night I dream of hunger. Hunger is the only bright ray in my hopeless life. If you would only know how I long for it! At times there rises within me the strength of a spiritual Samson, consumed with the longing to starve. When that occurs I roam about the streets for a few days and I satiate myself with hunger. I devour hunger with all my being so that I may remember it during the seven fat years. The days when I go hungry are so rare now! Recently they have been very rare. Perhaps it is a sign of deterioration — of senility? To-day, Heaven be praised, shall be a day of hunger! That is why I am so happy!"

Dvoyrelè regarded him mutely. She saw a devouring sorrow in his eyes. Never had she seen that in any human being before. His mouth was distorted in a painful grimace as if he were weeping within. Already she had decided to accompany him wherever he would want to go and to wander light-heartedly with him wherever his pleasure would lead him.

"Then why don't you hunger, if it makes you so happy?" asked Dvoyrelè.

"Do you ask why? I am not permitted to do so!" shouted Freier, his voice trembling with pent-up rage.

"Who is it that doesn't let you?"

"Who? That scabby Jew — my conscience!"

"Conscience!"

"Yes! My wife and children."

"Are you married?"

"The first day that I was born I was already married."

Dvoyrelè regarded him with bewilderment.

"First I was married to father and mother. After that — to a wife and children. I don't remember the day when I was single."

Dvoyrelè kept silent.

"Why don't you say something?" he reproached her. "Are you afraid of me because I have a wife and children?"

"Not at all!" laughed Dvoyrelè uneasily. "Why should I be afraid of you?"

"I knew all along that you wouldn't be afraid," Freier complimented her. "I have already decided that you must become a 'member' of our society, which at the present time consists only of three: yours truly, Haskel Bucholz the sculptor, and another. I forget — you don't know Bucholz."

A brilliant idea suddenly struck him.

"Do you know what!" he exclaimed impulsively. "Suppose we call for Bucholz? He lives in a studio on West Four-

teenth Street. We pass the house on our way. Do you
mind?"

"We will do that later," said Dvoyrelè. "First tell me
about your society."

"Well, as I have already told you, our society consists
of three members, namely: Bucholz, I, and a certain original
who is only a common tailor but a very interesting person
nevertheless. I must introduce you to him. He is a wonderful worker — can do everything, but he has one very great
fault. He has a habit of sewing the buttons on the wrong
side of a garment. Do you think he does that because of
absent-mindedness or carelessness? All wrong! There is a
system to his madness. Our friend maintains that it should
be the sacred duty of every man to guard the integrity of
his will and that he must assert it at every possible opportunity.

" 'And as I am forced to sew buttons on garments against
my will,' says he, 'I must assert my will by sewing the
buttons on the wrong side. Otherwise of what earthly use
can my will be to me? Yet I must sew for I must eat too.
As for the damned buttons, I've got to sew them on the
wrong way.'

"Sooner or later our free-will advocate gets caught by
the foreman in his work of rebellion against law and order.
Then he is discharged without a moment's delay. Yet under
no circumstances would he join a labor union, for he is a
former anarchist and militates against every kind of individual or collective tyranny.

" 'A union,' says he, 'is like a police permit to maintain
a brothel.'

"So he goes without work for several weeks, starves until
he again finds employment. But the same thing repeats
itself endlessly. Although the garment that he sews is from
beginning to end a work of art — nevertheless, he sews the

buttons on the wrong side! Now, how do you like this tailor
friend of mine?"

"What is wrong with you to-day, Freier?" suddenly
asked Dvoyrelè, not answering his question.

"What do you mean by your question? Do you for one
moment think that I have invented my tailor? I swear he is
genuine and if you would like to convince yourself I will
introduce him to you."

"But why are you so depressed, Freier?" persisted
Dvoyrelè anxiously. "Surely something disagreeable must
have happened to you."

"To-day, Dvoyrelè, is my day of hunger and it is you
who are the cause of it," said Freier solemnly.

"I?" exclaimed Dvoyrelè much startled.

"Yes, you! You have awakened in me a dream that I had
thought had long died within me."

Dvoyrelè kept silent and walked by his side with down-
cast eyes.

"Aren't you at all curious to learn for yourself the nature
of the dream which you have awakened within me?" asked
Freier.

Dvoyrelè still kept silent.

"I have always cherished the dream that a time would
come when I would put everything aside, and buying myself
a barrel organ I would wander forth into the world.
Naturally, it would have to be in jolly company. Bucholz
would be one of those who will accompany me. He will lead
a little monkey attached to a chain. It will play its tricks
on his big shoulders. I will be the chief of the band and will
grind the barrel organ. Only one thing remains to complete
the dream: a beautiful dancer. It is she who will make the
whole expedition worth while. I have sought her but as yet
I have not found her. The dream has gradually evaporated
and I had become resignedly tranquil once more. But all of a
sudden you entered into the darkness that envelops my

life and my dream blossomed forth again. Do you understand now what ails me to-day?"

Dvoyrelè grew sad of a sudden. She wrinkled her little
forehead and remained silent.

"Why do you wrinkle your forehead so?" asked Freier.

Dvoyrelè did not answer. But after a moment she spoke:
"I will tell you the truth, Freier. Your words have made
me sad."

"How so?"

"Because you speak words to me that are not intended
for me."

"What do you mean?"

"In your present mood you would have spoken the same
way to any girl that would be walking by your side."

"What makes you think so?"

"I don't know myself. I just feel that way."

Freier said no more. Without exchanging a word they
continued their walk until they reached West Fourteenth
Street. They stopped before a dingy tenement house. Freier
led her into a dark, filthy hallway.

"You wait here for me," he said, "and I'll go to fetch my
friend Bucholz."

"No, Freier! Better let me go back to work. I am late
enough as it is."

"Why? I thought you had consented to come along with
me to the park!"

"I did so at first. But I regret it now."

"It's not nice to go back on your word."

"I know that very well but I can't help it."

"But if I promise you that I will not speak any more
about *that matter* — will you come?"

"I feel sad enough as it is," muttered Dvoyrelè.

"Please, Dvoyrelè, remain with me! On my word of
honor, I promise not to talk about that confounded dream
of mine again." Freier begged her like a spoiled child.

A Meeting

His pleading made Dvoyrelè laugh. So she nodded her head.

"Now I'll run up to Bucholz. I won't stay a minute. But please don't run away while I am gone."

And Freier mounted the dark stairs which wound in a spiral into a vast labyrinth of flats.

The instant Freier left her, Dvoyrelè felt a panicky desire to fly. Wouldn't it be much wiser if she returned to her work? Not that her conscience would torment her for idling away one day. But what Freier had said to her did not sound quite honorable, she suspected. Yet she was filled with great pity for him. She instinctively felt his suffering although its nature was such that it could not arouse within her any admiration for him. Nevertheless she remained rooted to the spot and waited for his return. She had to wait a long while. When he rejoined her he was out of breath. He had run down the stairs too rapidly.

"Please forgive me for keeping you waiting so long," he said. "It isn't such an easy matter to get to Bucholz. I had to scale a half dozen ladders until I reached his 'villa.' He lives quite near the sky. I found him undressed. He hadn't even washed yet. At home he walks about quite unconcerned like old man Adam before he ate of the blessed apple. But here he is himself! Dvoyrelè, I have the great honor to present to you the second member of our Hunger Society — Herr Haskel von Bucholz."

Before Dvoyrelè stood a young clumsy giant. His appearance was at once ungainly and comical at the same time. He looked as massive as an oak. He had broad shoulders and long sinewy arms and gave the impression of one who was used to heavy manual labor. The one soft spot about him was the manner in which his eyes closed when he laughed. Then he looked like a child and it was moving to see him that way.

Bucholz always laughed, with and without reason. His

185

eyes closed with merriment and he appeared then like a helpless, innocent child.

"Bucholz!" snapped Freier commandingly. "Bow to the lady! The Devil take you but why do you behave like a bear?"

Bucholz bowed clumsily and laughed sheepishly.

"It is three days already since he has last been out on the street," Freier enlightened her. "During this time he either lay in bed or else prowled about his room like a caged bear, without a stitch of clothing on his back."

Bucholz laughed.

"It was good so," he said.

"What was good?" asked Freier irritated.

"That!" growled Bucholz.

Freier laughed and apologetically explained to Dvoyrelè:

"All one can get out of this bear is either: 'this' or 'that'! There are no other words in his vocabulary."

Dvoyrelè now felt sorry for her new acquaintance.

"Why don't you leave him alone?" she rebuked Freier.

When they emerged into the street, Dvoyrelè cast a curious, appraising look at Bucholz. She first noticed the odd shirt he was wearing. It was   rough workman's shirt of an uncertain, dark color. Its tails gaped dangerously from his loosely hung, baggy trousers and bulged through the short sleeves of his coat. There wasn't a button about his person. With democratic impartiality neither his trousers, his coat, nor his shirt was guilty in this respect. . . . Through a rent in his shirt there gaped a dark patch of hairy chest. His neck, ruminated Dvoyrelè sourly, stood badly in need of a good, hard scrubbing with soap and washing soda. About it he had wound a curious sort of cravat which also served the purpose of a collar. His face obviously had not been shaved for days. His hair was disheveled and flaked with chicken feathers — just as if the down of a pillow had been emptied on his head.

A Meeting

"Bucholz!" commanded Freier sternly. "For God's sake stick the ends of your shirt into your trousers! Why must you disgrace me so?"

Dvoyrelè walked between the two hulking men. With her small, slim body she attempted to shield the helpless, lumbering giant from the nimble-witted, unscrupulous poet.

"Oh, I don't mind him at all!" Bucholz assured her with a good-natured grin. He stopped into the middle of the street and tucked the blundering shirt tails into his cavernous trousers.

"Where are we going?" Dvoyrelè asked finally.

"Didn't we agree to go to Bronx Park?" said Freier.

"Yes, yes!" nodded Bucholz vigorously.

"For that we've got to have money for fare. Have you any money, Bucholz?"

The great fellow reddened. He stuck his hands into his pockets and pretended he was looking for money.

"Sorry! I've got no money," he mumbled vaguely.

"Have you money anywhere else except in your pockets?" snapped Freier maliciously.

Here Dvoyrelè sprang to the rescue.

"I have twenty-five cents," she eagerly interjected. "Will that do?"

"It will be enough for one way. But what will we do for the return journey? We are three."

"I will go back on foot," grunted Bucholz simply.

Dvoyrelè gave him a bewildered look.

"I always do that," he commented reassuringly.

Without further thought about their finances, the trio of rebels against the machine age entered the subway and boarded a Bronx Express train.

Chapter 11

IN THE OPEN

■■■■■■■

THE subway trains that roared from the Bronx into the heart of the city were jammed with people. The returning trains, however, were quite empty. The car into which the "Hunger Club" entered was practically deserted. Very few people travel to the Bronx during the forenoon hours and these, for the greater part, are idlers. So the trio felt at ease.

The deafening clatter of the speeding train made it possible for Freier to enlighten Dvoyrelè about Bucholz, his life and character. He did so with thinly disguised malice. . . .

The more ungainly and idiotic Bucholz appeared to Dvoyrelè, the greater the sympathy that awoke within her towards his helplessness. She felt the need of defending him against Freier's sarcasms. Freier had told her that Bucholz was a butcher's son. He was to follow in his father's calling. But he felt an instinctive leaning towards art. He loved to draw and kneaded human figures out of lumps of bread. Discovering this preoccupation, his father tried to beat it out of him with his great fists. He dragged him by the scruff of the neck to his butcher shop. But Bucholz was as obstinate as a mule. One day, when no one was about he rifled his father's till and ran off to America. Here he worked at anything that turned his way. Once he worked as a porter. At another time he was a night watchman. But all the time he attended an art school in the evening. He had found himself a garret room in an old house and applied himself diligently to his art.

"In that garret room," said Freier, "he sleeps — not on a bed, but on the bare floor. He molds his crazy figures from clay and uses himself as his model for he can't afford to employ one. So he poses for himself in the nude during both hot and cold weather. Now he is working on a clay model for a heroic figure of Samson. But it has as much resemblance to Samson as I have to the voluptuous Delilah. Not so, Bucholz?" asked Freier with a sneer.

"That's not true!" laughed Bucholz. "I walk about naked in my room because of the great heat."

"Don't be a fool, Bucholz! What is there to be ashamed of?"

"I'm not ashamed."

"And when he is hungry," continued Freier, as if Bucholz were not present, "he crawls down from his garret room and goes out looking for work. Sometimes he gets a job on a moving van or in a shoe store. Or else he grinds a clothes wringer in a wet-wash laundry. He even worked as a crier for the busses that carry passengers to Coney Island.

"After he earns a few dollars to buy bread and to pay his rent, he purchases a sack of clay and drags it on his back to his 'studio.' Then he resumes his work on his sculptures, which no one can get a blessed sight of because he is ashamed to show them. It will surely amuse you to know that he can barely read or write. He has never read a book and he has never been inside a museum. He doesn't even know what an art exhibition looks like. How can one expect him to know of the new trends in art — of Rodin or expressionism, for instance?"

"Not true! I have seen!" mumbled Bucholz and vigorously shook his head in denial.

"What have you seen?" asked Freier ironically.

"Skyscrapers," said Bucholz, shaking with laughter.

The Mother

It was one of those rare summer days when sun and wind unite as a blessing for the harassed inhabitants of the great American metropolis. Although it was midsummer and the sun poured mercilessly down upon the earth, houses, streets, bridges and people alike, a cool, refreshing breeze blew from the sea and breathed upon the sun, like a cooling fan.

Bronx Park smiled in all its verdant beauty. And if one but penetrated into its sylvan depths there sprang up the illusion of having strayed into a jungle, overgrown with wild grass, climbers and tendrils. The feet trod upon virgin land of primeval and as yet unexplored America.

For a long time they wandered along the narrow paths walled in by aisles of closely growing trees. Bucholz knew every tree in the park and had he not been forcibly restrained by the others who were afraid of the possible arrival of a park watchman, he would have clambered up to the top of every inviting one.

For the first time since her arrival to America, Dvoyrelè saw before her the cheering aspect of green, growing things. It was for the first time as well that she became aware of the naked, unencumbered earth. She could touch the moist, growing trees, the fragrant, tranquil ground and the high, sweet grass. After these long months of confinement in her cellar home and workshops, contact with nature came as a shock to her. It intoxicated her. She flung herself upon the grass and buried her face in the growing life about her, as if she wanted to merge herself with it. She kissed the grass with her moist lips and became wrapped in joyful daydreaming. She succeeded in more than once startling her companions with her sudden, impulsive conduct. The constrained and ever silent girl of a sudden lost all her bashfulness. She gamboled among the trees like a mad young colt and defied the young men to catch her.

The latter tore after her in hot pursuit. Freier was the

first to give up the chase. Even Bucholz, who had powerful legs and advanced like a charging bull, and despite his determination to catch her, had to abandon the chase. At last she tired running and came back of her own accord.

"Heavens! Who taught you to run so?" asked Freier with begrudging admiration.

"Our goat in the old country is to blame for that," rippled Dvoyrelè.

"Your goat!" exclaimed Freier and Bucholz with one voice.

"Yes, our goat! When I was a little girl I was charged with the responsibility of taking the goat to the pasture. It was he who taught me to run. When he ran I ran too, holding onto the rope about his neck with all my might. You see, I was afraid to lose him."

"I would like to be a goat and to run away and have you pursue me," exploded Bucholz impulsively.

Without any warning he dashed away, imitating all the capers of a runaway goat, much to the amusement of Freier and Dvoyrelè.

"How about playing some game that I used to know in the old country?" suggested Dvoyreiè eagerly. Vainly she tried to recollect.

She suddenly grew sad. She could not remember the time when she ever played. She had been born old . . .

"Forgotten! Forgotten!" murmured Dvoyrelè with a forlorn look.

"Bucholz, do you remember any game?" ventured Freier.

"Yes, I know one."

"What is it like?"

"Standing on one's head. Who remains standing in this manner the longest time wins."

Without ado Bucholz balanced himself skillfully on his head. Not only Freier, but Dvoyrelè as well, tried to imitate him.

"Bucholz, do you know what I proposed to Dvoyrelè? That all three of us strike the open road in a jolly company. I will play the hurdy-gurdy, you will do the tricks and Dvoyrelè will dance. Do you know how to dance, Dvoyrelè? In this way we will earn our bread."

This time Dvoyrelè did not feel offended. Nor did she try to interrupt him. She knew that it symbolized something strange and luring that he wanted so badly to achieve.

"I am ready," said Bucholz simply.

"Are you?" asked Freier of Dvoyrelè.

"But how can I? I don't know how to dance."

"Even so," blurted Bucholz, "I will take you along with us."

"Oh, no! It is I who will take you," protested Freier with a slight irritation. "Tell us, Dvoyrelè, with whom would you rather go?"

Without deliberating Dvoyrelè pointed to Bucholz.

"With him," said she coquettishly.

"Now, what do you say to that, Bucholz, you lucky dog?" gasped Freier maliciously.

But the sculptor of a sudden grew grave. He made a grimace and throwing his arms about a great tree he embraced it savagely.

"What's gotten into you, you big bear?" gasped Freier.

"I would like to make things like that!" blurted out Bucholz.

"What did you say?" asked Freier, not believing his own ears.

"Yes! I would like to make such trees," reiterated the sculptor.

"Sculptured trees?"

"Yes, make such great, thick trees with immense spread of foliage. They stand erect in rain and storm as if they were guarding something."

In the Open

"What can you possibly express with such inanimate objects as trees?"

"Trees have faces, hands and feet, grown together like children in their mothers' wombs. Trees are like embryonic children that have turned into wood in their mothers' wombs, as if they are accursed of God or the Devil. Trees can laugh. They can also weep. Have you ever heard trees laugh?"

"Then what keeps you from sculpturing trees?" asked Dvoyrelè.

"Some day I will," answered Bucholz.

"Bucholz, what in plague is the matter with you?" exclaimed Freier. "You have always been a dumb brute and now you can't stop talking! A miracle has happened! Bucholz talks! Bucholz tells of his plans! Who would have ever believed it?"

And turning to Dvoyrelè, he shouted:

"It's all your fault!"

Dvoyrelè flushed deeply at these words and Bucholz, pouncing furiously on Freier, seized him in his strong arms and threw him to the ground.

"Shut up!" he roared like an enraged bull. "I'll crush you like an insect if you say another word!"

. . . .

Pangs of hunger began to undermine their good humor. Exercising in the open had sharpened their appetite for food. At first the young men very tactfully kept quiet about it. But Bucholz, who like a healthy child could not long dissimulate his natural passions, cried out petulantly:

"I am hungry!"

"Do you think you are the exception?" wrathfully asked Freier.

"So what's to be done?"

"I still have ten cents," Dvoyrelè shyly broke in. "We

193

can buy a loaf of bread for that. Of course, we will all have to get back home on foot."

"Splendid!" applauded Freier. "But, no!" he qualified. "Bread for only five cents — the other nickel for you to ride home."

"No! If one walks all must walk!" Dvoyrelè stubbornly insisted.

"How about it?" asked Bucholz naïvely. "I'll carry you home on my shoulders." And he smiled foolishly.

"You can believe him, Dvoyrelè. He is quite capable of doing the maddest things."

When they had left the park grounds and emerged into the street, Dvoyrelè was suddenly struck by a bright idea.

"Miss Isabel Furster, my night-school teacher, lives on this street. I visited her once before but I am afraid I've forgotten the number of the house."

"Have God in your heart and try to remember!" beseeched Bucholz.

"I believe the number is forty-something."

"We'll try every house bearing those numbers."

Dvoyrelè decided to call on Miss Furster alone. She had the men wait downstairs for her. She was afraid that seeing the Hunger Society in full muster, her teacher might possibly be constrained in her welcome. She would only ask her for the loan of a dollar and would cleverly explain that she had gone out with two gentlemen friends of hers and that unfortunately her friends discovered that they had no money with them.

Luckily, Miss Furster was in. Hearing Dvoyrelè's explanations, she burst into a merry laugh and ran downstairs to call the men up.

"Do come up!" she purred ingratiatingly. "I understand your predicament. The same thing has happened to me more than once."

Before Freier and Bucholz stood a radiant young creature

with laughing, almond-shaped eyes. She was dressed in a Japanese silk kimono and this made her look more Japanese than Jewish. She spoke Yiddish badly and with an American accent.

Freier she had previously met and Bucholz she had heard of.

"I have heard a lot about you," she said beamingly to the latter. "I was told that you are a great artist."

Bucholz grew as red as a beet. He did not know what to answer.

"Who told you that?" he stammered ill at ease.

"Oh, many people have told me that," evasively replied Miss Furster. "How did you happen to meet these people, Dvoyrelè?" she asked with some astonishment.

Dvoyrelè found it embarrassing to explain.

Miss Furster's room was very simply furnished. It contained a sofa and two wicker chairs, a few Japanese prints, two small cactus plants, a three-legged table on which stood a brass candlestick containing a half burnt candle.

Miss Furster called Dvoyrelè into her little kitchen to help her improvise a lunch for her guests. It consisted of lettuce, tomatoes, olives, and dainty slices of bread. The men did themselves great credit. They ate like lions. After which, their hostess playfully gave them money for their fare home. And before parting she urged them:

"Come to see me whenever you like. In case I am not at home, you will find the door always open. Don't be bashful — walk straight to the icebox and eat whatever you find there."

It was late when they arrived downtown. When he bade her good-by, Bucholz held Dvoyrelè's little hand for a long time in his big paw. He smiled foolishly, bared his strong, large teeth and could not utter a single word. Freier could not restrain a cynical jibe:

"Well! Why do you stand there like a damn fool? Tell

her what you want to say. Don't you see she is waiting for you to say something?"

Bucholz's eyes of a sudden began to flash daggers at Freier. Not knowing what to say or do, because of some inexplicable impulse, he suddenly spat with great vehemence and dashed off. Dvoyrelè stood looking after him in amazement.

When Dvoyrelè returned home she found every one fast asleep. Weird shadows of elongated beds and the gaunt limbs of the sleepers sprawled over the walls of the cellar. The sound of deep snoring filled the room. Only against the wall, where a ghastly gas jet was burning, the fierce, cadaverous shadow of a woman bent over her household work. It was mother standing at the sink and washing the breeches and shirts of her little ones so that when they would rise in the morning she could dress them spick and span for school.

More than on her own body, mother's exhaustion and debility were betrayed in her shadow. The harassed shadow on the wall had a long thin neck, lean baggy breasts, and a humped back that loomed to monstrous proportions and suggested the strain of many invisible burdens.

When Dvoyrelè saw mother she was seized with great pity for her. She wanted to take her in her young arms, overwhelm her with love and tenderness and weep upon her breast. But she keenly recognized the necessity for self-mastery. Instead, she approached her and gently pushed her from the sink.

"I'll finish the washing myself," she whispered to her.

Mother protested vigorously.

"Better go to sleep. You are tired."

"I am not tired, mother, for I didn't work to-day."

She drew up the sleeves of her dress and began to wash.

"Take off your dress — you'll get it wet!" admonished mother.

In the Open

Next morning Dvoyrelè did not return to her work at the Salkinds'. Instead, she arose bright and early and after dressing carefully she went to the office of the garment workers' union to inquire for a job.

It was during the hot summer months when many working girls had gone away on their vacations, and because the fall stock of clothing was being prepared it was not difficult for Dvoyrelè to find employment. She found it among hundreds of other girls in a stuffy, filthy shop that looked dangerously like a fire trap.

Chapter 12

NEIGHBORS

·······

ANSHEL half sat, half reclined on the stone steps that led down to his cellar home. His shirt was wide open, revealing his bare, hairy chest. He breathed with difficulty. With one hand he kept mopping his face and neck. With the other he fanned himself incessantly.

The night had brought the inhabitants of New York's East Side some relief from the heat which hung oppressively overhead like a leaden pall, bearing downwards with crushing weight upon all that lived and grew. The human body once more became subordinated to the will but, worn out by the excessive heat of the day, it was too limp and nerveless to exert itself. Humanity was dominated by only one powerful passion — water to quench an apparently quenchless thirst. The children, their faces besmudged and overheated, were hoisting to the upper floors of the tenements tins of beer and soda water tied to long pieces of heavy cord. To remain indoors was impossible. During the scorching downpour of the sun the brick walls had sucked in the heat like a sponge, and now when the night fell exuded it like from a hot, steaming furnace. Men and women, unblushing *en déshabillé,* were carrying bedding from their homes into the street. With a perfect lack of self-consciousness, as if they were in their own bedrooms, they sought comfortable spots on the pavements to bivouac for the night. Others sought release from the heat on the iron fire escapes as well as on the roofs of the houses. The

198

Neighbors

only ones in whom the joy of life pulsated were the young imps. Some of them gathered in great heaps all the egg boxes and newspapers littered on the street, and put fire to them. They made a merry blaze and added further to the already excruciating heat. Others picked up gasoline tins and discarded ash cans and beat on them a blood-curdling, ear-splitting din. From time to time could be heard the laughter of children playing in the long, dimly lit corridors of the houses or the insistent cry of a mother sticking her head out through a window from an upper floor and calling:

"Sammy! Sammy! Take the baby carriage upstairs!"

It grew late. The electric lights in front of the motion picture theaters had already been extinguished. The last of their audiences had long departed. Even the soda-water and ice-cream stands were beginning to look deserted. But no one thought of sleep. On the contrary, only now when the cool night air had set in, the exhausted people breathed freely. They became animated and exchanged neighborly pleasantries.

A gramophone suddenly burst into action. It was a Jewish cantor coquetting with a piece of synagogue *fioritura*. The loud conversations now ceased. In the streets, at open windows, on roofs and fire escapes, people became thoughtfully silent and listened to the singing. Anshel, sprawled over the steps leading to his cellar, also listened raptly.

"Surè!" he called into the cellar. "Come out just for a minute!"

But Surè made no answer. She was too tired to speak but lay without stirring on her bed with reddened eyes half closed in pain.

"Surè!" called Anshel again, this time more insistently. The gramophone was grinding out a holiday hymn.

"What do you want?" groaned Surè weakly and soon

appeared at the doorway with a wet cloth tied about her head.

"Just listen!" bade Anshel eagerly.

"That reminds me that the holidays will soon be here," sighed Surè.

"What is ailing you, Surè?" asked her Anshel anxiously. "All night long you have done nothing but groan and sigh. Why did you insist on sitting all day long at the machine?"

"I don't know what's ailing me," ruefully replied Surè. "For a long time already I have felt a sharp pain in my side. It makes it so hard for me to move about."

"I know exactly what is the trouble with you," volunteered a distinguished gossip and woman of the world living on the same block. She had listened with great curiosity to the conversation between Anshel and his wife. "It's all due to an enlarged liver. My mother, of blessed memory, suffered from the same malady," she insisted on her diagnosis.

"You're just talking nonsense," interrupted another neighbor who regarded herself as a great medical authority. "Our family doctor says that a pain in the side means only rheumatism. He ought to know. He is the doctor of the lodge of which my husband is a member."

Surè's pain in the side now grew to the dimensions of a public discussion. One woman leaned out of a first-floor window and gratuitously shouted down her piece of expert advice.

"Mrs. Zlotnik," she cried. "Don't you listen to those ignoramuses! Take my advice: go to Coney Island and take a few ocean baths. The pain will stop as if by magic."

During the short time that she had been living on the block, Surè had managed to adjust herself to the lives and habits of her neighbors. She knew them all and they knew her. But this acquaintanceship most often proved of little practical value. It was torn up before it had time even to take root. It was difficult enough to break the conventional ice between one's neighbor and one's self, to harmonize all temperamental differences, to wax friendly even. Then along came the spirit of unrest and carried off the neighbor and a new one would move into the vacated tenement. The process of adjustment would have to be repeated, often amidst incessant quarreling and mutual annoyance.

To every new neighbor in the tenement house Anshel would apply the Biblical expression: "The one who knew not Joseph."

Yet life in the New York tenements does not permit one to stand aloof and self-sufficient. Every one has to participate in the struggles and fortunes of the others. There is no place for secrets. Each knows the most intimate happenings in his neighbor's life. Every one on the block was well acquainted with the fact that Mrs. Zlotnik had many children and that they were well-bred and clever. Anshel was held in the greatest respect because of his learning and dignified bearing, and all the housewives never tired of singing the praises of Moses, formerly "The Ox," who guarded his mother "like the apple of his eye." Now when they heard of Surè's complaint they did not hesitate to lavish upon her all their medical wisdom culled from a vast history of personal and family illnesses. Poverty and adversity draw the discordant hearts of men together into a firm bond.

The following morning when it was time for Surè to rise to prepare breakfast and the lunches for the menfolk, she found it impossible to get out of bed. The same incident had already repeated itself a few times that summer. Her legs felt heavy as lead. They did not respond to her will, try as she would. Anshel had even with a rude tenderness in his voice bent over her bed and whispered:

The Mother

"You must lie in bed all day, Surè! If you will rest you will feel better."

"Woe is me!" lamented Surè. "There is no one to prepare breakfast! I'd better get up."

A great pity seized her for those helpless menfolk and for Dvoyrelè. How hard they all worked!

Again she made a desperate effort to rise. But she sank back with a groan that was half a sob.

Dvoyrelè made coffee and set the table. Then she prepared the lunches for those who went to work.

"Who will wash the dishes?" called Surè from her bed in a weak voice. "They have been lying piled in the sink since yesterday."

The matter of washing the dishes after dinner developed into a serious problem for mother. She recently began to feel such exhaustion when night set in that she reluctantly left the washing of the dishes for the following morning. Solomon, however, instituted a new practice to meet the emergency. Whenever the boys stayed home from school they were obliged to perform this household duty for mother.

"That's the way it's done in all good American homes!" explained Solomon.

But the boys did not relish this delectable task. They were cunning enough to invent all manner of tricks to evade it. For instance, when the time came to wash the dishes, they suddenly were seized by a soul-stirring piety and began to pray with fervor. The rogues well knew how happy mother was to see them in such religious throes. She would not for all the world dream of interrupting their prayers. So mother washed the dishes herself.

This time as well, when the boys heard mother express concern over the unwashed dishes, they leaped for their prayer-books. But Anshel frustrated their fraud. He grew angry and cuffed them on the ears.

Neighbors

"Just look at my saints!" he cried. "All of a sudden they have become religious! It is always so: when mother falls sick they think of nothing else but God! ..."

"Please, Anshel, do leave the boys alone! I'll wash the dishes myself," called mother from her bed. "I'll get up in a minute."

This smote the boys with great force. They felt remorse and were filled with pity for their mother. They would not let her get out of bed.

"Never fear, ma!" they comforted her. "We'll wash the dishes all right."

So they ceased their pious pretending and turned to the dishes with alacrity. One washed and the other dried and without uttering a word they good-naturedly exchanged a shower of well-aimed kicks.

When it grew late already and it was time for mother to go out shopping for dinner, she scolded herself: "Why do I lie in bed now? What's the great celebration about?" Then she tried getting out of bed. But she grew faint and dizzy and fell back into bed. The older children were at work and the younger ones were out playing on the street. So she waited until her youngest, little Feigelè, came in.

"Go, Feigelè, and call a neighbor," she moaned.

Feigelè returned with Mrs. Barkin, a stout, good-natured Galician who had left her cooking and with flushed face and rolled-up sleeves ran to Mrs. Zlotnik's assistance.

"What ails you, Mrs. Zlotnik?" she asked.

"I don't know, Mrs. Barkin. My head just turns with dizziness. The children will soon be here and I haven't bought anything yet for dinner. And it's getting late."

"It all comes from the liver, Mrs. Zlotnik!" insisted Mrs. Barkin pleasantly. "My sainted mother, may her soul rest in peace, suffered from the same trouble. A few salt baths will fix you up fine."

Here Surè made another ineffectual effort to rise.

The Mother

"Better lie still, Mrs. Zlotnik. It's not good for you to move," chided Mrs. Barkin.

"But I've got to cook dinner! Anshel and the children will soon be home and they'll be so hungry!" said Surè with a groan.

"Don't you worry, Mrs. Zlotnik. We'll manage somehow. I'll go out shopping for you right away. Does Mr. Zlotnik like calves' liver? I've seen some lovely calves' liver at the butcher's to-day. Shall I buy a pound of it for you? I've cooked a delicious soup. I'll bring you some of it."

After a few minutes, Mrs. Barkin returned bearing with her a pot of soup. This time another neighbor, Mrs. Rabinowitz from the third floor, accompanied her. It was the same Mrs. Rabinowitz who had advised Surè that her ailment was only a rheumatic pain and recommended that she consult her husband's lodge doctor. She had brought with her a bottle of ointment that the latter had once prescribed for her. It was a cure for all bodily ills. But Mrs. Barkin took matters into her own hands and rather crustily interrupted her medical ruminations:

"Mrs. Rabinowitz, I'll let you put the house in order while I'll go shopping for Mrs. Zlotnik."

"Feigelè! Where is Feigelè?" called Surè weakly from her bed.

"I'll send Feigelè in to you, Mrs. Zlotnik," said Mrs. Barkin. "Whatever you do don't move out of bed! If you'll excite your liver it will grow bigger. That it is all a case of 'bad nerves' is very clear to me."

Mrs. Barkin put on her shawl and went out shopping and Mrs. Rabinowitz started cleaning up. In a short while the former returned leading Feigelè by the hand. She put her to peeling potatoes while she busied herself preparing dinner, in the meantime not neglecting to talk about Surè's liver, as well as about the liver of her sainted mother, may her soul rest in peace, who died from its enlargement.

Neighbors

Surè offered no protest to her neighbors' kindly service. On occasion she had performed the same neighborly duty for them.

When Anshel returned from work and found Surè in bed, he grew frightened. This had never happened before. Of his sons, only Solomon was at home. Although he lived apart from his folks and worked in his prospective father-in-law's shoe store, he often came home on a visit. Moses now worked for a country customer-peddler and was away all the week, carrying his pack of merchandise from village to village in the outlying states near New York. Gedaliah too had found employment in a boarding-house in the Catskills for the summer. He did that in order to save enough to enable him to continue his studies during the rest of the year.

Anshel did not know what to do. He stood despairing before his wife's bed, and pulling at his beard with nervous fingers, asked:

"What ails you, Surè?"

"It's nothing," answered Mrs. Barkin for her, deprecatingly. "It's all due to an enlarged liver. My sainted mother, may her soul rest in peace, suffered from the same ailment. She'll be all right after she will have taken a few salt baths in Coney Island."

"Don't you feel well, Surè?" asked Anshel again in a trembling voice.

"Oh, I am feeling better already," murmured Surè, dissimulating.

"Now have your dinner, Mr. Zlotnik," wheedled Mrs. Barkin. "I am not sure whether you will like my cooking as much as your wife's, but that can't be helped."

But Surè had more pressing concerns than to be ill.

No sooner did Moses arrive from the country and discover that mother was ill and that the neighbors recommended sea baths, than he insisted that she travel to Coney

Island for the purpose. Once, on a Sunday, when all the children were home, they persuaded her to accompany them to the seashore. She returned home more dead than alive.

For two days after her excursion to Coney Island she went about with a cold compress tied about her head. Her experience with the great crowds, the noise and the sea bathing evoked nothing short of a nightmare within her mind. She had barely succeeded in ridding herself of the disagreeable memory when a strange occurrence took place which completely made her forget everything including her illness. And it all happened because of a "book."

Moses, a business man, even in the old country, had no sooner reached American soil than he began to think about his future. Alert and resourceful, endowed with business acumen and imagination, after considerable observation and solid thinking, he came to the happy conclusion that the greatest opportunity the new world could offer for a future lay in peddling.

"Peddling is the stepping-stone to something better," he would say with far-seeing eyes. "Every day I earn a couple of dollars and better yet, I am my own boss at that."

When he succeeded in attaching himself to a customer-peddler it was almost impossible for the latter to get rid of him. He carried his heavy packs of merchandise and ran his errands. He never minded how hard the work might be nor how long and irregular the hours. Ahead of him he saw a goal toward which he was working. He would often go on short trips to small villages in southern New York State and eastern New Jersey to supply the farmers with the merchandise they needed. He was strong and active, had muscular legs and broad shoulders. On his shoulders he carried one heavy pack. In his hand another. In this manner he tramped from one farmhouse to another selling his wares.

Peddling in the country also gave him an opportunity

to do a little business on his own account. Of course in a secretive, roundabout way, without the knowledge of his employer. He would sell the farmer cheap trinkets on installment, alarm clocks and cutlery. These accounts he kept duly recorded in his own "private book." A time came when he had actually put by one hundred and twenty dollars in a savings bank. Although he was exceedingly generous by nature and deeply devoted to his mother, yet he well knew the need of saving money. He deprived himself of many necessities, never indulged himself any ordinary luxury. He had a goal to reach....

About this time an unusual opportunity came his way. A certain customer-peddler, who was beginning to feel his old age and infirmity and found it difficult to tramp from village to village with his heavy packs of merchandise, decided to sell his "territory" and his "book" of accounts for the sum of five hundred dollars. He asked for two hundred and fifty dollars in cash and the rest to be paid off in installments within a year's time. When Moses heard of this wonderful opportunity he knew that Fate was knocking at his door. But alas! He possessed only one hundred and twenty dollars in cash.

True enough, if only he could acquire from the peddler "the book" he would have little difficulty with the Canal Street wholesalers to advance him merchandise on credit. But for that he needed guarantors. The most vexing problem, however, was how to obtain the necessary one hundred and thirty dollars in cash to add to the one hundred and twenty dollars which he already had. There was no time for delay. The route was a good one, a well-to-do neighborhood among New Jersey farmers. Purchasable "books" were rare those days and there was a dearth of buyers.

As in the past, this time too it was necessary to turn to Solomon for help. He had not been married yet but waited until the kitchen of his little flat would be furnished.

The Mother

The parlor and the bedroom stood ready to receive the
bride and the groom, but that was because the former had
paid for the furniture. The few hundred dollars Solomon
had saved he had invested in his future father-in-law's shoe
store of which he aspired to become a part owner. To
advance his brother Moses the required sum of money
for his customer-peddler's "book" was only possible by
withdrawing his interest in the shoe store. Could he risk
it? That, God forbid! might perhaps result in an unforeseen rupture in his relations with his girl! As it was, her
parents were very much displeased with him for spending
so much money on his greenhorn family. "You ought to
think about the welfare of your future wife a little more,"
they rebuked him. They had another grievance against him
on account of the diamond ring he presented to their
daughter. They thought it was too small. . . .

When Moses came home one day and announced to his
mother the speedy redemption that would come to the entire
family as a result of his obtaining his "book" from the
old customer-peddler, and that it was the chance of a life-
time, mother lost no time in going out to seek her eldest
son's aid. She pleaded with him, then kissed and embraced
him, and even shed tears. Was he not obligated by the
holiest ties of the blood to come to his younger brother's
aid and help him purchase the "book"? But it was as she
had expected at first. Solomon would hear none of her pleas.
He once more lamented over the fact that his own flesh
and blood stood in the way of his getting married and
would now jeopardize every chance he had by forcing him
to withdraw his money from the shoe store. Was there not
a definite understanding between him and his prospective
father-in-law that no marriage was possible until he had
saved enough money to earn a quarter interest in the
business?

Hearing which, mother went to see her future daughter-in-law. She kissed her hands and with tears in her old, faded eyes implored her to intercede with Solomon that he lend his brother the necessary money for the purchase of the "book."

"He will listen to you much sooner than to his own mother," said Surè, wistfully. "His heart already belongs to you — not to me."

All this she kept from Anshel. He was such a hothead and might in a moment of excitement want to have it out with the girl's parents. After all, they were not over-enthused with the prospect of having Solomon as a son-in-law! That would put an end to all her son's marital plans.

Under these circumstances, how could she possibly think of Coney Island, she asked herself? Or of ocean bathing?

To coddle her illness would be too great a luxury for her.

PART THREE

Chapter 1

THE FAMILY MOVES

■■■■■■■

ONE evening when the Zlotnik family sat down to dinner, mother, without any apparent rhyme or reason, suddenly let slip a remark which filled them all with apprehension.

"How will you manage without me?" she asked.

"Manage without you! What do you mean?" exclaimed Anshel with surprise.

"When I won't be with you any more," mother quietly elaborated with a smile.

"Don't talk nonsense!" chided Anshel sternly.

"After all, I am not going to live forever." Surè tried to explain, smiling sadly in the meantime.

At this Anshel became wrought up and forbade her to talk any more in that preposterous vein.

Of late Surè had been constantly dwelling on unpleasant subjects. One morning, on awaking, she declared that her sainted mother had visited her in a dream. At another time an ancient grandaunt had come to console her and bade her not to fear the Angel of Death.

Since all her children were preoccupied with their own affairs they soon forgot her strange words. At first these words had given Anshel a great scare. He tried to reassure himself by calling her a goose. But he too soon forgot about it although the one who dismissed it most completely from her mind was Surè herself. She chose to ignore the doctor's professional apprehensiveness over her condition and his admonition that she have complete rest and take ocean baths. Were there not more important things to do than to be ill, she had deprecatingly asked herself? Then came Solomon's forthcoming marriage which overshadowed everything else.

Solomon's bride-to-be stubbornly insisted on an elaborate wedding in a high-class hall where the unwritten law demanded attendance in frock coats for the menfolk. This deeply pained her thrifty parents who thought any expense besides that entailed by the marriage ceremony a great extravagance. It would cost a tidy sum and where was all that money to be gotten? Then the thought of the Zlotnik family coming to the wedding, looking shabby and like greenhorns, succeeded in depressing them. How would they look among their many well-to-do storekeeper friends wearing frock coats and shiny opera-hats? More than once before the day of the wedding, they had tremblingly adjured Solomon:

"Have God in your heart and see that your greenhorns don't put us to shame before our rich uncle!"

Solomon saw no way out of it but to outfit his entire family in new clothes. This caused much bad blood between him and his bride's family. Much acrimony and many bitter words were exchanged because of the expense it entailed. Surè was driven frantic with this incessant bickering.

At last the eventful day arrived. Because of the presence of the bride's rich uncle at the wedding Anshel passed quite unnoticed among the guests. At table he and his brood were seated in an inconspicuous corner near the door. Surè felt it her sacred duty to deport herself at the wedding in the good old way, as it was done in the town where she was born and raised, to serve the guests at table and to coax them to eat heartily of everything. But Solomon would have none of it. He was filled with mortification because of her and under his breath sternly bade her under no circumstance to move from her place.

Because he and his little flock were so thoroughly ignored, Anshel lashed himself into a fury of suppressed resentment. Immediately after the wedding ceremony he herded together Surè and their fledglings and gave the sharp word of command: "Home!" The youngsters, clustered about tables loaded with good things to eat, like flies over honey, were loath to obey him. Skillfully they wriggled out of his reach and he and Surè had to go home alone. Of all the grown-ups in the Zlotnik family only Moses remained. He enjoyed rubbing shoulders with the frock-coated "aristocrats" invited by the bride's family.

When Anshel returned home he vented his resentment and humiliation upon Surè.

"I always told you that our coming to America would bring us no good!" he cried.

Moses' close contact with the "aristocrats" at the wedding completely demoralized him. He could not endure living in the cellar any more. He strenuously urged moving "uptown" to a better locality. His parents regarded him with bewilderment.

"You've gone crazy!" exclaimed Anshel with heat. "We've hardly enough to pay for the rent here in this wretched cellar. How do you expect us to pay for an apartment uptown?"

"The first thing one must think of in America," rejoined Moses, "is to live like civilized human beings." Then with a subtle wink at Dvoyrelè: "After all, we have a marriageable young lady in the house and young men will soon come acourting and they must be welcomed to a better place than this pigsty."

"Of course you are right!" said mother, vigorously nodding her head.

"Well! Show us what you can do! It's your America,

not mine!" Anshel gave his parental sanction with a groan of resignation.

Conditions had improved somewhat for the Zlotnik family. Besides Anshel and Dvoyrelè, Moses was the only provider of the family. All week he tramped the highway, carrying his packs of merchandise from farmhouse to farmhouse. This made his visits home infrequent. Nevertheless he contributed toward its upkeep. Gedaliah was already well advanced in his studies. He was attending a preparatory school with the intention of matriculating at Cooper Union as a student of civil engineering. During the day he worked in a cigar factory. He no longer delivered newspapers. This "business" he had handed over to his younger brothers, Meyer and Nutè. The elder of these two worthies began to reveal particular business acumen and enterprise. This made Surè boast: "He is already following in Moses' footsteps."

Moses was impatiently waiting for Meyer's graduation from public school in order to take him along with him on his country route. Meyer was a poor scholar but had a passion for sports and athletics. One day he brought home to his mother a silver medal which he had won in a hundred-yard dash at school.

"Tut-tut!" said father with magnificent disdain. "Just look for what medals are awarded in America!"

Whereas Meyer distinguished himself in athletics, his younger brother Nutè was more inclined in Gedaliah's ways. He was timid and reserved and displayed unusual ability in his school studies. Because he was the youngest and the most helpless of her children mother loved him best of all. So he and Meyer delivered newspapers before and after school and earned enough to keep themselves in shoes and stockings. Moses, therefore, had reason for being extravagant and ambitious for his family. Things began to look quite rosy for them.

The Family Moves

One day he said: "Mother, we must look for new rooms."

"That's quite impossible!" answered mother. "The first of the month will soon be here. I am frightened when I think about it. Where will I get the money for rent? Don't forget that Solomon can no longer help us. We are in a bad fix as it is worrying about paying for the cellar without hunting for new trouble."

"Don't worry, mother!" comforted Moses. "Everything will turn out all right. Should you be short on the rent I'll make up the difference."

"May God reward you for your kind heart!" murmured mother with deep feeling, and as always put her arms about him and kissed him fondly.

Early one Sunday morning he and Dvoyrelè went out apartment hunting "uptown," which for East Side dwellers in those days extended no further north than 14th Street. On Third Street near Avenue B they at last found three rooms which they thought adequate for their needs and which they could have for a monthly rental of eighteen dollars. One room was large and light, another small and dark and the third, a tiny one, served as a kitchen. As the trolley line ran through Avenue B the locality was convenient for those who had to travel to work.

When Moses and Dvoyrelè returned home with the good news Surè once more began to waver and to have apprehensions.

"Whereto do you want to lead me, children?" she asked, trembling. "Everybody knows me here. When I have no money I can get credit at the grocer's and the butcher's. But I will be a stranger and helpless on Avenue B."

"Don't worry, mother!" Moses reassured her. "You'll get credit on Avenue B too. It's all one America."

Therefore one bright Sunday afternoon, a day before the first of the new month, when the whole family except Anshel was at home, Moses fetched a peddler's wagon and with the aid of the others began loading the furniture and other household goods on it. What a pitiful spectacle they made, the rusty broken beds, the pillows and the featherbeds bundled in soiled bed sheets, mother's ancient pots and Dvoyrelè's sewing machine.

Surè left her humble cellar home with a heavy heart. It had been her first home in the new world. She had become attached to it, in fact, she almost loved it. It gave her a sense of security and protection. But toward her new and "expensive" apartment she felt only mistrust and fear.

"Our cellar took us to its heart like a mother!" she lamented, touching the walls with a tender caress of farewell. "It served us as our first shelter in this cruel new world."

Although moving day is no novelty in New York's Ghetto, Surè's neighbors came out into the street to bid her Godspeed. And those who could not leave their household duties for long, stuck their heads out of their windows and showered their best wishes upon her.

"May you enter your new rooms with your right foot first!" they piously wished.

Some of her neighbors envied Surè. They silently prayed:

"May the day come soon when we too will move uptown!"

It was painful for Surè to part from her neighbors. They had been her only friends in the new world. They read her emotion and said with feeling though not without some vainglory:

"May you find no worse neighbors when you move into your new rooms, Mrs. Zlotnik."

Then the boys harnessed themselves to the shafts of the peddler's wagon. Moses pushed it from the tail-end. Surè followed close behind, carrying the red Sabbath wine flagon which she had brought with her from the old country. Beside her walked Dvoyrelè, bearing gingerly the piece of cut glass which Moses had bought to impress Solomon's girl with when she called on them for the first time. Both she and mother dared not trust the boys with these fragile, precious objects. So they carried them themselves.

Anshel was not at home when the household moved. Being a Sabbath observer, he worked on Sunday instead. His absence was regarded as a stroke of great fortune by every one. Toward nightfall, when he descended the stairs of the elevated station from work, he was met by Nutè who guided him to their new home. Anshel could hardly believe his own eyes when for the first time he stepped into the large light room which mother designated as the "poller." Despite the fact that the room was still in disarray and piled high with the unpacked bundles of bedding, he lost no time in penning a letter then and there to the Rabbi of his home town in Poland with whom he kept up a steady correspondence. He wrote:

"I have already written you how I crossed the Red Sea and the torments I endured before I reached the Promised Land. But that was nothing compared to my bitter bondage under Pharaoh, King of Egypt, meaning of course the shirt factory in which I am enslaved by my boss and the foreman and all the other plagues with which one must put up at first in America. But after one has passed through the fires of Gehenna it is but inevitable that one reaches ultimately the land flowing with milk and honey.

"I now occupy a new dwelling in which, God be praised, one room is as large as the interior of your synagogue. When the gas chandelier is lit at night the room becomes illuminated as if the sun were shining into it during the middle of the day. The physical conveniences we enjoy are too numerous to mention. They are so cleverly arranged that they are a source of endless pleasure to us. If I choose I seat myself in a chair which can be rocked deliciously like a cradle. When I feel but the slightest chill I have to do nothing more than turn a little valve and lo!

and behold! out pours a stream of warmth which instantly heats the room. Similarly I can make me a fire in the gas stove or draw water from the wall in quicker time than it would take you to blink an eyelash. In conclusion: God is good and I will sing His praises all my days."

Chapter 2

SAMSON

■■■■■■

ONE Saturday afternoon, when the entire family was at home, the door suddenly opened and there entered a young man, dressed in a brand-new suit, the newness of which dazzled the eyes, and wearing dilapidated shoes and a hat full of holes and grease spots.

"Does Dvoyrelè Zlotnik live here?" he asked.

Dvoyrelè looked at him and she turned all colors. Her heart beat like a sledge hammer. It was Bucholz!

To Anshel's and Surè's astonishment and grief she arose and without uttering a word took the young man's arm and led him out into the street.

"There — there is your crazy America!" blurted out Anshel in disgust. Mother bit her nails to steady her nerves.

When they had emerged into the street Bucholz said:

"I've got a few dollars with me so I've come for you. I'd like to take you out for a good time."

"How did you find out my address?"

"I looked for you everywhere — did not know where you lived. I was given your address at the shop where you worked last."

"I am not working there any more."

"Good!"

"Why so?"

"Because Freier comes there often."

Dvoyrelè laughed.

The Mother

"Where did you get the money from?" she asked. "You are wearing a new suit."

"It cost twelve dollars. How do you like it?"

Dvoyrelè noticed that the collar was too large and the sleeves too short.

"Yes — it's very nice," she said. "But how did you get the money?"

"I worked."

"At what did you work?"

"I got a little job at coal."

"Coal!" echoed Dvoyrelè astonished. "What did you do with coal?"

"What's the difference? I wanted a new suit and a few dollars for spending money. I wanted to take you out, Dvoyrelè," explained Bucholz bashfully.

Dvoyrelè laughed.

"What do you propose we do now?" she asked.

"I have already fixed the program. First of all we will take a bus ride on Fifth Avenue. We will look at the shops and the passers-by. I love to look down from the top of a moving bus. Then we will hire a boat and go rowing on the Central Park Lake. Perhaps you would like to eat first? Aren't you hungry? At night we will go to a moving picture show. How about it? A cowboy picture is being shown at the Apollo Theater to-night. I love cowboy pictures — Western life, men on horseback. Or perhaps you would like to go to a Yiddish theater instead. Mogulesco is playing to-night in *The Alright-nik!* What do you say about going instead to a dance hall? I love to watch people dance."

"I don't know myself what I would like to do," answered Dvoyrelè in a quandary. "You want to do so many things at one time."

"I have thought so long about taking you out for a good time that I don't know where to take you first," laughed Bucholz. "At one time I very much wanted to take you

222

to the Yiddish theater. At another time bus riding on Fifth Avenue. And now when I actually find you with me, I want to do all those things at the same time."

"How is your work progressing?" she suddenly asked.

"My work! What work?" asked Bucholz puzzled.

"Your 'Samson.' "

"Oh! You mean *that!* He sleeps.

"What do you mean — he sleeps?"

"I got sick and tired working on him. So I put him aside. He stands in a corner and sleeps. But he is broken. I punched a hole through his stomach."

"Why did you do that?" gasped Dvoyrelè.

"I wanted a new suit and to take you out for a good time."

"So for that you broke your Samson!" said Dvoyrelè reproachfully.

"Why not? He prevented me from working for a living. Then again we wrestled with one another to determine who was the stronger. So with one solid punch I smashed a hole through him."

"What mad things are you saying?" murmured Dvoyrelè in consternation.

"On second thought I think I will throw sculpture away altogether."

"Why so?"

"What for do I need it? I will learn instead some useful trade so that I can earn some money, a lot of money. I know already what trade I would like to learn."

"In other words, Bucholz, you are giving up the hunger strike that you pledged yourself to carry through," said Dvoyrelè, laughing loud. "I never asked you to buy yourself a new suit of clothes or to take me out for a good time."

"But I wanted it myself!" insisted Bucholz. "I so longed to take you out for a bus ride on some Saturday afternoon when all workers go out with their sweet —" (He could not finish the word.) "All I needed was a new suit and a few dollars in my pocket."

"Well, Dvoyrelè," — he interrupted himself — "what do you say? Shall we take a bus ride on Fifth Avenue, move among the crowds, have dinner together and afterwards see a moving picture show or perhaps a Yiddish show?

"God! How impatiently I have been waiting for this!" he exclaimed fervently.

Dvoyrelè did not answer. A light kindled in her eyes. She looked at him wonderingly. She leaned heavily toward him. They walked side by side. He heard her rapid breathing and he felt her small, palpitating body press eagerly against him. He suddenly grasped her hand and began to run.

"Let's run, Dvoyrelè!" he said.

"But it doesn't look nice, Bucholz!"

"What do you mean — not nice? Are you afraid of what people will think? What do I care about their opinion?" cried Bucholz, pointing a finger at the streams of people thronging the avenue. "They are like water and we two are like fish and we swim and drift along with their tide."

The day was clear and golden — a typical autumnal day in New York. The gold suffused the air and tinted the sky. The air was like strong drink. And when the wind blew it wafted the fragrance of ripe apples through the streets.

Saturday afternoon. The streets are thronged with busy shoppers. Happy faces everywhere, eagerly looking into shop windows, much conversation and gusts of laughter. To-morrow is a day of rest and one can sleep late. The day is young yet and a carefree night still to be spent in relaxation and pleasure. The streets are jammed with automobiles and busses and the sidewalks are crowded with endless streams of passers-by. Everybody merges in the mass and everything swirls in a rhythmic chaos.

Dvoyrelè and Bucholz floated with the stream. Bucholz

held her hand tightly clasped in his. He liked her pleasant
silence. Covertly he looked at the patches of olive skin
that were visible on the nape of her neck through her
hair. He gloated with his eyes over the fullness of her arms
and shoulders and rejoiced over her sweet chasteness and
the aura of holiness that hovered about her.

Every time he thought of the few dollars snuggled in his
vest pocket he became panicky for fear of losing them. He
constantly put up his hand to feel them and he gave a sigh
of relief when he found them intact. God be praised!

At first they thought of boarding a bus and from its
elevation look down upon the swarming sea of humanity.
In the end they decided to walk and to look into the shop
windows.

They stood in front of a silk-goods shop. It looked like
an Oriental bazaar. In the show window, under multicolored
silk tents and on expensive Eastern rugs, squatted lifeless
manikins dressed as Arabs. From between their hands unrolled exotically colored silken fabrics, fine Near East stuff.
Some of it was scarlet as blood — blue as the night sky —
silver-toned and shimmering like luminous deep-sea fish.

"If you like," burst out Bucholz with a baffling earnestness, "I'll steal into this store at night and carry off enough
silk stuff to dress you like a queen."

Ah! So she thought he was joking! He would prove to
her that he was capable of such a daring act!

They moved on and stopped again before a magnificent
fur establishment. The show window was piled high with
expensive furs. They conjured visions of vast frozen spaces,
unexplored islands and dark mysterious forests. If Dvoyrelè
only would agree, reiterated Bucholz, he would break into
the fur store at night and carry away for her a fortune of
the most expensive sables and minks. He also volunteered
to do her the same service in other shops before which they
halted. He was only too eager to steal for her an expensive

The Mother

automobile and in it, he suggested, they would go touring over the whole country in a care-free manner! Or if she liked (they were standing in front of a Japanese jewel importer's) he would throw a brick wrapped in a newspaper through the window, and seize a handful of lovely jades and ivories. She'd look just enchanting in those beautiful amber beads!

Dvoyrelè laughed. She enjoyed his nonsense. . . .

Then Bucholz suggested that they go to Childs' for buckwheat cakes and coffee. After Bucholz had paid the bill he discovered that of all his money there was hardly enough left to buy two gallery seats in a Yiddish theater. Hearing this Dvoyrelè registered no enthusiasm for further entertainment. So Bucholz cautiously inquired whether she would not prefer to go up with him to his studio. At home he had a little gas stove on which they could make tea and for the money he still had left he could buy some corned beef, bread and sauerkraut.

Dvoyrelè readily assented to his suggestion:

"I would like you to show me your 'Samson' and your other works," she said.

Bucholz looked dubiously at her.

"Would you really like to see my work?" he queried.

"What a question? I have been thinking about it for a long time already."

"Very well! Let's go!"

When they entered the dark hallway in his house and commenced to climb the rickety stairs, she timidly slipped her little hand into his. And he pulled her after him through a labyrinth of corridors and up seemingly endless stairs and ladders. Finally he led her into his garret "studio" that was separated from other rooms by thin partitions. Besides a small window with thickly coated panes, the room was lit up by a skylight through whose unwashed glass a strong light poured down. Dvoyrelè took a mental

226

inventory of the sculptor's possessions. She noticed old trousers, galoshes, soiled shirts and tattered underwear. They lay in a heap and waited for a redeemer. A few broken chairs, a table on which lay an open razor and a shaving brush as well as an ancient petrified looking crust of bread, a dilapidated sofa, a dirty quilt, a heap of colored draperies, pieces of coal and a barrel of clay, were strewn over the room. A gigantic figure reaching to the very ceiling and swathed in moist cloths, reposed in a corner. It looked like a stage ghost.

"What a mess!" cried Dvoyrelè, hardly believing her own eyes. And before Bucholz could offer a protest she began to put the room in order.

"Oh, leave things alone!" besought Bucholz. "You'll never be able to make any order out of all this junk."

"Is that 'Samson'?" asked Dvoyrelè curiously, pointing to the swathed mummy.

"Would you like to have a look at him? I'll let you decide his fate. If he will please you I'll let him live — if not, I'll twist his neck off," said Bucholz grimly.

He now pulled the moist cloths from the statue and before Dvoyrelè stood revealed a colossal, naked figure. It resembled Bucholz somewhat and represented a broad-shouldered, muscular, overdeveloped giant, with broad chest and long, powerful hands. But the face was that of a child and a naïve, childlike smile hovered in the corners of the mouth and in the half-closed good-natured eyes. He looked so clumsy, so powerful and helpless!

The first thing Dvoyrelè noticed about "Samson" was his thick, muscular neck which grew out of his shoulders like a tree trunk. She could not at all visualize the sculptor's boast that he would twist his giant's neck off. How silly! "Samson" looked so lifelike that she would not at all have been surprised had he at that moment lifted his powerful arms and wrecked the house like the real Samson did to the Temple of the Philistines.

"How will you ever twist his neck off?" asked Dvoyrelè teasingly. "Will he let you?"

"Oh, I'll fight him and just knock him down!" bragged Bucholz vaingloriously.

"He's stronger than you."

"I fought with him once already and there you see I punched his belly in."

"Why did you do that?"

"I don't know myself how it happened, but once, while lying in bed at night, I saw him standing over there, bathed in the moonlight which streamed through the skylight. He then appeared very ridiculous in my eyes. Why did I ever want to make him? Who needs him, anyway? Besides, have you ever seen a more idiotic face than his? He looks as if he himself doesn't know what he wants."

"That's why I think it is so splendid," enthusiastically cried Dvoyrelè. "He is a hero, a child. Every hero is a child. He is strong for himself and does not know what to do with his strength."

Bucholz became lost in thought.

"Strong for himself?" he wonderingly asked. "What do you mean by that?"

"I mean just that. He is like a violinist who plays for himself and for himself alone."

"You are right, Dvoyrelè. He is strong for himself alone. He plays with his strength. That's exactly what I wanted to express!" Bucholz cried jubilantly and grasped her hand. "A Samson who plays with his strength! He is not a mere hero, like Bar-Kochba, fighting to liberate his people from the oppressor's yoke. He is more than that. He is strong for himself and plays with his strength. He sportively puts fire to the crops of the Philistines in their fields, steals one of their prettiest wenches for himself, makes a feast, sings and dances. In short, a strong man, a hero, a child. That's Samson! Now he stands in that corner over there with his mighty arms hanging clumsily to his sides. Like a man who doesn't know what to do with his life, he doesn't know what to do with them. That was what I wanted to express with my statue."

His last words moved Dvoyrelè deeply. She began to recognize his self-portrait in "Samson." . . .

"Does he please you?" asked Bucholz furtively.

"I don't know," answered Dvoyrelè, looking doubtful. Then she sank into a melancholy state of mind.

"What are you thinking about?" he ventured timidly.

"I don't know myself. Your 'Samson' has made me sad."

"Why?"

"I believe because he is so unhappy. With all his great strength he remains unhappy."

"Please don't be sad, Dvoyrelè!" he implored her.

She moved near to Bucholz and looked earnestly into his eyes. He became embarrassed.

"Why do you look so?" he asked.

"I feel as if I have known you for a very long time, Bucholz."

"I have felt the same way about you since the first minute I saw you."

Both fell silent.

"Why have you all of a sudden become so sad, Bucholz? God has blessed you with such great strength!"

"I am not sad!" remonstrated the sculptor and his mouth puckered up to laugh. But no laughter issued.

"Tell me, why are you so unhappy?" insisted Dvoyrelè. "Have you had very unhappy experiences in your life?"

"I have nothing to live for," murmured Bucholz, turning his face away. The puckered, strained smile on his lips now turned into a horrible grimace of anguish.

"If you have nothing to live for, then I don't know

who has!" Dvoyrelè rebuked him. "You create such great masterpieces. You are so strong. God has blessed you."

"Blessed me!" laughed Bucholz hysterically.

"Yes!" nodded Dvoyrelè with conviction.

"What makes you think so?"

"I know. That's easy to see. You will continue to create your beautiful works of art. Some day the world will give full recognition to your great talents."

"Beautiful works of art! Beautiful works of art!" repeated Bucholz with hysterical self-mockery. Then he impulsively pressed his big face against her slender little throat. She made no effort to move her head away. A stream of tears burst from her eyes and when he raised his head to look at her she offered her lips to him with pleading eyes.

Chapter 3

IN THE FOG

▪▪▪▪▪▪▪

WHEN Dvoyrelè made it her practice to stay out night after night until the early hours of morning, mother's sorrow and anxiety knew no bounds. Where in God's name could the girl be spending her time? Father lectured and abused, mother pleaded and wept — to no avail. Even Solomon, who was hastily summoned home and apprised of the dreadful happening, could offer no constructive advice.

"Mother dear, forget about it!" he begged. "Remember that this is America. Things are done here just this way. When a girl 'keeps company' with a boy, her parents have no right to interfere. It is better so."

True, mother did not know why it should be better so, but if that was the custom of the new world it would avail her little to object. Anshel too had given up wondering about it. He quite reconciled himself to the inevitable. He had only one thing to say:

"America is not ours. It's theirs. Therefore they have a right to do anything they please."

One thing, though, Surè found hard to understand. She confided the matter to Solomon:

"If Dvoyrelè does keep company with a young man, why doesn't she get herself some new clothes like other respectable girls would do in her place? She hasn't made for herself one new dress, or bought a new hat or a pair of shoes since she goes out with him. Instead, she walks about in perfect rags. Now what I would very much like to know is what she does with all the money that she earns. After all, she only contributes a few dollars to the house! It is also hard for me to understand why she doesn't bring her gentleman friend to see us."

Solomon answered nothing but at the first opportune moment he broached the matter to his sister:

"Dvoyrelè," he said, "you know very well that mother is still green and doesn't know much about the way things are done in this country. Of course, I know better. You are now keeping company. All right! We have nothing against that. But why don't you bring your boy friend to see us? Why don't you introduce him to papa and mamma if you know that his intentions are perfectly honorable?"

Dvoyrelè turned ghastly pale. She couldn't utter a sound.

Surè's apprehensiveness grew. Every day she came running to Solomon in his shoe store.

"What shall I do, Solomon?" she implored.

What could Solomon advise her to do?

Whenever Dvoyrelè returned home late at night, she invariably found mother had not gone to bed yet but was waiting for her.

"Where have you been at such a late hour?" Surè sternly rebuked her. And mother and daughter would exchange angry words which they would later regret. When Solomon heard of this he lectured his mother:

"What are you doing, mother? I know that it's bad enough as it is. But how will you feel if Dvoyrelè will decide altogether to move away from home? Don't forget, we're in America now!

"And furthermore," he added, "perhaps she doesn't confide in you because she really has nothing to tell you. She may not be as friendly with her young man as we are inclined to think. I am convinced that if she will come to a real decision about him she will lose no time in letting us know of it."

Solomon's words frightened mother into silence. She never said anything more to Dvoyrelè. Only at night she lay awake and kept endless and anguished vigil.

.   .   .   .

Every day when Dvoyrelè left her shop, Bucholz was already waiting for her outside. He stood guard near an Italian fruit stand on the corner of 27th Street. She always greeted him with a bashful smile and eyes brimming over with happiness. Then leaning heavily on his arm and pressing her little body close against his, they made their way through the crowded streets. He walked along with his great arms swinging and with mouth wide open as if he would have liked to swallow her in one big gulp. Where were they going? What difference? As long as they walked, and together.

The winter night descends upon New York. The cold is hardly felt. A light snow spray begins to fall and all the people in the streets turn their collars up. The sidewalks overflow with jostling throngs. Every one hastens — not to work but in pursuit of pleasure. All faces are alight. From restaurants, stores and motion picture theaters pours a flood of electric illumination which brilliantly lights up the iridescent snow-carpeted streets. The little tables in the restaurants, bedecked with dazzling white cloths on which glisten the large glass water bottles and cutlery, invitingly appeal to the hurrying passers-by. Amorous couples with arms intertwined run laughing through the snow. The atmosphere palpitates with a pale yellow tint because of the glistening falling snowflakes that are blurred by the stream of electric light. The streets take on a festive appearance. They radiate happiness.

Bucholz and Dvoyrelè felt themselves jostled by the good-natured, hurrying crowds. They felt gay and light-hearted.

233

The Mother

Walking arm in arm through the streets, Bucholz, like the overgrown child he was, prattled away about all sorts of grandiose plans for their future. Every night he breathlessly communicated to her a brand-new plan. Once he planned that they both go to Paris. Surely an artist stood in need of atmosphere! And since they had to starve while living in New York they might as well starve more pleasantly in Paris instead. At other times he settled upon Rome and Florence as the ideal setting for the future life. Wouldn't it be just wonderful to see the works of the old masters — sculptors like Michelangelo and Donatello?

One night, Bucholz, breathless with excitement, told her how a friend of his, a Yiddish journalist by the name of Rubinstein, had come to see him and informed him that he had just been speaking to the Jewish art patron and collector Sachs, of Kohn, Sachs and Co., and that the latter had consented to purchase his "Samson" for ten thousand dollars. He also proposed to send Bucholz to Paris at his expense. As happened to all his other plans, this never materialized. He shouldn't have taken that fantastic liar, Rubinstein, so seriously, he explained to her apologetically!

His imagination ever fertile, he became obsessed suddenly with a great and original idea. He would create what would be a new and startling conception of Adam and Eve. He would delineate Adam as a tree, a man-tree, not with two arms but with six, that grow out of his body like branches. That was to be a symbol of all the races of man that sprang from his loins. Eve he would portray as a negress, swarthy like Mother Earth herself. She was to appear pregnant and heavy with child.

Bucholz was chafing to put all his other work aside and to journey South to seek models for his new works. Besides, one could subsist there principally on sugar cane. That, he insisted, he had been told by a man who had been there. In the meantime he suffered from a healthy appetite for food. That, unfortunately, could not be overlooked. Invariably, Dvoyrelè would fish out a half-dollar or even a whole dollar from her pocketbook and they would go looking for a restaurant where food was inexpensive and where it was served in heaping portions. . . .

Occasionally they would attend a concert given by the New York Philharmonic Orchestra. That, of course, depended on how flush Dvoyrelè was with money. But whenever a Wagner program was announced, the price of admission had to be found somehow. Yes! Bucholz was just crazy about Wagner's music! He had a fine appreciation of music but he interpreted it in his own original and naïve fashion. One composition suggested to him a stormy sea on which twelve four-masters in their full panoply went down majestically to the depths. Another he interpreted as a stormy sky in which the mutinous clouds took on wings and turned to battle with one another. Or was it perhaps a forest being destroyed by a conflagration?

According to Bucholz he never enjoyed music as much as when he heard it with Dvoyrelè.

"When you sit near me at a concert," he said, "I can concentrate better on the music."

"How is that?" she asked, ingenuously looking into his eyes.

"I don't know why, but that's how it is. When I look at your hair and your shoulders I understand the music better."

Often Bucholz would take a job for a day or two in a wet-wash laundry or in a lumber yard and towards nightfall, when Dvoyrelè left her shop, he would advance eagerly to meet her, waving jubilantly the money he earned at his work.

"I've got money for tickets to the Philharmonic, Dvoyrelè!" he cried.

Dvoyrelè looked searchingly into his face and reading

fatigue in it, readily understood that he must have been doing heavy manual labor that day. She grew sad.

"It interferes with your art!" she rebuked him.

"That's not at all the case!" he protested. "As a matter of fact, I did not feel like modeling to-day."

Dvoyrelè laughed. They went to the concert.

Leaving the concert hall, Bucholz patiently began to interpret the music they had heard to the admiring Dvoyrelè. He modeled the music for her.

"You see, this is the way it is," he began, proudly conscious of his appreciative audience. "Great masses of people, entire nations, are passing through a dark, gloomy forest. They hew down the trees in their way, awaken the slumbering wild beasts with the thud of their axes and their shouting. They infest the great forest with an unspeakable dread. On the summit of a mountain clusters a city. By the ruddy glow of the setting sun its inhabitants behold the steadily advancing hordes of the enemy. The alarum sounds mournfully through the city, calling its inhabitants to the walls. Soon they appear upon the parapets and buttresses of the encircling fortifications and a battle is fought to the death."

Occasionally on a Sunday they would pay a visit to Miss Furster in the Bronx. She was their only friend. She had seen Bucholz's "Samson" and believed that he possessed great talent.

"America will be proud of him some day," she prophesied.

She was wrought up against American art patrons who spend millions annually upon fake old masters that are specially manufactured for them in Europe and at the same time have no sympathy or understanding for their contemporary native art. They permit their own artists to struggle bitterly and to starve. She promised that she would bring a friend, an art critic, to view his work. Perhaps he might interest himself in his behalf and obtain for him some stipend so that he might go ahead and perfect himself in his art.

When Miss Furster discovered the new intimacy between Bucholz and Dvoyrelè her interest in them became intensified. She was a radical and took a keen delight in helping those who were in trouble. She encouraged Bucholz to continue in his art and urged Dvoyrelè to inspire and strengthen his undisciplined spirit. By doing so she would reap a great reward, she promised her. Dvoyrelè was puzzled by this. She did not grasp her meaning readily.

Each time Bucholz conceived a new plan for a colossal and original work, for which he was ready "to consecrate his life" because he thought it would be his greatest masterpiece, his enthusiasm for it lasted only until a newer idea, still more colossal and more original, arose to overshadow it completely. And that change often took place during the few minutes' walk to Dvoyrelè's shop where he was to meet her at closing time. The germ for a new work had of late been taking firm root in his mind. He never tired of talking about it to Dvoyrelè. The new work that he was planning was to be called "Mother." He did not want to portray a mother of children — only a little girl, a thin, helpless mite, with as yet barely perceptible breasts and a tiny round belly, and slender, frail feet. In one of her hands she was to hold an apple, symbolizing Eve. All that is motherly, tender, protecting and long-suffering was to be expressed in her attitude, but at the same time a subtle smile was to hover over her lips in luring play: Lilith the Temptress. . . .

"That is the way I imagine Eve looked when she tremblingly first came to Adam and offered herself to him," said Bucholz to Dvoyrelè. "She must have been then but an undeveloped child with a small head. Yet into the curve of her belly had already been poured all the motherhood of the ages: the leitmotif of all mankind — the lust of our mortal lives."

"What keeps you then from making your 'Mother' look just the way you want her to look?" asked Dvoyrelè.

"I don't know how," gloomily answered Bucholz. "I question if I will at all be able to express the universal, the eternal motherliness in the little, undeveloped belly, and all the sorrows of motherhood, love, sin and carnal lusts in the subtle, melancholy smile on her childish lips."

Dvoyrelè became lost in thought. She did not answer.

"Sometimes it appears to me," continued Bucholz, "that I understand the idea so well that to put it into execution would be the next logical step. But at other times it recedes further and further from me and if I were to begin work I would probably produce a silly and meaningless clay figure."

"I know you can do it," remonstrated Dvoyrelè with conviction.

"Do you really think so?" asked Bucholz, his gloomy face lighting up. "Of course, I know I can do it and believe me, I'll do it! Wait and see! I'll immediately begin work on it to-morrow. So you do like my idea? Great idea, isn't it?"

"Of course it is!" loyally agreed Dvoyrelè.

"So you do understand my conception, do you?" asked Bucholz happily. "The beginning and the end joined together — just like in a wheel — mother and child forming the connecting links in an endless cycle."

"No, Bucholz! I'm afraid I don't understand that at all. But I do think that your idea to represent your 'Mother' as a child is very lovely. She really is so."

"Do you think people will understand what I mean to express?" asked Bucholz doubtfully. "I am afraid 'Mother' will also remain standing neglected and forgotten in the corner of my studio and gather on the dust of the ages so that the rats will take pity on it and gnaw it up for their dinner."

"You should worry, Bucholz!" Dvoyrelè consoled him. "You are not modeling for them — it's for yourself alone — not so?"

"But where will I get the money for the marble?" asked Bucholz with despair in his voice. "It must only be done in marble."

"We'll get the money for it somehow, never fear," promised Dvoyrelè recklessly.

When Bucholz heard Dvoyrelè utter the word "we" he melted with delight and grasping her hand he cried impulsively:

"Dvoyrelè, if you want me to, I'll make 'Mother.' Honest I will!"

"I wish nothing better," rippled Dvoyrelè happily.

"If so then come and live with me," stammered Bucholz with a great effort.

For an instant Dvoyrelè remained standing where she was. Then hanging her head she continued walking without having answered his question.

"When you are near me, I always know what I want," Bucholz almost shouted.

Dvoyrelè still did not answer. For a moment they walked in silence. Then Bucholz suddenly burst out laughing.

"Why do you laugh?" murmured Dvoyrelè sadly.

"Forgive me, Dvoyrelè! I really didn't know what I was talking about. I was only joking," he laughed with painfully quivering lips.

They did not exchange another word after that and hastily bade each other good-by.

Chapter 4

DVOYRELÉ'S WAY

■■■■■■■

A FEW days passed. They did not meet. Every day
Bucholz awaited her at the entrance to her shop. She
did not come out. He decided that she was angry with him
because of his suggestion that she come and live with him.
What an idiotic thing to have said! What could she possibly think of him now? Most likely she believed him to
be some disreputable loafer or even worse — who could
tell? To ask a delicate, refined creature like Dvoyrelè to
come and share his rat-hole was nothing less than imbe-
cilic, he told himself reproachfully.

Bucholz now went through a period of self-disillusionment. At such times he found a perverted delight in tormenting and reviling himself. He was convinced of his
unworthiness to live, branded himself as a faker, liar, hypo-
crite and what not. He was always deceiving others, and
what was much worse, deceiving himself with the pretension
that he was an artist. Of course, he was nothing but an
ignorant lout! He felt an irresistible temptation to seize
a mallet and break all of his sculptures to fragments. Let
there be an end to all this mockery! Since he had no trade
or calling, he came to the conclusion that all he was good
for was to be a tramp. He even decided to hit the road
and wander from city to city and leave everything to
chance. Or even hire himself out to a country customer-
peddler and carry for him his great packs of merchandise

from farmhouse to farmhouse. The mere thought of confining himself within the four prison walls of a factory, day in and day out, like all other people of his acquaintance were doing, filled him with terror.

For several days Bucholz continued in his self-torment. The last conversation between him and Dvoyrelè, which ended with his extraordinary proposal and, what was far worse, that it was answered by her with a look of consternation and silence, convinced him of his own worthlessness and insincerity. More than that, even his idea for the immortal work he wanted to create, "Mother," that was to be the consummation of all his artistic striving, he began to regard as insincere, a mere pose to make himself appear a great man in her eyes, in fact, to deceive the innocent girl with false pretensions. In reality, what did all that signify but that he was spiritually empty and bankrupt? Were his artistic conception actually motivated by an inner impulsion he would not have babbled about it so much, he was convinced. Indeed, how could he now possibly think of it as being honest and sincere?

Whenever he felt in a depressed mood, Bucholz stretched himself out on his dilapidated sofa, dressed in his khaki shirt, coat and slippers, and covered with all the sheets and rags that he used to swathe his clay figures to keep them moist. It was so cold in his studio that the small coated window-panes, some of which had been broken and were replaced by squares of corrugated paper, were now filigreed with ice-traceries. Even though the sun was shining, it only cleared for itself a small circular space in the center of the ice-encrusted window, like a round moon. On a chair, near where he lay, languished what had once been a loaf of bread. The crust had been torn away from so many sides that it now had the appearance of a misshapen mass. He had bought it on credit the day before. For twenty-four hours he had been lying on the sofa and not once did he think of getting up. His "Samson" and "Adam," upon which he had already commenced work, as well as other completed statuary, stood like frozen corpses wrapped about in their moist shrouds.

He was now confronted with the necessity of finding some employment for himself. For what was he best suited? He thought of many trades to which he might apply himself for a livelihood: a clothing salesman on Canal Street, or perhaps a chauffeur. The latter calling pleased him best of all. How nice and interesting to fly about the city streets with loving couples inside his taxicab or to park his vehicle before the elegant hotels on Times Square, or before the Metropolitan Opera House and watch the beautiful, richly dressed women enter. Also, how intriguing it would be to drive suspicious-looking, amorous couples to hotels in Coney Island some late summer evening....

Perhaps he would do best of all as a hotel clerk? He would even compromise and become a bell-boy or a porter, for there is much to be seen and heard in a large city hotel. People gather there from every part of the country and one may meet interesting characters. He would come in close contact with beautiful girls exquisitely dressed in furs and diaphanous evening gowns. He would have the opportunity of observing their delicately modeled feet tripping gracefully on magnificent Persian rugs. How thrilling!

"But what the Devil!" finally thought Bucholz with exasperation. "Why must I have a trade altogether? As a matter of fact that is the last thing I want. Instead I would like to become a hobo, steal rides on freight trains, or tramp the highway from village to village in search of adventure. I will meet many people and experience much. Every day I will be in another town and meet with something new to interest me. I will wander through wild mountain regions out West and see California where oranges grow all year round and where there is eternal summer.

Dvoyrelè's Way

I will see cowboys on horseback and Mexicans and —"

His daydreaming was suddenly interrupted by the opening of the door. Noiselessly, without knocking, some one stole into the room. Bucholz stared in astonishment. He thought he was still dreaming.

Dvoyrelè stood before him. She was dressed in her little hat and coat on which the fox collar already looked well frayed. She carried something in her hand. Was it a valise or a bundle, wondered Bucholz?

He lay without moving, taut and silent. He saw that her hat was covered with snow and that strands of her black hair were moist and clung to her face. "It must be snowing outside," thought Bucholz and still lay on the sofa silently regarding Dvoyrelè.

She placed her valise on the floor near the door and brushed the snow from her clothing. Then she approached him. With her characteristic, melancholy little smile she asked:

"Why do you lie in bed at this time of day?"

Like a bolt he sprang to his feet.

"Dvoyrelè!" he cried.

"Yes," said Dvoyrelè simply, nodding her head. "I have come to live with you."

Bucholz looked dazed. He did not seem to understand what she was telling him. He stood with mouth agape.

"Dvoyrelè!" he cried once more.

"You wanted me to come and live with you,— didn't you?" murmured Dvoyrelè, smiling into his face with eyes blinded by tears.

Still Bucholz stood silent. He did not know what to do. Then he picked up her valise and scrutinized it without seeing it, from every angle.

"What a lovely valise!" he muttered.

"I brought it with me from the old country."

"It looks so familiar and homelike!"

243

"Just look at the mess your studio is in!" she cried with feigned disgust. She then commenced to put things aright.

"My grandfather once owned a valise that looked just like yours," rambled on Bucholz rather pointlessly, admiringly handling her bag. His voice shook slightly.

.   .   .   .

A little while later and they sat beside the little coal stove that supplied the heat to the room. How Bucholz managed to get money for coal will always remain a mystery. Due to Dvoyrelè's capable exertions the studio looked quite transformed now.

She swept the floor, and with the help of Bucholz deposited both "Samson" and "Adam" in a corner. The table which had lain collapsed in a corner now stood firmly in its proper place on all its four legs. She hid his soiled clothes from improper view and collected all the books that lay strewn over the floor and deposited them on their shelves.

Bucholz told her of his plans anew. But they were not the same plans about which he had rhapsodized to her before. He was somewhat more practical this time. He was anxious to make money. Rubinstein, that fantastic Yiddish journalist, had proposed to him a deal with a Jewish book-dealer downtown. The latter had consented to purchase his "Samson" on condition that he pour for him miniature replicas of it in plaster of Paris. These he would sell on a large scale at a dollar apiece. The sculptor was to collect from these replicas ten percent royalties.

"To-morrow I will see Rubinstein. He will have me meet the book-seller and we will close the deal. Now, there are three million Jews in America." Bucholz waxed ecstatic of a sudden. "Three million 'Samsons' means three million dollars. How much is ten percent of three million dollars, Dvoyrelè?"

Bucholz suddenly stopped and looked guiltily at Dvoyrelè. "I know," said he, "that I am talking a lot of nonsense.

Dvoyrelè's Way

You mustn't mind me even if you hear me profane my most sacred artistic ideals with such sordid chatter about money. You mustn't forget that I am the son of a common butcher and that I was also intended to be a —"

He stopped short. Dvoyrelè fixed him earnestly with her eyes.

"What about it?" she asked.

"Well, you see," he stammered. "I possess only strong lusts and evil instincts. I am not capable of feeling any of those refined and sensitive emotions which you are capable of. As a sculptor I can create only huge, powerful and rude works. Freier once tried to explain it to me. He said my art was only a mirror of my own true nature. Do you think so too, Dvoyrelè?"

She regarded him mutely and with an overwhelming pity. Her eyes brimmed over. She stroked his hair.

"How could you ever suspect me of such a thing!" Dvoyrelè reproached him.

"You see, everybody thinks that of me. I hear it so often said that sometimes I actually begin to believe they are right — that I am nothing better than a butcher with ugly impulses and that I am incapable of anything finer."

"I have never noticed any ugly instincts in you," said Dvoyrelè softly. "Only people who are ugly themselves could ascribe such a nature to you."

"Do you actually mean what you say?" asked Bucholz with incredulity. "Isn't it true that I lured you with lying words to come and live with me?"

"That is not the case at all," replied Dvoyrelè heatedly. "You haven't lured me. I have come to live with you out of my own free will."

"Out of your own free will?" asked Bucholz, not understanding.

"Yes."

"Then why have I such a guilty conscience?"

"Probably because you are not happy with my coming," said Dvoyrelè, with a coquettish toss of her head.

At this Bucholz sank to his knees, and burying his head in her lap, he wept.

"Dvoyrelè!" he moaned between his sobs.

"What is it, Haskel?" she asked, calling him by his first name for the first time and tenderly stroking his hair.

"I don't know who I am," he lamented.

She laughed gayly into his face.

"You are Haskel — Haskel — Haskel," she cried, almost chanting.

.   .   .   .

A little while later they went down into the street. They celebrated their reunion over buckwheat cakes and maple syrup at Childs'. Bucholz was now in an excellent humor, laughed immoderately and bared his strong white teeth.

But when they returned to the studio and were about to enter, Bucholz suddenly remained standing before the door.

"You'll sleep in the studio," he said. "I'll stay over at Freier's."

Before she could utter a word in protest he dashed down the stairs.

"Haskel, come back!" she cried.

"No! It's better this way," he shouted back, thundering down the rickety stairs.

Chapter 5

NO RABBI MARRIED THEM

■ ■ ■ ■ ■ ■ ■

NEXT morning, when daylight began to stream through the studio window and skylight, Dvoyrelè prepared to leave. What worried her most was where to place the key so that Bucholz would find it on his return. This problem became definitely settled when the door opened and Bucholz entered. He looked disheveled and wild-eyed and gave the impression of not having gone to bed the previous night. Up and down the room he paced with suppressed excitement. He could not bring himself to utter a word. Dvoyrelè gathered her things together and also said nothing. Finally Bucholz approached her and looked her questioningly in the eyes.

"Why are your eyes so inflamed?" he asked. "Did you cry?"

"No, I didn't cry," she lied.

"Yes, you did!" said he accusingly. "That's why your eyes are so swollen."

Dvoyrelè said nothing.

"Do you know what I am? A good-for-nothing!" burst out Bucholz savagely.

"Why do you call yourself such names?"

"Because I deserve them."

Dvoyrelè came close to him and touched him caressingly with her hands.

247

"What's wrong with you, Haskel?" she asked. "Where were you all night? You look a fright."

"I ran away on my wedding night," he cried hoarsely. "I wanted to be a dog instead of a groom. I felt like running wild through the streets and howling my pain and derision at myself."

Dvoyrelè began to tremble violently. She hid her face in her hands and wept unrestrainedly. Bucholz impulsively threw himself at her feet and in a passion of self-debasement kissed her shoes, feet, clothing and hands. In another moment he had lifted her up, and as if she were only a child, he paced up and down the room with her in his arms.

"My predestined one, my happiness, my only joy, that has come to lighten the burden of my life, tell me: what would you like me to do for you?" begged Bucholz in an outburst of happiness. "If you will bid me to jump down into the street from that window this very minute, I will do so without hesitation," he added somewhat extravagantly.

"You mustn't do such a crazy thing!" laughed Dvoyrelè through her tears.

"The truth of the matter is," added Bucholz on second thought, "I begrudge myself any possibility for happiness. Now do you understand everything?"

"Yes," said Dvoyrelè, with a wise nod of her head.

"Mother of my yet unborn children!" he cried out in a wild ecstasy.

Dvoyrelè placed her hand chidingly over his mouth.

. . . .

Once more they sat about the little coal stove talking over their plans for the future. Bucholz had bought bread, butter and coffee, and Dvoyrelè prepared the first eventful breakfast of their life together. She had not come empty-handed. Like the prudent little person she was she had brought along with her twenty-four dollars, which represented her previous week's earnings. She was, after all, her mother's daughter, and had sensibly packed into her satchel some sheets and towels. Bucholz could not see the necessity for such apparently useless things. He insisted that they should lose no time in refurnishing the studio. He therefore proposed an expedition to Little Italy on First Avenue, where household necessities could be bought on pushcarts for a song. The mere thought of establishing a home with Dvoyrelè fired him to a white heat of enthusiasm and made him decide upon a course of action that never, even in the most critical times, had he permitted himself to think about.

Bucholz had an older brother who kept a second-hand furniture business in a cellar on Allen Street. He was his only relation in America and the sculptor religiously kept away from him, because, as he contemptuously had explained to others, he was only an "alright-nik!" Both brothers found a satisfying need of avoiding one another. They had not met or written to one another for seven years although they lived within walking distance of each other. Bucholz, always next to starvation, never asked him for help. Now he decided to swallow his pride and approach him. After all, was he not of his own flesh and blood? A plan formed itself in his mind. But Dvoyrelè was as yet to know nothing of it.

Bucholz shaved, put on his best shirt and adjured Dvoyrelè not to leave the studio until his return.

"I am calling on a friend to talk over a very important matter," he said. "I shall be back soon."

After he had gone, Dvoyrelè looked about her anxiously. How was she to make the studio a fit place to live in? All the rubbish that lay strewn over the floor she swept into a corner and began to sort the collars, shirts, slippers, books and picture frames into some semblance of order. She collected a few broken teacups and some rusty pots and pans as well as some plates, and safely deposited them in an orange crate which she placed in a corner. She was so absorbed in her work that she did not notice the door open. Bucholz entered, carrying on his back an iron folding bed and a new mattress. Behind him came a negro, bent double under the weight of a kitchen closet and a few chairs.

Dvoyrelè could hardly believe her own eyes. Where could he have gotten the money to buy all those fine things?

"Now come along, Dvoyrelè," said Bucholz with unrestrained enthusiasm, "and let's buy some dishes and cutlery! I've got twenty dollars."

Dvoyrelè laughed.

"What do we need dishes and cutlery for? We don't intend to eat at home."

Dvoyrelè washed her face and hands at the sink and changed her dress. Then she went out with him.

When they passed a hardware store Bucholz stopped before a little gas stove that was displayed in the window. He took a great liking to it and wanted to buy it on the spot.

"But we don't need a stove!" protested Dvoyrelè. "Haven't we an oil stove at home?"

"Then what is it that we stand in need of?"

"Quilts," said Dvoyrelè shyly.

Accordingly, Bucholz led her to Little Italy on First Avenue. But instead of quilts they bought some highly colorful Oriental strips of cloth.

"They'll serve two purposes," said Bucholz. "They'll keep us warm as well as be decorative."

Dvoyrelè looked skeptical.

"They'll be decorative without a doubt," she said with a smile, "but I doubt whether they'll be very warm."

Then Dvoyrelè bought linens, sheets, towels, and other apparently needless things, at least so thought Bucholz.

No Rabbi Married Them

After which they returned, overloaded with their purchases, to the studio. They slowly mounted the stairs, Bucholz leading the way. Suddenly Dvoyrelè heard a very familiar groan. She stopped, frightened and confused. At the head of the stairs before the studio door sat her mother! A white compress was tied about her head. She sat on the stairs and swayed to and fro as if she were praying. And a few steps farther, against the door of the studio, stood Anshel with his arms folded behind his back and silently regarded them. Near by stood Solomon. He looked impatient. Obviously he was in a great hurry. He tried to calm his parents.

"All we've got to know," he said in a low voice, "is whether they have been legally married by a judge. That's how it's done in America."

At the last words Anshel nodded his head sarcastically. But catching sight of Bucholz and Dvoyrelè he grew frightened, turned pale and mumbled:

"There, Surè, comes your daughter, your son-in-law, and their household goods!"

Surè felt so crushed and broken-hearted that she could only echo pointlessly in a weeping monotone what Anshel had said:

"My daughter, my son-in-law and their household goods!"

At this Solomon grew angry.

"What's wrong with you folks anyway?" he asked with irritation. "Here in America every young man and woman has a right to do whatever he or she pleases. It's a free country!"

"I know, I know that far too well, my son," snarled Anshel.

Bucholz, utterly taken aback, looked at Dvoyrelè, perplexed and at a loss. But the latter recovered her composure and in what sounded to the sculptor an almost matter-of-fact voice, as if she had prepared herself for the scene all along, she asked:

"How do you all come here?"

"Oh, we came to see with what kind of man you eloped," ironically joked father. "No doubt he is a millionaire. In America one elopes only with millionaires! That's how it's done here. I know all about it. I read about it in the newspapers."

"Father, father! Please!" protested Solomon.

"Let's go inside. There we will talk it over better," said Dvoyrelè quietly. "The neighbors may come out and overhear what we say."

"Dvoyrelè is right," said Solomon.

Bucholz dug his hand into his pocket for the key to the studio, but as if the Devil himself had designed it, he could not find it. He emptied every pocket, in the meantime revealing to the watchful eyes of the Zlotnik family, all that they contained, which naturally could not raise him much in their estimation. At last he produced the key, and unlocking the door, led the way into the studio.

Father rambled over the room, studiously eying everything before him, the broken furniture, the sculptures and the moist cloths wrapped about them.

"When I look at a palace, I soon know what kind of a count lives in it," he dryly remarked as if to himself.

Surè now found her speech. She pulled a crumpled piece of paper from her pocket.

"You left me, daughter, a note in which you wrote that you were leaving home and that you will never come back," she tearfully began. "Have I deserved such treatment from you? What harm have I ever done you?"

Here Solomon interrupted and in order to ease the general constraint good-humoredly said:

"You have no right to complain, mother! No tragedy has befallen Dvoyrelè. Such things do happen in America."

No Rabbi Married Them

And addressing himself to Bucholz he continued apologetically:

"My parents are only greenhorns. They still think and live in the old way. Let us now talk business. My sister has left home. Now we have come here to discover for ourselves with what kind of man she is ready to throw her lot. We would like to know your intentions. We are her nearest relations and we have a right to know."

Bucholz stood in the center of the studio and did not know what to answer or do. He nodded his head foolishly to everything Solomon said just as if he were beating out the time for him.

"We want to know," demanded Anshel sternly, "whether you were married by a Rabbi in the Jewish way or whether by a judge in the American way."

"Dvoyrelè is my wife, my true wife!" cried Bucholz with tragic earnestness, beating his breast for emphasis. "Yes! my true wife!"

The last words Bucholz almost shouted so that Solomon quaked with fright.

"Well, I guess that makes everything all right," he said hastily, turning to his parents.

Then he went on to explain.

"That's the way things are done in America. When a young lady loves a man she is not obliged to obtain her parents' consent in order to marry him."

At bottom Solomon was pleased with Dvoyrelè's elopement. It did not cost him anything.

"What is all right?" demanded Anshel. "Have they been married according to Jewish law?"

"You've heard him say so yourself that they are husband and wife," said Solomon with a shrug of his shoulders, and addressing Bucholz he continued with great elegance and courtesy: "Please accept my congratulations! Allow me to introduce myself. I am Solomon Zlotnik, Dvoyrelè's brother, of the firm of Aronson Shoe Company. Dvoyrelè, why don't you say something or introduce me to your husband?"

But Anshel would not be silenced. Repeatedly he shouted:

"What's all right — what? Have they been married by a Rabbi? Tell me — yes or no!"

"Why do you shout so? Do you think this is the old country?" asked Solomon heatedly, anxious to impress Bucholz that he was not a greenhorn. "In America a marriage performed by a judge is just as good as one performed by a Rabbi."

Here mother burst into lamentation:

"Why is all this coming to me, Dvoyrelè?" she cried. "I always dreamed of the happy hour when I myself would lead you under the marriage canopy."

"Idiot!" snapped Anshel witheringly. "There is no necessity of your leading any one under the marriage canopy. Don't you know this is America? Come! Let's get out of here as soon as we can! I never want to look at her face again. Don't you see this is America? They have other customs here. Men and women live together without the sanction of God."

And Anshel seized Surè's hand and began pulling her toward the door.

"Why did you do it, why?" wept mother, with outstretched, pleading hands to Dvoyrelè.

"Idiot!" snarled Anshel, beside himself with rage and pain. "Why do you stand here? To whom are you addressing yourself? That creature has neither heart, pity nor conscience! Come away with me this instant, Surè!"

And Dvoyrelè turned her head away and murmured in a choking voice as her parents passed through the door:

"I'm sorry, mother! Believe me, I couldn't do it any other way."

"Greenhorns — not long in the country — you can well

see that!" apologetically explained Solomon to Bucholz as he retreated through the door after his parents.

.   .   .   .

When they were left alone, Dvoyrelè ran to Bucholz and laid her head wearily on his breast. He enfolded her protectingly in his arms.

Chapter 6

SURÉ IS CONFUSED

■■■■■■

DVOYRELÈ'S flight created an upheaval in Anshel's home. Little by little the new arrivals had begun to take root in the Ghetto life of New York but now Surè became convinced that the entire foundation of their lives was giving way. Anshel was constantly in a state of anger and excitement. He never spoke of Dvoyrelè. Yet it was apparent to all that the thought of her never left him for an instant but tormented him night and day. Needing an outlet for his growing pain he roundly abused Surè in and out of season. He expressed his disapproval of everything she said or did. The food she cooked was atrocious. Why was she not severer with the children? The work he did was killing him, he complained.

The relations between him and his children grew more tense from day to day. He quarreled with them incessantly although he stood somewhat in fear of the older children and let them alone. After Dvoyrelè's departure the financial burdens of the family were borne principally by Moses. As for Gedaliah, even though he studied at night, he nevertheless worked hard during the day in order that he might contribute towards his upkeep. The family would be in a fine pickle, thought Anshel gloomily, should his two financial pillars decide to move out of the house! The little ones, on the other hand, he did not treat with silk gloves. He raged at them at every opportunity and in that way gave vent to the accumulated bitterness and woe in his soul. He found fault with them of a sudden because they refused to say their prayers, although in the past he had resigned himself to the inevitable with a philosophic sigh.

"Tell me, please," he would say to one or the other of his boys with crushing irony, "when do you intend to elope with a Gentile wench? Are you seriously thinking perhaps of joining the Catholic Church? That's America for you! That is the way things are done here."

These polite sarcasms uttered half in jest often resulted in unpleasant scenes between Anshel and his boys, to the great unhappiness of mother.

He spent sleepless nights keeping anguished vigil. When he knew that Surè was awake he suppressed his woe but no sooner did he think her asleep than he tossed about in his bed groaning piteously:

"Father in Heaven! My daughter lives in sin! Have mercy!"

"What ails you, Anshel? Why don't you sleep?" mother would cry, starting up from her sleep. She well knew what ailed him without asking. It cut her to the heart to see him suffer so.

"I sleep — I sleep," muttered Anshel under his breath and he turned savagely to the wall so that the spring creaked alarmingly.

"Would you like me to speak to *her* again?" asked Surè hopefully.

"Idiot!" he barked back. "What good would that do? Would you ask her to leave him? That would make matters a thousand times worse."

"It isn't that!" explained Surè. "I will ask her to marry him according to the Law of Moses, like all good Jewish daughters."

"But didn't she tell you that she is already married in the American style?" continued Anshel with exasperation.

257

"I don't see what good you will accomplish by going to see her again."

"Why do you turn away from her?" Surè bitterly reproached him. "She is no apostate to the Faith!"

To all this Anshel could only rage.

"Cow, horse, sheep, hen!" he abused her, enumerating all the creatures in the animal kingdom.

Surè prudently held her tongue.

But she could find no rest. No matter what she was doing the obsession of her daughter living in sin with a man rose to torment her. She felt her body convulsed by a nameless pain. Her knees shook with terror. Her heart beat like a trip hammer. Often, moved by an impulse she could hardly explain to herself, she would hastily draw her kerchief about her head and run out to seek Dvoyrelè.

"Fool!" she would upbraid herself. "Where am I running?"

She did not even know where her daughter lived. The first and only time she had gone to see her, Solomon had led her there. So after running a few blocks, wringing her hands in frustration, she slowly retraced her steps homeward and resumed her washing at the tub.

"I will wait until Moses will return home from the country," she consoled herself. "Moses is clever. He will advise me what to do."

Whenever Moses arrived from the country, weighted down by his packs of merchandise, she would prudently wait until Anshel left for the factory in Brooklyn. Then she prepared his breakfast in the way he liked: eggs fried with sliced onions. And when she saw that he liked it she would approach him and say:

"Dear child, may God shower many blessings on you!"

Then in a coaxing voice:

"Will you take me to see Dvoyrelè? I must see her!"

"It's no use, mother!" he would say with pity in his

Surè Is Confused

voice. "Don't interfere! You'll make matters worse! She will have to sleep in the bed she has made for herself."

"But, Moses darling, I cannot find any rest!" mother moaned piteously. "I feel heartbroken when I think of her."

"You will accomplish nothing by your interference," stubbornly insisted Moses. "He might abandon her yet! We don't know exactly how things stand between them."

And mother wrung her hands in anguish and moaned:

"Dear child, I can find no rest when I remind myself that my daughter is living with a man in sin!"

"Don't speak this way, mother!" protested Moses reproachfully. "Isn't she his wife? Didn't they get married in court? Solomon told me that in America this is regarded as the proper way of getting married and just as if a Rabbi performed the ceremony. Now you can understand why I don't wish to take you to Dvoyrelè. You might spoil everything. After all, he is an American boy and may not understand your intentions. Just leave it to Dvoyrelè! Surely she knows what she is about."

"My child, I will give you no rest until you take me to Dvoyrelè," obstinately persisted Surè. "I am ready to promise you that I will not speak about this subject at all to her. Only I must see her! Isn't she my child too, my own flesh and blood?"

And Surè burst into convulsive sobs.

"Who ever said she isn't?" asked Moses soothingly. "Only you musn't interfere!"

Finally Moses had to give in. But instead of conducting her to Dvoyrelè's home he led her to the dress shop where she worked.

"What! Is she working?" exclaimed mother indignantly. "Did she have to get married for that? What kind of marriage is hers anyway?"

"There! You're beginning all over again!" complained

259

Moses wearily. "In America parents have no right to interfere in such matters. How do you know what their relations
are? And were he to decide upon leaving her, what will you
do about it? Would you like that better?"

"All right, son, I won't say another word about it, even if
my heart will break!" promised Surè tearfully.

Moses deposited his mother before the entrance to Dvoyrelè's shop. There she set herself to watch for her daughter
when she would emerge after work.

When Surè saw her daughter coming out of the factory
building still dressed in her faded old jacket that was
trimmed with yellow fox, bald in spots, and which Moses
had helped her buy for the last holidays, she grew sad and
heavy hearted.

"Where is your trousseau, daughter mine?" bitterly commented mother in her thoughts.

She then left her hiding place and hastily approached her.

"Good evening, daughter," she said, with affected calm.

At first Dvoyrelè looked alarmed. Then, with her well-
known little smile as if nothing had ever come between them,
she said, "What are you doing here, mother?"

"I have come to see you," said mother and she trembled
violently. Then in a bitterly lamenting voice:

"So you are still working, daughter! Married and working! What a life!"

And tears sprang to Surè's eyes.

"But you too work, mother! And aren't you married?"
asked Dvoyrelè, smiling, and put her arms about her.

"I work for my children," exclaimed Surè in extenuation.

"Well, I work for my husband," countered Dvoyrelè.
"Didn't you too work for your husband?"

"Now, Dvoyrelè, where is your trousseau? I see that you
are still wearing your old jacket with the fox collar," said
mother, a look of tender solicitude creeping into her eyes.

Surè Is Confused

"If you feel that way about it, mother, then why didn't you buy me a new outfit?"

"You never gave me the chance. I never had the slightest inkling of your intention to marry."

"Let that not worry you," laughed Dvoyrelè playfully. "Better tell me, mother, how you are feeling. Do you manage to make ends meet without me?"

"God knows it's hard for us to get along. I cannot tell you the half of it. When the first of the month arrives I am at my wits' end to know where I will get the money for the rent and the gas."

"What about Moses?"

"What can you expect of him? He does the best he possibly can and a good deal more than that. The new rooms we have taken are proving quite a drain on our funds. I dread to think what would happen to us at home without his assistance."

"In that case, mother, it might be desirable for you to take in a boarder in my place."

"That's what the menfolk advise me to do. Only I oppose their wishes. I still believe, hope and pray that you will return home again soon."

"Return home!" laughed Dvoyrelè gayly. "And if I return home who will take care of my child?"

"Your child?" asked Surè, bewildered.

"Yes, mother, you have your children to take care of and I have one of my own," said Dvoyrelè and she embraced her mother and kissed her with great warmth. "Now good-by, mother. I must run home and cook dinner. My child is waiting for me there."

Dvoyrelè suddenly noticed Moses standing half concealed behind a fruit stand and she was anxious to ward off further discussion about her marriage. So she hurried off, casting a tender look at her mother in parting.

"Dvoyrelè! Dvoyrelè!" Surè called piteously after her.

The Mother

"I will see you some other time, mother," shouted Dvoy-relè to her as she boarded a street car.

"Moses, son," wept Surè as Moses ran up to her, "I understand nothing any more — nothing — nothing! It is time that I die!"

Chapter 7

SURÉ'S POTS ARE SPICK AND SPAN

▪▪▪▪▪▪▪

SURÉ lay awake on her bed. She tried to imagine what would happen to her brood if she were to die. Most of her children could well take care of themselves. They needed her no longer. Solomon was married, also Dvoyrelè in her own way. Moses was doing a flourishing business as a customer-peddler and her scholar, Gedaliah, was also self-supporting. They too no longer stood in need of her. They would grow to manhood without her aid and guidance. But what would Anshel and little Feigelè do without her? Who would wash the little one's frocks and dress her for school? How could Anshel possibly do without her? Surè shuddered in the dark.

And in the dimness of her consciousness arose the conviction that she was to go on a very long journey. For that journey she must prepare herself and leave everything behind her. Before her mind passes a procession of possible consequences. She sees Anshel rising at dawn. Instead of saying his prayers he prepares coffee for the children. At night he returns home, dead tired from his day's labor. He can hardly stand, so tired he feels. But instead of sitting down to a prepared dinner, he potters about the kitchen stove cooking the evening meal for the children. It certainly would never occur to him to take a strange woman into the house to cook for him!

Again she sees Anshel standing at the tub. He is washing

263

The Mother

Feigelè's little frock and underclothes so that she might look neat as a pin in school the next morning. Her dark ruminations were interrupted suddenly by a loud cough from Anshel. She was filled with wrath towards herself:

"How idiotic of me to think of such mad things! How can I depart from this life so soon? My time hasn't come yet."

It gave Surè pleasure to lie silently in the dark and let her thoughts drift like rudderless boats on the sea of consciousness, until she would fall asleep. She was tired and sleepy. Her limbs felt disjointed and lay limp upon the bed. How could she bring them together again, she wondered? Her weariness gave her pleasure. If only she could lie, lie that way and sink into ——!

The clock struck six. She knew it was time to get up. She had to get up! No doubt, thought Surè, Anshel was at that moment lying with open eyes and afraid to move lest he wake her. Of course she was up to all of Anshel's tricks! There really was no earthly use for her to lie in bed any longer. It was growing late. Yet Surè made no motion to rise. Why didn't she get up? "What kind of holiday is it to-day?" she raged inwardly. Nevertheless she lay inert in bed. It felt so pleasant to lie there! Never had it felt so pleasant to her before.

She watched Anshel dress. She heard Moses stirring in his corner where he lay. What was to be done? What ailed her? Nothing ailed her. On the contrary, her body, although tired, felt light as air. She abandoned herself to the pleasure of her weariness.

"Surè!" called Anshel apprehensively. "Aren't you feeling well?"

"I feel well," murmured Surè, "only I don't feel like getting up."

Anshel looked puzzled. He had never before heard Surè give such an explanation for lying late in bed.

"Well, if you don't feel like getting up, remain in bed" he advised her.

"But who will prepare breakfast?"

"Don't worry! It will be made."

Despite his assurance, Surè made an effort to rise but she fell back on her pillow.

"Anshel!" she groaned. "I don't know what ails me."

"You must have caught cold," Anshel comforted her. "Most likely, if you will continue lying in bed during the daytime, you'll feel much better by night."

"You are right," she said.

Anshel wondered much over her answer. Never before had she so docilely submitted to him in such matters. No, decidedly, it wasn't according to her wont! He became alarmed and going nearer to her bed he asked anxiously:

"What ails you, Surè?"

"Nothing, I'm only very tired."

"Then lie in bed and rest."

"I think I'll do so," she answered with a deep sigh and wearily stretched her limbs.

Anshel wondered much. That was not her way of doing things. No, not at all!

When night began to fall Surè again ruminated in the silence of her thoughts.

"Why do I lie now?" she raged within.

If she had indulged herself that luxury in her old home in the cellar, well and good. There were kind neighbors to take care of the children and the cooking. But here, in her new home, she had not yet had sufficient time to get acquainted with the neighbors. Anyway they were not her kind. How could she possibly impose upon them! She was a mere stranger to them. She decided to lie in bed until the children returned home from school. Little by little she sank into a stupor. She imagined that she had died and now it was well with her. She lay in bed and it was so pleasant

265

to lie still. There was no need for her to stir a limb or even to get out of bed. No more the need for worrying, to think with dread of the approaching first of the month, of the unpaid rent, of the washing and the children's shoes, of the grocer's and the butcher's accounts. All that concerned her no longer. There was nothing more for her to do but to lie in bed and never more rise from it.

Then incidents from her childhood rose before her. She saw her mother enter the room, attired in her magnificent Paisley skirt and her ancient pearl tiara on her head. Surè was filled with wonder at her mother's visit. Wasn't she dead and lying in consecrated ground in Lentshutz among her forefathers? How could she have crossed the ocean to America? A miracle then — a great miracle!

The room in which Surè lay now became transformed. The old home in Poland lived in its stead. In the center of the room, suspended from a thick rafter, hung the quaint old glass chandelier. And Surè was filled with astonishment.

"What is that?" she asked herself. "Where am I, in America or in Poland?"

She conjured up before her the twilight before Sabbath eve, so many weary years ago. Her pots hang on their nails, spick and span. In a corner of the kitchen stands little Dvoyrelè washing her hair in a basin of hot water. Dvoyrelè is still a little girl, Gedaliah but an infant, and Meyer yet "the suckling child."

Surè suddenly emerged from her stupor with a start.

"I must get up! Why do I continue to lie here? Anshel will soon come home from the synagogue."

When she opened her eyes she saw that little Feigelè had just come in with her schoolbooks.

"Heavens!" cried Surè with a start. "Where am I — in America or in the old country?"

And she again sank back upon her pillow, this time wide

awake, and looked at Feigelè. She only now began to understand what was happening to her.

"Who will take care of Feigelè, if I die?" she asked herself tearfully. "On whose hands will I leave her? Who will wash her hair?"

Thinking in this wise, with determination in her face, Surè rose in her bed and pulled the coverlet from her.

She had but taken two steps when she felt her knees sagging under her. She grew dizzy. Her head seemed to fly off her body and her senses whirled round and round.

"Mama!" screamed Feigelè, terrified. "What ails you, mama?"

And she ran to Surè who lay huddled up in a heap near the bed.

Surè did not answer.

Feigelè screamed in terror and opening the door into the hallway called for help. Some neighbors ran in and put Surè back to bed.

.   .   .   .

When Anshel came home from work he found Solomon and his young wife at Surè's bedside and, what was most alarming, a doctor who was holding a whispered consultation with his eldest son. The children walked on tiptoe or sat with frightened, pale faces in their corners. Surè lay in bed with a hectic flush on her cheeks. Wisps of her hair, which had already begun to turn gray, clung moist with perspiration to her forehead. Never before had Anshel seen her look so blooming and with such rosy cheeks. Only her lips had turned blue. She lay with wide open eyes. Their pupils were dilated. There was a look of frozen horror in them. When she saw Anshel standing beside her she looked guiltily at him with her great eyes as though she were asking his forgiveness for indulging herself in the luxury of an illness.

"Surè! What ails you?" asked Anshel, calling her by her

name which he never did except in moment of great tenderness.

"Anshel!" She moved her lips piteously and stretched out to him her hard calloused hands that appeared now so unnaturally bloodless and corpse-like.

"What ails you, Surè?" persisted Anshel. He was fairly livid and trembling.

"I don't know, Anshel," she answered wearily.

"What does the doctor say?" asked Anshel of his son in a choking voice. He tried hard to suppress his tears.

"The doctor advises that mother be taken to a hospital."

"To a hospital!" echoed Anshel wonderingly. He looked completely bewildered and overwhelmed.

"You see, the doctor doesn't know yet what is wrong with her. So he thinks it safer to have her under observation in a hospital."

"Doesn't know yet what is wrong with her!" Anshel listlessly echoed, as if in a trance.

Solomon and his wife left. Anshel alone remained. The children sat in the kitchen. Anshel seated himself near his wife's bed. His eyes wandered fugitively like hers, rapt in sickly thoughts and pale dreams. Mechanically he swayed to and fro just as he did when chanting the prayers in the synagogue. He said nothing but from time to time he would rouse himself and ask:

"Do you feel any pain, Surè?"

"No." Surè would silently shake her head.

Anshel sank back again into his trance and continued rapidly swaying to and fro just as if he were praying.

"Go and have your dinner, Anshel," gasped Surè, speaking with a great effort. "The children will prepare it for you."

But Anshel hears nothing and continues his swaying to and fro — to and fro — like the pendulum of a clock.

Surè's Pots Are Spick and Span

Moses arrived, weighted down by his packs of merchandise. No sooner did he enter the kitchen than he knew that some misfortune had happened to mother. He could read that in the children's drawn looks and silence.

"What has happened?" he cried.

"Mother is sick."

He threw down his packs and tiptoed into his mother's room. He looked at father and could hardly recognize him. During the few days since he had seen him, he seemed to have grown perceptibly older, grayer, shrunken. Frightened, he approached mother's bed. Anshel roused himself from his reveries and recognized his son.

"Is that you, Moses?" he asked.

"What ails mother?"

"Mother collapsed this afternoon. She will be taken to a hospital."

"Hospital," muttered Moses, turning pale.

Mother looked at Moses with her large fever-glowing eyes. She implored him about something, looked at him mutely like a dumb animal who cannot speak but can only look and look....

"Mother!" almost shouted Moses.

"Do you want anything, Surè darling?" gushed Anshel tenderly, putting his ear to her lips.

"My son!" murmured mother's lips.

"She says: 'My son,'" repeated Anshel piously.

.   .   .   .

No one slept that night in Anshel's home. No matter how much Moses pleaded with his father that he lie down and get some sleep and rest, the latter remained obstinate in his decision not to leave his wife's bedside. He sat there silent and thoughtful, swaying incessantly as if he were deep in prayer. Surè looked imploringly at him, urging him with her eyes to seek some rest. With almost imperceptibly moving lips she whispered:

"Anshel! Anshel!"

"What is it, Surè?" asked Anshel, putting his ear to her mouth.

"Go to sleep, Anshel," she continued weakly.

"No," answered Anshel determinedly.

Even though mother tossed about in a raging fever she knew everything that went on about her. Not for one instant did her eyes close. Deprived of speech, she spoke with her eyes and so communicated her wishes to Anshel and the children. They spoke with an eloquence that lips may never have. One moment they bade eternal farewell to her brood, in another they consoled or implored. Mother spoke the language of her eyes because they were best suited to what she wanted to convey. Moses understood everything mother felt and thought and he faithfully promised to fulfill her wishes and to care for the children until they would grow up. After this assurance Surè grew more tranquil. Now she could surrender her soul to God's keeping. Wearily she closed her eyes and gave the impression of having fallen asleep. But she did not sleep. Disturbed by some disquieting thought, she would start up again and turn her glowing, swooning eyes on Moses. He readily understood her request.

"Shall I call Dvoyrelè?" he asked.

"What an idea!" said Anshel, shocked out of his lethargy.

"Mother wants to see her," insisted Moses, looking at her for confirmation.

"There's plenty of time for that," said Anshel, his face distorted with pain. "It's still dark."

Once more Moses looked at mother to reassure her. Silently he nodded his head. Surè understood. Mutely she thanked him through her half-closed eyes. Little by little her eyelids drooped — drooped, like the setting of the sun upon the sea.

Next morning when the hospital attendants carried her down on a stretcher to a waiting ambulance, the weeping and shrieking of her children startled her for an instant out of her stupor. She tore open her eyes but she understood no more what was happening to her. When they carried her through the kitchen her eyes fell upon her beloved pots hanging on their nails over the stove. Never had she seen them look so spick and span and sparkling. She was filled with great wonder. Who had scoured them so for her in gracious token of the Holy Sabbath?

Chapter 8

CANDLES SPUTTER IN THE SYNAGOGUE

■■■■■■■

OUTSIDE the hospital, Surè's children wandered about disconsolately like lost sheep. Their eyes were red and swollen with weeping. They talked to one another in an undertone. At the entrance stood Anshel. The past few days, since Surè's illness, he had physically fallen away to a shadow of his former self. Unwearyingly throughout the day, he made many futile attempts to force his way into the hospital but each time the attendant on duty slammed the door in his face. He stood tense and distracted and kept on repeating to the impatient attendant:

"What do you mean, you won't let me in!"

"That's the rule, mister."

"What do I care about your rules! This is a matter of life and death."

Solomon, who had been whispering something to Moses, now came up to Anshel and tried to calm him.

"Don't worry, father!" he said. "I have just spoken to the hospital superintendent and have arranged with him that mother be transferred from the general ward to a private room."

"Transferring her! Transferring her!" almost shouted Anshel. "In other words, that means that — "

And Anshel bit his lips until they bled.

"Mother's condition is critical," said Solomon and put his hand over his eyes to hide his tears.

272

Candles Sputter in the Synagogue

"In other words — in other words — " mumbled Anshel almost with stupefaction, biting his lips. "Why don't they let us in now?"

"Be patient, father. They'll let us in soon," said Solomon, and burst into tears.

Moses hid his face in his hands and wept aloud. Gedaliah and the little ones, hearing their older brothers weep, could not restrain their own tears.

Only Feigelè was not there. Solomon's wife had taken her away to her home. Dvoyrelè stood apart, dressed in her faded little jacket, trimmed with yellow fox that was bald in spots. No one spoke to her. She alone did not weep. Her face looked frozen with horror and suffering but a strange little smile hovered bravely on her lips. She stood apart, ignored by everybody as if she had been cast out of the family. Every one felt that it was she who had caused mother's illness. She too felt that way but somehow without any qualms of conscience. So she stood apart and bitterly turned her eyes away from her kin.

Dvoyrelè had seen her mother twice since the latter's illness. On one of these occasions her mother had not seen her for she lay with closed eyes. Their second meeting took place in the hospital. Then Surè fixed her daughter with her eyes. But she said nothing, nor even moved her lips. As she looked, however, her great anguished eyes grew moist with tears. The children, who were present at her bedside, on seeing her weep also burst into tears. Dvoyrelè alone did not cry. She bent over mother and whispered:

"Do you recognize me, mother?"

Surè nodded her head slightly in confirmation.

At this Moses could no longer restrain his anguish and burst into sobs.

"See what you have done, Dvoyrelè, just see!" he lamented as the tears trickled down his freckled, weatherbeaten face.

The Mother

"Moses!" upbraided Solomon sternly. "Hold your tongue now!"

Anshel was not present at the time. He had purposely absented himself. He refused to have anything further to do with the daughter who had abandoned the religion of her forefathers.

And Dvoyrelè answered nothing. She stood silent and tragic. She alone did not shed one tear.

At the time when Anshel and the children were besieging the hospital entrance, Surè's mind began to wander. She thought that she found herself in a great synagogue. Long sand-filled boxes, in which were fixed huge memorial candles as during the Day of Atonement, filled the interior. Only the candles remained unlit. On the walls, suspended from iron pegs, hung many pots. They looked freshly scoured and glistened like mirrors. Surè was filled with wonder.

"What are pots doing in a synagogue?" she asked herself.

She looked closely at the pots. Why, good Heavens! Weren't they all her own beloved pots that she had brought along with her from the old country? One after another she recognized them. Why, if that isn't the large, round-bellied pot with the cracked bottom which she had acquired by inheritance from her sainted mother! And that one over there with the high glaze and cavernous bottom she had bought for special Passover use! But what were all her pots doing in a synagogue? For she readily could see that a great congregation of Jews were present. They were garbed in white robes and swathed in their prayer shawls. But why weren't they praying? They were waiting impatiently for some one. For whom? Among them, on the rostrum, by the side of the Rabbi, and before an unrolled Scroll of the Law stood Anshel. He too wore the white sacerdotal robe of a priest and he was wrapped in his prayer shawl. But why didn't he cantillate the sacred words of the Torah?

And Surè wondered much. What were they waiting for?

Candles Sputter in the Synagogue

And why did she have to lie in bed? It was certainly high
time to get up! But how could she? She felt chained to her
bed. Why was she chained to it? All of a sudden Anshel
disappeared from before her eyes. Now, where could he have
gone to? But where are the others, the great congregation
of Jews, wearing the white sacerdotal robes of priests and
wrapped in their prayer shawls? All had disappeared. Now
the synagogue was deserted. Only she was there — alone.

Four walls closed in about her — bare — empty — alone
— only she — alone.

Then opened a grave underneath her bed and it sucked
her in. Alone — alone — no more Anshel — no more children — no more anybody! Where were they all?

In terror she opened her eyes and looked about her. Then
she became aware of the presence of Anshel and the children at her bedside. All of the children were there, even
Dvoyrelè. And at the foot of the bed stood Anshel. He was
swaying to and fro as if in prayer and he was uttering pious
words. Surè saw everything and regarded each one separately. There stood her first-born and his wife who had presented her with a black lace shawl to adorn herself for the
synagogue. Impractical child! Where do I find the time for
going to synagogue? Surely God will forgive me my sin.
Had I not to prepare breakfast for the menfolk? Why was
Moses crying so? She felt an impelling desire to say to
him: "Don't cry, Moses darling!"

And who was it standing in the corner over there with
such a pale tragic face? God be praised! it was Dvoyrelè
herself! Surè wanted to tell her something important —
something that absolutely had to be told. All the time she
had been thinking about it and tormented herself with the
fear that she might forget it. And just now, of all absurdi-
ties, it had slipped from her mind! No! She had to recollect!
And she tore open her eyes by the command of her rapidly
failing will and looked at Dvoyrelè. How hard she tried to

275

remember! Almost — almost she recollected but the weeping and the clamoring of the others rose like a dividing wall between her memory and Dvoyrelè.

Surè's heart breaks listening to her children's cries, and the thought that she had forgotten that which she so yearned to impart to her daughter tormented her. Then she strained her mind until she felt it give way in a swooning weakness. Oh! God be praised! There she had it at last!

"Dvoyrelè!" her mind shouted although not a sound escaped her lips. "Dvoyrelè! I shall never lie peacefully in my grave if you will not live like a virtuous Jewish daughter!"

Thank God! She had remembered in time after all! Now Dvoyrelè had heard her and all was well. A terrible burden was lifted from her soul. Now she would be able to listen to her children's clamoring once more. And through mother's mind again flashed her final admonitions to her little flock and, as before, not a sound escaped her lips:

"Remember, Meyer," she tenderly pleaded, "that you must not fail to say your prayers every day and to recite the 'Kaddish' after my death. Also you must revere your father and be devoted to him. Promise me, children, that you will be good to father and not forget him in his old age."

God be praised! The children had heard her! They had promised her to fulfill all that she desired of them. Now her heart grew so light, so free, so joyful! It is good so. Now she may close her tired eyes and rest.

Wearily mother closed her eyes and turned her head to the wall.

Her children's cries would not let her depart so soon. She heard them. Her fledglings cried to her: "Mother darling! Mother!" She had to answer them! By a tremendous effort she tore her eyes open again and despairingly looked at her children. For an instant she recognized them. Then they became blurred and she saw them as if through a mist. But in her ears rang out sharp and clear the agonized voice of Anshel. He did not weep as did the others but his voice arose in fervent prayer. She sought him anxiously with her eyes but she could not find him.

"He stands at the foot of my bed and he is chanting the prayers for the dying," thought Surè, overjoyed.

Now she was afraid no longer. She grew tranquil, and submitted to her destiny with a loving smile. . . .

Soon the great memorial candles sputtered in their wooden sand-boxes in the synagogue. How wonderfully illuminated the synagogue looked! The elders stood garbed in the white sacerdotal robes of priests and swathed in their prayer shawls. Then they commenced the service. How fervently they chanted! And on the rostrum, at the foot of her bed, stood Anshel in his white priestly robe and prayer shawl and he cantillated Holy Scripture. Never had she heard him intone that way! An indescribable joy wrapped about her heart and she fell asleep to the ardent singing of Anshel's prayers.

Out of the dark night some one was coming to meet her. It was her mother. She was dressed in her beautiful Paisley skirt and on her head she wore her pearl tiara. And she said to her in the most caressing of voices:

"Child! Don't be afraid!"

After that her children's loud lamentations did not succeed in calling her back. . . .

·   ·   ·   ·   ·   ·   ·

Drawn by a cadaverous white horse, a black decrepit-looking hearse creaked its monotonous way through the noisy streets of New York's East Side. Close behind it followed on foot Anshel and his children. Their piteous cries and lamentations drew the attention of the passers-by. After them followed their countrymen, headed by Itzikel the Sexton of the Congregation. Bringing up the rear of the funeral procession came a black carriage in which rode Solomon's wife and her parents. Upon the special request of Moses, the procession wound its way through Allen Street so that Surè's old neighbors near her cellar home might have the opportunity of paying her the last honors as she was being carried to her grave.

Before their cellar home waited the neighbors and with many a groan and tear followed the hearse for a few blocks. But soon they reminded themselves of their household duties. With a mute look of farewell they returned to their kitchens to carry on the life of the living.

When the hearse reached the Williamsburg Bridge, all except the immediate family departed. Surè's children, wretched and tired, climbed into the carriage. But Anshel would not leave the hearse for an instant. Holding on to a hind bar he walked the entire weary stretch on foot to the cemetery in Cypress Hills. And when the passers-by hurried along on their business, and cast an indifferent glance upon the creaking hearse that was followed by a solitary weeping man, they did not realize that a great heroine was being carried to her eternal rest. . . .

.   .   .   .

One evening when Dvoyrelè came home from her work she found the door of the studio locked and the key in its customary place. There was nothing surprising in that. Bucholz had done the same thing many times before. What made her wonder though was the cold stove in which no fire had burned that day. It was clear that Haskel had not been home all day. First she set about making the fire as usual, then she busied herself preparing dinner. In any case, she expected his arrival at any moment. But as the evening drew on and he had not come, she became restive and uneasy. The thought of eating alone was distasteful to her, despite her hunger. She decided to wait for him. So she seated herself by the little coal stove and folding her hands over her breasts even as mother was wont to do when she had some important problem to solve, she fell into deep thought. Mostly she thought about Haskel and herself. She also thought about one other matter but that frightened her and she tried hard but vainly to dismiss it from her mind. . . .

Of late, a terrifying suspicion had begun to haunt her: Haskel was not happy with her. Of course he loved her, but it was a joyless sort of love. That could be well seen. How different were her expectations of happiness from their union! She had rhapsodized about it so long until she could visualize their marriage only in the most magical hues of romance just the way it was described in novels. Her cherished dream was to work for him so that he might be free to devote himself entirely to his art. He would then be able to create all those wonderful works he had so often discussed with her as they walked through the streets on her way home from work. Was it not for this that she had broken away from all those dearest to her in order that she might come to live with him? But ever since the day she came to him he had done nothing — nothing at all. His uncompleted sculptures stood in a corner, covered and dusty. Depressed and silent he would tramp the city streets for hours at a time or spend the night with his cronies at Sholom's Café on Rutgers Square. He had altogether forgotten his work. He neither began any new work nor did he complete any of the old ones. Not a word about them ever passed his lips. Once he asked Dvoyrelè to pose for him in the nude. Listlessly he made a few sketches of her but he never completed any and nothing ever came of them.

Yes, she well knew that he was unhappy with her. His melancholy look and his despair betrayed his feelings to her. Ofttimes he tried to drown his misery in a wild abandonment of sexual love for her. . . . But of what little avail! The gray dawn in its everlasting coming rouses the night from its dreams of drunken slumber.

Why then did she stay when she knew that she was giving him no joy? Why did she stand in his way? By what moral right could she find it in her heart to return home to the studio from work every evening?

Perhaps it would be best for her to go away. She could probably take a room with another girl and continue to live away from home.

She did not try to imagine how things would be with her were she to leave Haskel. Her concern was principally with him. The question she had to answer herself was: What was better for Haskel — that she continue living with him or that she leave? Yet she feared that without her he would go to ruin, because of his helplessness. He would probably return to work in some lumberyard or wet-wash laundry and would, without a doubt, be sucked in by them so that all hope for a better life would be extinguished. Or worse yet — he would sell his art for a mess of pottage and accept commissions from some disreputable art dealer to make portrait busts from photographs. That would certainly be the last straw, thought Dvoyrelè with alarm.

Of course Haskel needed her, now more than ever! Could there be any doubt about that? Therefore she had no right to desert him. As long as he stood in need of her, whether he was happy with her or not, she felt that she had no moral right to leave him. To protect him against the world and against his own helplessness was the sacred duty she set herself to perform.

Only after it had become clear to her what would be best for her to do to further Haskel's interests and happiness, Dvoyrelè began to think about her own troubles. Her little brow wrinkled, and under the hideous light of a gas jet the barely perceptible line which during the past few weeks had become etched about her sensitive mouth stood out in painful relief. For some weeks past she had been aware of the fact that she was pregnant. Were she to let matters take their natural course she shuddered to think what the consequence would be for both of them. . . .

She still had developed no definite attitude towards the growing life within her womb. She felt only dread and a sinking feeling in her heart. Who could tell but that it might yet destroy forever all that which had appeared so necessary and holy to her and for which end she stood in such joyful readiness to bring herself as a living sacrifice! And that end was to make Haskel absolutely free so that he might be enabled to grow to his full stature as an artist. To help him realize his ideal she had left her home, had destroyed all her bridges behind her in order that she might consecrate her existence to him whom she loved.

Dvoyrelè was afraid to succumb to the dormant maternal instinct now vaguely stirring within her. With all her power she tried to resist its undermining progress. It had all come so unexpectedly — so suddenly. She was altogether unprepared for this new feeling. She regarded it as an obstacle to what she had set out to accomplish. It frightened her. And this fear crowded out everything else from her mind.

What was she to do? The mere thought of it made her heart throb painfully. Yet on one thing she was determined: Haskel was not to know of her condition. Everything that was necessary to be done in order to prevent the catastrophe would have to be done by her and by her alone. . . .

For a long time she sat thus harassed by her gloomy thoughts and haunted by a sense of inescapable doom. Her little brow became deeply wrinkled and her heart throbbed painfully. At last she heard Haskel's approaching steps. She did not see him enter — only heard him. Since the day that she had awakened to the realization that she was to become a mother her love for him had grown a hundredfold. She was happy to hear his footsteps, to feel him near her, not to see him but with closed eyes listen to his voice and to dream about her great happiness to come. . . . In the half-darkness of the studio, she now sat with closed eyes and a happy smile hovered about her lips as he entered.

"Is that you, Haskel?" she murmured.

"Yes!" he answered.

"Where have you been so long? I have been very anxious about you."

"I have found work — a job."

"Work! Job!" wondered Dvoyrelè. She opened her eyes and regarded him mutely. Then she became frightened. His clothes were in a terrible disorder, full of plaster, cement and mud. His face was bespattered with all the colors of the spectrum.

"I had my eye on that job for a long time already," he explained apologetically. "It's the kind of job at which I can earn a lot of money. If you don't believe me — there is the proof."

And he pulled some crumpled dollar bills from his pocket.

"What kind of a job?" asked Dvoyrelè accusingly.

"Tombstones."

"Tombstones!" she gasped.

"Yes, tombstones. I know the work well. I can get a job as a stonecutter any time. All I have to do is to join the union. The reason why I did not take a job until to-day was because there was no need for me to do so. When I stood in need of a few dollars to pay the rent or to buy myself some food I took on work for a day or two and that sufficed for me. But now I have decided to accept a steady job. I will have to join the union first, then I will begin making money and grow useful like all other respectable people. In any case I am afraid my sculptures will never be of any earthly use to me or to anybody else."

Dvoyrelè did not answer him. He felt the reproach in her silence. He wanted to justify himself.

Candles Sputter in the Synagogue

"The stone-cutter's yard is — far out in Brooklyn. That's why it has taken me such a long time to get home."

Dvoyrelè came near him.

"You shouldn't have taken that job," she lectured him severely and looked deeply into his eyes as was her habit.

"What then — would you have liked me better to make portrait busts from photographs? Does it really matter what I work at?"

Her head drooped.

"What about your art?" she upbraided him. "When will you find the time to model if you will become a worker?"

"Nothing will ever come of it!" he answered bitterly with a deprecating motion of his hand.

"Why do you speak this way, Haskel?" asked Dvoyrelè with a beseeching look in her eyes.

"But do be reasonable, Dvoyrelè!" cried Bucholz. "I've got to do something! It would be idiotic of me to continue wasting my time on these gewgaws and wait for recognition while you are slaving away in a sweat-shop!"

"What about the precious time you have been wasting until now?" she asked.

"That's an entirely different matter, Dvoyrelè. If I starved alone all these years — it was I who did the starving. It was no one's business what I did. If I chose I worked. If I chose not to work I lay up here in this hole like a dog in his kennel. When it gave me pleasure, I made all these clay gewgaws which you see about you."

"But why this sudden change of heart, Haskel?"

A bitter expression crept into his face.

"To-day," he said, "I feel as if a rope were tied around my neck, as if a heavy burden were weighing me down to the ground. I am powerless to turn once more to my modeling. What kind of man do you think I am, to have you sit all day at a sewing machine and earn my bread for me?"

283

These last words he fairly shouted. He was beside himself with self-disgust.

"If I work for you, I work for us," Dvoyrelè murmured almost guiltily. So low was her voice that he could hardly hear her. "Aren't we both one? You yourself have said so."

Bucholz was deeply moved at her words. It wasn't so much the words as the voice in which she uttered them. Impulsively he felt like taking her in his arms. But what would have been the use of his new resolution? Matters would have ended as they had always done before. He would have carried her playfully about the studio in his great, strong arms. Bucholz suppressed his impulse. He remained standing where he was, and angry with himself, he bit his lips.

"If you are so absolutely against my working, why don't you stop working too?" growled Bucholz at her. "In that case we will both starve. We will wander about through the streets like good-for-nothing tramps. But under no circumstances will I agree to stay home every day, eat out of your earnings and sit before the stove warming my aged carcass like a Russian Grand Duke. Under such debasing circumstances do you think it at all possible for me to do any creative work?"

"But I am no artist!" protested Dvoyrelè smilingly. "I do not need the proper mood and atmosphere for my work. What else can I do besides sewing dresses? I have nothing to complain of. I am happy when I can do something to enable you to devote yourself entirely to your art. Has my life any meaning without that?"

Bucholz remained adamant.

"I absolutely forbid you to return to your job," he insisted. "If you work I too must work. Either both of us work or both of us decide to do nothing."

Dvoyrelè laughed.

"Then how will we live?" she asked amused.

"So we won't live!" he answered with his usual consistency. "Must we live? We'll go hungry as we have so often done before. Is it absolutely necessary that one live, work and eat? My decision is final. Either both of us work or else both of us starve in company. Do you agree, Dvoyrelè?"

She nodded her head in smiling assent. The evening ended with his marching about the room with her sitting astride his shoulders and with self-deceptive dreams about a grandiose future.

. . . .

Next morning when Dvoyrelè prepared to leave for work, Bucholz barred her way. Determinedly he closed the door.

"I won't let you go to work," he said. "If you insist on going I'll follow you."

"But, child!" she tried to reason with him. "One of us has to work. Since you were made for something better than that, I take it that I am the one to work. After all, it is only for a short time until you will have completed your great works. After that it won't be necessary for me to work any more."

"Do you think so?" he asked incredulously.

"I do," she answered, earnestly looking into his eyes. "I believe that you are a great, a very great sculptor and that you were predestined to create great works of art."

Bucholz kept silent. He caught her hand and shook it vigorously. He wanted to tell her something but thought better of it. Instead he said:

"To-day, Dvoyrelè, you must not go to work. Only to-day, I beg of you. To-day we will tramp about the streets. Just see! snow is falling. Come quickly before the street cleaners shovel it away."

Together and with much hilarity they rushed out into the street.

Chapter 9

AN IDEA

∎∎∎∎∎∎∎

IT was high time for Dvoyrelè to do something. To wait any longer meant to court danger. The thought of what was coming filled her with terror. But worse than that was her fear that were she to delay much longer she might become attached to the awakening life within her womb. If that were to happen she would not be able to free herself from it. . . .

Her mind was definitely made up. She knew that she had to go through with it and that the less she struggled against it the better for her. At first she regarded the growing child within her as some inanimate object, a cancerous growth of which she had to rid herself immediately at all costs. But as the days sped by and she hesitated to take any action she began to fear that soon it would be too late to do anything. For a definite attitude towards her embryo child began to take form in Dvoyrelè's mind.

"At all costs I must get rid of it!" said she vehemently to herself. "If not for my own sake, I must do it for Haskel."

But how could she possibly do it? Tears welled up in her eyes. It would be mad to delay any longer. She must find some one to help her, some one to take counsel with.

One day, as she was thinking about it, Isabel Furster suddenly came to her mind. Why had she not thought of her before? Wasn't she a woman too and a radical? She

286

would understand — she would sympathize with her. Once Isabel had said to her:

"Little girl, each time you get into trouble come to see me."

Why not ask her advice? She would ask nothing of her but advice. In such matters only a woman can be of help.

With a hopeful heart Dvoyrelè went to see her former night-school teacher. She confessed to her everything and in justification for her decision to do away with her unborn child, she said:

"It is quite impossible. I must not give birth to the child. I have no right to enslave Haskel — to tie him down to a job. What will become of him? If he will find out that I am pregnant he won't let me work. He will accept commissions to make portrait busts from photographs. In that event, what will he ever amount to?"

Dvoyrelè could no longer restrain her tears, and she wept bitterly.

"Don't cry, dear!" said Miss Furster, putting her arms about her.

"I am not sure whether I am doing the right thing," continued Dvoyrelè, dabbing at her eyes with a handkerchief, "but I will never find any peace to think that because of me, Haskel's life and talents had gone to waste, that he had been broken by the struggle like all of us and beaten down from his exalted strivings to the inconsequential meanness of a worker's existence. I feel certain that he is a superior creature. He was made for something better than work. And he certainly is not going to be ruined because of me."

Dvoyrelè burst out weeping afresh.

"Don't cry, don't cry!" crooned Miss Furster, tenderly embracing her. "I understand you perfectly, dear."

"If you will not help me, I will have to find another way out. But I will never agree to have this child," declared

Dvoyrelè with resolution. Then she dried her eyes and grew calmer.

"I'll help you, Dvoyrelè," said Miss Furster gravely. "I understand you well and I absolutely agree with you that you must not have the child."

"In that case," cried Dvoyrelè joyfully, "it must happen during the holidays next week when Haskel will go to the country. I will have sufficient time to recover from the operation. But I want Haskel never to know of it."

"I have to make certain inquiries first," said Miss Furster thoughtfully. "Come to see me next Saturday and I will be able to tell you more definitely. I think that I will be able to manage it for you."

Dvoyrelè took her hand and with bent head murmured: "How can I possibly thank you enough?"

"Do you love Haskel very much?" asked Miss Furster suddenly.

Dvoyrelè nodded her head bashfully.

"And still you insist on undergoing the operation."

"I must! Even more than that — I want to."

"You are a darling!" exclaimed Miss Furster with enthusiasm and embraced her fondly.

.   .   .   .

When Dvoyrelè next called on Miss Furster she learned from her that she was to hold herself in readiness to enter a certain private institution during the holidays. She would have to remain there for several days. That institution had been founded by a well-known radical and birth control advocate, and was exclusively devoted to the interests of workers' wives.

The great difficulty now before Dvoyrelè was how to get Haskel out of the way. Recently he had become more observant than ever. He noticed that she was being consumed by some secret sorrow. Was she concealing something from

An Idea

him? One day he demanded of her to tell him what the trouble was. To which she evasively replied:

"The children at home are causing me a great deal of worry. I suppose I will have to go home for a few days and see what I can do for them."

"You ought to do that!" agreed Haskel wholeheartedly.

"But I am afraid that you will follow after me," said Dvoyrelè with cunning. "Remember, you mustn't do that. The folks are still angry at you."

"Rest assured, I won't come!" he promised her.

"If I were you," said Dvoyrelè coaxingly, "I'd go away to the country for several days. It must be very beautiful out there now. You will return strengthened and more cheerful."

The idea pleased Haskel. He grew enthusiastic like a child.

"A grand idea!" he said. "I'll go to my friend's farm in Connecticut."

"Just wait until the holidays next week," she begged him. "I won't be working then so that it will be possible for me to go home for several days. During my absence it will be fine for you to go to your friend's farm."

But it was far worse than she had expected. When the time came for Haskel to go he balked. With his usual contrariness he stubbornly insisted that they spend the holidays together. When she finally did succeed in packing him off to the country she felt limp and weak and all but a mass of protesting nerves. When she was reasonably certain that he had left the city she began making preparations for her impending ordeal.

On her way to the institution she had to pass through a small park. It was on a beautiful winter day. The sun smiled benevolently down upon the frozen earth. The park lay wrapped in a blanket of dazzling snow. Mothers, pushing perambulators before them, crowded all the footpaths. They

The Mother

held their babies, who smelled sweetly-sour from rich milk, up to the sun, crooned and played with them. Older children, bundled up in white woolen sweaters and mittens, made snow men and pelted each other with snowballs. For an instant Dvoyrelè stopped to contemplate the scene about her. Then quick as lightning there sped through her mind a curious thought. She saw herself among all these mothers, also pushing before her a perambulator in which lay her child. It had a short stubby nose with broad nostrils and a chin just like Haskel's. It was dressed in white woolens too. She wheeled the perambulator through the park and over the crisp dazzling snow that lay bathed in a downpour of sunshine.

Then Dvoyrelè shook off the daydream. The recollection of the tragic duty that she was about to perform made her hasten her steps.

Several days later Dvoyrelè returned home. She sighed with relief when she found that Haskel had not arrived yet. She had sufficient time to prepare for his coming, so that he might notice nothing wrong That same evening he arrived sunburnt and bubbling over with good spirits. The few days he had spent in the country had done him a world of good, he exulted. He therefore urged that in celebration of their reunion they go to see a motion picture or, better yet, make a gala night of it in an artistic café in Greenwich Village. As for money, she had nothing to worry about. He had helped his friend, the farmer, cut down some timber for which he had earned a little money.

To avoid suspicion Dvoyrelè readily assented to go with him although she still felt ill and so weak that she could walk only with great difficulty. Slowly she began to dress. She laughed much and helped to sustain his jolly mood. But soon he began to notice her pallor and her weakness.

"What ails you?" he inquired anxiously. "Why are you so pale? Aren't you well?"

An Idea

"What a silly idea!" she parried in confusion. "Of course I am well! I am only a little tired. I had so much to do at home."

Haskel looked relieved.

"How are they getting along at home?" he asked with obliging concern.

"They are getting along well enough without me," answered Dvoyrelè, growing sad.

"Why so sad?" asked Haskel, his apprehensiveness returning. "I don't know what is ailing you. I can see that some change has taken place in you since I left for the country. You look so ghastly!"

"You just imagine it, Haskel. I feel just fine."

"Perhaps it will be better if we don't go out to-night. We can postpone it for some other night. You look so terribly worn and tired."

"No! I'll go with you!" said Dvoyrelè with decision, and walking up to the mirror she began to comb her hair. "I would like to distract myself a bit."

He looked closely at her. How comically strange her feet appeared to him! He had often, in his boyhood, seen new-born calves stand that way. Her feet looked weak and crooked as if she were about to collapse. An idea suddenly recurred to him. He opened his eyes wide just as if he were regarding some wonderful phenomenon. He saw an image before him of one he had so often seen in his thoughts and dreams.

"That is how she will appear," he mused raptly within himself, "that is how my 'Mother' will appear — with crooked, weak legs, like a new-born calf."

"Why don't you say something?" she chided him as she stood arranging her hair before the mirror.

"Oh, nothing!" said he in a low voice. But his eyes remained riveted on her.

The Mother

Dvoyrelè grew weak. She felt that she couldn't stand up any longer.

"I am so weak!" she murmured with a forced little smile, as she looked for a chair to sit down.

With a great start Haskel suddenly noticed a dark red stain on the floor where she was standing. . . . A stabbing pain shot through his heart. He averted his eyes quickly so that she might not notice that he had observed anything. . . . Words, like red-hot coals, whirled through his brain: "Like a wounded animal."

"We are not going out to-night," said he quietly. He then took off his coat.

"Why not?" she asked with surprise as she sat inertly in her chair. "I'll soon be ready. I am only a little tired. It will surely pass off in a little while."

"I just don't feel like it," said Haskel with decision. "I would like to stay home to-night."

She tried to rise from her chair but he would not let her.

"Sit still!" he commanded.

"But I want to prepare something to eat."

"That's all right! Sit where you are. I'll prepare everything."

Dvoyrelè suddenly grew frightened. Had he noticed anything? With an ingratiating smile she asked:

"What is the matter with you to-night, Haskel?"

"I just want to prepare the dinner. What's wrong with that? Must you always do it?"

He then began to juggle with the furniture so that without her noticing it he covered the dark stain on the floor in front of the mirror. Then he pulled his coat on again in order that he might go out to do a little shopping. But before going out he pleaded with her:

"Please, Dvoyrelè, remain sitting in your chair! Don't you dare do anything. Wait until I return. I'll do everything."

An Idea

"But why? I'm not sick," protested Dvoyrelè weakly. Her heart pounded like a sledge hammer. Had he noticed anything?

"It will be a great pleasure for me to cook to-day — why must you insist on depriving me of the pleasure?" he countered. "Now do be a good girl! Remain sitting where you are. Imagine that you are a little princess. I'll be your slave — your strong Ethiopian slave who is in love with his mistress. I'll prepare food for you. Is it a bargain, dear? Say 'Yes'!"

"But what is the matter with you to-night, Haskel?" she asked wonderingly. Her alarm was increasing.

"I'll tell you all about it later," he grumbled. "I am drunk with a very great idea."

Then he dashed down the stairs.

Haskel was overwhelmed by an emotion that he had never felt before. It was the deep impulsion to give form to a perception of beauty which had slumbered in his soul for a long time. It was like giving expression to the very core of his being — that other people keep concealed from even their dearest ones. He felt the irresistible need now of creating a work that was to express the agonizing of all humanity as symbolized in "The Mother Who Bleeds."

He got drunk on the idea. It dominated him completely. He walked on thin air and as he walked from store to store on his shopping expedition he made his purchases without giving much thought to whether they were needed or not. So that when Dvoyrelè saw him enter with an extraordinary number of milk bottles she gasped with astonishment.

"Why have you bought so many bottles of milk?" she asked in stupefaction. "Who will drink all that?"

"I will!" He laughed mischievously. "I want to get drunk to-day on milk."

"Get drunk on milk! What for?" wondered Dvoyrelè.

"You see! It will be like a new-born calf that can hardly stand on its legs."

"Who?"

" 'The Mother' — naturally!"

Haskel then seized her in his strong arms and carried her to her bed. He pressed his coarse, unshaven face to her throat and breast and body and murmured some incoherent words. . . .

"What is the matter with you to-day, Haskel?" she asked him.

Haskel pressed her closer to him but did not answer.

Chapter 10

THE WORK

·······

FOR the first time since he had become a sculptor, Haskel felt that he was molding living flesh from the clay with his hands. He worked fast and furious on an armature of his own design. Nothing else mattered except his indomitable will to achieve his aim. He attacked all the problems facing his work with the authority of a master. He never faltered for a moment. He knew what he wanted to achieve. The idea of his "Mother" dominated his will, saturated his entire being and gave him a weapon with which to fight off the black demons of doubt towards his own talent. For the first time in his life he was working from the living model, a creature who was inspiring him. By his will he forced the living model to resemble her image which he saw reflected in the mirror of his own conception.

The few weeks Dvoyrelè posed for Haskel were the happiest and most harmonious in the entire period of their living together. Life had become charged with a new and significant meaning. All of Dvoyrelè's actions which in the past had been wrapped in obscurity and confusion now became clarified and understandable. They received moral sanction and purification in the radiance of her joy. And, moreover, every one of her actions which had caused pain to those she loved, and about which she was even afraid to think, now appeared to her as the result of a divine prompting. Instead of regret and repentance the thought of them only called forth from within her a feeling of satisfaction and pride. In fact she could almost boast about them. . . .

Haskel found the days too short. Dvoyrelè was away all day working in the shop. But whenever the opportunity lent itself she came home early so that he might have the benefit of her posing in the daylight. Saturday afternoon and all day Sunday were devoted entirely to work. It was difficult to make much headway working evenings. The gaslight blurred all contours. So they burned wax candles which threw a soft warm glow on Dvoyrelè's figure and helped to bring out its delicate, womanly curves. Haskel made numerous sketches of her at night to aid him in his work during the day. He had set his heart upon reproducing the statue in marble after he had completed the clay model. But where would the necessary money come from?

The work became fatiguing and nerve-racking. Haskel kept Dvoyrelè posing for him in the nude three or four hours at a time. What made it doubly difficult was the fact that the studio was draughty and poorly heated. She often turned blue with the cold. Nevertheless, it was a labor of love. She attended to it with piety, as if it were the performance of some religious mystery at which she was assisting, a sacred fast or an ecstatic praying. She devoted herself to it with all the glowing ardor and enthusiasm of her naïvely believing youth.

In the midst of their work they were rudely interrupted by the very dramatic appearance of the rent collector. The principal worry which always burdened Dvoyrelè since she had gone to live with Haskel was where to get the money for the rent? The same worry had made her mother spend sleepless, wretched nights as long as Dvoyrelè could remember. It seemed as if this business of worrying about where the money for the rent was to come from had descended by inheritance from mother to daughter. Dvoyrelè earned enough for food and the other household necessities and expenses. But when the first of the month arrived and the rent collector made his appearance she became distracted. How was she to raise the necessary money? No matter what firm resolutions she and Haskel made to put by a few dollars each week for the rent, some attractive concert would turn up or else Haskel would be tempted to have dinner in a restaurant, and then all their money would vanish like melting snow.

Dvoyrelè never worried Haskel about it. It might disturb his work and make him miserable. She resolved that were he to question her about it she would tell him a white lie — that it had been paid already. Unfounded was her fear. Haskel never questioned her. . . .

The clay figure began to fashion itself prodigiously under his molding hands until one fine day it stood complete. In some respects it resembled Dvoyrelè but in a transfigured sense. Her sculptured self appeared as if it had come from distant worlds and that it was conjured by Haskel by some power of enchantment which he alone possessed. Her face was familiar, so familiar that every one who looked upon it would exclaim "Where have I met this girl before?" Yet no one would ever succeed in recollecting.

Haskel was himself uncertain as to the results of his creation. Originally he had planned to delineate "a new-born calf with weak, crooked legs," but what he had made was something entirely different. He had fashioned the legs firmly as if they had been carved out of granite, only they were disproportionately long and thin to the rest of the body. It was clear that he had made them so deliberately in order to emphasize them. The hips came broad and strong and the belly was like that of a pregnant woman. On the face hovered a chaste smile although the expression in the eyes was arrogantly haughty. They were proud of the fact that in the womb a child had been conceived.

297

The Mother

Upon first sight the figure presented a comical appearance. But looking longer at it one grew accustomed to it and soon the indubitable feeling awoke that one had seen its living model before, perhaps in a dream. She was very, very familiar, but where one had seen her it was impossible to recollect.

Haskel was convinced that he had created a great masterpiece. He was drunk with joy and looking at the sculptured figure kept on repeating to himself:

"That's just what I wanted to make! It is winged like a bird. Do you understand? She is the mother of mothers. There has never been such a mother and yet she is to be found everywhere where women suffer and give birth to the races of men."

Soon a reaction set in. After a few days of the wildest elation and strutting he was attacked by the most blighting doubts and despair. He even wanted to destroy the figure.

"What a sculptor!" he ridiculed himself bitterly and heaped abuse upon himself and his handiwork.

It now became hateful in his eyes and he steadfastly averted his gaze, so that he might not have to look at it. But after a little while he began to long for the sight of it. Again he uncovered it and now it appeared to him as if it were a new work. But strangely enough he did not feel as if he were its creator. He was wholly struck with its originality and vitality. It made him happy once more.

"It is my creation!" he thought proudly. "That is the way I conceived it in my mind. Let others say about it whatever they please. It is my conception of the Eternal Mother, my mother, everybody's mother."

Afterwards came the "critics." Freier complained that Haskel was becoming too sentimental, too lyrical. He blamed it all on his marriage. The last remark he made to Rubinstein the journalist in an undertone so that Dvoyrelè should

The Work

not be offended. Then turning to Bucholz he said in his most sweeping manner:

"This time, Haskel, you have failed to create a work of art. It's entirely too lyrical and once you become lyrical, Haskel, it's bad — very bad. Your talent lies in virile and dramatic portrayals. You ought to model giants with broad, powerful shoulders. This sentimental figure does not do you any credit."

Rubinstein too became authoritative about it.

"It's not made according to the laws of composition." He sadly shook his head. "It is not harmonious. You should have modeled it like an ancient Greek temple from the bottom up instead of from the top down."

Haskel stood open-mouthed and did not understand what they were talking about. Was his work lyrical, he asked himself, or did it resemble a Greek Temple? How could he possibly tell? Why a Greek Temple of all things? But what was the use of asking? If Rubinstein said so he surely must know, for he had once studied composition. At bottom he felt pained because he had exposed his ignorance of the laws of composition. Nevertheless, he stubbornly resolved that the way he had made the figure was the only right way.

"That's how it is and that's how it ought to be!" he obstinately asserted.

"All right, have it your way!" sneered Freier. "When people who know something about art tell you that your work is too lyrical you ought to take their word for it. Just look at your Madonna! Where is her originality? I know I must have seen her somewhere, but exactly where I cannot recollect."

"Splendid!" cried Haskel, overjoyed. "That is just what I wanted!"

Dvoyrelè stood by silent. It pained her cruelly to hear Haskel's friends demolish his work with their barbed criticism. She felt herself an intrinsic part of the work, of her and Haskel's life together. Were they not directing their malice at them personally too? How she wanted now to hide the work from the eyes of strangers! How they defiled it with their coldly appraising, contemptuous glances! She felt herself outraged, humiliated. Hastily she approached the figure and covering it with a moist cloth, said jestingly:

"Haskel made this work for us two alone — for no one else. Not so, Haskel?"

Haskel was nonplused. He mused long over her words. Why had he not thought of it himself? Of course he had not created it for any one else but for himself and Dvoyrelè! And those who did not know what was in his mind while he worked on it, how could they possibly understand it?

He moved near the figure and pushed it gently in a corner behind a screen just as one does when concealing something precious and intimate from the prying eyes of strangers. And as he did so he kept on repeating Dvoyrelè's challenging words:

"I made this work for us two alone — for no one else."

It was at this moment that the idea of his great work became completely clear in his mind. It began to loom large in his own eyes....

Chapter 11

SURÉ FINDS NO REST IN HER GRAVE

∎∎∎∎∎∎

THE snow was descending swiftly and fell in great drifts over the countryside. Slowly and with great difficulty Moses plodded through it along the highway. His two immense packs of merchandise, slung over his shoulder and so balanced that one hung in front and one behind, almost dragged him to the ground. But all this caused Moses no disquietude. It was still early in the afternoon, and besides, he knew the road well.

He was on his way to call on one of his customers, a German farmer who owed him money on goods that he had bought on installment. As he had somehow learned that the German was celebrating his birthday that day, Moses hopefully expected his wife to purchase from him the half dozen fine linen towels and the bed sheets for which she had been bargaining a long time.

Moses was thoroughly acquainted with his territory, which was located in Staten Island. He knew every house lying between Red Hill and Tottenville, despite the fact that they lay far apart and that the neighborhood was desolate and overgrown with brush and forest land. Twice a week he covered his route. To-day was the fifteenth of the month when all his customers expected him to call for their semi-monthly payments. Moses well knew that were he not to call on his customers that day, they would fall hopelessly into arrears.

The Mother

He had lunched heartily at a farmhouse in Red Hill. That gave him a sense of well-being. His body felt warm and comfortable. And both the icy wind and the falling snow set his youthful blood aglow. He felt light on his feet, strong and energetic. So he trudged along bravely against the wind and pondered long on his plans for the future.

He had succeeded in putting by in a savings account the sum of two hundred and eighty dollars. His customers owed him an additional three hundred dollars. Besides which he possessed merchandise that was worth about one hundred and fifty dollars. The territory was good. Germans lived there. They were upright, thrifty and hard-working and paid promptly. Were he at all inclined to sell his "book" he could probably realize eight hundred or a thousand dollars on it.

Then the thought of marriage came to his mind. Why not get himself a wife, some clever immigrant girl who had some money besides? After all, what is more important for a business man than capital? Before his excited imagination now arose the vision of fabulous sums which his future wife would possibly bring him as her dowry: fifteen hundred, two thousand, three thousand. No! That was just one bit too much! He dared not dream beyond fifteen hundred dollars. What would even please him more than a wife with a dowry would be to find one whose parents were well established in some small business and who would not object to have him as their partner.

His thoughts of a future were suddenly interrupted rudely by the recollection of the solemn promise he had made to his mother on her death-bed that he would not marry until little Feigelè had grown up. Had he not promised mother? How could he ever think of being faithless to her and her sainted memory, he asked himself with deep emotion?

Then there awoke within him a feeling of great self-pity. Why must his own happiness wait so long? His mother's

face now rose up before him, sad, calm and earnest. Moses
no longer had any doubts....

His father too could not possibly manage without him.
The elderly widow who took care of the children had to be
paid. Gedaliah, struggling with might and main to pursue
his studies, stood badly in need of assistance. Moses loved
and admired his wonderfully learned and clever brother. He
would give away his last dollar to help him if it were
necessary.

Then his brother Solomon recurred to his mind. Why not
go into partnership with him? Of late, whenever his elder
brother came home on a visit he would complain bitterly
to Anshel:

"It's just rotten to have your father-in-law as your
partner!"

What for did Solomon need his father-in-law anyway?
Moses angrily asked himself with clannish loyalty. He'd
do wisely by withdrawing his investment from the shoe store
and go into some manufacturing business with him, Moses.
Before his eyes flashed a large sign upon which was in-
scribed in bright gilt letters the legend: "Zlotnik Bros."
Solomon would be the "inside man." He would manage the
factory end of the business and their workers, while he,
Moses, would be the "outside man." He would seek credits,
buy merchandise and function as office manager and salesman at the same time. When the business would be successfully established there would be no necessity for their
father to continue working. They would have enough money
to supply all of his needs and to rent a nice apartment for
him in Harlem. He would then be able to give all his attention to the upbringing of the children. Meyer and Nutè
they would take into their business. Only father and Feigelè
would remain at home. And in his bright imagination
Moses already saw his father promenading with an air of

superb dignity along Lenox Avenue, wielding a gold-headed cane.

Moses suddenly became conscious of the icy chill which now penetrated to the very marrow of his bones. The cold blast of the wind howling in the treetops struck his body fully and caused him to tremble. Carrying his heavy packs overheated him and now the perspiration froze on his body. He had remained oblivious to it all this time because of his preoccupation with the golden mirage of "Zlotnik Bros." He had even failed to notice that he had strayed off the road and that he was now plodding through softly yielding snow. When he became aware of his surroundings he was filled with consternation:

"Heavens! Where am I?" he exclaimed aloud.

There was no sign of any road. The falling snow had completely erased every trace of it. He had without knowing it strayed into the brush which now stood half buried in snow.

"Where the Devil is the road?" muttered Moses, cursing under his breath.

He started to retrace his steps, guided by his own footprints in the snow. He thought that in this manner he would find the road again. For a long time he waded through the snow until he began to feel what he believed to be the hard stony road under his feet. Relieved at having found his way again he walked more rapidly.

"It's getting late!" he mused uneasily.

Now he walked with the wind blowing behind him. It accelerated his speed and, as if commanding him, drove him on ahead.

Moses reasoned that thereabouts stood the red house of the Irish farmer whose land lay adjoining to that of the German. The Irishman, disliking Jews, never permitted Moses to pass beyond his gate. For that reason Moses usually avoided him as if he were the very plague. But now, with the snowstorm raging without, how could he possibly object to offering shelter to a living creature who had strayed to his door?

He looked searchingly about him to locate the Irishman's house. But there was no sign of a house anywhere. He forged his way ahead and once more sank deeply into the yielding snow. He hadn't been walking on the road at all, he discovered to his dismay. All about him protruded through the snow the stumps of trees that had been felled. He had blundered into the woods. How did he ever get there? Try as hard as he would he could not recollect ever having been there before.

"I'll have to get out of here!" he thought with desperation. "It's getting late and soon I won't be able to see at all."

Once more he retraced his steps, guided by his footprints in the snow. He walked with all possible speed, straining every ounce of energy, for night was falling.

Moses felt complete confidence in his sense of direction. He had no doubt now that he was going right. As yet he could not imagine the possibility of any danger confronting him. He did not feel cold. On the contrary, he felt over-heated and his body dripped with perspiration. The snow looked so white and flaky, pure and innocent. With what danger could it possibly threaten him? He walked on swiftly.

After he had walked about a half-hour and still did not see any sign of a house, nor meet with any human being, he began to be alarmed.

"Where am I?" he asked himself. His thoughts had become confused.

He felt exhausted now. His body was drenched in perspiration which the chill wind immediately froze. He began to feel a sharp numbness in his limbs. He laid down his packs on the snow and sank wearily upon them.

He noticed through the thickly falling snow that the light was beginning to dim. The drab gray in the sky grew

still more somber. Every object looked indistinct and
blurred and merged with the others into a confused mass.
And about this mass the snow continued to fall ceaselessly
like the threads of a spider's web entwining itself about a
victim. Moses felt that he was being enmeshed in the snow-
web and that nevermore would he be able to extricate himself. Night descended upon the earth. Now the snowflakes
no more looked white but were bluer and bluer.

"Why am I sitting here — night is falling?" Moses raged
inwardly.

He sprang to his feet and slinging his great packs over
his shoulder staggered on his way.

"Help me, mother!" he prayed aloud.

Suddenly he found his way barred by a wall of trees
which he had not noticed before on account of the increasing dark and the snowstorm. Moses' heart beat wildly. It
would be nothing short of folly for him to make his way
through the woods at this time of the day. He might never
emerge from them alive. Also to return by the same way
that he had come was out of the question. It would do him
no earthly good.

"Mother!" he cried aloud once more. "What shall I do?"

He felt stiflingly hot. The moist snow which had fallen
on him in heaps penetrated his clothes and coming in contact with his skin caused a steamy vapor to ooze from him.
He felt that his shirt, which had been saturated with his
perspiration, had frozen to his back.

What was he to do? It would be madness to enter the
woods. Far better to return by the way he had come. After
all, no matter how long it might take him, sooner or later,
he was bound to reach some habitation. There is an end to
every road.

"Help me, mother!" he prayed fervently and continued
on his way.

He had but gone a few paces when he heard the barking

of a dog. He stopped. The sound came from the woods. A cry of relief sprang to Moses' lips. He turned into the woods and blindly groped his way between the trees.

It had now grown so dark that Moses found it impossible to see more than a few feet ahead of him. He no longer walked, he ran. He stumbled and often sank helplessly into a deep snowdrift. But he was on his feet again, carried along by the hope the barking of the dog awakened in him.

With a cry of joy he noticed the roof of a house protruding from among the treetops. Reassured he stopped short and caught his breath. Then he approached the house.

No light shone in the windows. This surprised him. But in as much as there was a dog in the house, he conjectured, most likely there were people living there too.

The dog inside the house was now barking furiously. It had heard the crunch of Moses' approaching feet on the snow. Yet no one came to open the door for him. Moses tried the door. It was locked. The windows were shuttered.

Frantically he knocked upon the door. There was no answer. Only the dog raged savagely at the intruder from the other side of the barrier.

"Just like my luck!" commented Moses grimly to himself.

He decided to make the best of a bad situation and sought the doubtful shelter of the open porch. Standing on one spot proved tormenting. His teeth chattered with the cold. His legs felt as if they had been amputated from the rest of his body. All his clothes hung stiffly on him. They had frozen on his back. Sharp, stabbing pains attacked his toes and his fingers.

"Must I perish, mother?" he moaned amidst the awesome silence about him.

He now felt an overwhelming pity for himself and for those at home. Who would look after them now? How would they manage without him?

The Mother

"Help me, mother," he prayed. "I am so young to die!"

Tears blinded him. And through them, beyond the transparent web of the falling snow, he suddenly saw a face. That did not frighten him. It was the face of his mother.

"Mother!" he cried out in anguish. And he stretched out his arms to her for aid. "You will help me — you will help me."

Then throwing his packs over his shoulder he staggered like a drunken man through the dark forest. Swiftly he ran, often falling against stumps of trees and rocks. Half-blinded, he reeled through the serpentine course between the trees that through the falling snow had the aspect of elongated corpses wrapped in their winding sheets. Moses did not know where he was going. Only in his consciousness there loomed the certainty that somehow he would save himself from what before had seemed a certain death.

He suddenly stopped in his course and half-swooning for joy leaned against a tree for support. A light flickered in a house only a little distance from where he stood. Panting he ran towards it. Then he pounded frantically upon the door.

A tall, wiry man, with a weather-beaten face and red hair and beard rushed out to him. Moses saw him as if in a dream, for in another moment he sank limply to the ground and lost consciousness.

Years after, when Moses had already become the head of the well-known firm of clothiers, "Zlotnik Bros.," he never tired of recounting the story of the miraculous manner in which his mother came to save him from certain death in the woods.

"A miracle it certainly was!" he insisted. "Else, how did the red-headed farmer ever get there? I had never seen him before in my life, although I knew every inch of my territory."

Chapter 12

ISABEL

■ ■ ■ ■ ■ ■

I SABEL'S interest in Haskel's career grew constantly. Since Dvoyrelè had come to ask her aid in the matter of her unborn child, she had become intimate with both of them. She plotted unceasingly to make Haskel publicly known as a sculptor. For a long time she had been planning to bring some American newspaper men down to his studio to view his work. Something unforeseen always intervened. But one Saturday evening she arranged for a meeting in Sholom's Café between Haskel and a lanky Irishman, a news reporter, whom she called Gregory. Freier and Rubinstein, as Haskel's best friends, and as art connoisseurs besides, were also asked to be present. Isabel fairly glowed with amiability. She was animated and provocative and charmed all with her cleverness and enthusiasm.

How beautiful she looked that evening, thought Haskel, regarding her with an artist's appraising eye! But after a little while he discovered that his admiration for her was not altogether from the dispassionately æsthetic viewpoint. ... This thought made him sad and moody. He had never before seen her in such a seductive light. She awakened within him desires of whose possible existence he had never even dreamed.

Haskel regarded her now as if it were for the first time. He fairly devoured her with his eager eyes. Why had he never before seen her so beautiful and radiant? he asked

himself in wonderment. Surely he must have been blind as
a bat all along.

"Like a rose in full bloom," he silently commented as he
looked at her. Her supple, graceful body, draped in a wine-
colored gown, enticed him with an impelling allurement.
Her gown was *en décolleté* and her fresh rosy flesh filled
him with disturbing thoughts. ...

Everything in her seemed mature. Not only her full,
supple body with its finely rounded contours, but her intelligent, lively eyes as well pointed to an intellectual and
spiritual maturity. This even enhanced the voluptuous se-
ductiveness of her full-blown body.

Almost unconsciously he began to make comparisons between her and Dvoyrelè who sat so constrained and silent.
How shocking! Dvoyrelè looked so frail and delicate, almost
like a child. He had never consciously thought of her that
way before. How dearly he loved her! She was already a
part of his being, so precious, so near, like a sister or a
mother. He could not imagine his life without her. But what
an extraordinary contrast Isabel presented! She looked so
unattainable! She lured him with the fullness of her body
and the fullness of her mind. ... The voluptuousness of all
existence sang in her firm, rosy flesh. She wove a magic spell
over his senses and wafted him as in a dream to enchanted
worlds.

Thinking about her did not cause him to feel any sense
of guilt towards Dvoyrelè. On the contrary! It appeared to
him now that he and Dvoyrelè were not two beings apart
but one. She had so fused her identity with his that he
could not dissociate himself from her in any of his thoughts
or actions. They were but one being and now he liked to
believe that together they were daydreaming such pleasant,
sensuous dreams and together they were lusting after Isabel's voluptuous body. ...

He noted every one of Isabel's gestures and bodily movements. He devoured her with his eyes. How he would have liked to get drunk on her breath and on the fragrance of her blossoming flesh!

Haskel sat tongue-tied. His senses became overheated. He riveted his eyes upon Isabel's bare arms.

"How full and superbly modeled they are!" he mused admiringly.

When she stood up he looked at her feet. They were so delicate and she walked with such grace! Why had he not noticed that before? he asked himself with wonderment.

Each time that he had seen her she had left no particular impression upon him. In fact, something that appeared to him alien and unapproachable about her had kept him at arm's length. Her face he had never found particularly attractive. The tiny wrinkles about her eyes and the deep crease in her throat testified with mute eloquence to her age. He could only think of her as an old maid.

How differently he felt about her now! Everything that before had appeared as unattractive in her began to exercise a strange fascination for him. The crease in her throat captivated him. How much tender femininity lay poured in the lines of her full white throat, he thought! The deep crease that lay drawn through it like a thread of silk spoke mutely of untold pain and inner struggle. Her former strangeness and unapproachability lured him now. She was friendly and kind and lovable but nevertheless a certain reserve stood between her and others. Her poise, dignity and social talents filled Haskel with admiration and respect, and unconsciously he compared Dvoyrelè to her. He thought:

"Dvoyrelè would never know how to conduct herself with such elegance and poise."

This ungenerous thought filled him with shame and remorse. He bent towards Dvoyrelè and stroked her hair. But his eyes were elsewhere. They were glued upon Isabel's face and particularly on the crease in her throat. It seemed to him as if that crease had endowed her with an individual charm, had lent her the attractiveness of something that was elusive and incomparable at the same time.

Isabel suddenly noticed his fixed look on her and she returned him a beaming and appreciative glance. He turned red under the collar. Then turning persuasively to Gregory her friend, she said:

"Do come with me, Gregory, to Haskel's studio! I want you to see his work. I believe he is a great sculptor and you must help him."

"Sure!" agreed Gregory with a good-natured grin. "Just as you say. Come on, let's go!"

Haskel was now filled with a feverish desire to display his work. Never before had he felt such an urgent need for showing off his talents. That he meant it entirely for Isabel's benefit he very well knew. How he would have liked to make a great impression on her! He would have been ready to barter away all his future happiness for the sake of pleasing her that moment.

Impatiently he led the way up the stairs to his studio. With trembling hands he placed his statues before his visitors. One after another he unveiled them for their inspection. There stood his "Samson," "Adam," and in front of them "The Mother." In the gloomy light of the studio, half cast in shadows, the figures took on a fantastic appearance. Their contours became blurred and indistinct and in the semi-darkness they emerged like weird Sphinxes in some moonlit desert. "Samson" stood in all his heroic strength, laughingly playful like a child, and beside him the mystic "Adam" with his six pairs of hands upraised like branches of trees. In sharp juxtaposition to them stood "The Mother" with her wan little smile and thin, knock-kneed legs. She stood in an attitude as if she were straining to protect some one against an impending danger. They had the semblance

312

of ancient gods whom untold generations of men had worshiped since time immemorial.

The primitive force, imagination and originality of the sculptures impressed every one. Even Freier and Rubinstein became thoughtful and subdued. They abstained from making any criticism.

It was Gregory who broke the enchanted silence.

"To what school do you belong, to the classical or to the modern?" he asked naïvely.

Haskel was in a quandary. He did not know what to answer. Only Isabel, who all this time had been standing spellbound before his works, burst out into an enthusiastic eulogy:

"You are a great sculptor, Haskel!" she gushed, with shining eyes, as she extended her hand to him. "The vital force in your works is like that of a god."

Haskel kept silent. He flushed deeply and looked earnestly into her eyes. Her lips trembled convulsively and he forgot to release her hand.

Isabel became embarrassed. She averted her gaze and gently withdrew her hand from his grip.

"Gregory," she said to the reporter, "you've got to do something for Bucholz! Do it for my sake! He deserves it and you will never regret having helped him."

"Sure!" grinned Gregory, taking out his notebook. "What's the story?"

Isabel sat down with him in a corner of the studio and painstakingly explained to him the primitive force and vitality of Haskel's work.

"That's not the dope I need," grinned Gregory in his good-natured way. "I want a story. Tell me please — how old is he? What has he done until now?"

At this juncture Rubinstein interrupted:

"I know exactly what you need, Mr. Gregory," he said with a shrewd professional wink. "You probably want to hear something about Bucholz that would make spicy reading, something he has done that has human interest value. Well, one day an art patron came to look at his work. He suggested a certain lucrative plan to Bucholz which would have entailed the sacrifice of his artistic ideals. Although Bucholz at the time lived next to starvation he seized the offending Mæcenas by the scruff of his neck and kicked him down the stairs. There's a consistent idealist for you!"

"That's the stuff!" exclaimed Gregory with delight. "A starving artist throws an art patron down the stairs because he asks him to compromise his artistic ideals — that will make a first-class feature story!"

And Gregory feverishly made notations in his notebook. For the first time that night he evinced some enthusiasm for Haskel's sculptures. . . .

Chapter 13

THE GREAT FORTUNE

■■■■■■

SEVERAL days following Gregory's visit to Haskel's studio there appeared in the Sunday issue of one of the leading New York morning papers a featured article about Bucholz and his art. The news story concerned itself more with a fantastic account of the sculptor's life than with his work. The caption, which was printed in bold letters across the page, read:

"GREAT SCULPTOR DISCOVERED IN A GARRET."

The reporter then went on to describe in detail all that the sculptor had done, in what manner he earned his livelihood — his work as a wringer in a wet-wash laundry during the day and at night modeling his masterpieces in his garret studio. He had never attended any art school but was self-taught. The distinguishing element in his work was an extraordinary vitality and primitive force. Although he had received many flattering offers from art dealers and patrons he had rejected them because he would rather starve than betray his artistic ideals. He had chosen instead a life of toil and hardship and earned his bread by the sweat of his brow. Also, the reporter had not neglected to note that the sculptor's pretty young wife worked in a sweatshop to help him reach his goal.

The article finally closed with a highly dramatic account of the meeting between Bucholz and the art patron whom he had kicked down the stairs for tempting him to betray his artistic ideals. Photographic reproductions of Bucholz, his studio, and of his "Samson," "Adam" and "The Mother" accompanied the article.

The very same day on which Gregory's article appeared Haskel received an unexpected visitor. It was a Mr. Davidson, the director of an art gallery. He was a spare, energetic little Jew with an incredible diamond pin stuck in his tie. He made Haskel an amazing offer: to purchase from him all the works that he had already completed as well as secure an option on all his future works for a period of ten years. Mr. Davidson spoke very glibly and in the most casual manner mentioned tens of thousands of dollars as if they were mere bagatelles. He promised to introduce him to the President at the White House and have the latter sit for his portrait bust. Afterwards he would arrange for his modeling John D. Rockefeller, J. P. Morgan, Jacob H. Schiff and other financial magnates. And suiting the action to the words he produced a ready contract and with the most urbane of smiles urged him to sign. But Isabel stood guard over Haskel and sternly forbade him to sign.

Some days later other art dealers came, looked at the sculptures, held whispered consultations and like Mr. Davidson offered him ready contracts. When Haskel bluntly refused to sign they shrugged their shoulders and departed.

A few weeks later Isabel came to see Haskel. She had brought Gregory along with her — as well as an old woman and another man. The man, whispered Isabel into Haskel's ear, was the famous art critic Davis. He was a silent and taciturn personage and with an almost bored expression looked about him. For a long time he regarded Haskel's sculptures, but never said a word. But when he saw "The Mother" his bored expression made way for an intense look of interest. His eyes sparkled with a true æsthete's delight. He even waxed enthusiastic over the work and for a while absorbed himself with studying the statue from various angles. Then addressing himself to the old woman who had accompanied him to the studio, he said:

"Mr. Bucholz undoubtedly has an original and first-class talent. He possesses a highly individual and primitive force, a deep emotionalism and a sensitive perception for beauty, despite the fact that his work is crude and suffers from a lack of technical finish."

Afterwards he questioned Haskel. Where had he learned how to draw? Discovering that he had never received any art schooling he was filled with amazement.

"What Mr. Bucholz needs," said he to his woman companion, "is a trip abroad to Rome and Paris in order that he might see what others have done before him. So that every time he does something that he believes is original he should not imagine that he is another Columbus discovering America."

The critic smiled mischievously at Haskel.

"Do you think, Mr. Davis, that an exhibition would be advisable at the present time?" ventured Isabel diplomatically.

"Most certainly!" agreed Mr. Davis heartily. "These sculptures are works of art — particularly his 'Mother.' Of course the young man displays entirely too much self-confidence in his work. A little self-doubting would not be amiss, Mr. Bucholz," he chided good-naturedly. "And don't ever let a successful exhibition of your work turn your head."

At parting the old woman said to Haskel with a smile:

"We will see now, Mr. Bucholz, what we can do for you."

The critic shook his hand heartily and said with a playful grimace:

"You will learn a lot yet about art in Paris, Rome and Florence, Mr. Bucholz!"

Haskel did not know how to take all these encouragements. But when Isabel said good-by to Dvoyrelè she embraced her and joyfully whispered in her ear:

"The seven lean years are passed, Dvoyrelè. Now will begin for you the seven fat years."

.   .   .   .

A little while later Isabel brought to Haskel and Dvoyrelè the happy news that the old woman who had been up to see them with Mr. Davis was a well-known philanthropist and art patron, and that upon the prompting of the critic had consented to grant Haskel a stipend of five thousand dollars. This should enable him to stay abroad for two years. She also told them that Mr. Davis had succeeded in interesting a prominent art dealer on Fifth Avenue. The latter was ready to hold an exhibition of Haskel's works in his gallery.

"And now, Dvoyrelè," she concluded, "no more shop, work and troubles. Now will come Europe, Rome, Florence and Paris with the man that you love. Isn't it wonderful?"

Dvoyrelè did not answer her. An indefinable sorrow wrapped her about. She found it difficult to speak.

"Why don't you say something?" asked Isabel, surprised.

"I know only too well, Isabel, that all this is a great stroke of luck for Haskel. But strangely enough the thought of it doesn't make me happy. Instead I feel sad. I don't know how to explain it."

"Why is that?"

"I would rather that our good fortune should come in another way. Somehow I imagined it differently, quite differently."

"In any case, Dvoyrelè, Paris is very beautiful and you will love it."

Dvoyrelè's cold reception of the good news she had brought her somewhat offended Isabel.

"I know that Paris is very beautiful," murmured Dvoyrelè gratefully. "We owe you so much, Isabel!"

She pressed Isabel's hand. Tears sprang to her eyes.

"Don't worry about it now. You will thank me when you will get to Paris," said Isabel in a slightly offended tone, and drawing on her jacket she left the studio.

"Why did you do that? Why?" cried Haskel after she had gone. He paced up and down the studio in his excitement.

"I don't know why. That's how I felt," explained Dvoyrelè remorsefully. She well understood the cause for her feeling. . . .

.   .   .   .   .   .

Haskel's admiration for Isabel grew in bounds. He was overwhelmed by a feeling of the deepest gratitude for what she had done for him. Everything that she now said he accepted as gospel without questioning. The very fact that she interested herself in him and made efforts on his behalf meant more to him than the prospect of studying abroad and having his talents recognized. But being a misanthrope by nature he expected all his rosy prospects to end disastrously. Something would no doubt go amiss. His patron would either lose all her money, or a war would suddenly break out, or some other kind of catastrophe would happen to interfere with his good fortune. He knew he was ill-fated.

To his astonishment, one day he received a letter from his patron containing a check for five hundred dollars, also the notification that this money was to be used for making the necessary preparations for the journey. He was also requested to inform his patron's secretary whether he preferred having the rest of the money sent to him in quarterly or half-yearly installments.

When the letter with the money arrived, Dvoyrelè had already gone to work. Haskel's excitement was so great that he seized his hat and coat and ran off to her shop to inform her of the good news.

The Mother

Out in the street he was met by a flood of sunshine. The gay spring breezes blew carelessly into his face. The last signs of winter were fast disappearing and as he looked into the shop windows and saw the hurrying throngs, oblivious to everything except their business affairs, he felt a deep regret and pity. The world was so beautiful and made for people to play in the sun and to be happy!

He ran through the streets with great elation, and felt an irresistible desire to buttonhole every passer-by and telling him of his good fortune, produce the check as conclusive evidence. How rich he felt!

A disquieting thought arose in his mind. For an instant he succeeded in deluding himself into the belief that it was not to Dvoyrelè that he was hurrying to tell the good news, but to Isabel. It would be Isabel and not Dvoyrelè whom he would later take for a walk along Fifth Avenue. Together they would go shopping in preparation of their trip abroad. Then they would dine in a first-class restaurant, and go to the theater. He would hold her hand when the lights went out at the theater and feel her breath on his face, and perhaps — Haskel awoke with a start from his daydreaming.

"What a good-for-nothing creature I must be!" he reviled himself bitterly. "How can I possibly think of such wicked things?"

Nevertheless, while he was lashing himself into a state of remorse he already felt in his nostrils Isabel's fragrant breath and the tantalizing perfume of violets which emanated from her rosy bosom.

To drown out of his consciousness the temptings of the Devil, he increased his speed and dashing up the stairs to the shop where Dvoyrelè worked he had her called out to him.

"Put on your things and come along with me right away," he bade her breathlessly.

"What has happened?" asked Dvoyrelè, much upset.

"Just that," he answered, showing her the letter and the check.

Dvoyrelè couldn't quite see the point of his insistence that she stop working immediately.

"When I'll come home from work in the evening there will be plenty of time for us to talk about it," she argued in a matter-of-fact voice.

Her coldness offended him. He was prepared to celebrate his good fortune and here she came and dampened his good spirits. The thought of it enraged him.

"I don't want you to work any more!" he shouted. "You have worked enough as it is!"

Dvoyrelè was filled with remorse at having dampened his joy. So she smiled in a conciliatory manner into his eyes. Then she hurriedly pulled on her hat and coat and accompanied him into the street.

"Well, Haskel, what shall we do first?" she asked with feigned excitement, and she snuggled up to him like she used to in the beginning of their courtship, in order to bring him into a good humor.

Haskel's spirits rose in a remarkable manner.

"Let's do nothing yet," he said, excited as a child. "First let's walk through the streets and look into the shop windows. Let's pretend that we've got no money, just like in the good old days, when all the shopping we ever did was with our eyes. In case we will see anything that will please us very much we will buy it. What do you think about it, Dvoyrelè?"

"No, Haskel! I've got a better plan. First of all, let's buy a large bouquet of roses and carry it to Isabel. We must both thank her. Our good fortune is all due to her."

"That's a wonderful idea, Dvoyrelè!" cried Haskel with undisguised enthusiasm, and embraced her to the amusement of all the passers-by. "Suppose we ask her to join us in our celebration?"

Dvoyrelè hung her head sadly, without any reason as she herself thought. But Haskel failed to notice it. He was carried away by Dvoyrelè's suggestion that they call on Isabel. He hastened his pace.

"Come quickly, Dvoyrelè!" he said. "We've got to cash the check first."

And out of gratitude to her he embraced her warmly.

"How I love you, Dvoyrelè!" he gushed, and he fondly stroked her black curly hair.

Chapter 14

IN THE NET OF JOY

▪▪▪▪▪▪▪

HASKEL worked hard preparing for his exhibition. Isabel helped him a great deal. He consulted her on everything he did. So he spent very little time at home. Both that and the fact that he was constantly in Isabel's company appeared quite natural to Dvoyrelè. Why not? Isabel understood so much more about art, she tried in a spirit of fairness to justify her usefulness to Haskel. Strangely enough, she did not envy her. She respected and appreciated her intelligence and character. She had only one regret: that she could not be of help to Haskel like Isabel was nor be together with him as much as the other.

Dvoyrelè no longer worked in the factory which she would have liked to do. Life without any occupation was a dull affair for her. Also, she could not readily accept their good fortune as a fact. "Why was she wasting so many precious days in nothing better than idling?" she asked herself. Every time she protested, Haskel turned purple with rage.

"Why must you work when we sail for Europe right after the exhibition closes?" he asked. "We've got to get ready for the journey."

For some inexplicable reason which Dvoyrelè, try as she would, could not explain to herself, she had a premonition that she would not accompany Haskel when he went abroad. With almost fatalistic calm she prepared herself for the inevitable something which was to sever their relationship. Of course, she had no reason to doubt Haskel's motives, nor Isabel's for that matter. The relations between those two she had accepted as a matter of fact. She even shared Haskel's enthusiastic regard and gratitude for her. Then what made her so sad? And why was she so skeptical whenever Haskel discussed his plans for their stay abroad? It seemed to her as if Poverty were laying its viselike hand upon her and saying: "I shall always hold you within my power."

The days of idling and waiting for their departure were the unhappiest Dvoyrelè had ever experienced. Haskel did not know what to make of her taciturnity. He went about beaming with delight and hopefully picturing before her their roseate future together. But Dvoyrelè sat silent and glum. Gone was the familiar little smile about her lips which had given him so much pleasure in former days. Of that smile only the merest wraith remained, hovering about her tightly-pressed lips that looked as if they were convulsed by a suppressed desire to weep. The hectic luster in her eyes deepened and the rings about them grew still larger. She spoke less with her mouth and more with her eyes. . . .

·   ·   ·   ·   ·   ·   ·

Like the pendulum of a clock that swings from one end of the arc to the other, so Haskel oscillated in his love between Dvoyrelè and Isabel. This battle in his heart raged without ceasing. It remained ever undecided. Since that night when he had first recognized in Isabel the desirable woman, and despite his self-flagellation, remorse, solemn vows and self-justifications, he found no rest. Neither by temperament nor by character was he the sort of person to act consistently on any resolution. Carried away by his emotions neither his conduct nor his motivation ever had a rational basis. He had but barely resolved to attach himself with all devotion to Dvoyrelè when the desire for Isabel obtruded itself and gave him no peace. All things now became devoid of any meaning for him and utterly lifeless and futile. He could not conceive any happiness for himself without his passionate desire for Isabel's fragrant bosom being realized. When he finally did abandon himself to the new emotion he was in turn attacked by qualms of conscience and remorse which brought on a state of self-disillusionment and spiritual vacuity. When this occurred a ravening fear descended upon him. He felt as if the earth were giving way underneath his feet. Then in panic to drown out his fear he ran for sanctuary back to Dvoyrelè. . . .

"Why not have both?" he debated within himself with the petulancy of a spoiled child. "My love for both is so genuine and pure! But how can I?"

He well knew that neither Dvoyrelè nor Isabel would agree to a divided love.

"Why must that be?" he tormented himself. "Why must people so deliberately make themselves unhappy? Matters could be arranged so agreeably for everybody if only people wanted to. . . ."

Each time Haskel returned home after meeting Isabel he suffered deeply from a feeling of remorse. One day she had been particularly kind to him and had helped him arrange his sculptures in the gallery. Afterwards she had led him into a fashionable restaurant for tea. She smiled coquettishly at him and when she leaned forward to speak he eagerly drank in the fragrance of her breasts. He at last had his obsession realized. That made him happy. He was very reluctant to leave Isabel. But she, half in jest, bade him go home to "little Dvoyrelè."

When he arrived home he found Dvoyrelè sitting alone in the half-darkened studio. She looked so sad and forlorn

that he felt conscience-stricken. His fading love for her
stirred within him. In a voice full of tender solicitude he
asked:

"Why do you sit alone in the dark?"

"Just so," she answered with a forced little smile.

He now noticed what she was trying so hard to conceal
from him: that she had been crying.

"You have been crying, Dvoyrelè," he said accusingly
and impulsively he embraced her. He kissed her eyes and
tasted the salt of her tears.

"Why did you cry?" he demanded.

"Just so, for no particular reason. I just felt like crying,"
she tried to reassure him, smiling through her tears.

Her pathetic courage and struggling pride to conceal from
him her woe moved Haskel deeply. Solemnly he now swore,
and that for the last time, that henceforth only Dvoyrelè
would occupy a place in his heart. She was his affinity,
his predestined wife and his great fortune. That instant he
realized how much she and her deep devotion meant for him.
With all the tenderness that he felt capable of he strove
hard to convince her of it.

"Here I have gone and bought the steamer trunks for
our voyage and there you sit and cry!" he reproached her.

"I am not sure whether I'll go with you, Haskel," she
said almost in an undertone.

"What makes you think so, Dvoyrelè? Please tell me!"

"I don't exactly know why, but I just feel that way."

"Do you for one moment think that I'll go without you?
I'll let them keep their money and will rather go back to
my tombstones."

Dvoyrelè answered nothing.

Haskel took both her hands in his and looking deeply
into her eyes he pleaded with her.

"Dvoyrelè! Dvoyrelè!" he began, and then fell silent.

"What do you wish?"

In the Net of Joy

"Why do you speak this way? What makes such horrid thoughts enter your little head? Am I guilty of any crime? Have I done you any wrong? If so, please tell me!"

His questions sounded so childlike and naïve to her that all the protective instincts of the mother awoke within her.

"No!" she assured him with a smile.

"Then why do you speak so strangely? What can my life mean to me without you? What will I ever be without you? You have made me believe in myself and awakened within me all that was most worth while."

He laid his head in her lap and embraced her feet.

She looked into his face searchingly as the tears once more welled up in her eyes.

"Is what you say true, Haskel?"

"I swear it — on my soul — that my life without you will be empty!"

"Haskel! Haskel!" she half sobbed as she passed her fingers through his hair. "Why am I so unhappy? What you have said should have made me happy."

"If you loved me you would be happy, Dvoyrelè. Aren't both of us going to Europe soon — only you and I and no one else?"

She sank into his arms with a little moan of joy.

Again a night of abandonment of the senses. He carried her about in his arms muttering to himself strange and inarticulate words of love. Then he sat at her feet and began to paint for her a roseate picture of their future happiness. He waxed ecstatic over the innumerable delights of their forthcoming ocean journey — of their Paris studio in Montparnasse among thousands of other artists hailing from every country of the globe. Together they would promenade the gay boulevards, sip absinthe on the terraces of the cafés, travel over Europe, see all the ancient cities, and visit the museums. For two years they would live without care and bask only in the sun of beauty and happiness. He pictured them both as two drops of light, shimmering on a sea of joy. And Paris — the city of eternal dreams — sparkled and glowed and lured them both from the distance like a will-o'-the-wisp darting through an enchanted night.

"Why not?" thought Dvoyrelè to herself. "Why couldn't all that be possible?"

All her former doubts and gloomy premonitions she now forced from her. Had she no right to be happy? Why had other people and not she?

And in all sincerity Haskel continued to daydream before her and led her unsuspectingly into radiant mirages. . . . In an atmosphere of beauty and charming relaxation, surrounded by great works of art and culture, and inspired by her love and faith in his talent, would he not create works of lasting merit?

"You will infect me with your enthusiasm and with your faith in me," he exulted. "I was worthless and futile until you came to me and made me aware of my true self. And when all laughed at me you believed in me and strengthened me."

Tears gushed from Dvoyrelè's eyes in an endless flow. She could not stop crying.

"Then why am I so unhappy, Haskel?" she persisted in her forebodings. "Why do I fear the future so and doubt so much that things will turn out for us just as you say they will?"

"You must believe — believe — believe!" he chided and kissed her streaming eyes.

And Dvoyrelè believed. . . .

.   .   .   .

Next morning they arose early and went out shopping for the voyage. Haskel crowed with delight over every new purchase and went to great lengths to explain the necessity and virtue of each article to Dvoyrelè. His good spirits had their desired effect on her, so that she actually began to accept the idea of their trip abroad in earnest. The new life which awaited them both glowed deeply for her and it gently and irresistibly drew her on to a world of light and joy — a world, she had tearfully told herself repeatedly, that was not intended for her. . . .

In the afternoon Haskel took her with him to the galleries where his exhibition was to be held. There they already found Isabel talking excitedly to the reporters of some large dailies. Her charm and her cleverness succeeded in arousing their enthusiasm where Haskel's sculptures left them puzzled or indifferent. Isabel's devotion and loyalty to Haskel once more aroused Dvoyrelè's gratitude and admiration. Yet she did not know how to make it manifest to her. So she stood at a distance, silent and constrained, feeling somewhat ill at ease in the elegant galleries. When Isabel noticed her she came tripping up, put her arm affectionately about her and drew her into a chair beside her.

"Well, Dvoyrelè — are you all ready for the journey?" she asked full of concern.

"Yes, I am," answered Dvoyrelè in an embarrassed way, "that is, Haskel has bought me many things, only I don't know — I think that —" and she paused.

"What, Dvoyrelè?" urged Isabel.

"I don't see why all this good fortune is coming to me."

"Nonsense! You deserve every bit of it. You have worked hard enough for it."

Isabel's words moved Dvoyrelè deeply. She looked intently at her and without any deliberation said to her:

"It is you, Isabel, and not I who ought to go to Europe with Haskel. You are so good — so good!"

Isabel was completely taken aback.

"I!" she laughed in embarrassment. "I! Haskel can't take me along. I am not his sweetheart, you dear, darling girl!"

Much moved, Isabel embraced Dvoyrelè.

Chapter 15

THE EXHIBITION

·······

THE day of the exhibition arrived. The newspaper that had first discovered Haskel was interested to make it a success, and so it had prepared its readers for its advent. Davis, the art critic, did his share in bringing down the artistic élite and the connoisseurs. For that reason a large and distinguished gathering turned out at the opening. Among them were men and women prominent in the cultural and social life of the city, artists and art patrons, æsthetes and collectors, critics and intellectuals. All were eager to view the works of the new East Side wonder. As usual in such cases, there were also present the inevitable number of East Side social workers and politicians anxious to turn the exhibition into a "Jewish triumph."

Like all newly discovered artists, Haskel had as yet made no enemies among his colleagues. Nothing but lavish praise and enthusiasm for his talents was heard in the galleries.

The galleries were decorated with palms and flowers. This was all Isabel's work. Among the green palms arose the heroic figure of "Samson," proud of his mighty shoulders, powerful torso and muscular limbs, yet softened by a naïve, almost childlike, smile. Close by stood the "Adam" with his outstretched numerous arms whose puzzling symbolism caused many a fantastic speculation among the spectators. But most conspicuously placed was "The Mother." It stood in front of a natural screen of yellow chrysanthemums surrounded by smaller works, portrait busts, and figurines. For the first time, placed under the proper light of an art gallery, it appeared to advantage. The statue's resemblance to Dvoyrelè now became clearly evident. "The Mother" appeared so young and fragile, treading the earth proudly and sending before her the protuberance of her belly as if she were heavy with child. She knew she was pregnant and she was proud thereof. Her eyes, wide open and earnest, gazed straight ahead of her with the calm dignity of one who has just achieved the unattainable. Nevertheless her little mouth was tightly closed and the lips convulsed in a grimace of pain as if she were then and there experiencing the agonies of childbirth. Many smiled with amusement, seeing her widespread curved thighs, bent as if about to be delivered of her child.

The work that aroused the greatest interest, though, was "Samson." It was easy to understand, being such obvious art. But the critics and the cognoscenti agreed that "The Mother" was a work of the highest artistic merit. For that reason it was always surrounded by the greatest number of people, such as were afraid to betray their ignorance of art. They stood admiringly before the statue, chanting their praise for it.

Isabel stood at the entrance and received the invited guests. She was perfectly familiar with all the social amenities and carried herself so well that Haskel's admiration knew no bounds. She was dressed in a blue velvet gown that was sleeveless and deeply décolleté and revealed her firm little bosom and delicately chiseled neck and throat. Her bare arms, perfectly modeled, insinuated the satiny softness and rosy allurements of the rest of her body. Greeting the arriving guests with radiant smiles she escorted them through the galleries, interpreting this or explaining that with the greatest tact and charm.

Haskel stood in a secluded corner, looking constrained

and bewildered, and did not know how to manage with his arms and legs which somehow always got in his way. His heart jumped an extra beat or two and he began to find his new suit of clothes excruciatingly uncomfortable. His shoes felt too tight and so he constantly shifted his weight from one leg to the other. When Isabel saw him standing so wretchedly aloof she drew her arm through his and, pulling him forcibly after her, began introducing him to those whom she shrewdly believed important and influential.

Haskel flushed red. He felt Isabel's bare arm pressing his and he inhaled deeply the scent of violets which floated from her bosom. Her proximity at that moment meant more to him than the entire exhibition, the guests and their effusive congratulations. If only he could divest himself of those tight shoes and the stiff collar that was strangling him, there would be nothing left to be desired, he thought, heaving a deep sigh.

"It seems to me, Haskel, that you were born with a silver spoon in your mouth," whispered Isabel into his ear. "Few artists have ever achieved success with a first exhibition."

Without himself being aware of it, he took her hand in his and looked fascinatedly at her fingers.

"I can feel your soul through your fingertips," he murmured with a surprising gallantry that made her flush.

Slowly she withdrew her cold fingers from his warm eager hand. Then in a chilling, almost matter-of-fact voice, she remarked that Dvoyrelè was sitting alone and was looking in their direction. She hastened to her.

"Where have you been hiding, Dvoyrelè?" she reproached her. "I have been looking for you all this time."

Until the very last minute, Dvoyrelè had been reluctant to go to the exhibition. She feared that she would feel uncomfortable there. Of course, she rejoiced over Haskel's success! Had she not been prayerfully waiting for it all this time, and believed it inevitable that it should come? Now when at last success had come to him, she felt an irrepressible desire to run away and hide herself from everybody's sight.

That morning Haskel seemed to go about in such a state of excitement and he begged her so to accompany him to the exhibition that she did not find it in her heart to refuse him. He unreasonably fell into a misanthropic mood, looked forward apprehensively to the afternoon and foretold complete failure for his exhibition. His gewgaws would only make people laugh, he feared. It was in vain that Dvoyrelè reminded him that all those who had seen his work had been enthusiastic about it and that the newspapers had printed eulogies to his talents. Haskel became skeptical. It was all a terrible mistake, he insisted. Dvoyrelè saw how much he stood in need of her just then. So she dressed carefully in her new black silk dress which Haskel had bought for her and wrapped about her little shoulders the gypsy shawl that he liked so much. Then she put on her strings of beautifully colored beads, and taking a last look at herself in the mirror she went with him to the exhibition.

But when she entered the galleries and saw so many important-looking and fashionably dressed people, she became frightened and immediately after that fell into a constrained and unhappy silence. As Haskel was soon appropriated by Isabel in order to present him to all the important-looking people, she found herself an unobtrusive corner and stood at a loss, not knowing what to do.

Dvoyrelè regarded Isabel from a distance. She saw her busily engaged in making every one feel at home and in directing everything to a successful outcome. How lovely she looked, and how charmingly she smiled at every one! Her first reaction was that of a deep-welling gratitude to her. She thought:

"Why does she do all this for us? How good she is!"

Then this feeling was displaced by highly disguised envy which gnawed at her heart and made her wretched.

"Where was there the need for this exhibition?" she asked herself.

And she thought regretfully of the happy time when she worked in the shop and Haskel devoted himself to his art.

"How much happier we would have been had we continued that way!" she bitterly ruminated in her thoughts.

Then she thought of Haskel and said to herself:

"How foolish of me to think that I can keep him all to myself? Was he then made for me alone?"

Nevertheless, she could not free herself from the jealousy which she suddenly discovered herself feeling for Isabel. She envied her for her lovely clothes, polished manners, glib speech, charming ways, and helpfulness to Haskel.

"What kind of upbringing did I ever have?" she lamented silently. "What kind of education did I ever receive?"

Then she began to pity herself and in retrospect pondered moodily upon the circumstances of her hard life, her poverty, and her early environment.

Dvoyrelè's heart went on fire; her eyes began to glow with a hectic brilliancy. Then she grew ashamed of her thoughts.

"How vicious I must be!" she reviled herself. "She has done so much for Haskel and I think nothing but evil of her."

Despite all her efforts, she could not free herself from her jealous obsession. Why could it not be she instead of Isabel who should be so helpful to Haskel? This thought drove her frantic. She felt that she was hot and feverish. She became irritable and angry and bit her lips.

"All this was not necessary!" she ceaselessly repeated to herself. "Things would have been much better for Haskel without her help."

Yet deep down in her heart she knew that she was wrong. Haskel, like all artists, stood in great need of the practical help and encouragement that he was receiving as a result of Isabel's efforts. How happy he was over the prospect of going abroad! What sleepless nights he had spent in eager anticipation as well as in painful trembling over the opening of his exhibition! And against her will there suddenly came a terrifying thought: Isabel would make a better wife for Haskel. She could help him live his life and reach his artistic goal. As for Dvoyrelè herself, how could she help him? All that she could do for him had already come to a finish. Now he no longer stood in need of her. Worse yet — she could bring him no happiness. She knew nothing at all about art. Isabel was so educated and cultured! She could help him much to an artistic career.

Her thinking became confused and already she saw Haskel not as her husband, but as her brother, or a dear, a very dear friend. And she became concerned over him and pondered upon what would be best for him. Comparing herself with Isabel, she came to the conclusion that it was the other who should accompany Haskel to Europe and not she. She was so beautiful, good and educated and knew how to behave in good society. He would be so happy with her!

"God! What am I thinking of?" she suddenly awoke to herself with a start. "That can never be! He is mine and never will I let another woman take him away from me. It was I who recognized him when no one knew him. He himself has said so. I alone! Without me he would never amount to anything."

Would he be unhappy without her were he to marry Isabel? This thought persistently throbbed in her brain. Her heart grew cold and she closed her eyes in terror. Then she heard the friendly voice of Isabel purring solicitously:

"Where have you been hiding, Dvoyrelè? You and Haskel must come to my apartment to-night. I am giving a party in honor of Haskel's success. All our friends will be there, including Rubinstein and Freier. Then there will be other people whom I am anxious to present to Haskel."

Just then Isabel noticed a new arrival:

"Please excuse me, Dvoyrelè, I've got to introduce that man who has just come in to Haskel. He is a newspaper editor and can do a great deal for him. Well, so long, dear, until to-night!"

She tripped away carrying off Haskel with her.

"I won't go to her party!" Dvoyrelè firmly resolved in her mind.

Then she grew sad although she knew that there was no justification for it. Without being noticed by any one she slipped out of the galleries into the street.

Fifth Avenue was thronged with people and a steady stream of automobiles and carriages. The sun genially caressed everybody and everything. Dvoyrelè looked up at the sky and saw that it was bluer and vaster than ever and that gauzy little cloudlets sailed serenely overhead only to be devoured by a gray cloud that was rapidly out-distancing them. This made her unhappy. Why was she thinking so much about the gray cloud, she asked herself angrily?

Of a sudden she was filled with a deep regret.

"Why must all this be?" she lamented silently.

Then she began to deride herself. "How foolish I am!" She laughed bitterly.

She felt the need of remaining alone, to conceal herself from the eyes of all people. So she climbed to the top of a bus going downtown.

A dizzy array of houses, shops, passers-by and vehicles speed by. Noises rise up and as suddenly die out. Half in a trance, Dvoyrelè repeats to herself: "Why must all this be?"

Tears well up in her eyes. She dabs them away with a handkerchief.

Arriving home she flung herself upon her bed and buried her face in the pillows.

The Exhibition

"Why? Why?" she moaned disconsolately.

All that she had experienced in her life with Haskel she now relived in retrospect. Then came the agonizing thought of her unborn child which she had destroyed so that her loved one might be free to pursue his art.

"It cannot be! It cannot be!" She struggled frantically against her self-imposed destiny.

Then she grew angry with herself.

"Why do I think such dark thoughts?"

She jumped off the bed, washed and carefully combed her hair, smoothed her crumpled dress, and drew from the clothes chest the colored gypsy shawl which Haskel loved best. Then she put on her trinkets again and sat down to wait for his coming.

One hour passed and still he had not arrived. Her depressing thoughts came back again. She wanted to drive them away but she could not. Once more she threw herself upon the bed and buried her hot face in the pillows and agonized until she again got control of her emotions. Then she dried her tears, adjusted her clothes and hair and sat down to wait for his coming.

At last she heard him charging up the stairs. Her heart began to beat violently. She did not know why.

He burst into the studio radiant and boisterous. His stiff collar unbuttoned, the shoes unlaced and his tie in his hand.

"I have just taken Isabel home," he gasped all out of breath.

Then he recollected.

"Where did you disappear?" he asked, a little peeved. "We looked for you everywhere. I thought that all three of us would have dinner together in some nice restaurant. But Isabel wouldn't think of it unless you came along."

"I was so tired," she began lamely. "Then I couldn't see what the use was for my staying there any longer. I couldn't help you like Isabel. I can't speak to people as nicely as she does."

"Isn't she wonderful?" Haskel went into raptures. "You should have heard her talk to all those important people and have watched her introduce me to them! She did it so skill-fully and with such elegance! She charmed them so that she could do whatever she pleased with them."

"You've got much to be grateful about to her, Haskel," said Dvoyrelè.

"I am glad you agree with me!" exclaimed Haskel jubi-lantly. "Nothing would have happened without her. She did everything."

"Isabel can do much for you," commented Dvoyrelè earnestly. "She, more than any one else."

"Isn't that so!" chimed in Haskel enthusiastically. "She looked so beautiful to-day! Every one who saw her and her well-bred manners was captured by her."

Dvoyrelè did not answer and became lost in thought.

"You're not angry, Dvoyrelè, are you?" he asked in a conciliating tone.

"Why should I be angry?"

"Because I speak so warmly about Isabel."

"Isabel is a fine and lovely girl."

"How I love you, Dvoyrelè, for that!" expanded Haskel in his enthusiasm. "You cannot imagine how I love you."

He placed his arms about her and kissed her pas-sionately.

"Why do you kiss me so?" she asked in an injured tone, repulsing him.

"But I do love you, only you — only you, Dvoyrelè!"

She averted her gaze. Her disillusionment now came to stay with her and would not leave her.

Chapter 16

THE MOTHER

....

DVOYRELÈ was firmly resolved not to go to Isabel's party.

"To-night, Haskel," she said, "I would like that we two remain alone together. There should be nobody else with us — only we two. If we have at last lived to see the day of your triumph, don't you think it right we should do that?"

"You are right," Haskel interrupted her eagerly. "We should spend this night together and alone."

Then he recollected and a look of dismay spread over his face.

"But what shall I do about Isabel?" he asked. "She expects us and she has invited her friends to meet us. The party is in my honor, after all."

"You can send her a telegram saying that I am ill and that you cannot possibly leave me alone," advised Dvoyrelè.

"Good! I'll send her a telegram or a letter by messenger," he agreed.

Then, a moment later: "Do you think she will feel offended?"

"If you will write to her that I am ill and that therefore you cannot leave me she will have no cause to feel offended."

"Very well, I'll write her so."

After a little while Haskel thought of another plan.

339

"I have been thinking, Dvoyrelè, that I would very much like to have everybody know that whatever success I am having is all due to you and that to you I owe more gratitude than to any one else. So like a good little girl come along to the party. They are all waiting for us and it won't be nice to disappoint them. Gregory will be there and many other useful people. I wouldn't for the world like to offend them nor make a fool of Isabel. How about it? Let's go to the party to-night — anyway we'll have plenty of nights ahead of us to spend together."

"No, Haskel! I really cannot go. If you like, go alone. I will remain at home."

"I won't go without you," said Haskel with resolution, and seated himself beside her.

But when the hour for the party arrived, Haskel became restless. A disturbing sorrow and a longing filled his spirit. How much he would have liked to see Isabel once more in her blue velvet dress! Dvoyrelè read his suffering and frustrated desire in every one of his movements. As always, she could not remain indifferent to his pain. She was filled with pity for him. Before her eyes he now appeared like a helpless little boy aggrieved over his failure to get what he had set his heart upon.

"Haskel," said she kindly, "I see that you want very much to go to the party. Please go! I'll remain at home."

"Come along, I beg of you — do come along!" he pleaded.

"But why can't you go alone?"

"I would like to show off with you to-night before everybody — to have them know that all the credit for my success must go to you."

"I cannot go! Believe me, I cannot!"

"Come, if only to please me, Dvoyrelè. You have no right to mar my joy — particularly on this night."

She began to relent. She herself became anxious that he go to the party.

The Mother

"Please go, Haskel! You will do me the very greatest favor if you will go. I have a bad headache and I think I'll go to bed."

"Come along, I beg of you, come along," he pleaded like a child.

Her mother's heart was almost overcome by his childish plaint. So she steeled herself and resolved not to go.

"You must go, Haskel! How will it look if you won't go? Isabel has done so much for you. You must not offend her. The party is, after all, in your honor."

"And will you assure me that you won't feel badly if I go alone?"

"Why should I feel badly? Is it because you wish to go to Isabel? You talk like a child now."

"I'll soon be home, Dvoyrelè. Don't you worry! I won't stay there long," he murmured half in guilt.

Then he kissed her and muttered placatingly:

"You look so lovely to-night, dear!"

"Come!" she said with forced gayety. "Let me fix your tie for you. Your hair looks disheveled too."

Haskel was in a great hurry. He was afraid that he would arrive at the party very late.

"Wait a moment, dear," she said, taking from a vase a bunch of violets which Haskel had bought her on their way to the galleries in the afternoon. "Give these flowers to Isabel and tell her, please, how sorry I am not to be able to come along with you."

"I'll tell her," muttered Haskel, hastening away with the flowers.

  · · · · · · ·

When Dvoyrelè was left alone all grew dark before her. The room receded. She felt as if she were wandering in a storm-swept wilderness. The wind buffeted her about like a leaf and she did not know in which direction to go. Soon this feeling gave way to a more compelling one: to the thought of Haskel.

"In what does his guilt lie?" she pityingly asked herself. "He is only a child, a helpless, blundering child!"

Then the mother within her awoke and she concentrated all her thoughts on how to serve him best. She readily recognized Isabel's significance for him. Soon she began to see herself as one outside him, as one who must objectively think only of his welfare. Once more she drew a comparison between herself and Isabel. She found herself wanting.

"I have nothing to give to Haskel," she thought despairingly.

She could view the entire situation soberly. Of course Isabel would be useful to him! He stood in great need of her. She would accompany him to Europe, teach him foreign languages. What an interesting companion she would make! She knew how to behave properly in good society and with her charm and wit make herself well liked by everybody. Haskel would be happy with her and proud of her. She would have to be altogether blind not to see that he cared for Isabel. He longed for her and could find no rest until he went to see her. Of course, she had noticed how sad he had become when the prospect of not going to the party loomed large before him. His world had grown dark for him.

But her sober judgment and objectivity did not long endure. Soon she was swept by an emotion that left her cold and trembling. She suddenly visualized Haskel and Isabel traveling together. She imagined that she saw them depart for Europe and that she remained standing alone and bereaved on the pier watching the steamer carry him and her happiness away — never to retrieve them again. A deep yearning now consumed her heart. Her nerves, taut and jangling like so many fine electric wires, began to break under the strain. She began to beat her tiny hands forcefully against her face, moaning piteously:

"I love him! I love him so! I don't want to let another woman take him away from me! Why? Why must it all be?"

And like one drowning she frantically clutched at the empty air.

Then Dvoyrelè fought desperately against the dark flood of despair which was sweeping her away.

"But nothing really has happened!" She strove to reason her suspicions away. "How can I be certain that anything has taken place between the two of them? She pleases him because she is a lovely-looking, clever woman. When we will both go abroad he will surely forget her. Of course he will forget her!"

Only for a little while she succeeded in dispelling her tormenting thoughts. Then her cold reason painted another and even more distressing picture of their future life together. Although Haskel would live with her he would constantly be longing for Isabel. She already saw him go about in a highly excited and dazed manner. He sat near her but his thoughts were far, far away. . . . Then he learned to hate her.

"Ah!" thought Dvoyrelè with anguish. "Better that I were dead than that he should hate me!"

Her thoughts once more got out of control. She saw him now living with Isabel. He was already famous. He did not know where she was nor what had happened to her. Sitting in his beautifully furnished studio his thoughts reverted to her, Dvoyrelè, and of the days when they had lived together, of their dire poverty and of their occasional joys. Then no one knew him — no one. And a deep longing seized him to see her again.

Once more her eyes became blinded by her tears.

"In other words, it's all ended, ended for all time!"

The Mother

The word "ended" frightened her. Yet she plainly could see that his heart was no longer with her.

"But it has to be so!" the stern reality persisted.

"Then let him rather long for me — being with her, than hate me, living with me and longing for her!" her pride rebelled.

Yet the heart would not resign itself to the inevitable without further struggle.

"Nothing final has happened yet. It is still time to avert the tragedy," she countered to her fears.

Then impulsively she arose and threw her head back with a brave toss so that the coils of her dark hair loosened and fell in an avalanche over her shoulders.

"It is for his happiness — therefore I am happy!" she murmured aloud.

A resolution formed itself in her mind. She smiled an enigmatic smile.

.   .   .   .

Isabel felt disappointed that Dvoyrelè had not come to her party. She insisted that Haskel should go back and fetch her. But he, with the greatest sincerity, assured her that it would be of no use as she could not possibly come, being indisposed. Isabel suspected that the cause was jealousy and felt a slight irritation toward Dvoyrelè. How absurd and childish, she thought, but as the party became animated as the evening progressed and more liquor was consumed, she, as well as Haskel, soon forgot about Dvoyrelè.

Toward midnight, made feverishly gay and expansive by much drink, the guests paired off and sought the comparative seclusion of dimly lit corners. Even the candles in the tall brass candlesticks flickered sleepily and enveloped the room in half shadows. Made sentimental and amorous by wine, there was much love-making.

On a sofa in a corner sat Isabel and Haskel. Her hair,

usually dressed very neatly, had now become slightly disheveled and fell over her naked shoulders. Her silk gown clung so closely to her body that its supple contours were clearly outlined. All the evening Haskel had been pursuing her, devouring her with his hungry eyes. Each time he came close to her he felt her breath on his cheek. He placed his arm about her waist, and felt the warm throbbing flesh through her dress. Skillfully she maneuvered out of his embrace and moved away from him each time on a different pretext, leaving behind her the subtle scent of violets and a smile to tantalize and goad him with desire.

Haskel had the suspicion that she was only luring him on — encouraging him to greater intimacies. Another time he would never have mustered sufficient courage to follow her with such persistence. The success and laurels he had been crowned with that day had given him unwonted daring. The liquor he had drunk had gone to his head and the scent of violets floating from her bosom enticed him and lured him. He forgot about everything and dared everything.

At last, when he found her half reclining on the sofa, looking worn and half dazed, he seated himself beside her.

She did not try to run away.

Suddenly he was seized by an irresistible desire to fling himself at her feet and to take them in his hands and fondle them. Still he forebore. His heart beat like anvil hammers. Dark little fires blazed in his eyes. And when he looked at her it was with an unuttered prayer. He murmured:

"Isabel!"

She did not answer him. Her eyelids drooped sleepily.

"Isabel!" he murmured again.

"What, Haskel?" she whispered drowsily.

Haskel's courage rose. He thought that he no longer heard any resistance in her voice. The fragrance of her body made his blood sing madly. He drew nearer to her and took her in his arms. How cool and firm and satiny was her flesh, he thought with rapture as he strained her to him and passed his burning hands over her in a rude caress!

"Isabel!" he murmured beside himself with desire.

She did not turn away from him. Only he felt the tremor that shot through her body. Her eyes were languorously closed and her breath came in short and piteous gasps.

They sat that way for a long while. At last he no longer saw nor heard what was going on about him. He slid to the floor on his knees and wildly began to fondle and kiss her small feet.

Slowly and with determination she withdrew her feet from Haskel's hands.

Again he seated himself on the divan beside her and in a choking, almost doglike voice, pleaded:

"Isabel!"

"Why do you do this, Haskel?"

"I don't know."

"Can't you see, Haskel, what a calamity it would be were I to fall in love with you? After all, I am only human," she added with a sad smile.

Haskel thought he heard tears in her voice and it filled him with remorse.

"What am I to do then?" he asked in a trembling voice.

"I am only human — only human!" reiterated Isabel beseechingly.

"Very well, then what am I to do?" he almost shouted.

"Go back to Dvoyrelè," she advised.

"You are right," stammered Haskel and he fell into a moody silence. Then he lifted his eyes and looked at her with the pleading helplessness of a child tormented by desire.

The Mother

"But I cannot — I cannot!" he lamented.

"You must!" she insisted coldly. "Dvoyrelè has sacrificed everything for you — more than you yourself imagine. Only I know it — only I!"

An angry glitter crept into her eyes.

Haskel hid his face in his hands.

"You are right, Isabel, you are right!" he repeated penitently.

She felt sorry for him now.

"Haskel, be a man!" she adjured him almost tenderly. "Both of us must be strong. I am only a woman and you must help me. Dvoyrelè must not suffer on account of us. You must promise me, Haskel, that you will protect her against yourself."

"You are right, you are right!" mumbled Haskel mechanically in contrition.

"Give me your hand, Haskel," said Isabel softly. "We will always remain good and devoted friends — but friends only."

Haskel pressed her small hand to his hot face.

"Be strong and remember Dvoyrelè," she continued in a coaxing voice.

"Dvoyrelè is my sister," he mumbled guiltily.

Isabel burst into a rippling laughter, revealing her small white teeth.

"You are not much of a brother to her, I am afraid, Haskel!" she good-naturedly jeered. "Nevertheless let us both remain good, dear friends."

She again extended her hand to him. How cold her fingers lay in his now, he thought bitterly! And again desire swept over him. He threw all caution to the winds and abandoned himself to his surging emotion.

"I feel your soul in the tips of your fingers!" he gushed.

Isabel looked impatient and annoyed.

347

The Mother

"You must never speak of this matter again, Haskel," said she in a forbidding voice.

She rose quickly and walked away from him.

.   .   .   .

On his way home, Haskel thought only of Isabel. Dvoyrelè was completely obliterated from his consciousness. He dwelt long and feverishly on Isabel's supple body which he had touched through her thin silk gown. The thought of it drove from him all other thoughts, feelings, recollections and obligations. His breath was full of the fragrance of her skin and the memory of her cool satin body wove about his senses a flaming net from which he could not extricate himself.

"I shall never have her!" he silently lamented. "My hands shall never caress her body and I shall never drink her breath, nor press her hair to my lips. Her smile and her voice will be for others — nevermore for me."

He could not reconcile himself to the loss of her.

From under a smoldering heap of ashes glowed a dying ember. That ember was Dvoyrelè. From time to time it flared up in Haskel's conscience and gave him no rest. But its flaming was too pale and feeble. It was dying by degrees. The fragrance of Isabel's breasts filled his nostrils and made him drunk.

It was near dawn when Haskel entered his studio. He did not strike a light but sank limply into a chair.

"Is that you, Haskel?" called Dvoyrelè tremulously.

"Yes," he muttered in a hollow voice.

Never had she heard him speak in that voice before.

"Why don't you undress and come to bed?" she reproached him gently.

He arose unsteadily and sat down on the side of her bed without uttering a word.

"What ails you, Haskel?" she asked with tender solicitude.

348

The Mother

In the darkness of the room he could not see her face nor could she see his. They were merely aware of each other's presence.

"Dvoyrelè!" he whispered and bowed his head towards her. She took it tenderly in her hands.

"What ails you, Haskel? Please tell me!" she begged him.

"Aren't you, Dvoyrelè, my sister, my everlasting, eternal sister?" he asked humbly.

"Of course I am your sister! You know it," she answered in a hoarse voice.

"And I am your brother — your only brother!" he added chokingly.

For a moment she kept silent. He heard the frantic beating of her heart.

"Please tell me, Haskel," she finally asked him in a barely audible voice, "are you in love with Isabel?"

Haskel did not answer and like a helpless child seeking the protection of its mother, he pressed his feverish face against her breast.

"Would you like to go with her to Europe?" she mercilessly continued.

Haskel put his fingers on her lips to silence her. But she brushed them aside.

"Why are you ashamed to tell me?" she rebuked him gently, trying hard to control her voice and pressing his head closer to her. "Why can't we speak openly about it? For a long time already I've been thinking that it would be better for you to marry Isabel. She is more educated, better and prettier than I. I would only stand in your way. Isabel could help you reach your goal."

"Don't speak this way, Dvoyrelè!" broke in Haskel mournfully.

"Why not, Haskel? I have wanted to tell it to you for a very long time. You would do best in taking Isabel rather than me to Europe. I don't want to go with you. I'll better remain where I am."

"Don't you love me any more?" asked Haskel in an injured tone.

Dvoyrelè laughed.

"Of course I love you, you big baby!" she chided him. "Only I cannot go along with you to Europe. Isabel ought to go instead. She is more suitable for you as a wife than I. You'll be happier with her."

"Please don't say any more!" implored Haskel. He began to weep.

"Why can't we discuss this matter intelligently?" persisted Dvoyrelè with hectic cheerfulness. "There, there, you mustn't cry! It's not nice to see a great big man like you cry like a two-year-old."

"But what will become of you?" he moaned despairingly.

"Don't you worry about that, Haskel! I have already made up my mind to return home to my folks. My father is lonely and the children are still small and need taking care of. I am the only one that can look after them."

"Won't you come with me to Europe?" he begged her.

"No, Haskel! I cannot go with you. I once thought that it was possible. Now I understand differently. My conscience won't let me. Better go with Isabel."

"What mad things you are saying, Dvoyrelè!" he cried, weeping bitterly.

"Don't cry, I beg of you, Haskel darling!" she crooned to him like a mother and drew him tenderly to her breast. "I don't like to see you cry."

.   .   .   .

When Haskel rose from sleep a little later he found that he had undergone a complete change of heart. He now deeply regretted the confession of love for Isabel that he had made to Dvoyrelè. And now he swore by all things holy that he loved only her — Dvoyrelè — and it was her he wanted to accompany him abroad. He was even ready to go to Isabel then and there and let her know of his decision.

Dvoyrelè listened to all this with a good-natured smile — nodding her head approvingly the while. For an instant Haskel thought he had noticed a significant subtlety in her smile which he had never seen before. Then he dismissed it from his mind.

When he had gone to tell Isabel of his new-found love, Dvoyrelè quietly brought down her battered old valise from a shelf in the closet. She packed into it her few personal belongings and musing deeply she left the studio to fulfill her secret mission whose burden she had inherited from her mother. . . .

THE END